PRAISE FOR
BLACKWATER SPIRITS:

The third book in the critically acclaimed Glynis Tryon historical mystery series.

"Satisfying historical fare whose proto-feminist spin feels just right."
—*Kirkus Reviews*

"Glynis [Tyron has] a substantial personal history that gives credibility to the choices she makes."
—*The Drood Review of Mystery*

"Rich in historical background and Native American lore, vibrant with characters who are as engaging as they are individualistic . . . *Blackwater Spirits* is one of the most marvelously written mysteries I have ever read."
—*Kate's Mystery Books*

"Ms. Monfredo demonstrates a real appreciation for the drama in our history, and is very skilled at translating the social and political ferments of the times . . . into immediate problems for her characters."
—*Mystery News*

"Excellent courtroom scene . . . A very fine historical novel."
—*The Poisoned Pen*

"Monfredo excels at capturing the mood and spirit of the times, especially in her delineation of what it meant to be a woman of that day."
—*The Purloined Letter*

continued . . .

PRAISE FOR
NORTH STAR CONSPIRACY:

While most of the town of Seneca Falls is focused on the opening of a brand new theater, Glynis finds high drama of her own investigating the suspicious death of a freed slave.

"A solid, classically crafted puzzle that combines the best of Agatha Christie and Walter Mosley . . . This book is a treasure."

—*Syracuse Herald American*

"Stimulating fare . . . that effectively parallels the powerlessness of slaves and women—the disenfranchised—building to a dramatic courtroom sequence."

—*Kirkus Reviews*

"An excellent blend of history, mystery, and love story . . . A fascinating glimpse into the issue of slavery in the 1840s . . . An outstanding read."

—*MLB News*

"[An] intricately plotted, historically vivid, thoroughly satisfying mystery."

—*Publishers Weekly* (starred review)

BLACKWATER SPIRITS

Miriam Grace Monfredo

BERKLEY PRIME CRIME, NEW YORK

BLACKWATER SPIRITS

A Berkley Prime Crime Book / published by arrangement with
St. Martin's Press

PRINTING HISTORY
St. Martin's Press hardcover edition / February 1995
Berkley Prime Crime mass-market edition / June 1996

The Putnam Berkley World Wide Web site address is
http://www.berkley.com

ISBN: 0-425-15266-9

Berkley Prime Crime Books are published
by The Berkley Publishing Group,
200 Madison Avenue, New York, NY 10016.
The name BERKLEY PRIME CRIME and the BERKLEY PRIME CRIME
design are trademarks belonging to Berkley Publishing Corporation.

PRINTED IN THE UNITED STATES OF AMERICA

10 9 8 7 6 5 4 3 2

ACKNOWLEDGMENTS

Those who have engaged in historical research will know how much an author owes to others: to reference librarians, town and county historians, and additional informative and helpful people. I am fortunate to have access to numerous fine libraries in western New York: the Rare Book Division of the Rush Rhees Library, University of Rochester; the Rochester Public Library, Rundel Memorial Building; The Strong Museum Library; the Seneca Falls Historical Society, and particularly the Rochester Museum and Science Center, with its material on the Iroquois.

I am especially grateful for the Edward G. Miner Medical Library's History of Medicine division at the University of Rochester, and I wish to thank librarian Christopher Hoolihan, head of special and technical services.

I am also indebted to those individuals who have made unique contributions: Betty Auten, Seneca County Historian; Ellen Brown, former owner of The Shoestring Gallery of Art; Francis Caraccilo, Seneca Falls village planner and director of Seneca Falls Urban Park, and Gail Caraccilo, planning assistant; Gene Holcutt, refuge manager of the Montezuma Wildlife Refuge; G. Peter Jemison, Seneca artist and historic site manager for Ganondagan State Historic Site; Dan Hill, a Seneca/Cayuga, for his introduction to evocative Native American flute music; David Minor of Eagles Byte; and Nancy Woodhull and Bill Watson for loaning Glynis Tryon their historic (1840) Cayuga Street residence in Seneca Falls, New York.

Special thanks to my husband, first reader Frank Monfredo, for his invaluable assistance with legal history and trial development and for after-dinner strategy sessions; and to my daughter, Rachel J. Monfredo, of the Museum of Fine Arts, Boston, Department of American Decorative Arts and

Sculpture, for everything from dulcimers to women artists, soup to nuts and then some, including gourmet meals. Also to my father, Horst J. Heinicke, M.D., for medical information. And abiding gratitude to my editor, Ruth Cavin.

And to my friend and companion of seventeen years, my little West Highland lassie, Shaduff Balman Lyrae: Rest In Peace.

AUTHOR'S NOTE

The major characters in *Blackwater Spirits* are fictitious, but actual historic figures do appear from time to time. The interested reader will find them annotated in the Historical Notes at the end of the novel.

For reasons now obscured by time, there are two bodies of water named Black Brook in Seneca County, New York. The Black Brook referred to in *Blackwater Spirits* has its source near the village of Waterloo and flows east to the village of Seneca Falls, then north to an area known today as the Montezuma National Wildlife Refuge. These entities are factual, as is Black Brook Road. Black Brook Reservation is entirely fictitious, however; there is no Native American reservation in Seneca County.

An explanation is in order concerning the two different spellings of what has been variously translated as "people who build an extended home," or "people of the longhouse." The present-day Iroquois spelling of this is *Haudenosaunee*. Lewis Henry Morgan's work *League of the Ho-de-no-sau-nee, or Iroquois*, published in 1851, used a phonetic spelling that resulted from Morgan's desire to appeal to the primarily Anglo-American reading audience of the mid-nineteenth century.

BLACKWATER
SPIRITS

PROLOGUE

WINTER 1847

THE ICE. O-WE'-ZA. The ice could crack.

But the trail had ended. He *must* cross the river. The young half-blooded Iroquois ignored the warning murmur of spirits beneath the frozen surface of Black Brook, and urged his horse over the ice to the trail beyond as fast as he dared. Halfway across, the ice cracked.

The youth heard a sharp report at the instant his horse drew its hindquarters into a crouch, struggling for purchase on the river's shifting skin. Repercussions like musket shots split the cold air. Instinctively the youth loosened his grip on the reins; here the horse knew better than he. The animal faltered before it recovered its footing and lunged forward, snorting in fear as it scrambled up the bank of the river. With a roar the ice behind gave way.

But once more on the hard-packed dirt of a trail, the horse unexpectedly shied. Only then did the youth acknowledge that he had been shadowed. And while *tah-yoh-ne,* the gray timber wolf, followed closely now, it would not attempt to cross the broken ice-capped span of water; the wolf could sense danger where the human could not.

The youth twisted in his saddle to look back, and he called to the shadow. On the river's far side, the wolf would not show itself, but glided as unseen as a ghost through snow-dappled underbrush. The youth again urged his horse forward. The trail eventually curved south while the river beside it narrowed to a stream, and then faintly, from somewhere beyond, came the anguished screams of women. Reining in, the rider quickly dismounted. The horse hung its head wearily, steam rising from its nostrils.

Crouched at the far edge of the streambed, the wolf raised its muzzle to search the air as if to confirm the scent of only the one human. Then it cleared the stream in a single leap. The young Iroquois sensed the wolf closing the distance between them, and he turned the horse to give its rump a sharp slap. As the horse cantered off, the youth again called to the wolf, before he began to run.

He moved with the litheness and strength of his Iroquois forebears. And as swiftly as if he bore wings. His moccasins barely grazed the snow, a silent drum of *my brother, my brother, my brother,* steadily beating the rhythm of strides. Measuring every footfall.

Beside him, wind-stripped branches swept the stream's frozen surface, and where the ice was thin or broken, water glittered like black glass. Now and then the runner eyed the water warily, but his attention centered on the path ahead. And what he would find at his destination. He remained only marginally aware of the gray shadow now at his heels; but when the trees began to thicken, to become dense forest, the youth slowed and glanced back. The eyes of the wolf, outlined with black markings, had become luminous golden ovals. It raised its muzzle to howl.

The runner checked his stride to watch as his protector veered up a small hill, its outline stark against the milky winter sky. With a flick of tail the wolf vanished. The runner picked up his pace and entered the domain of Ga'-oh, spirit of the winds.

Towering hemlock now loomed over the footpath, their snow-weighted boughs curving like claws toward the forest floor. Amid the hemlock rose sacred white pine of the Iroquois. The pine thrust their branches upward as if to ward off the taller trees' threat; as if to guard the runner on the path below. High above the earth-bound creatures, an eagle shrieked its warning.

The youth's acute sense of hearing, like that of his kindred spirit, the wolf, now caught again the sound of women's anguish, long before they could be seen. Quickening his pace still more, he raced over the footpath, his way guarded to either side by the white pine. By Ga'-oh, whispering through their branches. Ahead of him, cries of grieving rent the near-twilight to rise on the air like his own frosted breath. *My brother, my brother.*

The forest suddenly thinned. The runner slowed, then paused at the edge of a clearing, his eyes on a solitary oak ahead, and on the two women under it on their knees. Above them, a body dangled from a rope noose. The youth took this in even as his peripheral vision scanned the clearing for signs of the lynching party. There remained only churned snow. Bootprints and hoofprints.

The two women, one young, one aging, got to their feet and pulled their graceful, shawl-like blankets around themselves while the youth went toward them across the roiled snow. Despite the tears on her weathered cheeks, he saw in the eyes of the older woman a hard light. And when she spoke, hers was a voice that rang with the harshness of knife against stone: "You come too late, Walks At Sundown. Too late for your brother."

The young, sweet voice of the other woman came to him now, raw with pain. "They took him. They did . . . *that* . . . and then they hanged him! But their law says—you *told* us—that first there must be a trial."

"Trial!" The older woman spat the word, and brushed her eyes with the back of a leathery hand. "White man's law! Law that you, Walks At Sundown, think we should honor. What should we honor, when this law lets white men drag your brother from the longhouse? Take his manhood. Ask *him*"—she pointed to the man at the end of the rope— "ask what *he* thinks of this law! But he will not answer . . ." The woman's voice broke, and she sank to her knees, gazing up at the body of her elder son.

Walks At Sundown raised his own eyes to see above him the cruelly battered face and, below the belt of his brother's tunic, a dark stain spreading over the buckskin leggings. Blood still dripped from between his legs, one slow drop at a time, into the snow.

For a long moment, Walks At Sundown remained with gaze fixed on the body swinging slowly above him; then he moved toward his mother. On her knees, she bowed in grief. Walks At Sundown stood over her, stared down at her hunched shoulders, and wiped his palms over and over again on his leggings.

At last his mother straightened and looked up at him, saying, "You, Walks At Sundown of the Wolf Clan, are bound by the code of your ancestors. You, who were born

Haudenosaunee, People of the Longhouse, know what it is you are required to do.''

Their eyes met, mother and son, and between them a fresh antagonism surfaced. But Walks At Sundown said nothing; there was nothing his mother would hear. He took several quick steps backward and then, with a running leap, grabbed a low branch of the oak to swing himself up into the tree.

He drew his knife from its quillwork sheath. Sharpened on whetstone, honed razor-keen, the knife severed the hemp rope with a single slash. Still grasping the length of hemp, Walks At Sundown lowered his brother's body into the arms of the women below.

When they had lain the dead man on the ground, his mother went to the edge of the stream, where she lifted her face to the Great Spirit. Walks At Sundown and the younger woman waited. The snow-bleached sun dropped behind the pines.

While the three figures stood as motionless as a tableau sculpted in ice, neither Walks At Sundown nor the women turned their heads toward a faint sound beyond the clearing. There, cowering behind a tree, a white-skinned girl choked on the tears that coursed down her face. But before she might be approached, she rose to flee through the forest.

She ran until her lungs failed, then hurled herself against the nearest tree, grinding her forehead into its rough gray bark until the snow under her feet reddened. Long strands of fine yellow hair whipped back and forth in her frenzy before they snagged on the bark, wrapping themselves around the tree trunk. The girl moaned softly as she tore the captive strands from her scalp.

At last, when the spirits of darkness began to gather, she threw herself into the snow. If she lay there long enough, she could die. She *would* die. Like the hanged man in his mother's arms. Just as cold.

SOME TIME LATER, a horse emerged from the trees. Its rider reined in, stared down at the still form dusted with snow, then dismounted to look more closely. A thread of vapor issued from between the girl's lips.

*   *   *

WOLVES HOWLED IN the forest. Dark water murmured beneath the frozen surface of the stream, and the wind spirit Ga'-oh sighed through the pines. But He'-no the Thunderer, spirit of vengeance, remained silent.

For now.

ONE

As our territorial history recedes from us, each passing year both deepens the obscurity upon the Indian's footsteps, and diminishes the power of the imagination to recall the stupendous forest scenery by which he was surrounded.
— LEWIS HENRY MORGAN, *LEAGUE OF THE HO-DE-NO-SAU-NEE, OR IROQUOIS*, 1851

AUTUMN 1857

THE LOW-PITCHED toot of a boat horn sent Glynis Tryon's gaze to the tall windows that faced the canal. She was seated at her desk in the Seneca Falls Library, and thus could see only the crowns of aspen that grew along the towpath below, their autumn-gold leaves shimmering in a breeze off the water. Beyond the trees, the sky shone with the blue brilliance of stained glass. A perfect September day.

Glynis pushed back her chair, rose, and went to stand at a mullioned window. On the canal below, one of two flat-bottomed boats, both loaded with grain and riding low in the water, was in the process of passing the other. This meant several minutes of intricate maneuvering, as teams of mules and their drivers were some two hundred fifty feet ahead of the boats and connected by long tow lines. Tangled lines could halt canal traffic for almost interminable periods. But on this occasion, as on most, the procedure was accomplished cleanly. And a good thing, too, Glynis thought, as more boats began to appear from the locks upriver; the harvest was a busy season in western New York.

Coming east from the village factories, the boats carried large crates of parts, which were labeled COWING FIRE ENGINES and GOULD PUMPS. The canal boats would head northeast to join the Erie Canal system, then either travel west or continue east to New York City and the ocean beyond. It gave Glynis acute pleasure that these goods manufactured in Seneca Falls were shipped all over the world. For might not someone, necessarily a very small someone, hide herself inside one of the crates and find herself in, say, England or even Peru?

Glynis smiled at this whimsy and remembered how, when she'd been younger, the thought of seeing Europe could set her daydreaming for hours. And yet she had not done much traveling in the years—fifteen it was now—since she'd graduated from Oberlin College and settled in Seneca Falls. And though she'd had times of regret, difficult times, most often she felt fairly satisfied with her choice of education and career rather than marriage and children.

Behind her, a low murmur of male voices ceased abruptly. She turned from the window to see her assistant, Jonathan Quant, bending over an open book that was held by Jeremiah Merrycoyf. Glynis suddenly recalled an illustration from Dickens's *Pickwick Papers,* prompted by Jonathan's earnest young face under a thatch of unruly hair, his rumpled sack coat and carelessly knotted neckcloth and, beside him, lawyer Merrycoyf's short, rotund shape straining the buttons of a frock coat, the stem of his unlit pipe jabbing at the page before them.

"Exactly what I wanted," Merrycoyf said at last. "Thank you, my boy, for locating it with such dispatch."

Jonathan nodded happily, prodding with his index finger the thick-lensed spectacles that had slid down his narrow, well-shaped nose. He returned to his tidy desk on the far side of the open room while Merrycoyf snapped the book shut, placed it under his arm, and lumbered toward Glynis.

Watching him cross the wood-pegged floor, Glynis thought, No, not Dickens but Clement Moore. She never saw the lawyer but that she wasn't reminded of Saint Nicholas. Short white beard, round cheeks that barely supported the wire-rimmed spectacles perched on them—his nose being far too small for this—Merrycoyf customarily looked content with his world. "You found it, then, Jeremiah?"

"Indeed yes, Miss Tryon. The efficient Mr. Quant has once again come to my aid. Now if you would be so kind as to sign this out . . . But tell me, my dear, do you get much call for Morgan's work on the Iroquois?"

"Not much." Glynis smiled in reply as she bent over her desk to sign the card. "But at least it's here when we do." She nudged aside the usual clutter on her desktop to find a small Seth Thomas clock, and straightened. "If you're leaving now, Jeremiah, I'll walk out with you. I have a small task to perform for Abraham Levy. A welcome task," she added in response to Merrycoyf's raised eyebrows. "I'm to meet the afternoon train that's bringing the new doctor."

"Ah, yes." Merrycoyf's brows lowered. "A young cousin of Abraham's, isn't it?"

Glynis nodded, and plucked her broad-brimmed straw hat from the hall stand beside the door; settling the straw carefully over her topknot, she gave its brim a rakish tilt. But then, after catching a glimpse of Merrycoyf's amused expression, she rearranged the brim to a more modest angle. While tucking in stray wisps of reddish hair, she called over her shoulder, "I'll be back in a bit, Jonathan."

Merrycoyf swung open the door. He stood aside while Glynis gathered in her long, full skirt and petticoats to accommodate the opening, then followed her out. In the far distance a train whistle sounded as they climbed several shallow steps to the wide dirt road that was Fall Street.

When Glynis hurried off in the direction of the station, Merrycoyf stood watching a black Morgan horse, with Constable Cullen Stuart astride, turn into the road behind her. The constable dismounted, caught up with Glynis, then walked along beside her.

Merrycoyf shook his head and could be heard to mutter under his breath, "That man's been waiting for years now—wonder if she'll ever make up her mind to marry him."

HER FOREHEAD CREASED in a frown, Neva Cardoza reluctantly turned her attention back to the train window. Although the people inside the passenger car had proved more interesting than the monotonous landscape outside, she supposed they were entitled to some privacy—the right not to be inspected by a disapproving stranger. But since her recent graduation from the Female Medical College of Pennsylvania, she had seen practically no one other than the diseased and dying, and now found she rather resented these travelers, who looked so robustly healthy. This somewhat disturbed her. Had she become more comfortable with the ill than with the well?

Neva's frown deepened as she watched yet more acres of dense forest stream past her window. Wasn't there anything other than *trees* in western New York? An hour after the train had pulled out of New York City, she had seen trees enough to last a lifetime. Mile after mile of the things. There were no majestic stone buildings, no crowded, bustling streets, no tidy parks. No omnibuses or elegant carriages, concert halls or museums. No Fulton steamboats, or wharves swarming with dockworkers whose muscled, sunburned backs, glistening with sweat, always unsettled her, made her turn away lest they notice her watching.

All she had seen from the train since it left the Hudson River valley was one other river—with the odd Indian name of Mohawk—hundreds of streams, a few small towns, scattered farmhouses, and many thousands of cows. And trees!

How had she gotten herself into this? She had never before set foot outside cities, those of New York and Philadelphia, yet here she was: an educated, reasonably intelligent, young Jewish woman headed full-steam toward the outer reaches of civilization. But of course she knew very well how she had gotten into this. Papa. Papa and Jacob Espinosa. Papa and Jacob Espinosa and a dowry. A dowry discussed before she, Neva, had even been consulted!

"Why do you want to disgrace me?" Papa had shouted. "Why do you think you can be a doctor? How did this happen—that my *daughter* wants to be a doctor? You should want to be a wife. And a mother. A respectable woman, as you have been taught by your own mama. Didn't you teach her this, Sheva?"

"I taught her," Sheva Cardoza said, gazing with annoyance at Neva. "She didn't listen. She never listens."

"But *you* are the one"—Papa now accused Mama, which Neva thought to be only fair—"the one who let your cousin Ernestine send her to that deceitful school. A school that would teach girls they can do just the same as boys. What were you thinking, Sheva?"

"I was thinking," Mama retorted, "that after Neva saw

what it was about, she might give up this foolishness of doctoring.''

"But, Papa," Neva began, mostly to interrupt their incessant arguing about who was to blame, not that it would do any good, "Papa, you don't understand. You won't even *try* to understand.''

"What is to understand?" In high drama, Papa flung his hands in the air, then brought them back to clutch at his chest. This, Neva knew, was to inspire guilt when, because of her, he finally succumbed to heart failure. But at the moment, he somehow managed to go on, "Jacob Espinosa, a fine, fine boy from a prosperous family, wants to marry you. But no! No, you would rather disgrace me. That I understand!''

And so it went. Day after day. While they waited, all of them, for her to come to her senses: Papa, Mama, her two older brothers—who both had decided long ago that she was unbalanced—and her younger sister Esthera. Beautiful Esthera, all the while crying her eyes out because Papa said she couldn't marry until Neva did, and nice boys wouldn't wait for her, Esthera, *forever,* and why did Neva *always* have to ruin *everything*?

During all of this, Jacob Espinosa hovered at the core of Neva's misery, wringing his hands solicitously. Jacob, with his sickly-looking white skin and his small, nearsighted eyes. His musty odor of old wool. His unbearable *niceness*! Besides which, Jacob Espinosa had to be, without doubt, the dullest person Neva had ever known. The thought of having to listen to his tedious monologues for the remainder of her days, and the image of his perpetually perspiring hands, his long, clammy fingers crawling over her body . . . Neva shuddered.

No! She would learn to *like* trees!

Her head came up with a jerk. The engine wheels were shrieking like banshees, which meant the train was about to stop again. It had stopped, so far as Neva could tell, at every village and hamlet in western New York. But this stop should be hers: Seneca Falls. She looked through the window at a squat brick station house coming into view, while a few brown chickens ran squawking from the track, feathers swirling in their wake.

She hoped this Abraham Levy who was supposed to meet her had received the last wire, the one that said she would be taking an earlier train. Abraham Levy was a fourth cousin—on her father's side. So Neva had been told. She'd never met him. She didn't want to meet him now, since to have voluntarily left New York City he must be a lunatic.

Still, Neva reassured herself, even in the middle of nowhere people got sick. And Dr. Blackwell had said—she'd *promised*—that if Neva worked in Seneca Falls for a few months' time, she, Elizabeth Blackwell, would guarantee her a position in the Infirmary when she returned: the New York Infirmary for Women and Children which had opened just a few months before. Begun by Elizabeth and Emily Blackwell and Marie Zakrzewska, it was the first hospital ever to be run entirely by women doctors. Neva wanted desperately to be *there*. But Elizabeth had insisted that the recent graduate needed still more education, more exposure to "the lessons of life"—whatever *that* meant! But how she could learn anything in Seneca Falls, New York, which didn't even have a hospital, Neva couldn't fathom.

And this Dr. Quentin Ives she was supposed to train with—what if he turned out to be one of those condescending know-it-alls who hated the very idea of female physicians? Not that Neva wasn't accustomed to them. Well, Dr. Ives would soon find out she wasn't a simpleton or a servant—a glorified nursemaid fit only to empty chamber pots.

When she descended to the station platform, Neva saw no one who appeared to be looking for her. So where might Abraham Levy be? She would wait only a few minutes. Why should she have to depend on some man who, from the looks of it, couldn't even tell time? Surely the Ives house wasn't very far; the town didn't look big enough for anything in it to be far.

As Neva glanced around, she experienced an unfamiliar anxiety. A sense of insignificance. This was a town that didn't even show up on some maps! Who would know if she lived or died? Who would even care? Maybe Papa had been right. Maybe she *was* a bad-tempered, stubborn girl who deserved to be alone, and who certainly didn't deserve someone as nice as Jacob Espinosa. But if she gave up now and went back to New York, without training and without a job, she'd almost have to marry Jacob. Even if she didn't deserve him!

She fought back an unexpected rush of tears. No, she would *not* cry. She would pick up her two valises and walk into town. Casting about for the baggage cart, she saw two people coming around the station house: a woman, and a man holding the reins of a black horse. They both looked her way and then started toward her. The woman, who smiled warmly at Neva, had an intelligent face, expressive, with large, alert gray eyes and lovely pale skin; high cheekbones were surrounded by strands of reddish hair escaped from under her broad-brimmed straw hat. Probably in her late thirties, she was not what one would call exactly pretty, this woman, but arresting. Someone who would be noticed in a crowd.

The man walking beside her reminded Neva of the rugged-looking Texas Rangers she'd seen in magazine illustrations: rangy and strong-featured, with thick sand-colored hair and mustache. As good-looking a man as Neva had seen in the flesh anywhere.

As they neared her, Neva stood waiting with a nervousness that she tried to conceal with an impatient frown.

WHEN ABRAHAM LEVY had asked Glynis Tryon to meet his cousin, he'd sounded apologetic. But surely Neva Cardoza would understand, Glynis had said, that Levy's Hardware store couldn't close in midafternoon during the harvesting season. Glynis would explain this and bring Neva back with her. Besides, she was eager to meet the young woman physician. The town desperately needed another doctor.

When Cullen had joined her on Fall Street, they'd gone on to the station together. "I think that must be Dr. Cardoza now," Glynis told him as they'd rounded the station house. "Standing next to the baggage cart."

"Let's hope it's *not* her," Cullen said. "She looks mad. You sure she's the one?"

But the young woman fit the description Abraham had given: slender and small, not much over five feet; dark brown crimped hair, pulled back severely into a knot; and widely spaced dark eyes. And Cullen was right. She looked angry.

"Neva Cardoza? Are you Dr. Cardoza?" Glynis asked. When the young woman nodded, Glynis extended her hand, introducing herself and Cullen. "Abraham Levy has a sick employee, and he can't leave his store untended. So he asked if I'd meet you."

"How *very* considerate of him!" Neva responded with a toss of her head.

Glynis sensed Cullen's immediate irritation, and felt a little of her own. But she then realized that the young woman would have no knowledge of life in a farming community.

And Neva Cardoza immediately apologized. "I'm sorry—I'm tired and out of sorts from the train ride," she explained. "And I do appreciate your coming. It's certainly not your fault that Mr. Levy is so—"

"Busy," Cullen interjected, so smoothly that Glynis glanced at him, expecting sarcasm to follow. But he went on, "Harvest time's busy for Abe—and he works hard." Cullen pointed at the two bulging valises. "Those yours?"

"Yes," Neva answered, her voice sounding considerably less peevish. "Yes, and they're very heavy, I'm afraid."

But Cullen had already lifted the valises and begun walking with them toward a farm wagon. "John," he called to the wagon's driver. "Could you drop these off at . . ." Cullen turned back to Neva. "You staying with the Iveses?"

"Yes, for now I am."

Cullen nodded, swinging the valises into the wagon as if they were feather pillows. Glynis thought Neva Cardoza looked impressed. That wasn't unusual; most women found Cullen impressive. But Glynis suddenly wondered what this young woman from New York City had expected to find here. Nothing but country bumpkins? No, that was unfair; Dr. Cardoza probably had no such preconception, no idea of what she'd find. And she must be overwhelmed, so far from home. Who wouldn't be anxious and uncertain?

"On the way, we can stop at Levy's Hardware so you can meet Abraham," Glynis told her as they began to walk. "It's just around the corner from the Ives house."

"That's not necessary," Neva replied swiftly. "I'm in no hurry to meet him."

Glynis didn't look at Cullen beside her. She didn't have to look; she could feel his disapproval of Neva Cardoza. But Glynis thought the young woman, despite their explanations, probably didn't understand Abraham's absence and felt hurt by his seeming lack of interest. Glynis thought she herself might feel that way, coming into a strange town to be met by strangers. And she wasn't ready to pass judgment yet on this badly needed doctor.

They reached the wide dirt road that ran through the center of Seneca Falls; Fall Street, and the Seneca River, which ran parallel to it, divided the town north and south.

"That's my library over there," Glynis said, gesturing to the small fieldstone building at the far corner of Fall and Cayuga streets. "It's just above the walled canal section of the river. Most of our mills and factories are on the other side, across the bridge there."

She paused, noticing that the woman was studying her intently.

"*Your* library?" Neva asked. "Then you're a librarian?"

When Glynis nodded, Neva said, "I think, now, that I've heard about you from my cousin Ernestine—Ernestine Rose?"

When Glynis nodded again, Neva went on, "Yes, and you write a newspaper column, and you're involved in women's rights. Miss *Tryon,* of course! I didn't recognize your name at first." And with that, Neva Cardoza smiled at last, a wide and generous smile that transformed her rather plain face into one that was extremely appealing.

Glynis didn't believe that Cullen had caught this transformation; he looked distracted, undoubtedly thinking that just exactly what the town needed was one more suffragist!

They walked west on Fall Street, moving around horses and farm wagons and elegant buggies, pony carts and light-weight runabouts and phaetons. Glynis pointed out to Neva the newly constructed hotel; a watchmaking and jewelry store; Erastus Partridge's Bank of Seneca Falls, with its new plate-glass windows and brass tellers' cages; Cuddeback's grocery; the drugstore, the bakery, the tailor's; Jeremiah Merrycoyf's law office; Hoskins's Dry Goods on one side of the road and Lathrop's Dry Goods on the other; and the Wayne County Mutual Fire Insurance Company.

Neva stepped onto a wood plank sidewalk to peer into the windows of the Widow Coddington's millinery shop. "I've never liked hats much," she said, her eyes going to Glynis's straw. "But I'll need one here—no buildings to blot out the sun!" The attractive smile flashed again.

Glynis started to comment, but was interrupted by a shout. "Constable! Constable Stuart—wait!" An obviously agitated, heavyset man hurried across the road toward them.

"What's the matter, Jack?" Cullen said when the man reached them.

"Where you been, Constable? I need to talk to you—right now!" the man panted, winded by his sprint across the street. He ignored the women if he even saw them, as his eyes were locked fast on Cullen.

"This is Jack Turner," Glynis said to Neva. "He has a farm north of town," she explained, attempting to introduce him.

Turner's attention was elsewhere. "Constable, you got to do something," he panted. "You got to!"

"Slow down, Turner," Cullen said. "What's the trouble?"

"Somebody means to kill me, Constable, that's the trouble. And you got to stop it!"

"It? What're you talking about, Turner?"

The man looked furtively up and down the street. "Constable Stuart," he said anxiously, "can't we go to the lockup—your office, I mean." He jerked his head toward Glynis and Neva. "I mean *alone*?"

Glynis couldn't imagine what Neva Cardoza might be thinking, but she herself wondered if Jack Turner had lost his mind—or, more likely, had lifted a few too many pints in the Red Mills Tavern.

Cullen, possibly wondering the same thing, just nodded

good-naturedly. "O.K., Jack. C'mon to the lockup." He turned to Neva. "Welcome to our quiet little town, Miss . . . that is, Dr. Cardoza. Nice to meet you." And he gave Glynis a wry, glad-to-get-out-of-*here* grin, before starting up the street with Jack Turner.

Glynis realized that all this time the young woman beside her hadn't said a word. Although faintly uneasy herself about Turner's agitation, she smiled at Neva. "I'm sure it's nothing serious," she offered. "Jack Turner likes his beer too much, that's probably all it is."

Neva looked skeptical, but nodded. Although they began walking again, after a few steps Neva put her hand on Glynis's arm. "Miss Tryon, up ahead there . . ." She pointed to a shop set back from the street with a sign that read LEVY'S HARDWARE.

The space in front of the shop was filled with farm implements: threshers, harvesters from the new Auburn plant, John Deere plows, and Pennock seed-planting drills. Recently the hardware store had expanded to include the cooper's shop next door, where barrels of every size had been piled, open ends outward, to form a gigantic honeycomb.

Several tall, woven splint baskets placed beside the shop entrance caught Glynis's attention; she hadn't seen them there before. In front of the splint baskets were stacked a number of smaller baskets woven from corn husks. They looked like the ones made by Iroquois women that she'd seen at the Seneca County Agricultural Fairs.

"That's Abraham's hardware store," Glynis said now to Neva. "Are you sure you don't—"

"No! If you could just show me the way to Dr. Ives's house."

"Oh, I'll go with you," Glynis offered, and to reassure the young woman, she added, "I think you'll like both Katherine and Quentin Ives."

She waited while Neva skirted first chickens, then a lean brown goat occupying the middle of the road; it was eating something unidentifiable, and was eyed by Neva from New York City with great distaste. She had just given it wide berth when she pulled up short to stare at a sturdy, ruddy-cheeked man emerging from the hardware store. He headed toward the women with a vigorous stride.

Glynis braced herself, not having any idea what Neva's response would be. "That's Abraham," she said quietly. "I really don't think we can avoid him now."

They couldn't, and as Abraham Levy approached them, his mouth, above a short, curly black beard, curved in an engaging grin.

"Afternoon, Miss Tryon," he said. Then, "And since you look just like your father—*you* must be the little Neva Cardoza."

For a moment, a pregnant silence swelled. Then, finally, "Yes, I'm *Doctor* Cardoza," she said acidly.

"Well, you can't expect me to call you *that,* can you?" Abraham laughed. "You're hardly more than a girl—"

"Frankly, Mr. Levy," Neva broke in, "I'd rather you didn't call me anything. And I suppose it's because I'm 'hardly more than a girl' that you wouldn't trouble yourself to meet my train."

Abraham's smile withdrew. "I couldn't get away," he said shortly.

"Obviously not!" Neva shook some dust from the hem of her skirt with a snapping sound. "Well, don't let this *girl* keep you from your important business."

With dismay, Glynis watched the two strangers glare at each other, the space between them crackling.

She bit down on her lip and sighed quietly to herself.

LATER THAT AFTERNOON, Glynis made her way home to 33 Cayuga Street through a shower of bright yellow leaves, the first of the season to fall. Her landlady's boardinghouse, a two-storied Federal structure with a gable roof, sat across from the village park. When Harriet Peartree's other boarder had left town several years before, to join his daughter's family in Syracuse, Glynis and her landlady had moved to this smaller house from a Gothic cottage one block away. Both places had been left to Harriet by one of her three deceased husbands.

In the kitchen, over a supper of beef and kidney pie and stewed tomatoes, Glynis told Harriet of the encounter between Abraham Levy and Seneca Falls's new doctor.

"And it was embarrassing," Glynis concluded. "At least it was for me, though I doubt if either one of them noticed—they were too busy shooting angry looks at each other. And it's really too bad, Harriet. After all, the young woman doesn't know anyone, and I'd rather hoped Abraham would be able to show her around. Now there's obviously no hope of that! But Katherine Ives took to Neva right away."

"Katherine Ives takes to everybody," Harriet pronounced, spearing one of her own translucent watermelon pickles. "Young woman would have to be a witch for Katherine not to like her. Is she?"

"A witch?" Glynis smiled. "No, although some of our town's menfolk might like to think so. She's just a bit . . . well, I guess *outspoken* could be the word. But it's possible that what I saw of Dr. Cardoza today came as the result of fatigue. And her uneasiness at being in a strange place."

"I don't know about that." Her landlady grinned as she got up from the table and went to the stove. "Young lady sounds like she might have been born difficult!" Harriet's hazel eyes twinkled as she returned with a plate of baked apples smelling of caramelized sugar and cinnamon. "S'pect Quentin Ives will have his hands full."

"You know, Harriet, something odd happened on the way to the Iveses'. Jack Turner came running up to Cullen on Fall Street, insisting someone meant to kill him."

"Can't say as I'm surprised," Harriet stated. "He's a bully, that man Turner is." She passed Glynis the cream pitcher.

"Really? Why do you say that?"

"I know his wife, Sara. Poor little thing always has one bruise or another, sometimes more than one. She tires to cover up, explain it away by saying she's clumsy, that she's fallen or bumped into something. And the Turner youngsters—they always look frightened. It's a shame!" Harriet pushed silvery blond hair from her face as she shook her head.

"I didn't know that about Jack Turner," Glynis said slowly. "But surely he wasn't suggesting his wife would retaliate."

"No. No, of course not," Harriet agreed. "I just meant

that maybe for once Turner took out his bad temper on somebody his own size. Somebody who could have threatened him.''

"I suppose so. Well, I certainly expect it to come to nothing. By the way, Harriet," she said, wanting to leave the sad and not uncommon plight of the Turner family, "where did you get this?" From the table she had picked up a small, narrow-necked bottle made of some tightly woven material. "And what is it?"

Harriet smiled. "It's a salt bottle. Made from corn husks."

"A salt bottle . . . doesn't it leak?" Glynis shook it slightly. "No, I guess it doesn't." She pulled out the stopper, a section of corn cob, from the bottle's neck to pour a small quantity of salt into her open palm. "Doesn't it have a liner of some sort?"

"No, no liner. It's woven so tightly they say it can even hold water. But mostly it's for salt. The outer husks absorb moisture so the salt inside stays dry."

Glynis ran her fingertips over the bottle's dense surface. "Did you by chance get this at Levy's Hardware? I saw some baskets there today."

Nodding, Harriet motioned toward the heavy oak sideboard against the wall opposite the kitchen window; on its top sat a shallow woven basket mounded with waxy Northern Spy apples. "Got that, too. I was there when a young Iroquois woman from Black Brook Reservation came in with them. And Abraham told her she could bring more items for him to sell."

"Those women make beautiful things," Glynis said. "I've seen them at the county fairs—maybe they'll bring in some of their silver jewelry. And those quill-worked bags. But who was it brought the baskets? I know one or two of the reservation women."

"She called herself Sunlight Weaver," Harriet answered. "Told me that when she was first born, her mother—a weaver herself—put her into a basket she'd made. Sunlight coming through the splints wove a pattern on the baby's face."

Glynis smiled; this Iroquois method of naming an infant

had always seemed to her both poetic and logical, infinitely preferable to accommodating a wealthy great-aunt by saddling an innocent with the lifelong burden of Sophonisba or Tryphenia. And the Iroquois birth name could be changed later in life. Thus a skillful corn grower might become Plentiful Harvest; a fast runner might be Wind Chaser; a silent and reclusive man—Walks At Sundown.

"I think it's so hard," Harriet said, "the way some of those women go off by themselves—into the woods usually—to give birth alone. I couldn't imagine doing that myself."

Glynis couldn't imagine it either. But it was their custom, and had been for centuries. Many of the Iroquois held on to their ancient ways. Or were trying to.

She got up from the table and went to stand by the kitchen door while Harriet heated water for the dishes. Gazing out into the back garden, Glynis thought she saw, from the corner of her eye, a flash of white beside the chrysanthemum bed. No, it wasn't Duncan, she told herself sadly; the little white terrier, with her for years, had died last spring. But she still imagined she saw a trace of him now and again, as if a phantom Duncan still roamed the house and yard. His gravestone, though, lay undisturbed beneath the lilac bush.

As she turned back to the kitchen, Glynis brushed at her eyes. She missed him.

TWO

ᕦᕤ

Higher education for women produces monstrous brains and puny bodies, abnormally active cerebration and abnormally weak digestion, flowing thought and constipated bowels.
—DR. E. H. CLARKE, C. 1850

ON THE FOLLOWING afternoon, Glynis, having at last completed a lengthy acquisition order, shut the top drawer of her desk, turned the wick of her new engraved-glass, oil-fueled study lamp—a present from Cullen—and prepared to close the library. As she'd told her assistant, "There's no point in staying open any longer, Jonathan. No one will come in after four—not until harvesting is over."

Jonathan Quant, his curly, snarled hair just visible over the spine of a book, nodded absently. He'd been buried in this same book all day, and Glynis crossed the room to his desk to see what had so captured him.

"Mary Jane Holmes's new novel!" she said. "That's what has absorbed you?"

Jonathan's smile was sheepish as he put down *Meadow Brook* to gaze up at Glynis with myopic blue eyes made huge by his spectacles. "I thought I should take a look at it. And it's a good thing we've got two copies—everyone's reading it."

Perhaps not everyone, but half the women in Seneca Falls couldn't seem to get enough of Mrs. Holmes's sentimental novels. Or those of any of the other romantic female authors, now that the prejudice against women's writing had begun to diminish somewhat. That Mrs. Holmes lived in Brockport, New York, just west of Rochester, only added to her astonishing appeal. And this while Hawthorne and Melville sat on the library shelves gathering dust. Indeed, Hawthorne himself recently lamented that America had been "wholly given over to a d—— d mob of scribbling women."

"So, how is it—the novel?" Glynis asked.

"Not too bad, actually," Jonathan said. "You haven't read it yet?"

"No, and I probably won't. There are too many other things I need to—" She broke off as the library door swung open. Zephaniah Waters, who was Cullen Stuart's young deputy, burst into the room. "Well, Zeph—hello. What is it?"

"Miss Tryon," Zeph panted, sweat beading his somber, square black face and crisp, nappy hair. "Constable Stuart wants to see you right away. Didn't you hear the commotion up the street just now?" He tugged at the cuffs on his sleeves, which were too short, always, for the long adolescent arms inside them.

"No, I didn't hear." Glynis shook her head. "What's happened?"

"It's Jack Turner," Zeph answered, his bright jet eyes alive with excitement. He rocked back on his heels. "His wife found him just a while ago—found him dead. Dead as a doornail."

"*What?*"

Zeph's expression, as usual, indicated impatience. "I said that Jack Turner is—"

"Yes, I heard you say that, Zeph," she interrupted. "I just meant—well, how? How did he die?"

"Don't know yet. They took him—that is, took his *body*—to Doc Ives's office. And Constable Stuart wants you to meet him there. Right now!" he again urged her.

BY THE TIME they got to Ives's, a crowd had begun to gather. Glynis left Zeph and weaved her way from the street to the house through a score of onlookers. Once inside, she located Katherine Ives just emerging from the examining room, a room that had once been the Iveses' front parlor. "Katherine? Is Cullen here?"

"He's in there." Katherine pointed to the closed door. "Go on in, Glynis. If you need me, I'll be in the kitchen with Sara Turner."

When she opened the examining room door, Glynis's head jerked back from a smell like that of rotting cheese. She gritted her teeth and forced herself into the room, where she found not only Cullen, but Quentin Ives and Neva Cardoza, all three of them bent over the body stretched out on a long table. Glynis noticed that Neva's face had a pallor not there the day before. The young woman looked up to give Glynis a brief nod.

Cullen straightened and moved from the table. "Glynis, I need you to talk to Sara Turner. She's been like somebody struck dumb since she got here, and there are things we need to know."

"But, Cullen, what happened? How did Jack Turner die?"

"That's what we're trying to find out," Quentin Ives answered. He opened a cupboard to pull from it two jean-cloth aprons, one of which he handed to Neva. "Turner obviously vomited before he died," Ives continued. "The front of his shirt's covered with it. We've got to learn what he ate today, and possibly his wife would know."

"Dr. Ives?" Neva said hesitantly. Although she looked pale, her voice sounded steady enough, Glynis thought. There was also an unexpected note of deference in the voice. "Dr. Ives," Neva said again, "the vomited matter looks rather peculiar. Almost black."

Quentin Ives nodded. "Yes. And notice the dark blue particles—they look a little like soot. What might that indicate to you?"

Having tied the bibbed apron around her waist, Neva bent again over Turner's body, while Glynis swallowed hard and turned away to edge toward the door. Cullen followed her out into the hall.

" 'What might that *indicate* to you?' " Cullen mimicked. "Sounds like a classroom in there."

"Well," Glynis offered, "Neva is supposed to be training with Quentin."

"Good! And when they get done admiring the colors of the 'matter' on Turner's shirt, then maybe they can consider what the hell happened to him."

"I think that's what they *are* doing, Cullen. And in light of what Jack Turner said to you yesterday . . . By the way, did Neva tell Quentin Ives about that?"

"I don't know. Until just a minute ago, she'd been

speechless, which was certainly a relief.''

''Cullen! Don't be so hard on her. She's only just arrived here, remember.'' But Glynis knew Cullen's annoyance stemmed from frustration, or even perhaps some sense of accountability for whatever had happened to Jack Turner.

Cullen shrugged and motioned toward the kitchen. ''Try to find out what Turner's wife knows, will you? Katherine Ives doesn't want to pester her with questions, but I assume you can be more hardhearted about it.''

Glynis did not find this assessment of herself a particularly attractive one, and it crossed her mind that just a few years before she would have taken issue over it with Cullen. At the moment, however, it seemed relatively unimportant.

She headed for the kitchen.

Sara Turner, small and gray-looking, sat slumped in a straight-backed wooden chair, staring at her hands, clasped around a small Bible. She didn't look up when Glynis entered. Katherine Ives, standing just inside the door, shook her head in sympathy.

''Poor little thing hasn't said a word since she got here,'' Katherine whispered to Glynis. ''She's clearly in shock. What a dreadful thing this is—and Sara's not in any shape to face Cullen Stuart's questioning.''

Glynis decided she'd better talk to Sara alone. Cullen had been right—Katherine would be too softhearted to press the woman. ''Would you mind, Katherine, leaving me with Mrs. Turner for a few minutes?''

Katherine's eyebrows lifted, but she nodded and left the kitchen as Glynis went to sit beside Sara Turner.

''I'm Glynis Tryon, Mrs. Turner. I think we've met before.'' This brought no response. In fact, the woman seemed to shrink further into herself, and Glynis had the feeling that Sara Turner might before long disappear entirely.

''Mrs. Turner,'' she tried again. ''This must be very painful for you, and I wish I didn't have to ask, but we need to know what Mr. Turner might have eaten today. I'm sure you want Dr. Ives to find out why your husband died.''

With this, the woman finally raised her eyes to Glynis. ''I don't care,'' she said thickly.

Glynis hoped her face didn't reveal her shock. Not only

at Sara Turner's words, which were shocking enough, but at the discovery—now that Glynis could clearly see her face—that the woman was hardly older than herself. Sara's whole demeanor had suggested advanced age and infirmity. But Glynis saw that the slack jaw, the round-shouldered slump, and the lackluster eyes were those of a woman perhaps forty years old whose life must be exceedingly harsh. Indeed, Glynis wondered if Sara Turner had the strength to care about anything. She wished desperately that she could leave the poor woman alone, but proximity to death rarely allowed for that. Especially sudden, unidentified death.

"Mrs. Turner, I'm really sorry to intrude—but if you could just answer a few questions?"

Sara Turner sighed heavily and gave Glynis the briefest of nods before her gaze went back to the Bible she fingered.

Glynis bent toward the woman. "Were you with your husband when . . . when he became ill?"

"No. I just come home—found him a-lyin' there. With no breath. I knew he was dead."

"Ah, where had you just come home from?"

"Been to Waterloo, most all the day. Margaret—that's my sister—she's expectin', you know?"

Glynis nodded encouragingly. "What time do you think that was?"

"Don't rightly know—somewheres around three, maybe."

"So when you got home, Mrs. Turner, what did you do first?"

"Stabled the horse. I sees that Jack's in from the fields, 'cause his horse is there, and I was hurryin' so's he won't get mad 'bout his dinner not bein' hot—you understand?" She gave Glynis a searching look.

"Yes, I understand." Perhaps more than the woman realized. By this time, Glynis had seen the bruises on Sara's jaw, the broken blood vessels in her hollowed cheeks, and the hand that hung from a wrist no longer sound.

"So you went straight to the kitchen then, Mrs. Turner?"

"Found him there on the floor. Covered with puke—he'd been sick on himself, see . . ."

"Was he sick often?" Glynis inserted.

"Never. Never got sick. Not a day, even after he'd been drinkin' all night."

"You said, a minute ago, that you knew he was dead right away. What did you do then?"

"Went down the road for help. Neighbors, they brung him"—her head bobbed toward the hall—"and me into town here."

"Was there anyone else at your farm? Any hired hands, for instance, or your children?"

"No. The kids're hired out, apprenticed in the next county. We don't need 'em at home no more, he says."

"Your husband said that?"

Sara Turner nodded. For the first time Glynis saw tears forming. "He says they got to work, so he sends 'em off. Says the farm's been doin' poorly of late, and we got no money for kids. Or hired hands."

Glynis did not want to think about this. About laws that gave fathers the absolute right to apprentice their children away, disown them, send them off—anything—without mothers having any say at all. And she had long ago become convinced that women stayed with abusive husbands because, without exception, men received custody of children in the few divorce proceedings that did take place.

She tried to disregard these thoughts, and said, "Mrs. Turner, do you know what your husband might have eaten today? For example, when you got home, was there anything in the kitchen that you yourself hadn't prepared?"

The woman started to shake her head, then seemed to hesitate.

"Yes?" Glynis prodded.

The hesitancy gave way to, "No, nothin'."

Glynis frowned, wondering whether to pursue this possible evasion. But she couldn't, the woman looked so fragile. So pathetic. "Just one last thing, Mrs. Turner. Yesterday, Mr. Turner told Constable Stuart that he believed someone meant to kill him . . ." Glynis stopped as Sara Turner's head jerked toward her.

"He said that?" The woman's mouth twisted. For a split second, Glynis even wondered if Sara Turner might be about to smile! But instead her mouth reset itself firmly, and she looked straight into Glynis's eyes. "I shouldn't be surprised," she said flatly.

Glynis felt her stomach tighten. "You aren't surprised at what your husband said?"

"Ain't surprised somebody wanted to kill him. That's been true for . . . for quite a few years back."

Glynis urged Sara to give her more explanation, but the woman refused to elaborate. She gripped her Bible and sank back into her enigmatic silence, relieved only by a sigh now and then.

At last Glynis leaned forward to clasp the woman's undamaged hand. "Thank you, Sara. I won't trouble you any more." It hardly seemed appropriate to offer further condolence for Jack Turner's death.

As Glynis left the kitchen, Sara Turner's head bent again over the Bible in her lap. Cullen, pacing outside the examining room's closed door, looked up as she came down the hall, then gestured toward the Iveses' back door. "Let's go out on the porch and talk," he said. "They're doing the autopsy in there."

Glynis heard from behind the door a sudden clatter of metal, as if an instrument had been dropped. Wincing, she walked quickly toward the back porch, wondering how Neva Cardoza was holding up.

As she and Cullen settled into the cushions of the wide porch swing, there came the murmur of voices from the street.

"Still a bunch of people there," Cullen said. "Folks never seem to get enough of calamity—long as it's somebody else's." His boots pushed against the porch floor, and the ropes holding the swing creaked softly.

Glynis felt her tension begin to lessen as the swing moved gently back and forth. "I don't think Sara Turner knows exactly what happened, Cullen," she said. She related her conversation with the woman.

When she'd finished, Cullen grunted. "That's all she says—she came home and found him dead?"

Glynis turned to look at him. "Yes. Why, don't you believe her? And if not, why not?"

Cullen shook his head. "I'm not saying I don't believe

her. But Jack Turner had a strong appetite for drink. He could get real unpleasant, and rumor has it he beat his wife and kids. Maybe Mrs. Turner came home and found him drunk, and—''

''And what, Cullen? She's a very small, frail woman— what could she have done?''

He shook his head again. ''I don't know,'' he shrugged. ''I'd think Turner died of something like heart failure, except for yesterday—what he said.''

''What *did* he say, after you left us?''

''Same thing you heard. He kept repeating that somebody meant to kill him. He seemed positive of it, Glynis. I must have asked him a hundred times *why* he thought that. He wouldn't—or couldn't—say. I finally decided beer had pickled his brain. Sent him off. And now . . .''

''Cullen, you can't blame yourself for what's happened. If he wouldn't tell you anything—''

She broke off because he suddenly sat forward, stopping the swing's motion with a sideways lurch. ''Turner did say one thing, come to think of it,'' Cullen said thoughtfully. ''He muttered something like if he got killed, it'd be because . . . because of the brook. Then he clammed up. Acted like he was sorry he'd said anything.''

''The brook? What brook? That doesn't make sense. Unless he meant some legal issue—but it still doesn't make any sense.''

''No. No, of course it doesn't, and I told him so. And he lit out right after that.''

''Well,'' Glynis sighed, ''maybe the autopsy will provide some explanation. It did seem bizarre, though, Sara Turner so calmly announcing that she wasn't surprised somebody wanted to kill her husband.''

They heard Quentin Ives call, and when they got back inside, the physician stood in the hall outside the examining room, removing a blood-spattered apron. Neva appeared just behind him; she looked even paler than she had earlier.

''So?'' Cullen said. ''You find anything?''

''Oh, yes,'' Quentin answered quickly. ''We certainly did find something.''

Neva stepped forward and took several shaky breaths.

"Could we go outside? I really need some fresh air."

Glynis didn't doubt it.

They trooped back out onto the porch, passing the kitchen where Sara Turner still sat, still staring at her lap.

Quentin Ives leaned against the porch railing. "Turner had no heart problems that I knew of, but I looked for that kind of thing first." He shook his head. "Nothing there that could have caused his death. Heart looked good."

Cullen made an inarticulate sound, and Glynis knew he didn't want to hear all the things that *couldn't* have caused Turner's death. Quentin must have gathered this also, because he said, "All right, Cullen, I guess you want an answer."

"Right. What *did* you find?"

"Found inflammation of the stomach, small intestines, and colon. Badly inflamed, stomach full of grumous fluid and blood. But most telling were the particles adhering to the stomach lining."

With that, Glynis had a grim premonition of what might be coming, and Cullen repeated, "Particles?"

"Particles of arsenic."

Glynis sagged against the porch railing to catch her breath. At the same time, Neva Cardoza gazed at Quentin Ives with what only could be described as admiration.

". . . and you're telling me," Cullen was saying, "that Jack Turner died from poison."

"Little question about it," Quentin said firmly. "It would take about three grains of arsenic to kill someone Turner's size. Even considering the fact that he'd vomited, we found the equivalent of that. Would you agree, Dr. Cardoza?"

Neva seemed startled, and flushed slightly. "Oh, yes. Yes, I would agree!" But her voice sounded tense.

It must have been hard for her, Glynis sympathized, to have this occur on only her second day in town. But she certainly appeared impressed with Quentin.

Cullen gripped the porch railing and stared off at the sky. But Glynis, recalling her questions of Sara Turner, asked, "What time do you think he died?"

"Hard to tell," Quentin said. "Arsenic retards decomposition, so it could have been any time in . . . well, say the last twelve hours.''

"So we have to find out," Cullen said, turning back to the porch, "what he's eaten since this morning."

"Or drunk," Neva spoke up unexpectedly. "Arsenic can be masked by any number of things."

"Such as?" Cullen said to her.

"Well . . ." Neva hesitated, turning to Quentin.

"Go ahead," Quentin told her. "You seem to know a great deal about poison."

Neva flushed again, but said to Cullen, "Just about anything that's bitter can mask the taste of arsenic. Like chocolate or rhubarb, lemon flavoring—or wine or beer."

"Oh, great!" Cullen slapped his hand palm down on the railing. "That's just great. Jack Turner made his own wine."

"But," Glynis said, "he also bottled it. If the arsenic *was* in the wine, couldn't we find sediment traces in the bottle?"

"And then what?"

"Well, we could . . . I don't know," she floundered. "But surely it would be useful to know if arsenic *was* in the wine or not. And in the wine he made."

"True," Cullen said, "or his wife could have baked him a nice chocolate cake full of poison before she so conveniently left town. That so, Quentin?"

Quentin Ives frowned. "Didn't find any evidence of chocolate. Any food at all, as a matter of fact."

Glynis followed this with, "I don't see why you're so anxious to blame Sara, anyway, Cullen. Isn't it likely that Jack Turner, when you asked him about it yesterday, would have mentioned that it was his *wife* who intended to kill him?"

Cullen shrugged. "Not if he thought she was sick and tired of getting beaten—don't think he'd have mentioned that. At any rate, we're not going anywhere with speculation—I'd better take a ride out to Turner's. See what I can find."

He went down the porch steps, leaving the others to stare at one another in silence.

*   *   *

NEVA WATCHED CONSTABLE Stuart stride off around the corner, as Glynis and Quentin Ives went back inside. Still feeling shaky, she remained on the porch. She found she was also wretchedly tired. Just one day in this "quiet little town," as the constable had phrased it, and already a murder—even if nobody had actually called it that. Maybe it wouldn't be quite as boring here as she'd feared. But the most agreeable aspect of Seneca Falls so far was Dr. Quentin Ives.

He seemed nothing like the self-important doctors at the medical school. After she'd unpacked last night, they had sat, she and Dr. Ives, on this same back porch while he'd asked questions about her education, about what she wanted to do with it, and even listened to her answers. As if they were important. He'd discussed—*discussed,* not preached— areas of medical controversy: the current dispute about which was the better anesthesia, ether or chloroform; whether dentistry should be a profession separate from medicine and surgery. Things like that. Quentin Ives had talked with her as though she were entitled to have an opinion.

He had broader knowledge than did most of the physicians by whom she'd been taught in Philadelphia. She guessed this came from not only having a good mind, but being a country doctor who had to know something about everything. Quentin Ives couldn't afford to concentrate in just one or two areas of medicine, as many physicians were now beginning to do. And he didn't have many professional colleagues to assist in diagnosis; he was the only surgeon in Seneca Falls.

Neva's thoughts were interrupted by Dr. Ives and Glynis Tryon coming back out on the porch, then greeting someone who had just rounded the house. Neva looked over the porch railing to see Abraham Levy coming toward them.

"Had some trouble this afternoon, I heard," Abraham said, standing below the porch steps. The coarse blue cotton of his work shirt strained over his shoulders, and where the top button was undone at his neck, a few curly black hairs glistened with sweat.

Neva quickly looked away, listening, however, to the others explain the "trouble." She herself didn't intend to say anything to Abraham Levy. The minute she'd laid eyes on him the day before, she could tell—even if she hadn't known beforehand—that he was related, no matter how distantly, to her father. He had the same arrogance, the inflated sense of himself, the dogmatic I-am-right-about-everything attitude. She didn't like it in her father. She liked it even less in this man.

After all, he wouldn't even bother to meet her train—probably felt it beneath him.

Neva suddenly realized all of them were staring at her. "I'm sorry," she said to Glynis Tryon and Dr. Ives. "I wasn't paying attention. Did you say something?"

"Yes," Abraham Levy answered, as if she had addressed *him*. "I asked how you were doing?"

"I am doing *just fine*! Why shouldn't I be?" She pretended not to see Quentin Ives's eyebrows rise, or the look he gave Miss Tryon.

"No reason," Abraham Levy said, his mouth tightening. "Just thought our fresh air might have made you more agreeable. Guess I was mistaken."

As Neva sucked in her breath, Abraham pivoted on his heel and began to stride toward the road. But he turned to say to Quentin Ives, "Your grass here's getting tall. Better bring your scythe in for sharpening."

Neva missed Dr. Ives's reply; turning her back on the insufferable Levy, she had shoved open the porch door. Her cheeks burned, and she pressed them hard with her clenched fists, before entering the house and escaping the sound of his voice. Behind her, the door slammed noisily.

THREE

The only religious sect in the world, unless we except the Quakers, that has recognized the equality of woman, is the Spiritualists. They have always assumed that woman may be a medium of communication from heaven to earth. . . . The Spiritualists in our country are not an organized body, but they are more or less numerous in every State and Territory from ocean to ocean.

—HISTORY OF WOMAN SUFFRAGE, EDITED BY ELIZABETH CADY STANTON, SUSAN B. ANTHONY, AND MATILDA JOCELYN GAGE

"IT'S GOOD OF you to come with me," Neva Cardoza said to Glynis while they waited on Fall Street, outside Boone's Livery. "I either walked or took the omnibuses at home—in Philadelphia, too. I doubt I'll ever learn to drive one of those contraptions." She gestured toward the small, two-seater, four-wheeled phaeton to which a bay horse was being harnessed by one of Boone's young stable boys.

"You'll learn," Glynis said, and smiled. "We've all had to, those of us women who need to get places on our own—and who don't have the means to hire drivers. Why don't I give you a lesson today?"

Neva looked dubious, Glynis thought, but the young woman agreed readily enough. She had now been in town for little less than a month, and Quentin Ives had decided she should be seeing more of his patients. Dr. Cardoza was certainly qualified, he'd said, to handle the more routine things a rural physician encountered.

Neva had come by the library the day previous for some books on western New York's history. "I guess if I'm going to be here awhile, I should know something about the area," she'd said.

Glynis applauded this interest and, while locating materials, had noted that the young woman had lost her sallow complexion. Neva's cheeks glowed with a becoming ruddiness.

Glynis extracted two heavy books from the shelves beside her desk. "This first one, *The Jesuit Relations*," she explained, handing it to Neva, "is a collection of reports—letters and journals mainly—sent back to Quebec and France during the seventeenth century by Jesuit missionaries. It's thought that missionaries were the first whites to have contact with American Indians. At least they were the first to chronicle the contact."

Neva made a small face. "Jesuit missionaries? You mean Catholic priests?"

Glynis nodded. "And you should keep that in mind when the Indians are described as heathens and barbarians, because, of course, the Jesuits came to convert these people to Christianity. But the Iroquois—the only Indians I'm familiar with—already possessed a rich, spirit-based religion.

"The other book," she went on, "*League of the Ho-de-no-sau-nee, or Iroquois,* was written by Lewis Henry Morgan, a Rochester lawyer; Morgan did his research assisted by Ely S. Parker, a Seneca Iroquois."

"*Seneca* Iroquois?" Neva echoed. "I thought the Indians around here were *all* Iroquois—"

"It's a Confederacy," Glynis interjected. "If we can find some time in the next few days, I'll try to explain what I know of it."

"I have to make some calls with Dr. Ives today," Neva told her, "and tomorrow morning I'm supposed to go to the . . . the Grimm farm, I think it was. Do you know how far that might be?" she asked, her expression one of misgiving, "Because I'll probably have to walk—I don't know how to handle a carriage."

"It's too far to walk, but I'll go with you, if you like," Glynis offered. "Young Pippa Grimm has been sick, and I should take her some more books."

"Pippa—she's the one I'm supposed to see," Neva said. "Quentin—that is, Dr. Ives—" she corrected herself, flushing slightly, "said she'd had scarlet fever. The last time he saw her was several weeks ago, and he wants to be sure she's recovered without complications. To tell the truth, I rather hoped you'd offer to come with me.''

Her smile had been a grateful one.

Now, on Saturday morning, Glynis flicked the reins of the carriage horse, and they wheeled across Fall Street to turn north onto another, narrower, dirt road.

''This becomes Black Brook Road,'' Glynis said, ''and to the right over there is Black Brook itself. Notice how the water looks stained or dusky? That's because of tannin in the leaves and wood from the trees along its banks.''

''Is that where the word *tanning* comes from?'' Neva asked.

Glynis nodded. ''There are a lot of streams and brooks named 'Black' something or other, wherever there are oak woods. This particular Black Brook flows east to Seneca Falls village, then heads north, getting deeper and wider, until it empties into swampland called the Montezuma Marsh.''

Despite the autumnal color of the leaves, a soft October wind seemed almost as warm as that of high summer, and it lifted the brim of Neva's new straw hat. She grabbed at the hat, retied its long green ribbons under her chin, then took a deep breath. ''Well,'' she said, exhaling, ''the air here certainly smells different from New York City's.'' She said this somewhat reluctantly, Glynis thought.

''Are you very homesick?'' she asked Neva, the reins loosely held while the road remained flat. ''I should think you might be, by this time.''

Rearranging her small black leather satchel under her feet, Neva didn't answer immediately, and Glynis glanced sideways to see if she'd heard the question. But then Neva said, ''No, oddly enough, I'm not.'' She spoke slowly. ''I even had to think for a minute about what homesickness feels like. Guess I've been too busy to notice.'' Her face darkened abruptly. ''Yesterday, that Mr. Levy asked me the same thing.''

Glynis thought it probably best not to comment on ''that Mr. Levy.'' But then, to her surprise, Neva asked, ''How old is he, do you know?''

''Ah, well . . . let's see.'' Glynis found this question intriguing, coming as it did from someone who, by all accounts, appeared to loathe Abraham. "I think he must be around thirty-five or thirty-six."

"Has he ever been married?" Neva's voice was so faint, Glynis had to lean toward her to hear. Well, well—such singular curiosity about Abraham Levy!

"I heard that Abraham was betrothed when he lived in England—that's where he grew up," Glynis said. "But his intended died. I'm afraid that's all I know about it. I did hear that his mother was Spanish."

"Oh, yes," Neva broke in. "I know that! Not that I really care anything about it," she added emphatically. "I shouldn't have asked, Miss Tryon . . . I really don't know why I did."

Didn't she now, Glynis thought, swallowing a smile. Then, mostly to reassure Neva that she herself hadn't given the questions a second thought, she said, "Why don't you take the reins for a time? Here."

Neva reached for the reins without hesitation; the next minutes were devoted to driving technique. Their horse was an unfamiliar one to Glynis, possibly new to Boone's Livery, and while this made her a shade uneasy, the animal seemed complacent enough about the various tuggings and the inexpert poking with the whip. "Very lightly," Glynis instructed, "only enough to make him aware that you want a change of gait or direction. For example, just ahead where we want to bear right alongside Black Brook."

Neva negotiated the curve and smiled broadly, like a child mastering a difficult task. "Is that it ahead—the Grimm farm?" She pointed left with the whip.

"No, that's the Turner place."

Neva's smile disappeared. "Oh," was all she said.

They drew parallel with the Turner farmhouse; its roof and porch sagged badly, and sections of the fence fronting the road were missing altogether. Several sheep, their summer fleece matted and grimy, grazed on what appeared to be merely stubble. Small wonder that Sara Turner indicated the farm had been doing poorly.

"We should stop on the way back," Glynis said, "to see how Sara's getting on."

Neva murmured agreement.

She handled the horse with increasing confidence, so Glynis relaxed and sat back to watch. When they were a quarter of a mile past the Turner farm, they came abreast of several dilapidated structures to the right of the road. The blackened wooden skeletons of a farmhouse and barns were barely visible under a wrapping of wild grapevine and ivy. Several lilac bushes flourished beside the ruins of the house.

"What happened there?" Neva asked. "Fire?"

"A terrible fire," Glynis confirmed. "Four or five years ago. I remember that night, and seeing from my bedroom window what looked to be the whole northern sky ablaze. It was a real tragedy—Cole Flannery, the farmer who owned the land, and his hired hand, Dick Davis, both died in that fire. Fortunately, Cole's wife, Mary, and their children were away, visiting family in Syracuse when it happened, or they all might have perished."

Glynis shook her head; she still found the memory of that night disturbing.

The carriage now clattered up a moderate rise where the roadbed narrowed to become not much more than axle width. "The Grimm place is about half a mile up the road, on the other side of this hill," Glynis told Neva. "You're doing very well—why don't you take us all the way there?"

"The road's gotten so cramped, though," Neva said, peering ahead. "What happens if we meet another—"

Interrupting her, and making her concern all too real, came the sound of pounding hooves on the far side of the hill. Glynis sat bolt upright as a horse and carriage appeared at the top of the rise, racing directly toward them.

Neva gasped, and gripped the reins tightly. "Flex on the right rein," Glynis directed, "to pull his head around. Right rein! The other carriage will pass to the left."

"But there's no room!" Neva said between clenched teeth. She jerked her head to the right; the bank beside the road rioted with waist-high goldenrod.

"Neva," Glynis said anxiously, "slow the horse! Flex the reins with both hands: pull and release, pull and release. One, two, one, two . . . Never mind!" she said suddenly, glancing ahead at the rapidly approaching carriage. "Just haul back on both reins to make him stop. Use the hand brake!"

But the left rein slithered from Neva's grasp. The horse surged forward, while the oncoming carriage barreled toward them, clearly not about to give an inch.

"*Neva!*" Glynis shouted over the sound of rattling wheels. "Neva, use your whip—tap his left—*left*—hindquarters. *Left hindquarters! And use the brake!*"

Neva fumbled for the hand brake, nearly losing her seat. Glynis sucked in her breath as Neva brought the whip down, at the same time hauling on the right rein. Abruptly the horse swerved right. The carriage gave a great bounce, nearly throwing out both women as the horse scrambled directly up the shallow bank. The vehicle tilted precariously, jolting from one side to the other. Glynis grabbed at its low side and winced as her head repeatedly struck the canopy. They jounced ahead, plowing through goldenrod, pollen spewing into the air and blossom heads flying. At last the drag of the carriage proved too much for the horse. He came to a quivering halt.

Glynis's fingers ached from gripping the side panel of the phaeton. She rubbed them while watching the carriage on the road below pass swiftly. And although its driver must have seen their predicament, it did not even slow. Glynis managed to catch a glimpse of a woman's face, flushed and angry-looking, gazing straight ahead while she repeatedly whipped her horse. The woman looked vaguely familiar.

Neva sat very still, her face white and moist with perspiration. But Glynis had learned about her something that was extremely telling—the young woman hadn't thrown up her hands helplessly in panic, as many would have done. While she climbed down from the carriage to retrieve the lost left rein, she glanced with sudden affection at the silent Neva. Glynis struggled through the weeds in her long skirts; the horse's head swung toward her, his muzzle sprinkled with golden specks. He acted as if nothing unusual had taken place. "As if," she said when she returned with the rein, "he just stopped along the way for some sweets."

Neva gave her a shaky look and tried to refuse the rein Glynis handed up to her. "I don't think I should drive," she said unsteadily. "I almost got us killed."

"It wasn't your fault," Glynis said with firmness. "As a matter of fact, you kept your head and did very well."

"How can you say that?" Neva argued. "The horse would have done fine if I hadn't confused him!"

"Perhaps," Glynis said doubtfully. "But you can't depend on the reasoning power of a horse. Horses are none too bright. Beautiful, yes—but not bright. Though they're not as stupid as some people." She gestured toward the dust just settling behind the other carriage, now vanished.

"Did you see the driver?" Neva's voice had an edge.

"Barely. She reminded me of—that is, she looked like someone I should know." Glynis shook her head, frowning. "Can't remember where I've seen her."

"Perhaps a lunatic asylum?" Neva offered.

Glynis smiled ruefully and nodded. "Perhaps. Now, are you ready? I'll guide the horse back to the road. But then you should drive," she insisted.

Once again on the road, the carriage jerked briefly while its wheels unburdened themselves of goldenrod debris. Glynis glanced sideways at Neva, startled to hear the young woman begin to laugh softly.

"I was just thinking," she answered Glynis's unspoken question, "how shocked my family would be if they could see me now. I'm afraid I'm not too tolerant of people who get themselves into dangerous situations. It always seems to involve just plain stupidity on their part. But look at what I did!"

Neva's voice, not sounding particularly chastened, trailed off as the southern edge of the Grimm farm came into sight. Sturdy fences enclosed grazing flocks, reminding Glynis of a landscape scene by the artist Susan Catherine Moore Waters, whose favorite subject was sheep. Grass grew lushly green. Black Brook meandered to the right of the road, then curved to flow under a wooden bridge that vibrated noisily beneath the carriage wheels.

"Before we reach the farm," Glynis said, "I should tell you a little about the Grimms. They're . . . well, let's say they're a somewhat unusual family." Neva's raised eyebrows had made Glynis decide on *unusual* rather than *peculiar*.

"Unusual? Why?"

"For one thing, they're very reclusive. Hardly ever come into town, any of them but Molly. She brings Pippa with her to the library occasionally."

Neva nodded. "Pippa, the one I'm to see?"

"Yes, Molly's daughter. When Molly was widowed—I'm told her husband died shortly after their marriage—she returned to her home and the Grimm family name. Obadiah Grimm, Molly's father, is the patriarch of the family; everyone thinks of him that way, I guess, because he resembles the Moses of Michelangelo: shoulder-length white hair and flowing beard, strong, rugged features—an impressive-looking man. And quite an intimidating one."

Neva was frowning, and now said, "All those old biblical males were intimidating! That's one reason I renounced religion—like my cousin Ernestine Rose, although she's had more success in renouncing her *family* than I have." She glanced at Glynis with an inquiring expression.

Glynis wondered if Neva thought she'd be shocked. "Well, yes, I know about your cousin," she said, smiling with what she hoped would convey understanding.

But Neva's frown remained. And when she didn't say more, Glynis continued with the Grimms. "There's also Almira. She's Obadiah's wife and Molly's mother, but you should draw your own conclusions about *her*. And then," Glynis went on, "there is Molly's brother, Lazarus."

"Lazarus?" Neva's frown deepened. "Strange name."

"According to the New Testament, Jesus was supposed to have raised him from the dead. Lazarus Grimm, however, is rather"—Glynis strained for charity—"let's just say he has the reputation of a rascal."

"A rascal? You mean a ne'er-do-well, et cetera?"

"Et cetera. Yes, you might say that. In any event, Lazarus Grimm left town several years ago, and hasn't been seen since, although it's been rumored that he joined some spiritualist community—I myself can scarce believe that, it would be so out of character for him. But the rumor simply adds a touch more mystery to the family's reputation, which comes, as I said, mostly from their reclusiveness, and from the fact that they're not well known in Seneca Falls. But I do know Molly, at least a bit better than the others, and I quite like her." Glynis smiled. "Perhaps I like her because she uses my library now and then."

The carriage was passing flocks of mottled gray sheep, and Neva gestured with the whip. "Those are merino sheep, aren't they?"

"Yes, they are," Glynis said with some surprise. "But how—"

"They originated in Spain, that's how I know. My father—he's Spanish—said they're the oldest breed of sheep. That's the kind of thing my father would find satisfying. The oldest, the strongest, the richest, the 'est' of anything, he'd boast about." Neva gave Glynis a brief, unreadable look. "That's my father!"

Glynis didn't have the leisure to consider this, as the Grimm farmhouse appeared to the right of the carriage. "Turn into that drive," she directed Neva.

The dirt drive took them past a large but otherwise ordinary-looking gray farmhouse to its far side and an open area ringed with birch clumps. Some distance beyond was a gray barn, in front of which post-and-rail fencing formed numerous pens. Neva pulled the horse to a stop under autumn-yellow birch leaves rustling in the warm breeze.

"There's Billy Wicken," Glynis said, and motioned toward the Grimms' hired hand, who, apparently unaware of their arrival, was shuffling toward an isolated sheep pen. But shuffling wasn't the right word for Billy Wicken's gait; he dragged his left leg behind him as if it were an afterthought. Even from a distance the man reminded Glynis of an elfin creature—Shakespeare's Puck, perhaps. The tips of Billy's large ears protruded through a tousled mop of straw-colored hair, his sharp nose and chin pointing the way ahead of him. Glynis involuntarily glanced at the clear sky; Billy's eyes would reflect its color exactly, eerily changing from one day's blue to another's dark gray. And in winter those mirror eyes became almost ice-white.

Neva, too, was watching Billy. "Has he always been like that?" she asked.

"You mean his limp? Yes, ever since I've known him. And he's worked here at least as long as I've been in Seneca Falls—that's almost sixteen years."

Neva nodded. "Does the paralysis affect his brain? Is he feebleminded?"

"Some say so," Glynis answered. "I'm more inclined to believe he's just slow. He has, after all, learned to do a great many things on this farm. But he is childlike."

"Still," Neva said, continuing to watch him, "there are varying degrees of feeblemindedness. How old is he?"

Glynis smiled. "He could be any age. The first time I saw him I thought he was somewhere around thirteen—and he still looks the same way."

Billy had paused, his hand on the gate of the pen; although the hand looked withered, the arm seemed normal enough. He gazed off, jerked suddenly as if he'd just recalled something, then limped along the fence, peering over the top rail. Despite his affliction, Billy Wicken could move surprisingly fast. He was also quite strong, Glynis recalled.

Glynis climbed from the carriage to follow Neva, who, carrying her black satchel, was already moving toward the man and sheep pen. The pen was occupied. A gray woolly back heaved up and down, accompanied by loud panting, and when Glynis reached Neva's side, it became clear that the merino ewe inside the pen was in labor.

Billy, at the pen's far side, looked across the fence at the two women. "Long time," he said finally, scratching his blond head. His forehead furrowed with obvious concern.

Neva moved toward him and pointed down at the ewe. "You mean she's been like that for . . . for *how* long?" she asked.

"Long time," Billy said again, after pausing to study Neva.

Glynis glanced around for some sign of the Grimm family. "Where is everybody, Billy?"

Shifting his gaze to her, he grinned in apparent recognition, then gestured with his right hand in the direction of Black Brook. "Gone."

Glynis wondered how the whole family could have disappeared. But then she remembered that Billy tended to ignore everyone but Molly Grimm and her daughter, Pippa. So Obadiah and his wife, Almira, could be inside the house. But where was Mead Miller, the hired hand who took care of the sheep?

Neva spoke softly. "I don't think Billy's particularly feebleminded. He's childlike all right, but he answered our questions appropriately enough. I wonder if he had a severe head injury—that is, rather than having been born that way." She now said more loudly, pointing to the gasping ewe, "Billy, has she been like that since early morning?"

Billy Wicken seemed to consider this. "Early morning?" he repeated, then bobbed his head. "Sunup."

At that moment the ewe went down on her knees, then rolled over on her side. Neva headed for the gate, lifted the latch, and yanked it open. Going directly to the suffering animal, she knelt beside it, opened her satchel, and pulled from it a small, trumpetlike wooden stethoscope.

Neva bent over the ewe's swollen belly, listening. Finally, she removed the instrument from her ears and straightened to say, "I think there are two lambs. Is that common?" She addressed this question to Billy Wicken.

Billy, staring at Neva's stethoscope, turned to Glynis with a worried expression. "Why is the lady poking a stick at—"

"No, Billy," Glynis interrupted him. "That's a tool to hear heartbeats." Billy did not look enlightened. Answering Neva, she said, "Yes, two lambs are common enough."

"But aren't lambs usually born in the spring?"

"Your father didn't tell you?" Glynis smiled. "Merinos are one breed that can lamb anytime of year."

"Fertil*est*," Neva said with a twitch of her lips. She rocked back on her heels. "Where's the one who takes care of these animals? Billy, do you know? Because this ewe's in trouble."

"Gone." Billy looked around, then repeated, "He's gone!"

Neva sighed heavily. Then, to Glynis's surprise, she unbuttoned the wristbands of her cotton blouse and began to roll up her sleeves. Billy watched for a moment, then took off toward the barn.

"Neva," Glynis began, "are you sure—"

"Yes. In medical school we students once delivered a lamb. It was a training exercise—and rightly so—before we were allowed to deliver human infants. Sheep are usually pretty docile, especially merinos. I don't think this one will give me much trouble. Problem is, I think the first lamb in the birth canal is positioned wrong."

"Wrong? Then what—"

"Have to find out," Neva said, with more confidence than Glynis felt. "It's supposed to be positioned with its head crouched between its forelegs. I might have to turn it . . ."

Neva broke off as Billy limped back across the yard with a plaid blanket under his arm, the handle of a water bucket in his undamaged hand. "Oh, good, Billy! Thank you."

Billy spread the blanket just behind the ewe. Still kneeling, Neva moved onto it before she plunged her right arm into the bucket, then drew it out dripping and began to insert her hand into the panting ewe.

Glynis quickly turned away. "I'll leave you now, if that's all right," she called over her shoulder. There was no reply as she walked toward the house.

By the time she reached the porch, a dog had begun barking somewhere behind the house. Following the sound, she walked toward the rear yard, to be met by a black-and-white collie bounding across the grass, his tail wagging enthusiastically.

As Glynis reached down to stroke the dog's head, she heard a muffled cackle, silence, then another cackle. Searching for its source, she saw a curtain swing across a first-floor windowpane. That cackle could belong only to Almira, so Glynis waved at the invisible woman and started back around the house, the dog beside her.

"Miss Tryon?" Her name floated from the direction of Black Brook. "Miss Tryon . . . here!"

Glynis turned to see Pippa running toward her, hair the color of corn tassels floating behind like a long pale streamer. On the bank of the brook, Molly Grimm appeared, arms laden with wildflowers, and began to follow her daughter across the grass.

"Miss Tryon," Pippa gasped as she reached Glynis, "what are you doing here? Oh, I know—you've come to pick up your books."

"No, I came mostly to see you, Pippa. And you certainly seem to be feeling better than a few weeks ago. Dr. Ives will be glad to hear that." As she spoke, Glynis found herself, as always, drawn to the girl's sweet nature and her uncommon prettiness. Despite the pale hair, Pippa's eyes shone a deep chocolate and her skin, now flushed with exertion, had the color of ripe peaches. Glynis smiled at her choice of description and added, "You look good enough to eat."

Pippa smiled shyly and turned as her mother approached. In dappled sunlight filtering through the birch leaves, Molly Grimm's hair spun a gold much darker than her daughter's. The armful of coarse stems she carried bore flat white flower clusters, and watching Molly approach with her long, rose-colored skirt swinging gracefully, Glynis had the impression of a Flemish oil painting suddenly come to life.

"Molly, hello," Glynis said. "What have you been gathering? It looks like boneset."

Pippa answered, "It's Indian sage. That's what the Indian lady said, and it's—"

"Pippa," her mother interrupted, "Miss Tryon's right. It's called boneset or teasel."

"Or feverwort, isn't that also a name for it?" Glynis asked.

Pippa again started to answer, "Yes, that's why we got it. For tea. The Indian lady told us to—"

"Please, Pippa," Molly Grimm broke in with a patient smile, "take these to the kitchen for me. They're scratchy, remember, so be careful." She reached forward to unload the herbs into Pippa's arms, but fumbled and dropped most of them. Awkwardness was so uncharacteristic of Molly that Glynis had a sudden sense of something strangely amiss. After Pippa had retrieved the fallen stems, Molly watched her daughter run with them toward the house. The dog barked joyfully at her heels.

Molly's soft blue eyes were as full of love as ever for the girl, Glynis observed, but the woman's expression also had a strained look. A tenseness not part of her usual composed appearance. Something *was* wrong.

"Pippa looks wonderful," Glynis said, wondering if Molly's tension could be caused by lingering concern over her daughter's illness. "Hardly as if she'd been sick at all."

"Yes," Molly agreed, "she does seem to be recovered."

But Glynis felt that the woman's eyes held more worry than she was admitting.

"Molly, I've brought a young physician with me. She's going to be in Seneca Falls for the next few months, training with Quentin Ives, and she'd like to examine Pippa."

"*She?* A woman doctor?" Molly gave Glynis an uncertain look. "I don't know if . . . but I suppose a woman would be all right now that Pippa's recovered."

Glynis decided not to comment. This certainly wouldn't be the first time Neva Cardoza had run into doubts about her competence. And Molly Grimm was known to be ferociously protective of her daughter. Well, let her see for herself.

As they began to stroll toward the house, Glynis remarked, "By the way, Molly, Dr. Cardoza and I had a rather unpleasant experience on the drive here. I wonder if you had an earlier visitor today? By any chance a woman?"

Molly's face stiffened. "Why do you ask?"

"Because she ran us off the road," Glynis explained. "She seemed to be in a great hurry. Odd thing is, her face looked familiar to me."

Molly abruptly stopped walking. "Oh, she was familiar to you, all right. It was Lily Braun."

"Lily Braun?" Glynis echoed. "No wonder I didn't recognize her. I haven't seen her in years. Not since she left Seneca Falls after . . ." Her voice trailed away as she recalled the disturbing circumstances of Lily Braun's departure.

"Yes!" was all Molly Grimm said. But Glynis heard anger in that single word, and she was about to ask more when Pippa burst out of the house.

"Mummy, there's lambs down there"—she pointed toward the far side of the house—"I saw them out the window.'' And she took off in a run toward the sheep pens.

The two women followed. Glynis made a mental note to inquire further about Lily Braun, but then quickly forgot about her.

FOUR

❧

*Take incense and pigeon's dung and wheat flour, a pinch of
each, and temper with the white of an egg; and whereso the
head acheth, bind it, and it shall vanish anon.*
— A LEECHBOOK OR COLLECTION OF
      MEDICAL RECIPES OF THE FIFTEENTH
      CENTURY

WHEN GLYNIS AND Molly Grimm reached the sheep pen,
Pippa was hanging over the fence, watching Neva and Billy
Wicken attempt to introduce a small gray lamb to its mother.
They were meeting with no visible success, as the ewe re-
peatedly butted the lamb away, concentrating instead on her
other, larger offspring.

"Why doesn't she like the little one?" Pippa asked anxiously.

From her kneeling position, Neva rocked back on her
heels to answer the girl. "The bigger one came first, after
I'd turned it and helped it out. The mother began licking it
clean, and when the other one came, a few minutes later,
the ewe ignored it. I don't know how common that sort of
thing is with sheep."

"It happens occasionally," Molly Grimm volunteered.
"Then usually Mead Miller takes the rejected lamb to another ewe, one that's lost her own. But right now there
aren't any other ewes that have lambed recently. And, in-
cidentally," she asked Billy Wicken, "where *is* Mead?"

Billy slowly shook his head. "Gone. Mead's gone."

"We can see that. Where's he gone to?" Molly said to
him.

Billy's face flushed, and he looked away.

"Billy, where is Mead?" Molly persisted.

His face flushed darker, and not looking at Molly, Billy
shook his head again.

Just then Neva, still trying to induce the ewe to nurse the

smaller lamb, jumped back as the ewe nipped not only at her offspring but at Neva as well. "We obviously have an impasse here," she said unhappily. "Perhaps I did the wrong thing when I wiped this one dry"—she gestured to the rejected lamb—"because the mother might not recognize its smell."

They watched as the lamb tottered again toward its mother; this time the ewe's head shot forward, nipping it hard. The lamb let out a plaintive bleat and crumpled to the grass as its unsteady legs gave way.

"Please do something," Pippa said softly, her eyes bright with tears. "The poor little thing."

Neva looked from the unfortunate lamb to the girl. "You must be Pippa," she said, getting up from the grass. "I'm Dr. Cardoza."

Glynis saw that Neva's green skirt had bloodstains on it, but the young woman didn't seem to notice as she brushed off grass and twigs. "I suggest," Neva said to no one in particular, "that we try to find this Mead Miller. If he's the one in charge of these sheep, he certainly isn't doing his job." She gazed at the lamb, now pitiably trying to suck a corner of the blanket.

"We have to get some nourishment into it," she said to Molly Grimm. "Is there anything we might use as a feeding bottle—and make some sort of nipple arrangement?"

Molly nodded. "Yes, up at the house we can probably find something."

"I need some water to wash up," Neva added, "and then I'll take a look at you, young lady." This was directed at Pippa with a smile.

"Come along to the house," Molly told her. "And I'll ask Father if he knows where Mead Miller could be."

Glynis stayed behind, watching an obviously reluctant Pippa follow her mother and Neva toward the house; the girl glanced over her shoulder again and again at the forsaken lamb. Billy Wicken, on the other hand, had not taken his eyes off Molly and Pippa, and now gazed after them with a troubled expression.

"Billy," Glynis said to him, "I think you know where Mead Miller is, don't you?"

Billy pulled his gaze from the departing women to stare at the toe of his boot stubbing the grass. And he didn't answer.

"You know that lamb won't live long," Glynis insisted, "if we don't do something for it. We have to find Mead. Did he ask you not to tell where he'd gone?"

Billy finally looked up at her to nod unwillingly. "Said he'd come back soon. Not to tell. He'll come back."

"When did Mead say he'd be back?"

"Soon."

Glynis sighed, shook her head at Billy, and followed the others to the house.

WHILE PIPPA AND her mother and Neva were upstairs, Glynis sat for what seemed hours over a cup of cold tea at the kitchen table, while Almira Grimm darted in and out of the adjoining pantry. The thin little woman didn't remain in one spot for long, and Glynis's head began to throb as she watched Almira hover, flutter like a hummingbird, then shoot off in another direction. Almira's hair also brought to mind small birds: a few graying brown strands were caught back in a bun, but the rest stood out from her head like the bent twigs of a poorly constructed nest.

Suddenly the outside door swung open, and Mead Miller strode into the room. "Billy says you all been looking for me." He scowled at Glynis. "Don't see why."

"One of the ewes lambed—" Glynis started.

"Yes, yes, and she's dandy," the man interrupted. "So why the dustup?" Broad-shouldered and muscular, Mead Miller stood with arms crossed over his chest, feet apart, straddling the kitchen floor like Colossus. Glynis just stared at him, not sure where to begin. He hadn't so much as glanced at Almira, who now fluttered beside Glynis, wringing her hands.

"They're mad at you, Mead Miller," Almira whined. "You best be careful now—you know what happens when *he* gets mad!"

Glynis assumed "he" must mean Obadiah Grimm, and she wondered what *did* happen when Almira's husband got mad. Mead Miller, however, ignored Almira as well as her implied threat, and said to Glynis, "So who's this here lady doctor? And why's she delivering *my* lambs?"

A door behind Glynis swung open with Neva's announcement, "I'm Dr. Cardoza, and if you're so concerned about *your* lambs, why weren't you here to deliver them yourself?"

Mead Miller's mouth opened and closed rapidly as if he were attempting speech. Glynis pressed her lips together so she wouldn't smile, and decided she really did like Neva Cardoza. The young woman moved on into the room just as the outside door opened.

Obadiah Grimm stopped just inside the sill to glare at Neva. "Who are you, and what are you doing in my house? And *who* do you think you are talking to?" he thundered, his heavy-browed eyes flashing ominously.

For a moment it seemed as if no one even breathed, and Glynis stole a quick glance at Neva, who, her small jaw thrust forward, was moving resolutely around the end of the table until she stood within a few feet of Obadiah Grimm.

"If you're addressing me, my name is Dr. Neva Cardoza." Her chin lifted. "What I am doing here is checking on your granddaughter—that is, of course, if you are Mr. Grimm."

Obadiah Grimm's long, lean body and face, crowned with abundant white hair and beard, stiffened. He spoke harshly, "It is said in Proverbs that 'a foolish woman is noisy; she is wanton and knows no shame.' You are not welcome in my house, woman. Not you or your witchcraft. The girl is fine—we don't need you interfering. I expect you to be gone when I return!" With that, Obadiah brushed Neva aside and went through the inner door. Moments later, his boots could be heard stomping up the stairs.

During his speech, Glynis had watched Neva's hands clench at her sides, and was relieved when she said nothing more. "I imagine we should be on our way now," Glynis suggested. "Have you finished with Pippa?"

"Yes," Neva said. She glanced at the closed door through which Obadiah had passed. "She's recovered very nicely, and there don't seem to be any lasting effects that—"

Her voice broke off as from the upstairs came a series of sharp exclamations in what sounded like Molly Grimm's voice. Although the words were indistinguishable, there was no mistaking the anger in her tone. Glynis felt something unpleasant streak down her spine; coupled with Molly's odd reaction to her own earlier inquiry about Lily Braun, she wondered what recently had occurred to so agitate the woman.

However, a few minutes later, as Glynis and Neva walked back to the sheep pen, Molly came after them. Her face looked composed, if somewhat pale. "I'm sorry about my father's rudeness, Dr. Cardoza," she said a little breathlessly. "It's just that he doesn't like strangers. But we're grateful, Pippa and I, that you came out."

Neva nodded. "Pippa looks very healthy. There's no vision problem and no hearing loss, which can sometimes occur with scarlet fever—she apparently came through it well. But I'm curious as to what Pippa told me about the medicine woman from the reservation." Neva pointed north. "Black Brook, is it?"

"Oh, that was nothing," Molly said quickly. "Just some herbs for tea she brought Pippa."

"I didn't know there *was* a medicine woman at Black Brook," Glynis said.

Molly hesitated, and her response seemed overlong in coming. "Well . . . she isn't always at Black Brook. She travels back and forth from the Cattaraugus reservation, near Buffalo."

"Who is she?" Glynis asked.

Again Molly hesitated. Finally she said, "Bitter Root—her name's Bitter Root."

"That's an appropriate name, I'd say," Neva commented. "Pippa sounded very fond of the woman. I think I'd like to meet her myself. Some of the old herbal remedies seem to work as well if not better than patent medicines. Of course," she added, "there are male physicians who think these things are dangerous, and others believe they're some kind of witchcraft." She looked pointedly toward the house.

Molly went a shade paler and began to reply, but she stopped as they'd reached the sheep pen. Pippa sat cross-

legged on the grass, holding the orphaned lamb in her lap.
Billy Wicken was feeding it from a glass jar of fluid, topped
with what looked to Glynis like the thumb of a leather glove.
The lamb tugged at the improvised nipple with surprising
strength.

"Sugar water," Billy answered in reply to her question.
"That's what Mead Miller said to give it. He said maybe
the mother will feed it later." He grinned down at the lamb
in Pippa's lap.

Glynis and Neva took their leave and began to walk with
Molly toward their carriage. "Do you remember my brother
Lazarus?" Molly asked Glynis.

"Yes. Yes, of course I do," Glynis answered, wondering
what sort of mischief Lazarus had been up to now.

"He's coming home," Molly told her, "in the next few
days. He wrote that he's had a spiritual awakening, and
wants to share it with us."

Glynis couldn't deduce from the woman's enigmatic expression whether she accepted her brother's words at face
value, or suspected some shenanigans. She herself simply
smiled noncommittally at Molly, and nodded.

Under the first of the birch clumps, Neva and Molly stood
talking, while Glynis went on for the carriage and horse,
and suddenly stopped cold in her tracks. An eerie howl
drifted from the woods north of the Grimm property. A wolf
howling—at this time of day? The hair on the back of her
neck rising, Glynis walked forward a few paces before
drawing in her breath. There, some distance ahead at the
edge of the woods, stood a large black and white paint
horse. It was as motionless as the man astride.

It couldn't be! Glynis shut her eyes tightly, then snapped
them open, assuming the ghostly vision would be gone. But
it remained, the man and horse. And some inner sense convinced her of their substance.

"Jacques." Glynis barely breathed his name. "Jacques
Sundown."

She took a few quick steps forward, then picked up her
skirts and began to run toward the horse and rider. But the
horse wheeled abruptly, and galloped into the woods.

Glynis ran a few more yards, then stopped. Might it have

been someone else? No, it was Jacques Sundown; she had felt his presence as surely as if he had been standing directly before her. But he had been gone from Seneca Falls for three years. Why had he returned now?

GLYNIS DIRECTED THE bay horse onto the dirt road, and they headed away from the Grimm farm. Several times she glanced to the north, but no black and white horse and rider reappeared.

She could feel Neva's eyes on her, and after a moment or two, the young doctor said, "Just before we left, I heard a very strange sound coming from those woods."

Glynis nodded. "Yes, it was a wolf."

"A wolf?" Glynis turned to see Neva's shocked look. "There are still wolves around here?"

"Not many. For a long time there's been a bounty on wolves. Most of them have been killed."

"You sound as if you're sorry!" Neva's voice held incredulity.

"I *am* sorry. They're beautiful and intelligent animals, and it doesn't seem right to exterminate them. There's never been any evidence of them attacking humans. Wolves are very shy, and they try to avoid people. The farmers hate them and insist that they kill their livestock. But they only go after old or sick animals. And the wolves were here first . . ." Glynis's voice trailed off as she realized how absurd this must sound to someone from New York City.

Neva began, "But they look dangerous—"

"So do the men with guns who kill them!" Glynis bit down on her lower lip, startled by her own anger. "Forgive me, Neva, I have a bit of a headache—and I'd rather not talk about it," she murmured, hoping this wouldn't hurt the other woman's feelings. But she still felt unsettled about seeing Jacques Sundown. *It had been so long.* So long without hearing anything from him, as though he'd vanished from the face of the earth. She'd never allowed herself to consider that he might have died, so she hadn't realized, until she saw him, how afraid she'd been that he had.

Neva remained silent, and Glynis gradually felt the initial jolt ebb, receding into a less complicated, and more manageable, puzzlement. How long had Jacques been here? Did Cullen know—and if so, why hadn't he told her? And, finally, why—why had Jacques Sundown come back to Seneca Falls?

Neva, at last, made a great show of clearing her throat. "Are you better—I mean your headache?" she ventured.

Glynis felt foolish for having tried to deceive a doctor. "Oh, that." She made herself smile. "I'm sorry, I hope I didn't offend you."

"No, no—not at all," Neva protested. "It was just unexpected, because you always seem so composed, so self-possessed."

"Me?" Glynis laughed. "If you only knew how hard I fight shyness! All the time."

Neva gave her an unmistakably skeptical look. Then she shrugged lightly and said, "Well, if you feel up to it, I'd like to know something about the Iroquois—the Seneca Iroquois."

Glynis shot her a quick glance. Surely Neva hadn't seen Jacques Sundown. But even if she had, she couldn't have known, not from a distance, that Jacques was Seneca. *Half-Seneca,* Glynis corrected herself.

"I'll try," she began, her eyes on the road ahead, "at least to give you a brief background so those books you borrowed will make some sense. I guess no one knows the exact origin of the Indian tribes that lived here for centuries—'here' being the territory that lies more or less between the Hudson and the Niagara Rivers. But according to Lewis Morgan's research—he's the author of one of those books—the tribes were at war continually with one another. Sometime during the sixteenth century, the five largest tribes created a confederacy. And by the way, today they prefer to be called *nations* rather than *tribes.* In any event, they called this confederacy the League of the Iroquois, or Haudenosaunee, meaning People of the Longhouse. A symbolic longhouse in this case."

"Longhouse—what they lived in?" Neva asked.

Glynis nodded. "The nation farthest west in the original five-nation league was the Senecas. In the 1700s, a sixth nation joined the League—the Tuscaroras, living in what's now Ohio—but the Senecas continued to control all of New York from west of Cayuga Lake to the state's western border; they were the guardians or Keepers of the Western Door of the Longhouse. East of the Senecas were the Cayugas. And then the Onondagas, the Oneidas, and finally, the Mohawks, Keepers of the Eastern Door.

"Individually these nations were not strong enough to avoid the warfare I mentioned earlier, but once united under the one symbolic roof, they constituted a near invulnerable force. That's why western New York had so few white settlers until well after the Revolutionary War."

"So what happened?" Neva asked. "How did the Confederacy lose its power?"

"It's a long, tortuous story, but the final death blow came when five of the six Iroquois nations sided with the British during the war. So the colonial army made a sweep from Pennsylvania up through western New York and virtually destroyed the Iroquois farms and villages. The descendants of those Indians who survived are now either in Canada or on reservations in this country."

For a time Neva stared off, apparently deep in thought, at the ancient passing landscape. "How many Iroquois were there before they were driven out?" she asked.

"Morgan places the number at somewhere around twenty-five thousand or more; today there are far fewer than half that many, and not all of them, as I said, are in this country. But some *are* still here, at the Black Brook Reservation, for example. They're mostly Cayugas and Senecas; the Cayugas ended up with no land at all, and so are considered guests, so to speak, on the Seneca reservations."

"The spoils of war," Neva said.

"No, not exactly," Glynis shook her head. "It's more an issue of treaties disregarded. But that's a more complicated story." And a sad one, she thought, reminded of what was happening to the wolves.

She slowed the horse now as a lightweight buckboard, coming in the opposite direction, turned in front of them and rattled off down a rutted path to the west of Black Brook. Peering after the buckboard in a futile attempt to identify its driver, she explained to Neva, "That road goes to Jake Braun's farm. And Jake Braun happens to be the uncle of the woman who earlier ran us off this road.''

''I thought you said you didn't recognize her.''

''I didn't at first,'' Glynis said, ''but Molly Grimm told me it was Lily Braun. Lily's a woman with a . . . well, to put it politely, a somewhat checkered past.''

Neva immediately sat up straighter. ''You mean you actually have those here in Seneca Falls—checkered pasts, I mean?''

''Oh, we have them, all right. Doesn't every place?''

Some distance after they again passed the burned remains of the Flannery farm, they turned into a drive, overrun with weeds, that led to Turner's. As they drew closer to the farmhouse, Glynis could hear hammering. This proved to be an adolescent boy nailing up braces to support the sagging roof of the front porch; he glanced sullenly at the two women when they climbed from the carriage.

''Is Sara Turner about?'' Glynis asked him.

''What d'you want with 'er?'' The boy's wary eyes didn't meet hers, but focused on a spot somewhere over her left shoulder. His speech slurred due to the nails he held between his lips. ''Who'r'you?''

''My name's Glynis Tryon, and I just want to see how Sara's doing.''

''She's doin' fine.''

''Oh, well, good. Ah, may I have your name?'' Glynis waited while the boy took the nails from his mouth; he stood looking at the women as if deliberating whether or not he should yield this information.

Finally he said, ''Name's Jed Turner, if it makes a difference. And I dunno where she is—''

''Mrs. Turner's not home?'' Neva interrupted brusquely. ''That is, if you don't find that too demanding a question.''

Glynis restrained a smile, but the boy's sullen expression didn't change, and he gave no answer.

''Then I guess,'' Glynis said, ''we should probably be on our way if she isn't here. Would you tell her that Dr. Cardoza and I stopped . . .''

''Doctor? You're a *doctor*?'' the boy blurted; his eyes widened, and he blinked at Neva. To Glynis's surprise, his expression became even more guarded, as if he was frightened. And at that moment the front door opened, and Sara Turner stepped out onto the porch.

"It's all right, Jed. I know 'em. G'day, Miss Tryon."

Glynis nodded, too startled at Sara's changed appearance to say anything. The woman looked very nearly healthy. And taller somehow. Glynis glanced at Neva from the corner of her eye to see her reaction. Neva looked as surprised as she.

Sara came down the porch steps. "Guess you met my boy here."

"Your son?" Glynis asked. But hadn't Sara said her children were sent away by their father?

"My son!" Sara repeated, the gladness in her voice unmistakable. "Got him and his brothers back yesterday."

"Sara, that's wonderful," Glynis declared, while Neva simply nodded. "You must be very happy about it."

"Guess I am, truth to tell," Sara said, but despite the circumstances, her expression had, for some reason, become as guarded as her son's. Surely Cullen's suspicions about Sara having a hand in her husband's death were not warranted. So why did she appear so uneasy?

Neva, her eyebrows raised, might have been thinking along the same lines because she threw Glynis an odd look, and turned toward the carriage. "Guess Mrs. Turner is doing fine," she muttered.

"We are *all* doin' fine," Sara said, the wary look still in place. "Don't you fret none about us. "But," she added, "it was real nice of you to stop by. And you be sure 'n' give my regards to that Dr. Ives." Glynis could have sworn Sara laughed softly under her breath.

By this time, Neva had climbed back into the carriage. Glynis, still standing in the drive, attempted to delay their departure by grasping the harness of the horse and turning him as slowly as possible toward the road. She knew Sara and Jed Turner were watching her, but she had no idea why she herself felt so uneasy. It was silly! The feeling that something was wrong here must be just her imagination. She shook it off with a shrug and began to climb into the carriage.

Without warning, Sara Turner called out, "It's not nearly the end of it, y'know, Miss Tryon," she said with a scowl. "Not nearly the end."

"End?" Glynis felt a chill. "Not the end of what, Sara?"

"Death. It ain't done yet."

"What do you mean?" As Glynis stepped toward her, Sara Turner moved several paces away. Then she whirled abruptly and started for the house. Both she and the boy climbed the porch stairs quickly, but before she went inside, Sara turned to say, "Mark my words—there'll be more death. You'll see."

"Sara, wait!" Glynis, trying frantically to form questions, had followed both Turners to the stairs. As she put her foot on the first step, Sara Turner went through the door, slamming it shut.

Glynis heard the latch drop firmly into place.

FIVE

. . . and no such [liquor] license shall be granted except on the petition of not less than twenty respectable freeholders of this state, residing in the election district where such inn, tavern or hotel is proposed to be kept. . . .
—CHAPTER 628, SECTION SIX, OF THE LAWS OF 1857, ENACTED BY THE EIGHTIETH SESSION OF THE NEW YORK LEGISLATURE

ALTHOUGH THE DAY had been fair, later that evening a brief but violent storm whipped through the village. Water now chopped angrily against the walled canal section of the Seneca River, while a half moon riding the chill October wind barely lit the towpath behind Serenity's Tavern. Those hurrying along the road that fronted the tavern cursed the unpredictable weather; pulling their collars around their ears, they rushed through the oaken door when it swung open to admit them. Inside, the aroma of whiskey and tobacco, the crackling flames in the great stone fireplace, and the heat of closely packed bodies drove the cold from their bones.

On the first floor of the tavern, scores of lanterns hung over the long mahogany bar and gaming tables, while smoke rose in hazy blue strands toward the beamed ceiling. The small rooms above on the second floor held fewer lanterns, as what transpired there required little or no illumination. The tavern was also a brothel.

Serenity Hathaway, her starched petticoats and taffeta skirt rustling crisply, wound her way among tables as she crossed the sawdusted floor to the bar. She slipped onto a stool beside a black-haired young man who greeted her with very blue and very besotted eyes. Before Serenity propped her elbows on the bar, she tossed abundant hennaed hair over her bare shoulders, then, fingers arched under her chin, offered the young man a view of creamy breasts spilling over the scant bodice of her gown. Brendan O'Reilly sighed.

"Brendan, my lad," Serenity began, her smile not quite reaching her sharp, kohl-lined eyes, "in case you haven't noticed, we are running out of time. How many more signatures do we need on that petition?"

Brendan O'Reilly sighed more fulsomely; whether this was a consequence of Serenity's question or of her bare proximity was unclear. "Three. We need three," he answered glumly. "And maybe two more are possible, but . . ." He shrugged.

Serenity's smile faded. "I depend on you, Brendan my lad. In fact, I more than depend. I pay you generously, wouldn't you agree?"

Brendan wiped beads of sweat from his forehead. "Serenity, I've tried to tell you—"

"No!" she interrupted. "No more excuses. That bloody damn law passed in April, more than six months ago. Constable Stuart's been in here every week since. And he's not come to gamble! Until we have those twenty signatures, he's got the right to close me down."

"Serenity," Brendan began again, "Stuart doesn't want to close you down. If he did, he'd have done it by now!"

"Wrong!" Serenity's tone reflected more than a little impatience with her handsome admirer. "That temperance female from Rochester—the oh, so virtuous Miss Susan Anthony—has been here rabble-rousing again, and now Stuart's got every self-righteous crackpot in town on his back. So far he's kept them at bay, but that can't last forever."

Her eyes narrowed. "Now, Brendan, you hear me well— *I want those signatures!* I don't care how you get them. I've already spent a fortune on payoffs, but those we can't get that way, we have to get another. And get them fast, laddie, or no more job. And no more Serenity either."

Brendan's tragic expression almost made Serenity retract her threat, but a sudden lowering of the tavern's noise turned her attention from the bar. Utter silence settled over the room.

One glance told Serenity why: Cullen Stuart had entered

to stand just inside the door. He gave a cursory look around, but once he spotted Serenity, he nodded briefly at the men seated at the gaming tables, and started toward the bar. The noise gradually resumed.

"Evening, Constable," Serenity greeted Cullen when he reached her. She tapped the stool beside her, saying, "Sit a spell."

Cullen swung himself onto the stool. "Whiskey," he said to the bartender.

Serenity slipped off her stool to move behind the bar. "I'll take care of the constable," she told the bartender, and reached for a bottle of Alleman's finest. "On the house," she said to Cullen when she handed him the shot.

Cullen grinned. "Serenity, I'll take your whiskey, and I'll thank you for it, but that doesn't mean—"

"Naturally not," Serenity smiled, "I know you better than that by this time, Cullen Stuart. Never hurts to try, though."

"So how's the petition coming?"

"Don't waste words, do you, Constable? Well, my young friend here"—she gestured to Brendan O'Reilly, who had been scowling since Cullen sat down—"he tells me we're almost there. Just a couple more days'll do it. Right, Brendan, my lad?"

Still scowling, Brendan muttered, "Yeah, right." His knuckles whitened around the tankard he lifted and drained.

Serenity ignored him, and instead studied Cullen Stuart's face. Her tavern's prosperity, she often told herself, was due in no small part to her success in reading men; that she hadn't yet discovered this particular man's weakness annoyed her to no end.

She leaned over the bar toward Cullen. "What's it take, my good man, to get you to overlook a few signatures? Tell me! I'll be happy, more than happy, to oblige." The smile was her most persuasive.

Cullen Stuart didn't seem to notice. "It's not up to me, Serenity. I've treated yours like any other business in town. But there's folks around here think liquor's a bad influence. And maybe it is, not that I think any law is going to fix it. But it *is* the law. So get your license. End of problem."

"Maybe," Serenity acknowledged reluctantly. "Now, these temperance troublemakers you're talking about—besides the meddling Miss Anthony, do you by any chance know a woman doctor—*Witch* doctor is more like it—name of Cardoza?"

Cullen grinned and nodded. "What's she done now?"

"She's been in here—"

"Here? In the tavern?" Cullen broke in. "She's been in *here*?"

"Here. Twice. Ranting about women and children. As if it's my fault that men drink too much and go home and beat up their wives and kids. This Cardoza's feisty as hell, like a little bantam rooster. Last time, I had Brendan here escort her to the door. Told her I'd have her arrested for disturbing my peace."

Cullen laughed. "Yours isn't the only peace she's disturbed since she got to town. What with her and Lily Braun . . . and by the way, have you seen *her* recently?"

"No!" Serenity snapped. "Lily comes in here, she'll get tossed out. Told her that years ago, when I fired her. But I heard she's all of a sudden got respectable; found herself a nice little deal when Dooley Keegan's widow sold her house. Lily moved into it a couple days ago. You know about that?"

"Just that I heard it, too. But I can't believe Lily Braun's become respectable—not by a long shot—so who's the man paying for it?"

Serenity shrugged, a gesture that dropped her bodice several inches. She didn't move to pull it up, but leaned farther over the bar toward Cullen, fixing him with a smile. "I'll be happy to find out for you, though, Constable. In return for—"

"For ignoring the petition, right? No thanks, Serenity. You just bustle out and get your signatures like a good, law-abiding citizen—"

He was interrupted by an explosive shout from across the room. More shouting followed, and chairs scraped the barroom floor as cardplayers jumped to their feet, backing away from the poker tables. A big man, his back to the wall, stood brandishing a knife.

"You goddamn cheating bastards!" the man yelled. He lunged forward with the knife, slicing the air in fast, choppy strokes.

"Brendan!" Serenity's voice got lost in the shouting, but Brendan O'Reilly had already leaped from the bar stool and was sprinting across the room. Grabbing a nearby chair, he hoisted it in front of him, then moved in on the knife-wielding cardplayer. Parrying with the chair to avoid the other's knife thrusts, Brendan managed to pin the man against the wall, while onlookers rushed to disarm him. The man then sank to the floor.

Brendan yanked the man up, twisted his arms behind his back, and wrestled him toward the back door. Cullen, who had started to draw his pistol, now shoved it back in its holster; shaking his head, he asked Serenity, "Mead Miller ever do anything like that before?"

Serenity frowned up at him. "Nothing like *that*! But he's been acting strange for weeks now."

"Strange? What do you mean, strange?"

"Edgy, like he's all the time looking over his shoulder. And he takes offense real easy. Miller's been in here a lot lately, and he's drinking more than he used to. But he won't get in again for a while!"

She watched Brendan saunter back from the door. "S'cuse me now, Constable," Serenity said with a grin. "Got to go reward my hero." She blew Cullen a kiss and sashayed up the length of the bar.

When Cullen left the tavern a few minutes later, he looked for Mead Miller. Wind-whipped leaves flurried in the road, but the man was nowhere in sight.

THE NEXT MORNING, seated on a straight-backed Shaker chair beside Cullen's desk, Glynis protested, "But why didn't you tell me Jacques Sundown had come back?"

She could hear her voice scaling upward and glanced self-consciously toward the open door of Cullen's office in the rear of the firehouse. To her relief, she saw no passersby. After she'd gotten up to close the door, and then reseated herself, she began again. "I don't understand, Cullen, since you say you knew, why you didn't tell me about Jacques. Why?''

Cullen sighed heavily, banged shut the wooden file drawer, and slid into his desk chair. ''Guess I didn't think you'd care one way or the other. You and Jacques—well, you two didn't always get on so well.''

Glynis caught her lower lip between her teeth. To some degree, Cullen was right. In the beginning, she and Jacques had had some difficulty, rather a lot of difficulty. But then he'd left Seneca Falls for—what?—six years? When he'd come back, the two of them had made adjustments, and had begun to arrive at some sort of understanding. But then Jacques had left again, saying only that he was going to a reservation somewhere, to see his mother. She hadn't even known he *had* a mother.

''Glynis?''

Cullen's voice startled her. When she looked up, he was staring at her with an odd expression. ''What is it, Cullen?''

''I asked why you're so interested in Sundown's arrival.''

''Because I . . .'' Glynis paused, not entirely able to explain this. Finally she said, ''Well, why wouldn't I be?''

Cullen shrugged, and began pushing some papers around on his desk. Without looking at her, he said, ''To tell the truth, I'm a little sore at Sundown. He gets back maybe three, four weeks ago—doesn't even bother to let me know. He was my *deputy*. You'd think after three years he'd at least come by to say hello.''

At that, Glynis smiled. ''I can't imagine Jacques saying hello. Perhaps something like 'O.K.' Or, 'Good hunting weather,' but not hello.''

''No, guess not.'' Cullen, too, smiled. ''Anyway, I checked around some. Seems he's settled in at Black Brook Reservation. Built himself a log cabin. Looks like he's decided he's Indian after all, and doesn't want anything to do with us white folk.''

Glynis rose and went to stand by the open window. She glanced out before she said, ''But his father was a white man. A French trapper, he told you. And I just thought of something. Is his father still alive?''

''No. Died in Canada some years ago—that's why

Jacques went to Montreal after he left town the first time. At least that's what he said. You saw him yesterday?''

"When I went out to the Grimm farm. He was riding along the edge of those woods, the ones between Grimms' and Black Brook Reservation. I thought he saw me, but then he just rode off.''

"Sounds like Jacques. He never was what you'd call sociable.''

"No. No, he wasn't.'' Although what Cullen said was certainly true, Glynis still felt hurt by Jacques's apparent indifference. But she pushed the emotion aside and said, ''I also saw Sara Turner yesterday. She seems to have recovered from her husband's death very well. In fact, I'd say remarkably well.''

"That so?'' Cullen looked interested.

"Yes. She's gotten her children back from wherever Jack Turner apprenticed them, and one boy has already begun fixing up the place.''

"Yeah? Glynis, consider this—remember Jack's reputation for being tight-fisted? Well, apparently he left a fair amount of money. Sara Turner said she found it under a mattress, if you can believe that. All in all, I'd say the widow Turner has had a streak of good luck recently.''

"Cullen! You don't still think Sara had something to do with his death? Or do you?''

"Not something I can prove. Never did find whatever the arsenic was in. Searched the place pretty well, but no wine bottle. Nothing, that is, except a small sack of arsenic in the barn.''

"You didn't tell me that,'' Glynis said, surprised.

"Because Sara Turner swore it was for rats. And there's no evidence she's lying, at least none that any prosecutor would accept. No, either she's gotten away with murder, or . . .''

Still standing by the window, Glynis motioned him quiet. She'd just heard the rustle of an approaching skirt, and now she glanced out to say, "Here's Neva Cardoza.''

Cullen's low groan was unmistakable.

Neva, her face flushed a dark pink, came hurriedly through the door. She gave Glynis a quick nod, then stepped to place a sheaf of paper on Cullen's desk.

"You told me to get a copy of the new temperance law, Constable—well, there it is! *Now* will you do something about those taverns?"

Cullen, who had gotten to his feet when Neva entered, sighed and sank back into his chair as she went on, "I've read this thing all the way through, several times. It states very clearly that it's designed to curb intemperance and to regulate the sale of alcoholic spirits. If tavern owners don't have liquor licenses, and there's still some that don't, then according to Section sixteen, you, the constable, are supposed to shut them down." She picked up one of the sheets of paper to wave in front of his face. "Says so right here!"

"Dr. Cardoza," Cullen said, again rising from his chair, "the legislature just passed this law in April. No other state's got anything like it, so the tavern owners have been taken by surprise. They need time to comply."

"Why?" Neva interrupted, glaring at him.

"Why what?" Cullen's voice sounded strained.

"Why should they have *any* time? The law takes effect immediately, says so in Section thirty-four. Constable Stuart, if you'd bother to look at the misery that alcohol's inflicted on this town, you wouldn't wait a minute longer."

"Dr. Cardoza, I know that—"

"No! No, you don't! You know nothing about what happens when a husband and father comes home drunk every night. When he uses the money his family depends on, for their food and a roof over their heads, to buy liquor. But I *do* know." Her face flushing still more, Neva rushed on as Cullen tried to interrupt, "I've seen these wives and children. Malnourished. Beaten, and covered with bruises and sores. It's criminal. And you want to give tavern owners more *time*?"

"The law *also* states," Cullen said evenly, belying the color that had risen in his own face, "that to grant liquor licenses, commissioners of excise first have to be appointed by a county judge. Now that's been done, but just recently. So the tavern owners need the time—"

"The time for what?" Neva jumped in. "To buy off the

commissioners? And don't look so shocked, Glynis, it happens all the time.''

"Seneca Falls is not New York City." Cullen stressed each word. ''And if you're going to slander these . . .''

''I'm not slandering—''

''. . . folks, then you're also slandering me. And I don't take kindly to that, *Dr.* Cardoza!''

Neva continued to glare at Cullen. He, on the other hand, merely looked at her with irritation.

''I'm holding you personally responsible, Constable Stuart, for every woman and child that's harmed as a result of alcoholic excess. It's on your conscience!''

Glynis heard a sob catch in Neva's throat as the young woman whirled around and stormed from the office. Cullen stared after her with obvious exasperation. He shook his head, saying to Glynis, ''Now, where were we? Before the cyclone swept through?''

''You know,'' Glynis said, ''Neva does have a point.''

''Now don't *you* start in on me.''

''But since she's been here, Neva's spent much of her time with the poorer families in town. She knows what she's talking about.''

''That's not the issue.''

''It isn't? Then what *is*? That business owners, mostly men, are more important to Seneca Falls than the welfare of women and children. That—''

''Glynis, spare me, please. I'm not getting into this men-versus-women thing again with you. And I mean it.''

Glynis quickly got to her feet and went to the door. After she went through it, she closed it behind her very quietly.

SHE FLEXED THE reins to slow the pace of the small, dapple-gray mare, her personal favorite from Boone's Livery, and gritted her teeth as the lightweight buggy jounced over Black Brook Road's rutted surface.

After the previous night's cold snap had brought the season's first frost, the air had again turned balmy. Altogether it had been a lovely, unusually warm fall, Glynis reflected; perhaps there could be hope the coming winter would not be as fierce as that of the year before. But this was something for which western New Yorkers hoped every year.

On this particular afternoon, however, the slant of the late-October sun turned everything it touched a pale gold; there would be too few more of these days before snow fell, and the unexpectedly mild weather seemed to Glynis a reprieve of sorts. A gift of which one should take advantage.

Although Black Brook ran to the right of the road, the graceful willows, scarlet sumac, and cattails on its banks concealed the stream itself. As the buggy rounded a slight curve, Glynis could see a white horse standing in the high weeds, only its upper body and switching tail visible, and she guessed someone must be fishing along the streambed.

She flicked the reins over the mare's back, quickening their journey past the Grimm farm. But there appeared to be no activity there—which, this being a Sunday, did not seem particularly odd. No doubt the Grimms were all indoors for noonday dinner. Glynis was just as glad none were around to question her; she wasn't sure how she would explain this trip of hers to Black Brook Reservation.

And surely there was little to be gained, she thought uneasily, by questioning herself too vigorously as to the reasons that impelled her to seek out Jacques Sundown. Simple curiosity should be reason enough. And Cullen's remarks of that morning were not sufficient to satisfy her.

After another quarter-mile, she urged the mare up a long rise. At its crest she pulled back on the reins, and when they'd stopped, Glynis gazed down at the southern boundary of Black Brook Reservation.

The brook itself wound north through the heart of the reserve; some distance from the streambed, and on either side of it stood clusters of small log houses. Behind them lay fields dotted with orange pumpkins and hilled squash vines. Desiccated brown stalks rustled in the breeze. Outside each house, ears of corn hung by braided husks from drying posts in long festoons of gold and white, orange-red, and dark purple. Glynis had forgotten how many varieties of corn the Iroquois cultivated.

Gone were the great hickory and oak bark longhouses with their barrel-shaped roofs. Often as large as a hundred and thirty feet in length by some sixteen feet wide, a long-house once sheltered several generations under its one roof. These generations consisted of maternal families: mothers and their husbands, their daughters and daughters' husbands, and their daughters' children. The families had lived side by side behind a central row of circular hearths.

Also gone now was the central position held by Iroquois women of centuries past. Glynis had first heard the creation legend of Ata-en-sic, the Sky Woman, from a young Seneca woman who, for a number of years, had sold woven baskets, and moccasins and garments elaborately embroidered with beadwork, at the Seneca County Agricultural Fair. As this artisan related the legend, many ages past a wizard, jealous of women's power to create life, caused the pregnant Ata-en-sic to fall from the sky into a great, watery void. Sky Woman's fate would have been to fall forever but for the water birds that caught and carried her in their widespread wings. They held her until the muskrat deposited dirt on the back of Hah-nu-nah the turtle, the Earth Bearer. The water-birds then placed Sky Woman on his back. When the wizard had pushed her into the void, Ata-en-sic was clutching in her hands many seeds, which she now planted in the earth. She subsequently died, giving birth to twin brothers, the spirits of Good and Evil. Each brother claimed the Earth to be his dominion, and so began the endless struggle between strife and peace.

The Seneca woman had assured Glynis that, while the legend in its retelling had taken on variations over time, its essence had remained faithful to the lifegiving power of women.

It was for this same Seneca woman that Glynis now intended to look. It had been several years since she'd seen her, and Glynis couldn't be sure she'd recognize what now would be an older face, but her voice still must be unmistakable, rich and melodious, like the song of a wood thrush. Her name had been Small Brown Bird.

Glynis flicked the reins and the gray mare took off at a trot down the short hill to Black Brook Reservation.

SIX

❦

The Iroquois tribe . . . was not a group of families; neither was it made up of the descendants of a common father, as the father and his child were never of the same tribe. . . . Descent followed in all cases, the female line.
— LEWIS HENRY MORGAN, *LEAGUE OF THE HO-DE-NO-SAU-NEE, OR IROQUOIS*

AFTER GLYNIS TETHERED the mare to the branch of a willow growing beside the stream, she walked toward the first of the log houses clustered along Black Brook's west bank. An old woman sat alone on a sagging wooden stoop. Her gray hair, caught in the single long braid designating a married female, fell over the shoulder of a bead-trimmed deerskin tunic, and on her hollow chest shone a circular silver brooch with scalloped edges. She wielded in her gnarled fingers a wooden pestle, crushing sunflower seeds—for their oil, Glynis supposed—in a mortar held between her knees.

When she greeted the woman, she received a brief nod. "I wonder," Glynis said, taking a step toward her and smiling hopefully, "if you might tell me where I can find someone called Small Brown Bird?"

The woman's lips parted in a gap-toothed smile. She pointed the pestle toward a dirt path leading into a stand of shagbark hickory. Glynis thanked her and followed the path, shadowed by overhanging branches, until the trees began to thin, and she heard the chattering trill of women's voices.

Ahead of her lay a grassy clearing, beyond which a cornfield stretched into the distance. Small Brown Bird was easily recognizable; she looked almost as she had years before, as she sat with a number of other women on tree stumps beside a six-legged corncrib. Behind them soared a virtual mountain of unhusked corn. Stripped ears tied in neat bundles lay next to the crib, while the women braided together husks of others.

As Glynis approached, Small Brown Bird looked up from her lapful of corncobs. Her shiny black hair fell in two long switches indicating her unmarried status, and her dark oval eyes widened at the appearance of Glynis. She deposited the braided corn in a basket before gracefully rising to her feet.

"I don't know if you remember me," Glynis began. "We met several times at the County Fair. Although it has been some while."

But the woman had been smiling in obvious recognition. "Yes, Miss Tryon, I remember." Her flutelike voice was as beautiful as Glynis recalled. "You liked the beadwork I did. And you bought some moccasins."

Glynis nodded. "For my nieces, yes, and they loved them."

Small Brown Bird laughed shyly. The other women paused in their work to regard Glynis with pleasant if inquisitive expressions.

She stood there, feeling bulky and overdressed in long-sleeved, high-necked gray linen, tight-waisted over several petticoats that barely cleared the grass. The Indian women wore what she had heard called pantalettes, or leggings; most were of red broadcloth with a border of beadwork around the lower edges. The leggings hung straight to their moccasins. Over these, the women wore short tunics of brightly colored muslin or calico, gathered loosely at the waist. The garments looked comfortable and practical, reminding Glynis of the short-lived, long-lamented Bloomer costume that the suffragists had enjoyed before male ridicule had forced them back into their cumbersome dresses.

Small Brown Bird seemed to be waiting for Glynis to say something, her slender form bending forward like the willow at the edge of the stream. Glynis cleared her throat somewhat nervously. She was uncertain as to how she should begin, especially in front of the other women, and when she glanced toward them, found they were all watching her expectantly. She again cleared her throat. But shyness and the awareness of being an outsider made her tongue-tied.

Small Brown Bird gave her a gentle smile. "Every autumn after *onä'o'*, the corn, is harvested," she explained,

clearly to ease Glynis's embarrassment, "the women prepare it for storing. We are here"—she extended her arm to
include the others—"for *wadinowi'yǎ'ke'*, a husking bee. It
is said that if there had been no corn, there would be no
Haudenosaunee. But do you remember the story of Sky
Woman I once told you?"

Feeling somewhat more at ease, Glynis smiled. "Yes, I
thought of it, in fact, on my way out here."

Small Brown Bird nodded. "The Seneca legend says that
corn, and also beans and squash, sprang from the breasts of
Sky Woman when she gave birth to Good and Evil. And
so, even after her death, she provided her children with
food."

Small Brown Bird inclined her head to the other women
before she moved away, indicating that Glynis should follow. They walked toward Black Brook until Small Brown
Bird stopped in front of a small log house. She lowered
herself to the stoop, gesturing for Glynis to do the same,
then asked, "I think perhaps you wanted to talk alone with
me?"

"Yes," Glynis said gratefully, "but I don't quite know
how to put this." She hesitated, searching for words. "I
believe there's someone here—a man, that is—whom I used
to know."

But it was as if a curtain now descended over the other
woman's face. Small Brown Bird abruptly looked away and
gazed silently out over the stream. Although bewildered by
the woman's reaction, Glynis thought she had no choice but
to continue. "I saw—that is, I *thought* I saw—him several
days ago. Of course I might have been mistaken."

Small Brown Bird's eyes swung back to her. The woman's voice was almost a whisper when she leaned toward
Glynis to say, "Is it Walks At Sundown you look for?"

"Yes. Yes, it is." Glynis felt increasingly uneasy, but it
was too late now to disguise the purpose of her visit. "I
knew him as Jacques Sundown. Can you tell me if he's
here?"

Small Brown Bird rose from the stoop. "Please, Miss
Tryon, it's better that you don't look for him."

"But why?" Glynis, also getting to her feet, tried to ignore the voice inside her head: *Leave this alone. There's something wrong here. Just leave.*

But at that moment she heard a peculiar sound from the far side of Black Brook. A soft growling sound. Her skin prickled, and she sensed that if she turned to look, somehow a die would be cast. Some course determined. But despite the premonition, she was incapable of *not* looking.

She turned. On the opposite bank of the stream stood Jacques Sundown, light through the trees glinting off the coppery skin and glossy black hair, the fine, high cheekbones of his face.

His expressionless gaze from across the ribbon of water made Glynis inhale sharply. Seeing him again brought the disturbing awareness that she had sorely missed him. She hoped this was not laid bare on her face. But he probably knew anyway. And he must have known exactly when she arrived there at Black Brook; he had always known, by some arcane process, where she was or would be. She found it still startled her.

Behind her, a door creaked open, then slammed shut. Accompanied by hurried footsteps, a woman's harsh voice demanded, "What do you want here?"

Glynis broke from Jacques's gaze and whirled around. An aging woman now stood not three feet away from her, repeating, "What do you want?"

Glynis stared dumbly at the woman. The tall, wiry figure's leathery face held a mysterious but unmistakable malevolence. Glynis's immediate reaction was to step back. But she discovered that she was nailed to the spot by her boot heels, sunk into the marshy bank of the stream. She fought the urge to free herself by tugging at them, with the possibility of a headlong plunge into Black Brook, and instead concentrated on somehow mollifying this forbidding woman.

"Please. Please excuse me," she said, her voice as conciliatory as she could make it, "but I'm afraid I don't understand."

"You need to leave!" the woman commanded, her eyes, black and hard, fixed with implacable fury on Glynis.

What could be the reason for this? The hatred in those

hard eyes *must* have some reason. And yet . . . and yet it looked to Glynis as if the deep lines around the woman's eyes had been formed by timeless grief, much as everflowing water wears through rock.

Small Brown Bird, who had remained strangely silent, now spoke rapidly to the other woman. While Glynis was thankful for the temporary reprieve, she couldn't understand the words, which must have been in the Seneca tongue. Small Brown Bird seemed to be repeating herself, her voice rising and falling in intervals that sounded like musical recitative. During this, the other continued to glower at Glynis, who lowered her eyes to the woman's doeskin tunic and spectacular necklace. Suspended by a strand of small silver and glass beads, the flat, oval-shaped, seashell inlaid with silver lay in the cleft between the woman's breasts.

At the sound of Jacques's voice, Glynis raised her eyes with caution. And although the woman had been glowering still, she turned when Jacques, having crossed the stream by way of a narrow footbridge, approached them.

As he strode forward, he called sharply to the older woman in Seneca. This, in itself, surprised Glynis; she had never heard Jacques raise his voice, not in all the time she'd known him. And, in addition, instead of his jean-cloth trousers and the collarless, yoked cotton shirts Glynis had been accustomed to seeing, Jacques now wore leather leggings and a loose overshirt of soft pale doeskin fringed at the hem. He had always worn moccasins.

When he reached the older woman, his dusky brown eyes held their usual flat expression. He spoke a short sentence to her, and the woman responded in the same intonation as that used by Small Brown Bird, but higher. Glynis desperately tried to concentrate on the speech pattern rather than on her own anxiety. Failing this, she began as unobtrusively as possible to work her boots out of the damp earth. She would leave with as much composure as she could muster. Plainly it had been a mistake to come here.

But Jacques turned to her and said quietly, "Cross the brook. Cross over and wait for me."

Glynis caught his signal to Small Brown Bird, who, motioning for Glynis to follow her, started briskly for the footbridge. Behind them the other woman's voice again rose harshly.

Glynis felt shaken enough to keep her silence until they reached the far side of Black Brook. As they passed the last of the log houses and headed into a stand of gray birch, Small Brown Bird said to her, "I hope you will forgive my sister. She is very troubled by your coming here."

"I gathered that!" Glynis replied with some warmth, although she was startled to hear Small Brown Bird refer to the woman as her sister. But perhaps theirs was a clan relationship only, and not blood kinship. "Why should she be troubled?" Glynis asked. "She doesn't even know me."

"You are a white woman. For her that is enough to know."

Small Brown Bird led Glynis over a rough trail and on into a clearing some distance beyond the reservation. Just ahead, and barely visible over tall grasses, stood a small log cabin. Glynis saw that the isolated cabin had been so situated that the forest rose directly behind it, boughs of hemlock even brushing its bark roof. Irregular-shaped cones lay scattered over a carpet of needles, and the air was fragrant with the scent of fir.

"That belongs to Walks At Sundown." Small Brown Bird pointed to the cabin.

Glynis found she wasn't particularly surprised at the secluded location. Even when Jacques had been assistant constable of Seneca Falls, he'd stayed resolutely beyond the boundary of white society, and apparently he chose to remain in a no-man's-land here as well.

Since they had stopped walking, and since she was not satisfied with Small Brown Bird's earlier answer, Glynis now said, "Please tell me what exactly went on back there?" She motioned in the direction of the reservation. "Why did that woman, your sister, object so violently to my being here?"

Small Brown Bird looked off into the forest, and Glynis wondered if her question might have been considered discourteous. But finally, still not meeting Glynis's eyes, Small Brown Bird said, "You must not think it is only *you* she objects to. She would object to any white woman."

"But why?" Glynis repeated. "And who *is* she that Jacques—that Walks At Sundown even responds to her. I've never seen him give much notice to *anyone*—especially to someone who obviously opposes him."

Small Brown Bird's smile came swift. "That is true of him most of the time. But this woman is his mother."

"His *mother*?" That being the case, Glynis decided she had probably said enough. It still didn't explain the woman's behavior, but perhaps Seneca mothers simply didn't like white women anywhere near their sons. "Since you called her 'sister,' " she said to Small Brown Bird, "does that mean you're Jacques's aunt?"

"Your people would call me that, yes. But to Senecas, the word *mother* has a wider meaning. It means not only the birth mother but also all her sisters. Since Walks At Sundown's birth mother and I are of the same clan—the Wolf Clan—I also may be called his mother."

Small Brown Bird smiled and, apparently seeing Glynis's confusion, added, "Or you might say a mother-aunt, because I *am* the blood sister of Bitter Root."

"That was Bitter Root? Jacques's mother is Bitter Root?" Glynis asked incredulously. "Isn't she a medicine woman?"

"She is."

"But then I'm afraid I really don't understand," Glynis persisted. There must be more here than she was being told. "I know, for instance, that Bitter Root brought herbs to the Grimm farm recently, when young Pippa Grimm was ill. Not only that, but Pippa implied this was not the first time she'd seen Bitter Root. And Pippa and her mother, Molly, are white."

For a moment, Small Brown Bird didn't respond. Then she asked, "Are you certain Bitter Root did that in recent time—went to the Grimm farm?"

"Yes," Glynis said, now more puzzled than ever. "Pippa herself told me."

A slight frown appeared on Small Brown Bird's face. Again she hesitated before she said, "Bitter Root is not concerned about Pippa Grimm in the way that she is troubled by you."

"Troubled?" Glynis felt as if she were flailing around in

the dark. What could she possibly have done, in the short
time she'd been at the reservation, that could trouble Jacques
Sundown's mother?

Small Brown Bird sighed, as if about to undertake
something unpleasant. "You must not know," she said, now
looking closely at Glynis, "of Bitter Root's firstborn son?"

"Jacques has a brother?"

"He was Walks At Sundown's half brother." Small
Brown Bird's voice began to falter. "Many Horned Stag.
He is dead now, some years. He . . . he was killed. By white
men."

Glynis stared, stunned, at the woman, hoping she might
have heard incorrectly. Her next thought was that Jacques's
brother must have committed some crime. But what if . . .
what if he had died as the result of so-called "frontier justice"? Such things were done to Indians by angry mobs who
took the law into their own hands and . . . No! But then she
recalled that Jacques always had refused to talk of his family
or his past.

Needing to know, Glynis steeled herself. "Why was
Jacques's brother killed?"

Small Brown Bird studied Glynis's face with a look of
concern, clearly weighing a reply; but then she turned, her
eyes scanning the clearing behind them. And moments later
Jacques appeared, wading through the grass and holding the
reins of the dapple-gray mare. The buggy jounced behind.
From the closed expression now on Small Brown Bird's
face, Glynis knew no account of Many Horned Stag's death
would be given. At least not this day.

When Jacques reached them, he said something in Seneca
to Small Brown Bird. In response, she inclined her head to
frown at him momentarily, before she turned to Glynis. "I
will say good-bye to you now, Miss Tryon."

Before Glynis could reply, Small Brown Bird quickly
walked off across the clearing. The tall grass waved in her
wake.

Alone with Jacques, Glynis found herself inexplicably
stricken with sudden shyness, and to avoid looking at him,
she watched Small Brown Bird disappear into the far stand
of gray birch. But then, from behind the cabin, came a pe-

culiar sound much like a muffled bark. When she turned to look for its source, a large timber wolf suddenly materialized, loping from the forest. Its coat was dense, mostly gray, flecked with black and white guard hairs, and white markings on its muzzle and chest; black markings, as if drawn with a fine pencil, outlined its almond-shaped eyes, emphasizing an alert, intelligent expression. It came straight toward them.

"Jacques," Glynis whispered. "Behind you!"

Jacques registered no surprise. Indeed, with an unnerving display of nonchalance, he only muttered something under his breath. The wolf stopped in its tracks. Its ears pricked forward and and its muzzle lifted, searching the air, before its remarkable eyes came to rest on Glynis: fathomless, molten-gold eyes. It came to her with some surprise that she felt no fear. What she did feel was the presence of something benevolent. Something magical.

The wolf abruptly broke its gaze and turned to lope back into the trees. Then it vanished. It was there one moment, gone the next, leaving not even the shallowest impression in the pine needles to indicate it had been anything more than illusion.

Glynis let out her breath and looked with question at Jacques. His face held what might have been amusement. In fact, he looked as close to smiling as Glynis had ever seen him.

"He's a spirit," Jacques said. "Just a spirit."

"A spirit of your Wolf Clan?" Glynis asked. "But why was he here now?"

As soon as she'd said it, she realized how absurd it sounded—as though she believed Jacques's definition. He was once again making fun of her. And as if to confirm this, his face lost its subtle expression. It smoothed to a flat stare. The years fell away, and it might have been only yesterday when she'd last seen that maddening, enigmatic look.

However, she was older now. She would try to maintain some dignity, although this had never been particularly successful with him before. "Jacques, please don't let's start this again."

"Start what?" His flat stare swept her face; then it altered, just slightly, to look again as if he might smile.

Glynis felt heat flood her cheeks. Here she'd come all the way out to this place, simply to be ridiculed.

She took several deep breaths. What was the matter with her? Why did Jacques always provoke such exaggerated impulses on her part—always, ever since she'd first known him? She thought she'd convinced herself long ago that the tension between them resulted from the difference in their backgrounds, that he didn't intend, really, to embarrass her.

Armed with this, she would try again. "Jacques, let's at least make an attempt to understand each other."

"What do you want to understand?"

"Well, to begin with, why you didn't let anyone know you were back. Back in Seneca Falls."

"I'm not in Seneca Falls."

"But you're not on the reservation, either—not really. You've isolated yourself in these woods and . . ." Her voice had begun to rise, and she paused, unwilling to sound like his mother. She took a breath and went on, "Why didn't you come into town?"

"Why should I come into town?"

"Well, to say hello—or something! I suspect it hurt Cullen's feelings that you didn't. And I know it surely hurt mine!"

Glynis pressed her lips together; she hadn't meant to say that exactly, or with such emphasis.

Jacques's expression changed. The near-smile returned, and something moved in his eyes, like light rearranging itself. The cool, flat brown warmed to gold. He took several long, almost involuntary strides forward, but then stopped a few feet short of her, his hands clenched at his sides.

A sudden, vivid memory of another such encounter with him swept over her. At that time, the intimacy of the moment had confused her. Now it aroused something far more disturbing than confusion.

The sound of a twig snapping, and a harsh voice coming toward them, created in Glynis a rush of panic. She averted her eyes from Jacques's gaze, and hastened forward to climb into the buggy. Somehow she found the reins in her grasp— did Jacques hand them up to her?—and she flicked them harder than she intended over the mare's flanks.

The buggy jerked forward, and Glynis clamped her teeth together as its wheels rolled over the uneven forest path. She did not look back. She wanted to, and how she kept herself from doing so, she didn't know. But she riveted her attention completely on guiding the mare through the trees. All the way to Black Brook Road.

HER BREATHING HAD slowed, her heart no longer slamming against her ribs, by the time she saw the Grimm farm ahead. She needed to get back to town. To where she knew what to expect. She was *thirty-nine years old;* she had thought she knew everything about herself there was to know.

Apparently not.

She and Jacques Sundown came from wildly dissimilar circumstances. And she was at least ten years older than he. She felt embarrassed by her response to him, and disingenuous as well. She was not a young girl. In point of fact, she might be old enough to enter her change of life.

Perhaps that was the explanation. But did it mean she would now be capable of the startling things she had seen a few women do in this condition?

Like Moira O'Shaughnessy. Married in the Catholic church at seventeen, an exemplary wife and mother, Moira O'Shaughnessy at age forty-six had suddenly upped and run away to Utica with an itinerant scissors-grinder. Or spinster Sally Monroe, who, after fifty-two years of irreproachable— indeed saintly—conduct, had been seen one evening, dancing down Fall Street in her diaphanous nightdress. And a year later married a handsome young schoolteacher.

Glynis began now to laugh, remembering that at the time she had felt shamefully envious of such free spirits, unchained at last from the terror of unwanted pregnancy.

By the time she was half a mile farther down the road, she thought she was recovering some innate good sense. There could be no point in blaming herself for inappropriate feelings toward Jacques Sundown; those were entirely beyond her control, as she had learned, or should have, years before. She could, however, hold herself responsible for what she *did*.

And what she would do—oh, how remarkably simple it was—would be to never see Jacques Sundown again.

SEVEN

❦

I have sent books and music there, and all
Those instruments with which high Spirits call
The future from its cradle, and the past
Out of its grave. . . .
        —PERCY BYSSHE SHELLEY,
        "EPIPSYCHIDION"

THE LITTLE GRAY mare, heading for home and feed, took the buggy briskly past the first fences of the Grimm farm. Glynis held the reins loosely in one hand; the lowering sun shone directly into her eyes, and she needed a free hand to shade them. Granted, the days were shorter now, but how had it gotten so late without her realizing? It must be close to six o'clock. And the air had begun to turn cool.

She was reaching for the shawl on the seat beside her when the mare suddenly shied, then reared, fighting for her head. The reins jerked from Glynis's hand. The mare surged forward. Glynis was thrown backward against the buggy seat just as she saw a small, dark shape slip under the front wheels, immediately followed by a child's high scream.

Glynis grabbed for the reins only to have them whip away from her outstretched fingers. She lunged forward several times before she retrieved them and managed to pull the frightened mare to a stop. Then she looked back. Pippa Grimm was running along the roadside, and Glynis could hear the girl's panicky sobs.

Oh, dear Lord, not the lamb. She was clambering down from the buggy when Pippa screamed again. Glynis whirled in the direction of the girl, snagging her skirt on the buggy's hand brake. She yanked it loose, disregarding the sound of ripping linen, and hurried to Pippa.

The girl knelt in the road, the lamb's small body clutched to her chest, her face buried in its nappy gray wool. Glynis stood rigid with guilt. The thought crossed her mind that the wages of sin were now being extracted from her, and that she would rather burn for eternity than be forced to witness this; this heartbroken child cradling her dead lamb.

She never should have searched out Jacques. If only she'd left the reservation a half hour earlier . . . maybe just a few minutes earlier . . .

"Miss Tryon! Miss Tryon, look!"

Pippa's eyes gleamed up at her like ripe chestnuts. "Don't cry, Miss Tryon—he's all right. See? He's not hurt at all."

Glynis looked. And indeed, the lamb had begun struggling to escape Pippa's viselike grip, wagging its absurd, stumpy tail with vigor. It paused in its struggle briefly, however, to regard Glynis with what she could have sworn was reproach.

"Pippa, what happened?" Glynis choked out the words, guilt still grinding her between its teeth. "I didn't even see the lamb."

"I took him out of the pen—he hasn't been out in ages 'cause Mead Miller's been gone somewhere—and he just got away from me," Pippa explained, her voice high with joy. "He ran out into the road before I could catch him. But I guess the wheels didn't go over him."

"That's right, Miss Tryon," came a pleasant masculine voice from behind Glynis. "It's not your fault. Not at all!"

Glynis turned to look into the sympathetic eyes of Lazarus Grimm. Despite her distress, she couldn't help thinking, *And so the prodigal son returns. Offering absolution, no less.*

The lamb suddenly leaped from Pippa's arms and bounded off. The girl followed, laughing, as it dodged to elude her again.

Glynis sighed with relief. Now all she wanted was to get home, and she turned with some impatience to the man beside her. But as her guilty shock receded, she suddenly noticed how gaunt he looked. How different!

In the past, Lazarus had always appeared slightly bloated—some had termed it debauched—and the change in him was startling. For the first time, Glynis could see a square, clean-shaven chin, hollowed-out cheekbones, and a slender, patrician nose. Dark brown locks of hair curled over his forehead. There was about the hair, she decided, an artfully contrived negligence, although, truthfully, she didn't recall what his hair had looked like before. But his skin she did recall. Now pale, almost translucent, in the past it had been mottled as if he were constantly feverish. At the moment, Lazarus didn't look at all feverish. He looked, in fact, much like the marble bust in her library of a youthful Shelley: *The Poet kept mute conference with his still soul.*

Whence had gone the profligate Lazarus Grimm? The man standing before her looked positively aesthetic.

"Miss Tryon?" he said in the pleasant voice. "I'm Lazarus Grimm—perhaps you don't remember me."

Remember him? She couldn't imagine there were too many in Seneca Falls who would not. She hoped she hadn't been gaping at him, but the transformation was astonishing. Perhaps he had been ill.

"Of course I remember you, Lazarus. Your sister said you were coming back." Molly hadn't mentioned any illness. Maybe she hadn't known.

"Yes, I'm back home at last." Lazarus smiled. "Home to stay."

His wandering step, obedient to high thoughts, has visited the awful ruins of the days of old.

Forget Shelley, Glynis told herself. What stood before her was no aesthete. Lazarus Grimm had swindled aging widows out of money, hardworking men out of property, and persuaded a congregation in Buffalo to purchase from him, sight unseen, what proved to be a fourth of Montezuma Marsh for their new church.

And Lazarus didn't even own Montezuma Marsh. This was definitely a man to treat with caution. Glynis nodded politely to him and began walking along the roadside toward the buggy, where the mare stood placidly chewing clover. To her discomfort, Lazarus fell into step beside her.

"Are you still a librarian, Miss Tryon?" he asked. Glynis glanced at him from the corner of her eye. He looked sincere. This was undoubtedly when he was most dangerous.

"Yes," she said carefully. She probably also should mention that librarians did not make much money. But they both

turned as a voice floated from the direction of the Grimm
house. Molly was coming toward them.

"Glynis!" Molly's serene face looked apologetic. "I just
heard what happened. Pippa's been told and told not to let
that lamb out, but . . ." Molly gave Glynis the smile of a
resigned, forgiving mother. Pippa was fortunate.

"Oh, and your skirt's torn, too," Molly sighed. "I hope
you aren't very upset."

"I'm all right now, Molly."

Molly turned to Lazarus. "Did you ask Glynis? About
the theater?"

The theater? Oh, no, Glynis thought. Surely he hadn't
dreamed up some scheme involving The Usher Playhouse.
The love of Vanessa Usher's life—after Vanessa herself, it
was.

"It's getting quite late," she said, gazing significantly
toward the sinking sun. "I'm afraid I'll have to hurry to get
home before dark."

But the sun was not sinking nearly fast enough, because
Lazarus said to her, "I wonder if you would be so kind as
to give me an introduction to your neighbor Miss Usher. I'd
like to propose something to her about—"

"Perhaps we might speak of this another day," Glynis
broke in. "I really do have to leave now."

Lazarus smiled graciously. "Of course, Miss Tryon. I
have plenty of time. Plenty of time for the Lord."

Glynis assumed she hadn't heard correctly. Something
about being bored?

"You see, Miss Tryon," Lazarus continued, "I have had
a spiritual experience. A true awakening. I have renounced
my former ways and stand before you a man reborn. I have
seen the Lord's purpose for me. However, that you might
find this hard to believe, I can imagine."

He couldn't begin to imagine. Glynis threw Molly a questioning look, thinking she would confirm that her brother
had been ill. *Was* ill. But Molly stood smiling up at Lazarus
with a sister's blind, adoring eyes.

". . . find faith," Lazarus was saying, "and then we can
communicate with them."

"Excuse me?" Glynis asked, hoping fervently that what

she'd heard was not what he'd said. "Communicate with whom?"

"Our dear departed ones," Lazarus said. Said with reverence. "So you can understand the compelling need, Miss Tryon, to find a place for believers to gather. And I would like to convince Miss Usher that her theater could be that place."

Glynis looked to the sky. The sun, finally, sat as round as a ball on the horizon. *Thank you, Lord.* "I'm afraid I *must* leave," she said, pointing to the west.

As she started toward the buggy, Molly caught her arm. "Oh, Glynis, I meant to ask you"—her forehead wrinkled slightly—"have you seen Mead Miller today? In town?"

"No, I haven't. Why?"

Molly's frown deepened. "We haven't seen him either, not since early last night. Oh, well," she sighed, her forehead smoothing, "it's probably nothing to worry about. Mead does this occasionally. He doesn't have family hereabouts, so I can't imagine what he does on his Saturday nights."

Glynis wondered if Molly really couldn't figure out where a man like Miller might spend his free time. Or was this euphemistic language for her brother's benefit? In which case, given Lazarus's colorful history, it was surely wasted effort.

Before they could further detain her, she walked determinedly to the buggy. As she climbed in, and flicked the reins over the mare's flanks, she hazarded a glance backward.

Lazarus and Molly stood arm in arm, smiling beneficently at her. Lazarus lifted his hand in a wave. Or a blessing, perhaps? "I'll be into town to see you soon," he called to her. Molly beamed up at him appreciatively.

And here all this time, Glynis had believed Molly to be the one sane adult in the Grimm family.

She waved briefly, then turned her gaze firmly back to the road.

WHEN SHE PASSED the abandoned Flannery farm, the blackened ruins of house and barns stood starkly etched under clouds streaked by sunset to fiery crimson; the memory this evoked was not a pleasant one. But by the time she drove the game little mare past the Turners' place, the sky had begun to soften toward mauve. She should have left the Grimm's sooner. Yes indeed, *much* sooner! She smiled bleakly to herself. What a long and peculiar day it had been.

Later she would remember thinking this; it was just before she heard the high, piercing whinny of a terrified horse. Startled, she turned to look toward Black Brook. It was the white horse she had seen earlier, on her way out to the reservation.

The animal was rearing, again and again, and it continued to call in a high-pitched whinny. Glynis slowed the mare. Over the tall weeds, she couldn't see much more than the horse's head and its front legs pawing the air, but it was clearly in distress. Must have snagged its reins on something. She sighed, looking again at the sky. It would be dark soon. But the horse could lame or strangle itself before someone else came along, or its owner, some farmer no doubt, missed it. Much as she wanted to, she couldn't leave it. She'd already experienced guilt enough this day.

Reluctantly she pulled the mare to a stop and climbed wearily from the buggy to begin a trek through the weeds. She bunched up her torn skirt and held it as high as she could. Minutes later, her cotton stockings shredded and covered with burdock, she emerged from the weeds and stepped to the bank of the stream. Cattails rose from the water's edge like brown velvet pipe cleaners.

The horse shied away from her, but couldn't loose its reins tangled around a rotting tree stump. Glynis talked to it quietly, trying to soothe it, while watching her feet on the marshy ground. Suddenly she heard something sinister. A faint buzzing. She froze, peered cautiously ahead, then jumped back. The reason for the horse's terror became clear. Near its front hooves lay the broken, coiled body of a rattlesnake; it must have been seven feet long, as big around as a man's wrist. Its tail was still twitching spasmodically.

Glynis turned to bolt back to the road. But the rattler was dead. It couldn't hurt her if it was dead. And it was. She looked over her shoulder. Yes, without doubt. Dead. She turned back and, moving gingerly, her eyes half shut, she made herself step over the snake, while talking to the horse. She reached for the reins, and paused. Something smelled very odd. The dead snake? When she'd grasped the reins, she kicked the rattler a few feet away and had just begun untangling the horse when it abruptly reared. Its reins jerked her off balance. She had taken a large unintentional stride forward to right herself, when her shoe hit something soft. She regained her balance and then glanced down. An icy shock was followed by numbness that said what she saw was not there. *It couldn't be.*

Pressing her fists against her mouth, she turned away, instinct urging her to scream. And to keep screaming until someone came. So she wouldn't be alone with a dead man.

But she *was* alone. She took a deep breath, then another, before slowly turning back to look again. The man's upper body lay facedown in Black Brook, water lapping gently around his broad shoulders. Most of him lay concealed in marsh grass—the reason she hadn't seen him earlier. His boots were mud-caked, but the mud had dried. From the odor, she knew he had been there awhile.

The snake . . . the snake must have bitten him. But how could that be? He could have gotten help; snakebite took hours, sometimes several days, to kill.

She thought she heard something, and spun around. There *was* something, a whispering like someone moving through tall grass. Not the horse—he was standing quietly, his ears pricked forward toward the sound. She stood absolutely still, not daring to breathe.

"Leave." The voice came from directly behind her. "Leave now."

Heart leaping to her throat, Glynis whipped around.

Jacques Sundown reached out to grab the horse's reins before he looked down at her, no expression on his face, eyes level and dark. "You need to leave this. Get back to town."

In the wake of her fear, any resolve not to see him again vanished. And the alarm ringing in her head was silenced by relief. Her mouth, though, felt so dry she could barely talk.

"Jacques, thank God you're here. Look . . ." She pointed toward the body of the man in the stream. "He's dead," she gasped inanely, as if Jacques couldn't see that. "But I don't think it was the snake." She pointed now at the crushed rattler.

Jacques didn't even look toward the body. He stood staring at her with those flat eyes. What was wrong with him? Just an hour or two ago they'd been together . . . now he was looking at her as if she were a stranger. Did he think she was somehow responsible for the man lying there? Of course not . . . any more than she thought *him* responsible. But what *was* he thinking? He acted as if . . . She took a step backward. Jacques acted as if he already knew about the dead man. But how could he?

"Jacques," she said, her voice quavering. "What are you doing here? *When* did you get here?"

He didn't respond, but went forward until he stood at the water's edge beside the dead man. He didn't look at Glynis but at the body when he said, "You know him? Know who this is?"

"No. Well, maybe . . . I mean . . . how could I?" she stammered, gesturing toward the man's head, facedown in the stream.

Jacques thrust his foot under the man's right shoulder, then lifted until the body rolled over. Glynis gasped, closed her eyes, and turned away.

"You know him now?" Jacques's voice bore an unfamiliar edge. Glynis told herself that he couldn't be angry at her, that this must be the way Jacques sounded when he was upset. She couldn't remember his ever being upset before.

"Look at him," Jacques said again. "See if you know him."

Glynis shook her head. "I can't look. And yes, I know him. It's Mead Miller."

"Yeah. Guess it is."

"But how could he have died? Do you think he fell, leaning forward to get water from the stream? Maybe he was drunk . . . and hit his head on a rock. Knocked himself unconscious and drowned!" She was gathering strength from the logic of the words. Yes, that must have been what happened.

"You see any rocks here?"

She looked into the stream, at its edge, on the bank. Carefully she looked again. "No. No, there aren't any rocks here."

"See any wound on his head?" Jacques's voice, she noticed, had lost some of its harshness; instead he sounded tired. "Any sign of injury?"

"Well, no. But maybe there's a bruise on the back of his head."

"He fell forward. Facedown."

"Oh. Yes. Jacques, I don't know *how* he died. That's what I was asking you."

"You think I know?"

Glynis bit down on her lower lip. He still hadn't told her why he was here. It didn't make sense.

"You get back to town now. Get Cullen Stuart out here. Before it gets darker."

"What are you going to do?"

"Go back to the reservation. Nothing to do here."

"But, Jacques, should I tell Cullen that you . . ." Her voice trailed off. It had been dawning on her that it looked rather strange, Jacques appearing when he had. Unless he'd followed her to make sure she reached town safely. He'd done that before, years before. Once it had saved her life.

But could she explain that to Cullen? "What should I do, Jacques?"

Jacques shifted his weight, and reached for the reins of the white horse. "Do what you want."

He turned the horse in the direction of the road and gave its rump a hard slap. The horse cantered off. And Jacques himself began to walk away.

"Jacques! Wait . . ." Glynis felt dismayed, and irritated, at her fear of abandonment. "I mean, would you wait until I get to my buggy?"

"Planned to." He gave her a long look. "You should know that by now."

And he disappeared into the weeds. Like a scout or a guide, she realized.

Glynis stumbled after him up the slight grade. She could hear the sound of the white horse ahead of her as it plowed through the weeds, and she followed the path it opened to the road. Darkness was closing in fast. Finally she felt hard dirt under her feet and heard the little mare nicker. Her shoes were soaked, squashing with every step, and her teeth chattered wildly. She dragged herself up into the buggy. Drawing the shawl around her shoulders, she flicked the reins over the mare's flanks, and felt Jacques Sundown watching her.

"GLYNIS, WHAT IN hell were you doing on Black Brook Road anyway?" Cullen's voice was sharp as he untied the reins of his black Morgan. "You had no business being out there alone after dark."

He swung himself up into the saddle.

Even though she knew it to be concern he expressed, it sounded as if Cullen were scolding a naughty child. But she didn't have the strength to point this out. "I'd been . . . I'd been at Grimms' farm, and it got late faster than I realized. Then I saw the horse and . . ." Glynis sank to the railing of the Iveses' porch. She'd found Cullen there, talking with Quentin and Katherine.

"Quentin, I'll round up Zeph and some other men," Cullen said, turning the Morgan toward Fall Street. "Be back as soon as we find Miller's body. From what Glynis said, I think I know where along that stretch of Black Brook he is. Sounds to me like Miller drowned, but I'll need you to verify it."

"I'll be here when you get back," Quentin Ives said. "Dr. Cardoza, too. Most likely we should do the autopsy tonight, rather than wait for morning. Apparently he's been in the water there a while."

He looked at Glynis for confirmation. She nodded, and nearly fell from her railing perch.

"Glynis, sit in a chair," Katherine ordered, taking her arm and leading her to one. "You're exhausted. And it must have been terrifying to find Mead Miller, and you all alone like that."

Glynis hesitated before she answered. Cullen was about to leave; now was the time to tell him about Jacques. "Yes," she said finally. "Yes, it was terrifying."

It was all she said.

EIGHT

LILY BRAUN LEANED forward to instruct her carriage driver on the route she desired to take. After the driver nodded, touching his gloved fingers to the brim of his tall hat, Lily sank back against the soft leather cushions and smiled in satisfaction. She just hoped it wasn't too early in the day to be seen. Seen by everyone in Seneca Falls. *Look at me! Look at me, you smug little town with your smug little rules. Take a good look!*

She had defied the rules, and what had happened? Did anyone see her spirit broken? Impoverished and pleading for charity?

No, indeed!

Lily peeked around the ostrich feathers drooping over the brim of her white silk leghorn hat. There they were—bankers and lawyers and businessmen of Seneca Falls on their way to work. A few were her former customers. Good! They could hardly avoid seeing her. And women were out sweeping their porches, chasing their brats off to school, gossiping over their backyard fences. They'd really have something to gossip about *this* morning. Lily Braun. Lily Braun and her new, six-hundred-and-fifty-dollar, silk-fringed surrey with oil lamps, velvet carpet, and brass trim.

Lily ran her hand in its white kid glove over the rich leather seat, constructed by H. & C. Studebaker, one of the finest firms in the Carriage Builders National Association. The surrey had arrived in Seneca Falls by train from Indiana just three days past. It had been paid for, in advance, by a check drawn on the First Bank of Syracuse, New York, and signed by the bank president himself, John H. Stanhope.

Dear, sweet Johnny. She must find a particularly nice way to thank him for such a conspicuous drive through Seneca Falls. It was an event she'd anticipated for many months—anticipated, in fact, since the moment she had so fortuitously met John H. Stanhope. And, finally, here she was: the stylish lady of leisure taking the morning air.

She hadn't been up this early in years. The bright, clear light of morning had not always been agreeable to yesterday's Lily Braun. But that was then. Today's Lily welcomed the illumination.

Opening her beaded velvet reticule, Lily extracted a small looking glass; the sun's rays struck her reflection, and she indulged again in a smile. Soft curlicues of pale blond hair covered her forehead. On her ears sparkled clear, flawless emeralds—Johnny had exquisite taste—emeralds as hard and green as the kohl-lined eyes that beheld them. Eyes that could not be softened even by a satisfied smile. Who could mistake her now for an innocent? None could suspect that those shrewd eyes were formed not by her nature but by innocence savaged, after she had learned that love was kin to death.

It was thus with surprise that Lily saw in the looking glass a sudden glitter of tears. As if she were gazing at someone else. Someone who long ago had died.

Lily thrust the glass back into her reticule.

There, just ahead on the towpath, stood the tavern. Lily ordered the driver to slow the surrey. As ever, there were girls perched on the balcony railing and leaning out the open windows, brushing their hair in the sunshine and laughing about the previous night's customers. It was disappointing to Lily that her former employer, Serenity Hathaway, would undoubtedly still be lying abed. But Serenity would hear—oh, she would definitely hear—about the magnificent carriage. About the woman with pale, elaborately coiffed hair, who, dressed in elegant silk and feathers, had passed.

And surely by now all in town must know about the house—the house Johnny had bought for her from Dooley Keegan's widow. Lily smiled again, this time broadly. It was so right, so absolutely *right,* that she should have

Dooley Keegan's house. For as long as she needed. As long
as it took to accomplish what she had returned to do in this
wretched little town.

Lily rearranged her skirts so that her lace-edged satin petticoats were visible, and sat back. There was just one thing
about this morning that she truly regretted—that her father
was not alive to see her now.

The bastard.

GLYNIS TURNED ONTO Fall Street just as Seneca Falls's
church bells began tolling eight. She walked a little faster,
and immediately felt tightness in the muscles of her legs.
Small wonder, considering her activities of the previous day.
But she didn't slow her pace, since she wanted to reach the
Iveses' before Cullen came looking for her. She still didn't
know why she hadn't mentioned Jacques Sundown to him
the night before. She'd told herself it had been because of
exhaustion, that she'd been so tired she couldn't think
straight.

But that wasn't it.

Hearing a clatter behind her, Glynis moved closer to the
side of the road. She glanced back at the approaching carriage, looked again, then slowed for a still better look. There
were not many surreys in town, and none so ostentatious as
this one.

It was with astonishment that she recognized Lily Braun.
Glynis had not seen the woman since the day she'd run
Neva Cardoza and her off Black Brook Road. Now, looking
neither left nor right, Lily sat behind a liveried driver. Glynis
watched as the carriage went by, noticing that others on the
street stopped to do the same. If Lily wanted to create a
sensation, she had succeeded.

Glynis had lived in Seneca Falls only a few years when
she had seen Lily Braun for the first time. She remembered
Lily as a quiet, forlorn-looking young woman, unremarkable
except for the waist-length hair that swung around her like
silk veiling. Lily had returned to town, so it was said, to
attend her mother's funeral. This caused no end of speculation, since Lily had been conspicuously absent at her father's death a year or two earlier; no one seemed to know the

reason why. She had stayed in town just long enough to bury her mother; two older brothers had moved west years before.

The next time Lily made an appearance, four or five years ago, had been more interesting, if poignant. She arrived as a member of a traveling circus. The town was more than a little taken aback by Lily's new persona, that of a fortune-telling, palm-reading Gypsy called Madame Mysteriosa. The pale hair had been dyed black, a red kerchief and hoop earrings added, but underneath remained a profoundly sad-eyed woman. Her tragic look, moreover, simply heightened the Gypsy mystique—almost as if Lily had been employed for that very reason.

The night before the circus left town, some sort of dispute had occurred that involved Madame Mysteriosa and a circusgoer's money clip; the next thing anyone knew about Lily Braun, she'd been released from the lockup, her bail posted by Serenity Hathaway. Cullen had been markedly reticent about the whole episode, and Glynis thought she'd detected some pity in his attitude toward Lily.

Lily Braun's employment at Serenity's Tavern proved to be short-lived. This time neither Cullen nor Serenity was sympathetic to a charge of blackmail against Lily by one of the tavern's frequenters; the town never discovered the identity of the blackmailed man, although, Glynis remembered, it certainly had tried.

And now, here again was Lily Braun. Plainly this time her circumstances were very different. But why on earth would she come back? Glynis mused, as she came abreast of Levy's Hardware. Why return to a town that had very nearly ridden her out on a rail? It seemed irrational.

The hardware store hadn't opened yet when Glynis passed; arriving at the Iveses', she saw why. Abraham Levy stood on the porch with Cullen. Between them rested a long pine coffin. Glynis paused before climbing the steps, as she found herself still reluctant to tell Cullen about Jacques. And it might be too late. Cullen would justifiably wonder why she hadn't said anything the night before.

"Glynis, glad you're here," Cullen said, leaning over the porch rail. "There's a few more things I need to ask you—

about when you found Mead Miller's body."

"Oh?" Glynis said to him cautiously. "I told you last night what I saw."

"Yes, but we may need to go over it again. Your friend Dr. Cardoza thinks she may have found something. She's inside now, finishing up the autopsy."

"She's found something?" Glynis asked.

Cullen shrugged. "Don't know yet—but come on up here." He motioned to her. "Don't need to let the whole town in on this."

Glynis mounted the steps, assuming the whole town did not include Abraham Levy, since Abraham already looked fairly grim, as though worried about what Neva might have discovered.

Could Neva be the reason Abraham was here? Glynis wished she felt more like smiling.

"Morning, Glynis," Abraham said soberly. "Must have been hard for you, finding Mead Miller like that."

Glynis just nodded. Here was her opportunity. And if she didn't tell Cullen right now, right this minute, about Jacques's appearance last night, she risked having him find out another way, although how she couldn't imagine. But if Cullen did find out, he would realize she'd lied to him. Well, not exactly lied—simply neglected to mention a thing or two. *Lied.* But there was nothing to suggest that Mead Miller hadn't died accidentally. He'd drowned, simply drowned. So why was she being so secretive?

Because there was something malignant that she'd sensed about Miller's death. She couldn't put a name to it. But she felt it.

"Constable Stuart?" Neva Cardoza had opened the door and now stepped to the porch. "Constable, I think I know what killed that man. And if so, his death was no accident."

Glynis stared at Neva. Cullen and Abraham were staring too.

"Oh, Glynis, hello," Neva said. "They told me you found the man's body."

Miserably, Glynis nodded. "Yes, why?"

"Did you happen to notice the red spot on his neck?" Neva asked.

"Spot?" Cullen repeated. "What spot?"

Quentin Ives appeared behind Neva. "It's small," he said, "so I wouldn't be surprised if Glynis didn't see it last night."

"See what?" Cullen said. *"What spot?"*

"Made by a puncture wound," Quentin Ives said.

"Puncture wound?" Cullen sounded exasperated. "You want to relieve the suspense and just tell us what Miller died of?"

In response, Neva scowled and clamped her lips shut. Quentin Ives didn't seem to notice. "Actually, Dr. Cardoza should tell you," he said. "She's the expert in this area."

"What area is that?" Cullen asked.

"Poisons, Constable Stuart!" snapped Neva, as if she assumed Cullen couldn't believe she was an expert in anything. "In medical school I studied under an expert in the field, who had himself studied with Dr. Robert Christison." She gave Cullen an unpleasant smile, adding, "Dr. Christison wrote a definitive text entitled *Treatise on Poisons*."

Cullen's own smile looked equally if not more unpleasant than Neva's when he said, "I'm gratified to have your credentials, Dr. Cardoza! But all I want to know is what the hell Mead Miller died of."

"Very well, Constable. We found evidence of snake venom, but—"

"Snake venom?" Cullen interrupted. "You mean rattlesnake?"

"If rattlesnakes are what you've got around here," Neva retorted.

"There *was* a rattler near the body," Glynis said. "It's what frightened the horse. The horse had killed it, though, apparently just before I got there—the snake's tail was still twitching. But I didn't think snakebite could kill that fast. I mean to say, Mead Miller looked as if he had been dead for some time."

"So maybe," Cullen said, "the snake had bitten him hours before you got there. Maybe Miller . . . wait a minute! When I saw him Saturday night at the tavern, he was fairly drunk. Maybe, on the way back to the Grimms' farm, he stopped along the brook to get some water, passed out, and the snake got him then. Bit him, and Miller didn't even realize it. Died while he was passed out.''

"No, I don't think so," Neva disagreed, though her voice wasn't quite so testy now.

"Why not?" Cullen asked.

"Because," she said, "Glynis is right. It ordinarily takes quite a while for snake venom to circulate. Unless the victim is in poor condition. But Mead Miller was essentially a very healthy man. Our autopsy showed that."

"Yes, that's right," Ives agreed. "I don't think venom alone would have killed him. Not that fast, it wouldn't."

"How long do you think he'd been dead when Glynis found him?" Cullen asked.

"It's impossible to know exactly, but I'd say somewhere between fifteen and twenty hours," Quentin Ives said. "So he could have died shortly after you saw him—possibly on his way back to the Grimms' from the tavern. In any event, that's not what's behind our reasoning, Cullen. There's more to what we found."

Cullen sighed, and shot Glynis a long-suffering look. "Think you could just spit it out?" he said. "Sometime today?"

Quentin Ives smiled. Neva did not.

Abraham Levy, who as yet hadn't said a word, appeared to hide a grin behind his hand, and settled into the porch swing as if expecting to be there for some time.

Neva looked again at Quentin Ives. He motioned her to continue. "What we found first," she began, "was that Miller hadn't drowned as you, Glynis, guessed he might have. There was no water in his lungs, though he was lying facedown in the brook. We noticed the petechial hemorrhage." She paused, then explained, "The small red spot. But you couldn't have seen it if his head was in the water."

Glynis nodded. But what did that mean? It still sounded like snakebite.

"Significantly," Neva went on, "there was the puncture wound, with evidence of discoloration and swelling near the site. When we did an examination of the internal organs, we found evidence of kidney failure, swollen lymph nodes, and necrosis—dead tissue—"

"All of which," Cullen interrupted, "are signs of snake-bite. Aren't they?"

"Then this was no ordinary snake," Quentin Ives said, "to have bitten a tall man like Mead Miller in the neck."

"But couldn't he have been bending over the brook for a drink at the time?" Glynis asked.

"Possible," Ives answered, "but not probable. His head and neck would have been over the water. If he'd accidentally kicked or knelt on a snake, the bite would most likely have been on his torso or legs. That's partly why we believe, Dr. Cardoza and I, that poison was introduced by something other than snake fangs. And Miller's apparently swift death indicates that there must have been more than venom present."

"What?" Both Glynis and Cullen spoke, while Abraham Levy sat completely still, his gaze fixed on Neva.

"But most telling," Neva said, "was that the puncture wound was too large to have been made by a snake—I know because I've seen fang marks, and they're smaller than this was."

"So," Cullen said, "what *do* you think caused the wound?"

Neva looked at Quentin Ives as if for corroboration. Glynis felt unreasonable fear sweep through her, and decided she almost didn't want to hear the answer.

Quentin said quietly, "Dr. Cardoza believes—and I should add that I concur—that what killed Mead Miller was a combination of snake venom and some other highly toxic substance, given the damage we found in the internal organs."

"You want to explain that?" Cullen asked, looking as perplexed as Glynis felt.

Neva appeared uncomfortable. But Quentin nodded at her. "I remembered reading in medical school," she said carefully, as if she didn't expect them to believe her, "about American Indians who..." She paused, then added quickly, "I don't recall a specific tribe being mentioned, but they immersed their arrowheads in ground-up snake and venom. Or they would make a snake bite a rabbit liver, then steep the poisoned liver in toxic herbs before they used it for their arrows. That would be a pretty potent brew. Aconite was one of the most common herbs used because it's so toxic and so easily obtained from monkshood, which grows just about everywhere. And aconite by itself can kill rapidly, we know, if it's mistaken for wild parsley and ingested,'' she said.

"But surely," Glynis protested, "Mead Miller wouldn't have eaten it . . . oh . . . the puncture wound." She pressed her lips together before she could say more.

"Yes," Neva responded. "The poison *could* have been introduced by way of an arrow. It would have worked very fast if shot into a neck vein."

"No. Arrow point's way too big," Cullen immediately argued. "I would have seen that size wound in Miller's neck."

"It was dark, Cullen," reminded Abraham quietly.

Glynis remained silent.

"It didn't have to be an arrow," Quentin Ives said. "I agree that would probably have made a very noticeable wound. But it might have been something smaller . . . like a dart. Yes, in fact, a dart would have been just about the right size."

Cullen frowned at Ives. "I found a lot of burdock and thistle on Miller's clothes, but I didn't find anything else. As Abraham said, though, it was dark." Cullen turned to Glynis. "You didn't see a dart when you found him, did you?"

Glynis shook her head. She wished Neva hadn't mentioned American Indians. She knew Jacques hadn't killed Mead Miller, she knew that—and besides, why would he?—but it could look very odd if she mentioned his sudden appearance to Cullen now. She needed to think this through. And in the meantime she wouldn't say anything. Not yet.

". . . and I don't like this," Cullen was saying to Quentin Ives. "If what you're theorizing is true, then someone wanted it to look as if Miller drowned, or was killed by snakebite. And that means we've had two murders in this town in just a short time."

"Yes, Cullen," Quentin agreed, "of course I thought of that too. Although Jack Turner didn't die the same way."

"He was poisoned, though," Cullen said. "Seems to me what *kind* of poison doesn't make a whole lot of difference—both he and Miller are dead."

"And you know, something else has been bothering me," Quentin said. "Remember when Dooley Keegan died? About four years ago?"

Glynis looked at Quentin with uneasiness. She remembered Dooley's death, all right. The whole town had been shocked. Dooley Keegan, never sick a day in his life, had just keeled over during a hunting trip. He'd been with several other men who verified this. "I remember," she said now to Quentin. "But why do you mention it?"

"Because, at his wife's insistence, I did an autopsy on Keegan. She just couldn't accept that he'd died so abruptly. Natural on her part, I suppose—she maintained he'd always been in good health. But it looked to me as though he'd died of sudden, massive kidney failure. No reason to think otherwise."

"He wasn't very old, though," Cullen said. "We all wondered about that at the time."

Neva Cardoza had been listening attentively to Quentin. "But was there anything about that man's death," she asked, "which would make you think it was not as it seemed?"

"No," Cullen answered her. "Not that *I* remember, except . . . My God, Quentin, didn't you say something about a red spot on his neck? It's been so long, I can't recall exactly."

"Yes, it looked like a small puncture wound," Ives said, his face troubled. "I just now looked it up in my files. Couldn't remember until this morning, but I thought I'd seen, sometime in the past, the exact kind of wound that Miller had." Ives looked upset when he added, "Dooley Keegan! But at the time I assumed his neck puncture was something that took place while he was hunting; he was hiking through the woods, after all. I must admit, though, it bothered me some; but none of the other men could recall anything out of the ordinary happening to Dooley. And there was no reason to suspect anything sinister. But now I wonder."

"Yes," Cullen said, "I wonder too. It's unlikely we'll ever know the answer—Keegan's death was a long time ago."

"I thought you told me," Neva Cardoza commented, "that this was a quiet town, Constable Stuart." She stared at Cullen as though affixing blame.

"It was," Abraham Levy interjected, "until you arrived."

"Abraham . . ." Quentin Ives seemed on the verge of rebuke, but then apparently caught Abraham's grin. Neva just glared.

"You know, young woman," Abraham said to Neva as he got to his feet, "somewhere along the way you'd best find a sense of humor."

"I don't believe there's anything humorous about murder," Neva lashed back.

Abraham appeared to ignore this; he went to the pine coffin and lifted its lid. "You want some help, Quentin, getting Miller's body into this?"

Quentin Ives looked as if he couldn't quite believe the exchange he'd just heard between his friend Abraham Levy and his trainee Neva Cardoza. But he nodded briefly at Abraham and they went into the house.

Neva continued to glare at Abraham's disappearing back, then turned to Glynis. "Are you going to tell Constable Stuart about what Sara Turner said?"

Glynis had been about to do just that. "Neva and I stopped to see Sara on the way back from the Grimms', Cullen," she explained. "She was very odd—Sara Turner, I mean—and said something to the effect that her husband's death wasn't the end of it."

"End of what?" Cullen asked her, frowning.

"Death, was what she said. That there'd be more death."

"Seems she was right," Neva said, frowning herself.

"Didn't you ask what she meant?" Cullen said to Glynis.

"Yes, of course I tried, but she ran into the house before I could get her to say more. It was very strange."

Neva nodded in agreement. "And Sara Turner didn't look much like a grief-stricken widow," she offered. "Quite the opposite, I'd say."

"That your impression, Glynis?" Cullen asked.

"Yes, it was. But how could Sara know that Mead Miller, or anybody else, was going to be killed? Unless she knew the reason why. Which might mean she knows, or at least suspects, why her husband was murdered."

"Unless she's the one who did it," Cullen said.

"But would Sara Turner kill Mead Miller too? That makes no sense, Cullen." Glynis looked at Neva for possible suggestions.

Neva shook her head. "I agree with Glynis. It's one thing for Sara Turner to have killed a husband who was tormenting her and her children," she said. "At least that's understandable, some might say justifiable, but"—she hurried on as Cullen looked about to take strenuous exception—"for her to kill yet another man eliminates that motive. And anyway, I don't think Sara Turner killed either one of those men. She doesn't seem the type."

"Oh, there's a specific 'type' of person who kills?" Cullen said. "Tell me about this, Dr. Cardoza. It'll certainly make my job a whole lot easier!"

"I only meant," Neva snapped, "that someone like Sara, who has apparently endured years of mistreatment, doesn't suddenly transform from a victim into an aggressor. Not usually. At least I wouldn't think so."

"That's right, Cullen," Glynis said. "There are many women in Sara's situation, tragically, but they don't abruptly do away with their husbands."

"Or else," Neva added, "we'd have a whole lot more dead men."

Cullen's expression turned combative. Then, unexpectedly, he shook his head. "No, I'm not getting into another one of those pointless arguments. No!" he said firmly as Neva tried to break in. "I've got two murders to investigate. Now, if either of you wants to add anything about *those,* I'll listen. Otherwise, I'm heading out to the Turners'. And the Grimms'—see if they know why anybody'd want to kill Mead Miller.

"Glynis, you think Jonathan Quant can handle the library this afternoon? I'd appreciate it if you'd come with me. You know the people involved better than I do. And—"

He broke off as his deputy came running around the corner of the house. Zeph raced to the foot of the porch steps to sputter breathlessly, ''Constable . . . Constable Stuart, you need to come with me. Real fast! There's trouble. At Levy's Hardware.''

NINE

❧

*The trails of our Indian predecessors, indeed, have been oblit-
erated, and the face of nature has been transformed; but all
recollection of the days of Indian supremacy cannot as easily
pass away. They will ever have a share in our history.*
—LEWIS HENRY MORGAN, *LEAGUE OF THE
HO-DE-NO-SAU-NEE, OR IROQUOIS*

CULLEN STARTED DOWN the porch stairs. "What kind of
trouble, Zeph?" he asked the young deputy.

Abraham Levy had shot through the door and was down
the stairs and running in the direction of his Fall Street store
before Zeph could answer.

"It's the Indians," Zeph said. "They're at Mr. Levy's
store, and a bunch of folks are trying to make them leave—
I think you'd better hurry, Constable Stuart."

Cullen nodded and, with Zeph beside him, took off at a
brisk stride. Glynis followed at a slower pace. Even before
she rounded the corner onto Fall Street, she heard argumen-
tative voices; once in sight of Abraham's store, she saw a
small crowd gathered in the road around oxen yoked to a
rough dray wagon. Beside the dray stood four Iroquois
women.

Glynis recognized only Small Brown Bird and the wiry,
stern-faced Bitter Root. All four women wore broadcloth
pantalettes, flannel underskirts, and overdresses of bright
calico, but these were more elaborate than the ones Glynis
had seen at the reservation. The dresses were buttoned with
silver brooches; narrow bands of glass and silver beads
shimmered at the hems. From Glynis's vantage point, the
sparkle of beading and the bright fabrics made the four
women resemble colorful, exotic birds surrounded by a flock
of sparrows.

Cullen and Abraham stood on the front steps of the hardware store, being harangued by a heavy-framed white

woman who gestured toward the Iroquois and shook her head repeatedly. Glynis moved closer.

". . . and we don't want those savages in our town!" the woman finished. Glynis identified the speaker as Tillie Tyler. Standing beside Tillie, her much smaller husband, Lemuel, nodded his agreement after being poked by his wife's elbow.

"There's no law says these folks can't be here, Tillie," Abraham said reasonably. "Why're you raising such a dustup about this?"

" 'Cause you got their stuff in your store, Abe Levy, that's why," Tillie pronounced, arms akimbo, hands on her thick hips. "You just want to make money and you don't care how you do it. It's downright unneighborly and . . . un-Christian is what it is."

Abraham Levy's ruddy cheeks went darker. "I haven't noticed, Mrs. Tyler, that religion's ever stopped you from asking for credit in my store when you needed it."

Tillie started to reply, but her husband plucked at her arm in timid appeal, and wagged his head at her.

A tall, haggard man, a farmer whose last name Glynis recalled as Daniels, stepped forward. "Why're you dealing with these here people anyhow, Abe Levy?" Daniels gestured toward the four women standing quietly beside their dray wagon. "They're meant to stay put on their own land, not come on down here causing trouble."

"I don't see them causing any trouble," Abraham replied. "Seems like the only trouble is what you folks are making. These women have got quality goods for sale—"

"Yeah," interrupted bootmaker Sam Carson, "and they're competing with us white folks. They make their moccasins a lot cheaper than I can make boots."

"And they ain't gotta pay no overhead, neither," another voice chimed in.

Beside Abraham, Cullen stood with arms crossed over his chest, not saying a word. Glynis didn't think he would interfere as long as things remained relatively calm. Unless someone broke the law, Cullen generally didn't involve himself in disputes. Occasional squabbles were normal, he'd told Glynis more than once—some people just by nature were greedy and selfish and cantankerous. No constable was going to make them otherwise. In the past, however, Glynis had observed that Cullen's badge alone often worked to dissuade troublemakers.

"What's going on here?" asked a voice at Glynis's shoulder.

Glynis turned to find Neva Cardoza frowning at the restless and growing crowd. "Some think the Iroquois should stay on their reservation," she answered. "And they're angry, too, because Abraham is carrying the women's goods."

"That's ridiculous!" Neva said, so emphatically that several people pivoted to look at her. Neva ignored them. "I hope the unpleasant Mr. Levy isn't going to back down," she added, but in a somewhat milder tone.

Glynis had to ask. "Neva, why do you still insist that Abraham is unpleasant?"

"Because he still reminds me of my father."

Glynis wasn't sure how Neva's comment answered her question, but clearly this was not the time to pursue it. Especially since a buggy wheeling up Fall Street had stopped at the fringes of the crowd, and Lazarus Grimm was now jumping from the driver's seat. His pale, aesthetic face looked markedly eager. Molly and Pippa also began descending to the road, but Lazarus called something over his shoulder, and both climbed back into their buggy seat. Pippa, however, continued to eye the crowd with obvious curiosity.

Glynis wondered if perhaps Mead Miller's disappearance had brought the reclusive Grimms here this day. They might well have come to see Cullen about Miller. Had they by this time learned of the man's death? Perhaps not; the farm was so very isolated. Glynis felt a tremor travel the length of her spine as she considered the bizarre murder. She couldn't shake the sense that Mead Miller's death had to be linked to that of Jack Turner.

But other than the fact that the two men had lived on the same road, what could they have had in common to provoke murder?

To Glynis's chagrin, Lazarus had apparently spotted her, and now came toward her at a trot. "Looks like there might be trouble here, Miss Tryon."

Again Glynis noted that Lazarus looked remarkably unperturbed, perhaps even cheered, by this prospect. She concluded she should say nothing about Mead Miller; after all, she and Cullen were supposed to go to the Grimm farm later that day. She just nodded to him briefly. But Neva nudged her with insistence until Glynis introduced him.

"Ah, yes, the new doctor in town," Lazarus said. By all appearances, he seemed genuinely delighted to make Neva's acquaintance. "My niece told me of your visit to the farm."

He turned to gesture at the buggy. Mistaking this for acquiesence, Pippa again began to clamber down. Lazarus shook his head at her vigorously, and Pippa's face registered profound disappointment when her mother pulled her back up beside her on the buggy seat.

Whatever Lazarus said next was drowned in harsh shouts from those standing directly in front of the store. Glynis craned to see over their heads, and finally moved closer to the dray wagon. The shouts apparently had been prompted by Bitter Root, who'd begun toting baskets of moccasins to Levy's shop. The shop's two doors stood open and the space just inside was empty; presumably all the baskets previously there had been sold.

"Levy!" shouted Sam Carson. "You give those squaws space in your store, you can just forget about my trade!"

Abraham's face flushed a darker red, but he replied civilly, "If that's the way you want it, Sam."

"Or my business either, Levy," shouted farmer Daniels.

Neva, who had followed Glynis, said, "Isn't your Constable Stuart going to do something?"

"He probably won't unless it gets out of hand. So far, people are just shouting."

"So far," Neva said, looking skeptical.

"How come you let those squaws squat in your store?" another voice shouted. "They maybe giving you somethin' you can't get down at Serenity's?"

This was greeted with a few raucous laughs, which dwindled quickly to be replaced by stony silence. Most of the men there, irate as they might be, wouldn't condone that kind of talk in front of womenfolk. White womenfolk, at least.

Abraham spoke into the void. "These women aren't getting space free. They're paying me a commission to sell their goods. And as far as I'm concerned, they're entitled to be here so long as they do pay."

Mutters of surprise greeted this piece of news. To Glynis's relief, a substantial portion of the crowd appeared to shrug, if only figuratively, and began to saunter off. But Tillie Tyler wasn't satisfied. "Makes no never-mind, Abe Levy," she said belligerently, "no matter how much those Indians're paying you. They don't belong here, and that's the truth! Next thing you know, they'll be buying all kinds of liquor and shootin' up the town. You see if they don't!"

Abraham gazed down at Tillie Tyler with barely contained exasperation. "Tillie," he said wearily, "you are an ignorant woman—no, don't you interrupt me. I'm entitled to my say. You have never—I repeat, *never*—seen Iroquois women shooting up anything. Now, these folks have got the right to try and sell their goods here. You don't like it— don't buy it! But that's the way it is."

With that, Abraham Levy stepped down and lifted several baskets from the arms of Bitter Root, who was now on her second trip to the shop. Ignoring the crowd, which by then had diminished to a handful, Abraham deposited the baskets and moccasins, then headed back toward his store. Bitter Root started toward the wagon where the three other women had begun to unload more goods.

Glynis watched as the women made their way forward. Their woven baskets were filled with cornhusk dolls, salt bottles, carved pipes, and beaded bags and pincushions; black pottery of so fine a texture that it resembled stone, and earthen bowls, of which a few were faced with wolf heads. Various other animals had been carved on the handles of wooden paddles and ladles. Those townspeople who remained stood quietly, and their expressions showed curiosity more than hostility.

Glynis stole a quick glance at Neva, who was standing quietly beside her. She'd heard the quick intake of breath when Abraham began to speak, and now saw something unfamiliar on the young woman's face. Although Glynis couldn't identify it precisely, it might have been respect. She couldn't resist saying, "Well, I guess Abraham didn't back off."

"No. No, he didn't," Neva agreed surprisingly, her words coming slowly as if with some reluctance. "No, he stood his ground." She looked at Glynis with the merest hint of smile. "Aren't you going to say 'I told you so'?"

Glynis was about to say Yes, when Bitter Root, in front of the store and loaded down with baskets, suddenly began to cough. It was a painful sound. The baskets dropped when she wrapped her arms around her chest and bent almost double as, swaying precariously back and forth, she continued to cough.

Cullen stepped to the road with a look of concern. He moved to put an arm around Bitter Root's shoulders, but the woman thrust herself upright and, still hacking, flung off Cullen's arm.

"Keep away from me!" she gasped. "Don't need anything from white lawman."

Cullen took a step back as Small Brown Bird rushed forward and took her sister's arm to lead her to the steps. Once Bitter Root had been seated, the cough began to subside.

"I'm sorry," Small Brown Bird said over her shoulder to Cullen. "My sister was in distress, and so she was unkind in her words."

Bitter Root started to say something, but Small Brown Bird motioned to her with frantic gestures. Bitter Root's lips closed, but she stared straight at Cullen. Even from a distance, Glynis could feel the woman's hatred.

Cullen strode off down Fall Street, his face unreadable even to Glynis. And most of those remaining, while muttering uneasily, began to amble off.

"I wonder what that was all about?" Neva ventured.

Glynis shook her head. "I can't imagine, and—" She was interrupted by a familiar voice behind her.

"Glynis, what in the world is going on?" The clear voice rang accusingly as Vanessa Usher swept into Glynis's vision. Lovely, maddening Vanessa. Exactly the person they did not need here. And Neva, who had already met Vanessa several times, at once stiffened and adopted a wary expression.

"I *said,* Glynis, what is happening here?" Vanessa demanded.

"Oh, nothing you need concern yourself with, Vanessa. Anyway, it's over now."

"What's over? And just what do those outlandishly dressed squaws think they are doing?"

"Those *women* are simply minding their own business," said Neva sharply.

"Oh . . . well, if that's all they're doing, I shouldn't have bothered to stop," Vanessa retorted. "I thought something that might interest me was taking place." She gave Neva an airy wave of dismissal, then turned to leave.

"Ah, Miss Tryon, if you please?"

Glynis had forgotten Lazarus Grimm, who now hovered directly behind her.

"My dear Miss Usher," Lazarus said, bowing to Vanessa with a flamboyant flourish. "Miss Usher, I should very much like to speak with you on a matter of mutual interest. If you would allow Miss Tryon to introduce me, I would be forever grateful." He fixed Vanessa with an utterly charming smile.

Glynis had to give him credit; Lazarus had done precisely that most destined to pique Vanessa's curiosity. Vanessa who believed unshakably that all western New York men lacked even the most rudimentary knowledge of good manners; had only very recently shed their bearskins and emerged from caves.

She returned Lazarus's smile with equal charm. "Glynis, dear, do introduce this gentleman immediately."

Neva uttered an indistinguishable sound; while faint, it was somewhat louder than Glynis's sigh, hence the glare that Neva now received from Vanessa. "Of course," Glynis said, commencing to do as she had been commanded. But, my dear Miss Usher, she thought, don't blame me.

The introductions having been made, Lazarus bent over Vanessa's hand in a showy gesture. Glynis turned aside, determined not to laugh. She caught Neva's eye and saw that she, too, struggled for the solemnity this clearly historic meeting required. They both quickly moved away.

Glynis pressed her palm over her mouth. And under her breath, Neva muttered, "From what you've said about Lazarus Grimm, I'd say those two deserve each other."

Small Brown Bird had just returned from the shop, and Glynis walked to the dray wagon, saying, "I'm truly ashamed of the earlier scene here. Please don't think that all of Seneca Falls feels as those few people do."

"I don't think that," Small Brown Bird smiled shyly, "or we would not have sold so many things."

The two other women were still inside the shop, but Bitter Root had climbed with startling nimbleness into the wagon, apparently recovered from her attack. Glynis noticed that Neva had been studying the older woman with interest.

"Excuse me," Neva said now to Bitter Root, "but have you had that cough very long?"

Bitter Root moved her head to stare straight before her. But Small Brown Bird quickly said something to her in Seneca, and the older woman turned back to regard Neva with narrowed eyes.

"I told my sister that you are a medicine woman," Small Brown Bird explained to Neva, leaving Glynis to wonder how this information had been acquired. Then, as she saw Pippa coming toward them, she remembered that both Iroquois women had had contact with the Grimms.

"I could listen to your chest," Neva was telling Bitter Root. "In fact, I think I should. That cough sounds like something you should attend to."

But Bitter Root had turned at the sound of Pippa's voice, and watched intently as the girl came toward her. Glynis observed a smile spreading across the woman's face; a smile that planed the cold, rough lines and brought to Bitter Root's cheeks a copper warmth. With a start, Glynis realized that Jacques's mother must be considerably younger than she'd originally guessed—probably no older than her early fifties. That would account for her surprising agility. The Seneca woman's eyes, however, looked as ancient as the hills. An Old Testament image came suddenly, and for no obvious reason, to Glynis—that of Rachel and her lost children. *A voice was heard in Ramah, lamentation and bitter weeping;*

Rachel weeping for her children. . . .

Pippa had scrambled up onto the dray and thrown her arms around Bitter Root's neck, and received in response a warm chuckle and like embrace. Glynis watched this display of affection from the dour woman in astonishment. Then she heard Molly Grimm directly behind her.

"Pippa, come along now—we have to leave." Molly's voice held an urgent note. "Do get down from there!"

Pippa looked at her mother with a strangely poignant expression. She seemed about to protest, but when Bitter Root gave her a swift shake of the head and a soft nudge, Pippa descended from the dray dutifully but with obvious reluctance.

"Good morning, Glynis. And Dr. Cardoza," Molly said somewhat breathlessly, as though she'd run from the buggy. "I'm sorry to be in such a rush, but we don't have much time."

Time? Glynis thought. The woman had been waiting for the past ten or fifteen minutes without a murmur. But Molly seized Pippa's arm to pull her from the dray, while at the same time calling for Lazarus to hurry. Lazarus bent to pass his lips again over Vanessa's hand, then walked toward the buggy. Glynis's gaze returned to Bitter Root with curiosity; the woman was watching Pippa, her eyes glittering but relaying nothing specific in way of meaning. Glynis noticed that Small Brown Bird did much the same, before a sudden enigmatic look flashed between the two Iroquois women. It happened so rapidly that a moment later Glynis couldn't be positive she'd really seen it.

Voices coming toward the dray broke into her speculation. The two other Iroquois women had returned and now smiled tentatively at Glynis and Neva, while Small Brown Bird said, "These are my sisters. Or, in your custom, perhaps they would be called cousins. But we are all of the Wolf Clan."

She introduced Sunlight Weaver and a much younger woman, really just a girl, Glynis thought, called Silver Combs. Both smiled and nodded to Glynis and Neva, then climbed nimbly into the dray. Sunlight Weaver gave the reins of the oxen a quick shake; with her round face and flat nose, she looked so very different from the hollow-cheeked, sharp-featured Bitter Root, and from Small Brown Bird and Jacques, too, that Glynis marveled they could all be related, no matter how distantly.

The dray wagon creaked slowly forward.

As Glynis watched it turn onto Black Brook Road, she observed Bitter Root's long backward glance as well as a wistful look on the face of Silver Combs that touched Glynis with sadness. How much did Iroquois youngsters know of white culture, and if aware of how much was inaccessible to them, did they care? From Silver Combs's expression, Glynis thought the girl did care.

"Why do we see only the women in town and not the men?" Neva asked.

"From what I know," Glynis answered, her eyes still on the departing wagon, "I'd guess the men wouldn't participate in what they might consider women's work." She gave Neva a rueful smile. "That seems to be true anywhere."

"But from the books you loaned me," Neva said, "I gathered that Iroquois women had at least some small amount of power."

"Their lot has changed dramatically in the past five or six decades," Glynis explained, "mostly because of the Indians' confinement to reservations. In the past, women were in charge of the agriculture: planting and harvesting and storage and preparation. And they did have a certain stature within the tribes. Not, I think, as much as we've been led to believe by the European male chroniclers, who, no doubt, were flabbergasted at the idea of descent following the female line."

Neva nodded and grinned. "What a shock those first white men must have experienced! Can you imagine the authority they believed the women had?"

"Exactly," Glynis agreed. "But now the Iroquois men, having lost most of their hunting grounds, and no longer engaging in war, have begun to adopt whites' farming methods—very slowly, to be sure. Not that long ago, an Iroquois male wouldn't have been caught dead planting or harvesting; again, that was woman's work! Some of the men still refuse, especially when they might be seen. But the upshot is that the women, who once controlled use of the land, have been forced to give up that control.

"And believe it or not," Glynis went on, "Iroquois women at one time had more rights regarding divorce and inheritance, and most certainly their children's lives, than white women have today."

Neva gave Glynis a tight smile. "It's depressingly familiar. Those four we saw just now appear to be strong women—it must be hard for them, considering their history."

"Oh, I think it's hard for all the Iroquois, not only the women."

Neva seemed to consider this, then shook her head. "No, life's always harder for women; men don't bear children. And, speaking of that," she said, brightening somewhat, "are you or are you not going to join our women's march on the tavern?"

Glynis sighed. They'd been over this before. "No, Neva, I'm not joining."

She received a look of indignation.

Glynis sighed again, and said with frank regret, "Neva, I can't. Serenity and I have a past . . . ah, well, an association. Of sorts."

Neva's eyes narrowed. "You've been *associated* with Serenity Hathaway? Forgive me, Glynis, but that's a little hard to imagine."

"I know it must seem that way. But the woman has helped me out several times in the past."

"*What?* Glynis, is there something about you I should know?" Something sordid and shocking?" Neva's mouth twitched.

Shaking her head and smiling, too, Glynis said, "No, Serenity and I just happened to cross paths. It's a long story. But I can't participate in trying to close her tavern down. Not," she added quickly, "that I approve of her . . . business."

"Her *business*," Neva responded tartly, "is responsible for a staggering amount of misery. I don't understand how you can overlook that."

"I'm not overlooking it. I'm just not prepared to do

something that seems . . . I don't know . . .'' Glynis stopped. This was getting them nowhere.

But Neva pressed on. "That seems what? Disloyal? Ungrateful? Glynis, if the devil himself once inadvertently 'helped you out,' would you feel compelled to support *him*?''

"It's not the same, and I'm not supporting Serenity. I'm just loath to join in publicly embarrassing her. Now, please, Neva, let's just consider this a difference of opinion. And let it go at that.''

Neva now looked unmistakably angry. So angry that Glynis worried this would threaten their friendship. "Neva," she said carefully, "don't you think it's possible for us to disagree with each other occasionally, and yet still consider the other to be a friend?''

This seemed to shock Neva, as if it were an audaciously novel idea, but at least she appeared to be thinking it over.

At the sound of carriage wheels, Glynis glanced over her shoulder to see, for the second time that morning, Lily Braun seated in her elegant surrey. Catching the light with a sudden flash were the brilliant gems at Lily's ears. The jewels were the same green as the forlorn eyes that Glynis recalled, but given the emeralds—they looked like emeralds—and the beautiful carriage, she supposed Lily might not be so unhappy anymore. She certainly was not in poverty.

"Oh, I suppose so," Neva said, interrupting her speculation, and looking closely at her as if she were in another world somewhere, and might not have heard. "That reasonable people can disagree, that is," Neva explained. "But I didn't think we'd disagree, you and I, on something like a brothel. It's so . . . so . . .'' Evidentally at a loss for words, Neva shrugged.

But then she smiled, if very faintly. "You know what I think, Glynis? I think that what with murderers and bigots and exasperating hardware store owners, and librarians that tolerate brothel proprietors—well, I think that for a small town, Seneca Falls has more than its fair share of characters!''

*　　*　　*

LILY BRAUN HAD instructed her driver to take the carriage for one last turn around the village, just in case someone might have missed her earlier. She'd heard a crowd gathering at Levy's Hardware on Fall Street, but it had begun to disperse when the carriage drew near. Lily was in time, however, to see a buggy carrying members of the Grimm family swerve rapidly onto Black Brook Road. Maybe the almighty Grimms had heard she was out and about, and were trying to avoid her. Never mind, she told herself; they couldn't go fast enough or far enough. Not this time.

Lily's driver now abruptly pulled to the right to avoid a dray wagon rumbling from the hardware store. Lily's breath stopped when she saw its occupants. What were *they* doing here? She caught only a glimpse of the older woman seated in the wagon. Her face had grown more than ever like a meat-ax, Lily decided, but Bitter Root could have no ax to grind with *her*. Nonetheless, Lily turned her own face aside to be concealed by her hat brim when the vehicles passed.

When Lily again turned to look out, she saw two women engaged in conversation—obviously engrossing conversation, since neither glanced her way. Of the two, Lily recognized only Glynis Tryon; she had hardly aged at all, Lily observed with some envy.

Suddenly Miss Tryon turned to look in her direction. Lily's hands went to her ears, and she flicked the earrings to catch the light. As one of the very few in Seneca Falls who had been unfailingly kind to her, Miss Tryon had a right to see how well Lily Braun had managed.

Lily's hands flew from the earrings to her eyes. She brushed hurriedly at her tears before they could fall and spot the costly silk dress.

NEVA CARDOZA WATCHED Glynis walk away, heading toward her library. The surrey carrying the woman, Lily Braun, had just turned north off Fall Street, and Neva found herself alone; with the toe of her shoe, she traced a circle in the dust, and glanced guardedly over her shoulder toward Levy's Hardware. She had absolutely no reason to be dawdling there, so why was she doing so?

She took a few steps toward the shop.

"Interested in some baskets?" asked an affable male voice from behind her.

Neva turned to see Abraham Levy just coming from his store, carrying a number of empty wooden crates. Setting them down a few yards away, he began to separate an assortment of hand tools, tossing various of them into the crates. His blue cotton workshirt pulled taut over his muscular shoulders when he swung several large feed bags out of his way.

"Time to put some of these aside for the winter," he said conversationally, nodding toward the tools he was sorting. "Won't need them now until spring."

He didn't say more, and proceeded to winnow out various implements, apparently indifferent to Neva's presence. Well, why wouldn't he be? she thought with unaccountable disappointment. She supposed she hadn't made herself very congenial in the past. Her cheeks began to burn as his silence continued, and discomfort formed a hard knot in her throat. She knew she should leave, that she was making a fool of herself by simply standing there and gawking at him. *What was the matter with her?*

Clearing her throat loudly, she turned to go. But after several steps she paused. Wasn't he going to say *anything*? "Ah, Mr. Levy," she began, not turning toward him and thus speaking to empty space, "I just wanted to tell you . . . well . . . I thought you handled the . . . the earlier situation here very well."

She waited for a response. When he said nothing, nothing at all, she felt a humiliation so intense it made her light-headed. She took several shaky breaths and started to walk away. And jumped at his voice when it came from directly behind her. "I don't think I quite heard that," Abraham commented, standing so close she could feel his breath on the back of her neck. "What was it you said?"

Neva spun to face him. "I said I thought you handled the—"

She broke off as she saw the smile and, worse, saw it broaden. "I'm glad you find me so amusing, Mr. Levy. But please don't let me take up your valuable time."

"Woman," sighed Abraham, reaching for her hand,

''what is the matter with you?''

Neva swallowed hard as his fingers closed around hers, then tried to pull her hand away at the same time recalling that, not two minutes before, she'd asked herself the same question. She stopped resisting and stood very still. Abraham's hand felt strong and warm and dry, and she had a sudden unwelcome memory of Jacob Espinosa's limp, sweaty fingers.

''I don't know what's the matter,'' she said softly, biting the inside of her cheek in acute embarrassment. ''I don't know.''

''Well,'' Abraham said, with an expulsion of breath that ruffled her hair, ''that, at least, is a start!'' He gave her hand a gentle tug. ''I suggest we go inside and try to figure this out.''

TEN

SERENITY HATHAWAY LIFTED her voluminous skirts ever
so modestly before mounting the steps to the law office. A
brisk wind off the canal ruffled her gray wool cape and
fluttered the demure ribbons of her bonnet. She wasn't taking any chances; she'd even restrained her flaming hair in
a severe chignon. Her own mother wouldn't recognize her—
if the poor old thing could see her and hadn't drunk herself
to death years ago.

And Jeremiah Merrycoyf, upon opening the door, obviously did not recognize her either. Serenity bit back a smile
as he adjusted wire-framed spectacles and harrumphed several times, peering at her closely. At last he stepped aside
to usher her into his office with, "Have I had the pleasure
of meeting you before, Madame?"

"Surely have, Mr. Merrycoyf—I'm Serenity Hathaway.
And it's not Madame, it's *madam*."

She had to admire his self-control. He barely flinched.
With a slight cough, genteelly contained behind a chubby
hand, Merrycoyf gestured to a chair. Serenity lowered herself into it with utmost decorum, while thinking it a damn
shame that this man had never set foot in her establishment.
He was cute as a bug. She'd probably not noticed this before, because their only previous contact had been in a

courtroom. That kind of place did tend to put a damper on one's priorities.

"Miss Hathaway, madam; may I inquire as to why you're here today?"

Serenity grinned. Cute as a bug. "Mr. Merrycoyf, I need to hire your services."

"My services. I see." Merrycoyf had lumbered around his desk and settled himself in a large overstuffed chair. "I assume, Miss Hathaway, that you are speaking of legal services. Why are you in need of counsel?"

"To tell the truth, it's one hell of a thing, Jeremiah—I can call you Jeremiah?"

"Miss Hathaway, you are at liberty to call me whatever you wish. That does not, however, address my question. Your need for legal advice?"

"They want to shut me down. My tavern, that is."

"And who might 'they' be?"

"The self-righteous busybodies of this town, that's who."

"How do they propose to do this, Miss Hathaway?"

Serenity frowned, studying Merrycoyf at some length, before she said, "You'll pardon me for asking, Jeremiah, and I don't want to be crude, but—*don't you bloody well know the law*?"

He didn't miss a beat. "If you mean Chapter 628 of the New York State Code, which, as of the sixteenth of April this year, attempts to suppress intemperance and regulate the sale of intoxicating liquor—yes, I'm familiar with it."

Serenity exhaled with relief. "Had me worried there for a minute, Jeremiah. Anyway, these busybodies are pressuring the constable to shut me down. Because of that damn law."

"You didn't expect this to occur?"

"What—a mob of crazy women parading up and down in front of my tavern? No, sir, I did not! And that's what the scuttlebutt says is going to happen. Now, this kind of thing could be bad, real bad, for business. And I want to know how to stop them. I *can* stop them, can't I?"

Merrycoyf leaned forward. "Miss Hathaway, that is difficult to determine without more information. Happily, you are most fortunate in that, although I myself have pressing matters to attend in the coming weeks, I possess the name of—please, Miss Hathaway, hear me out before you protest—the name of a young attorney whom I shall personally request to take your case.''

Merrycoyf plucked a pen from its inkwell and began to write.

"Jeremiah, I don't want some kid lawyer still wet behind the ears.''

Merrycoyf kept writing. Serenity cleared her throat to create an irresistibly silken voice. "I can, of course, pay you well . . . in fact, any kind of payment you'd like.'' She smiled her most generous smile.

He continued to write, very fast. "My dear Miss Hathaway, that is a most beneficent offer. But my schedule simply will not allow me to pursue your interests. And I assure you, Mr. Adam MacAlistair will be eager to assist. He has recently returned to Seneca Falls from the law school of Virginia's William and Mary College, where he acquitted himself most admirably. Fear not, my good lady, you will be in the best of hands.''

Merrycoyf did not look up until he had signed the letter and sealed it in an envelope. Rising from his chair, he handed it across the desk to Serenity.

She couldn't remember ever having been so smoothly dispatched. She must be losing her touch. But she'd always known when to fold, and she did have to admire his style. "Make you a bargain, Jeremiah, darlin'. Just promise you'll watch over this Adam MacAlistair's shoulder, and I'll walk out of here nice and ladylike. Otherwise''—she smiled ominously—"there's no telling what I might do.''

Merrycoyf adjusted his spectacles. "With that possibility in mind, my dear Miss Hathaway, let me assure you I have already,'' he gestured to the envelope, "apprised Mr. MacAlistair of that very thing.''

Yes, indeed, she did have to admire his style.

"YOU WANT TO tell me what so riled that Indian woman this morning?'' Cullen asked as he guided the carriage horse onto Black Brook Road. "She looked like she wanted to string me up on the nearest tree.''

"I have no idea what was wrong," Glynis answered. "But it seemed very strange, I admit."

"Didn't think it was my imagination," Cullen said. "Guess the Indians hate all of us white men for what's happened to their land. Can't say as I really blame them."

Glynis glanced at Cullen on the seat beside her. And suddenly, for no apparent reason, the time he'd asked her to marry him came to mind. She'd refused, then immediately had second thoughts. But he'd said he wouldn't ask again. He hadn't.

That had been three years before. They had just gone on, the two of them, as always. Glynis had told herself over the years that if she were disposed to marry anyone, it would be Cullen. Which was undoubtedly the reason, she recognized abruptly, why she felt so uncomfortable about Jacques Sundown. She didn't even *know* Jacques Sundown—at least not in the way she knew Cullen.

"Glynis? You there?" Cullen had his you-aren't-listening expression.

"Sorry, I was just daydreaming. Can you remember an autumn ever being this fine? Almost November, and not even a really hard frost yet. It's still as warm as May."

Cullen now looked at her with his you-*weren't*-listening expression. "I asked if you knew anything about this march on Serenity's tavern?"

"Just that there's going to be one."

"When?"

"I don't know exactly. Soon, I expect—Neva is waiting to hear from Susan Anthony in Rochester."

"Those two are planning this together?" Cullen groaned. "What an unholy alliance that is! All the town needs, on top of two murders. The newspapers already are squawking about inadequate law enforcement. In other words, me."

Glynis tried not to smile. Though murder was not in the least humorous, Dr. Neva Cardoza and the temperance reformer Susan Anthony joining forces, on the streets of the same small town, could be a liaison Cullen might well lament.

He now eyed her suspiciously. "Are you taking part in this thing?" he asked in a wary voice.

"No, Cullen, I'm not."

"Thank God for that! Glynis, can't you talk Neva Cardoza out of this? It's just going to cause trouble."

"I don't have anything to do with it," Glynis again told him. "And I want to keep it that way. But, frankly, I don't see myself why you don't close Serenity down. From what I've learned about the new law, she certainly seems to be in violation of it."

Cullen groaned again. "You know, I really wish the state legislature could find something to do with itself besides passing more damn laws."

Glynis didn't think this was an adequate answer, but it was apparently all Cullen intended to say. They were now passing the Turner farm, and she searched for a glimpse of Sara. The place looked deserted. Sara's words came back to her—*Death. It ain't done yet*—and Glynis experienced a sense of apprehension. "Cullen, I think we should stop."

"Why? It looks like nobody's home," he protested. "Wait. There's somebody out in that field." He pointed to a garden plot beyond the house.

Glynis squinted in the direction of his finger. With considerable relief, she spotted not one but several figures bending over what looked like rows of cabbage.

"Looks like everything's all right," Cullen said. "There's no need to stop and wrangle more with her."

Glynis agreed, if he would insist on wrangling.

A few minutes later they came in view of the old Flannery farm. "Seems a shame," Cullen said, gesturing toward the fields now overgrown with weeds. "The land's just lying fallow. It's a good piece of property, even if the brook does run narrow there."

A sudden thought came to her. "Cullen, do you remember that night the farm burned?"

"How could anybody forget it?"

"It was in the fall, five years ago, wasn't it?"

"I can still see the corncribs billowing smoke, and they were full, so it must have been the fall. Yes, fall of '52. Why?"

"The other day I was telling Neva about it, and later on I recalled something about the barn door. It had been bolted,

I think, from the outside? It troubled you at the time.''

''It troubled me, all right.'' Cullen looked thoughtful. ''Only explanation that made sense was that the bolt had been thrown accidentally by one of the first people on the scene. Nobody could actually remember doing it, but what with all the confusion, who knows? And nobody realized until later that Cole Flannery and Dick Davis were still inside. Found their bodies right next to the door. The bolted door. And you're right, it bothered me.''

Glynis nodded. It bothered her, too, because while time had faded the memory, it now reappeared in stark relief.

''Glynis, why'd you ask about the fire?''

''On account of Jack Turner's death, and Mead Miller's. Isn't it a little strange that four men, four seemingly *healthy* men, have died in—''

''C'mon, Glynis,'' Cullen interrupted. ''As far as Flannery and Davis are concerned, quite a few people in town besides them have died.''

''That's exactly what I was thinking,'' Glynis said slowly. ''Dooley Keegan, for instance. Another supposedly healthy man. How many others like him have died, do you suppose?''

Cullen gave her a wry smile. ''People do die, you know. All the time. You sure you're not straining for some sinister connection?''

''There already *is* something sinister, Cullen. Two poison deaths in one month. Who's next?''

His expression indicated he had thought of this. ''But I can't find any logical connection between Mead Miller and Jack Turner. Nothing to make me think there's going to be another.''

''Sara Turner said there would be.''

''Sara Turner might have had damn good reason to say that,'' he responded. ''Throws suspicion someplace else, doesn't it? But I still think she's the one did in her husband. Though how I'm going to prove it . . .'' Cullen's voice trailed off as ahead appeared the Grimm farm.

Sara Turner might have killed her husband, Glynis acknowledged, but Mead Miller? And Cullen didn't fool her for one minute. He was more concerned than he let on, but didn't want to upset her. Well, he hadn't succeeded; she was upset. Especially so, after recalling the Flannery fire. But if there was some connection between the deaths, it might be so obscure they'd never find it. Or there might be no connection at all, if a madman was loose in Seneca Falls.

But in that case, how did Sara Turner know?

THE FIRST PERSON they saw, when they climbed from the carriage at the Grimm farm, was Billy Wicken, bending over the rail of a sheep pen. After he glanced up and saw them, he started in their direction. But, as if thinking better of it, he abruptly turned and limped toward the barn.

"Billy!" Cullen called. Billy seemed to hesitate, then kept right on going.

"Odd," Cullen said. "Wonder what's got into him?"

Shaking her head and also wondering, Glynis glanced around for Pippa; failing to see the girl, she looked for the lamb.

Pippa had a little lamb . . .

A door of the house opened, then slammed shut. Molly Grimm appeared and looked over the front porch railing in their direction. Her expression was clearly agitated. But when she recognized them, her face smoothed immediately, and she gave them a wave before descending the steps. As she walked toward them, Glynis caught, from the corner of her eye, a glimpse of something shadow-gray skittering into a nearby shed. When she looked again, it was gone.

Its fleece was . . . dark as coal.

"Glynis! Constable Stuart!" Molly exclaimed as she neared them. "I'm glad you're here."

Then why didn't she look it? Her face still reflected something Glynis would define as anxiety. Did she know yet about Mead Miller?

Her next words answered that. "We've only just found out about Mead Miller," Molly said tensely. "I can't believe it. I just can't believe it. He seemed perfectly fine when he left here."

"When?" Cullen asked her. "When did you last see him?"

Molly's reply came swiftly. "Saturday, late in the afternoon. He said he was going into town. That's all. That's all he said.''

"How'd you hear about him?" Cullen asked.

Molly's face went blank. Almost as if she were loath to let emotion, any emotion at all, expose itself. Glynis watched her closely, while the woman shook her head slightly as if trying to remember something.

Cullen was waiting for Molly to respond to his not very profound question. She finally let out a brief sigh. "I think we're all so shocked by Mead's death," she said. Not precisely an answer, but at least an explanation.

Cullen cleared his throat. "I guess I didn't hear you say who told you about Miller's—''

He was interrupted by a shrill shout from inside the house. Followed instantly by Almira Grimm bursting through the door to the porch.

For a moment, Molly stood frozen. Then, "Pippa! Where's Pippa?" she cried, and began to run toward the house. Glynis exchanged a puzzled glance with Cullen before they started after her.

"What the hell's going on?" Cullen muttered. "Why's she so worried about the girl?"

And everywhere that Pippa went . . .

"Cullen, wait!" Glynis stopped and looked toward the shed. "I think Pippa might be in there," she pointed, and began to walk to the low wooden structure. Cullen followed her. When they reached the shed, Glynis heard a male voice. She pulled open the shed door and, stepping inside, she smelled newly cut hay.

The lamb was sure to go.

On the dirt floor beside a wooden crate, the gray lamb lay sleeping. A shaft of amber light coming through a grimy window fell on Pippa; she stood on the crate, eyes closed, arms outstretched, the focus of a soft yellow radiance. Around her, dust motes flurried. Lazarus Grimm sat a few feet away on a three-legged stool. Gaunt face immobile, his gaze remained riveted on Pippa; Glynis didn't think he even heard them come in until Cullen said, "What's going on?"

Lazarus gave a start, sprang to his feet, and motioned frantically for them to be quiet. Glynis felt Cullen beside her tense, about to say something. Grabbing his arm, she shook her head. No, she mouthed at him, don't.

Cullen's eyebrows rose. But Glynis knew that if Pippa was sleepwalking, she shouldn't be suddenly wakened, and probably the same held true if the girl was in some sort of trance. And that was the way she looked.

Glynis glanced at Lazarus to confirm this, but he had turned back to watch Pippa, and his eyes were awash with tears. Anxiously, Glynis stepped forward to touch his shoulder. "Lazarus?" she whispered. "What's happening to Pippa?"

"She has it." Lazarus, also whispering, answered, "The child has the gift."

"What gift? What're you talking about?" Cullen said. Although his voice was at normal volume, it seemed to thunder in the confined space.

Pippa made a plaintive sound, and trembled slightly. Her eyes blinked open and shut several times. She looked around for a moment, as if disoriented, but when she saw Glynis, she smiled and hopped down from the crate. "Miss Tryon— why are *you* here?"

Lazarus sprang forward to clasp Pippa by the shoulders. "Do you remember anything?" he asked the girl. "Do you remember what you said?"

Behind Glynis, the door creaked open. Molly Grimm rushed into the shed, silencing whatever Pippa might have been about to answer. "Pippa, what are you doing in here?" Molly swung to her brother with an accusing look. "Why is she here—you're not doing *that* again, are you?"

Lazarus opened his mouth to reply, but Molly didn't wait. She grasped Pippa's arm and began to pull the girl after her. Lazarus took several steps toward them before Molly whirled around to cry, "No!" and dashed from the shed with Pippa locked in her grip, stumbling behind.

As Glynis followed them out, she heard Cullen behind her saying, "I'd like to know what was going on, Lazarus— and I suggest you tell me."

Since Glynis had a pretty good idea what had gone on, she headed toward the house behind Molly and Pippa, who were just climbing the stairs to the porch, where Glynis could see Almira huddled in a rocking chair. A few feet farther, and she could hear the woman humming "Rock of Ages."

"Go into the house, Pippa," Molly directed, "and wash yourself. You smell like hay."

Pippa seemed about to protest, but sighed instead. Giving her mother a dejected look, she went inside.

"Mother," Molly said to Almira, "what on earth were you yelling about? You scared me half to death."

Why, Glynis wondered, remembering what had occurred, should Almira's yelling make Molly think something had happened to Pippa? After all, Almira's behavior was frequently inappropriate.

"Because he's gone," Almira said dreamily. "He's gone, just like all the rest. Gone away."

"Who's gone, Almira?" Glynis asked, climbing the steps quickly, and going to stand in front of the woman.

Molly answered, saying, "I expect she means Mead Miller. My mother always did have a soft spot for him, although why I can't imagine." She then made an awkward move, apparently designed to insert herself between Glynis and Almira.

But Glynis stood her ground, refusing to step back to accomodate Molly's rather obvious intent. Did she think she needed to guard her mother for some reason? Glynis leaned forward. "Yes, Almira, Mead Miller's gone," she said. "But what did you mean, 'just like all the rest'?"

"Glynis, really," Molly protested, laughing lightly. "You know Mother isn't always . . . well . . . clear-headed."

Almira abruptly cackled, "Not like you, Molly, my girl. Oh, no; not clear-headed like you."

"Mother! Mother, you've had a shock—why don't you come inside and lie down?" Molly bent forward to help Almira from the chair.

The woman shrank back. And her face, under the hair like a wild bird's nest, twisted as if she were about to cry. Glynis hesitated to interfere in what certainly was a family matter, but Almira seemed unusually frail. And not quite as deranged as she ordinarily did. Still, Molly's mother must be a trial for her.

"Mother," Molly insisted, again reaching for her, "why don't you—"

"Leave me be, girl!" Almira shouted, shattering the illusion of frailty. "Go find the poor young'un to torment."

Molly gasped, her face blanching as she backed against the porch wall. Glynis saw tears in her eyes, and felt an upwelling of sympathy for this woman who was attempting, however ineptly, to care for the aged child her mother had become. She also began to understand why Molly kept such a close watch on Pippa.

Lazarus and Cullen had appeared, coming across the yard toward the porch. Glynis wanted to question Almira further about her curious remark, but then heard on the inside stairs a heavy tread. Molly's crumpled face tightened and her shoulders straightened. The door opened, and Obadiah Grimm stepped to the porch.

He said nothing, but stood and waited for the two approaching men; after they'd climbed the stairs, Obadiah stared in turn at each person there. The mass of white hair above the granite features seemed to quiver in indignation as, finally, his stare came to rest on Cullen. "Constable, you here for some reason—some good reason?"

"That's right," Cullen answered evenly. Glynis wondered how he could appear so unaffected by Obadiah's intimidating presence. At least *she* found him intimidating.

"I need to find out," Cullen said, "what you people might know about Mead Miller's death. Since Lazarus here has already told me what he knows, why don't *you* start?" He trained his gaze on Obadiah.

Lazarus gave Glynis and Cullen a brief nod before he escaped into the house. The door closed behind him with a soft click.

"Don't know anything," Obadiah stated. "Why should any of us? Man's dead, that's all."

"No, that's not all," Cullen said. "Miller was killed—"

From her rocking chair, Almira erupted with a shrill wail. Obadiah spun to fix her with a glare. "Quiet, woman! Go inside if you can't be still."

Glynis felt blood rush to her cheeks, and bit her lip to keep from saying something that would cause Obadiah to order her off his property. But she furtively reached down and pressed Almira's shoulder.

Cullen, however, had continued, ". . . and I need to ask a few more questions. Sorry, Mr. Grimm, if it offends you, but frankly, that's too bad. I can always order you to my office in town, if you prefer. Your choice."

Obadiah Grimm's eyes narrowed to slashes as he studied Cullen. There was a long moment of silence, during which Glynis wondered if anyone else's mouth was dry.

Obadiah spoke at last. "Night before the Sabbath, Miller always went to that den of iniquity to partake of alcoholic spirits." His voice rose alarmingly. " 'For their wine comes from the vine of Sodom, and from the fields of Gomorrah . . . for the day of their calamity is at hand, and their doom comes quickly.' "

Cullen didn't move a muscle. "You referring," he said, "to all the patrons of Serenity's Tavern, Mr. Grimm—or just Mead Miller?"

" 'For the Lord will vindicate his people,' " Obadiah declared. "And now, Constable, in retribution for his sin, the man Miller has met his doom. That's all I need to know."

He turned on his heel, yanked the door open, and went back in the house. The door slammed shut.

Molly, still ghostly pale, stepped cautiously toward the door and said, "I don't know anything, either." Her voice carried a tremor. "Please, Constable Stuart, I'd like to go to my daughter."

Cullen scrutinized her briefly, then nodded. And Molly quietly followed her father into the house.

"Nobody left but us chickens," observed Almira cheerfully.

"Almira," Glynis said, "I'd like to ask you again what you meant when you said earlier that Mead Miller was 'gone, just like all the rest'?"

Cullen frowned, but left any comment unvoiced.

Almira ducked her head to give Glynis a hooded look. "The rest of what?" she said, so extravagantly innocent-sounding that Glynis concluded the woman knew very well what she'd asked. Moreover, Glynis had begun to wonder if Almira Grimm's demented behavior was a ruse. Some stratagem of escape. And if she herself had been forced to live with Obadiah Grimm, Glynis guessed she'd try to escape, too. One of the few ways a woman could: into insanity, or what passed for it.

Cullen made an impatient sound. Glynis turned to him and said, "Wait, please, Cullen. Let me try."

Cullen shrugged and went down the stairs.

"Almira," Glynis began again, "I think you understood what I asked you about Mead Miller's death. And it's very important. Now, what did you mean?"

"Don't know," Almira said. "Don't never know what I mean." Her face then took on a coy expression, and she leaned toward Glynis with a confiding gesture, as if she were about to impart some dark secret. "That girl of mine—she got herself trouble, you know. Big trouble." And with a knowing nod, Almira leaned back and folded her arms across her chest.

Dropping to a crouch beside the woman's chair, Glynis asked, "Your girl? Do you mean Molly or Pippa?"

Almira threw her head back and brayed. "The young'un? No, ma'am, she never told nobody *she* had a husband! No, ma'am, not her!" Almira pounded the arms of the rocker before she slid out of it and scurried into the house. After the door banged shut, Glynis heard a bolt being thrown.

Frowning in bewilderment, she rose and went down the stairs. "Cullen, did you hear what Almira just said?"

"I heard enough," Cullen responded. He started walking toward the carriage. "I say we get out of this madhouse."

But Glynis, much as she agreed with him, now started for the barn. "I still need to see Billy Wicken," she called over her shoulder.

She found Billy just inside the barn door, standing beside a stall. He turned his head away from her, but not fast enough; his eyes were red-rimmed, and it was plain that he'd been crying. He rubbed his good hand along the stall's top rail, then ran it through his tousled, straw-colored hair. The withered hand hung at his side.

"Billy, you and Mead Miller were friends, weren't you?" Glynis asked gently.

His head bobbed.

"I'm very sorry about his death, Billy. It's terrible to lose a friend, especially that way."

Billy's head swung toward her. His odd chameleon eyes mirrored the grayish wood of the barn, and he dashed a hand across them. "Who killed Mead, Miss Tryon?"

"We don't know that yet. But Constable Stuart is trying to find the person responsible. Do you know anything that might help him?" He looked confused, and Glynis realized her question had been too general. "Billy, did you see Mead Miller leave the farm last Saturday night?"

Billy nodded.

"Did he say where he was going?"

"Going into town, he said. He always did that, Saturday night."

Apparently, Glynis thought, the entire Grimm household was privy to Miller's activities on Saturday nights. "Did you see Mead again, Billy, say later that night? Or the next morning?"

"No. I didn't see him again. Not ever."

Glynis heard footsteps, and sensed Cullen coming up behind her. She motioned him to stay quiet. "Billy, remember the day last week I came out here? With the young woman?"

"The doctor?" he asked. When Glynis nodded, Billy said, "She helped the ewe. And Pippa's lamb." He began to smile.

"Yes, that's right. And the reason Dr. Cardoza had to help was that Mead Miller wasn't here, remember?" Glynis saw his smile waver, but she went on, "I know Mead asked you not to tell where he went, and you kept your promise to him, but now—I don't think Mead would mind if you told me now. It might be important."

The last trace of Billy's smile vanished. He dug the toe of his boot into the stall's hay. "You don't think he'd care?" he said at last.

"No, I really don't."

"And it's important?"

"Yes, Billy, it could be very important. Where did Mead go that day?" Glynis bent toward him, willing him to answer.

"Well, I guess it'd be O.K." Billy sighed softly. "He went to see Jake Braun."

"Jake Braun? Do you know why?" More important, she thought, was why Mead Miller had been so secretive. But she didn't want to remind Billy of that. "Do you know why he went to Braun's?" she repeated.

As Billy shook his head, Glynis felt Cullen's hand on her shoulder. He said quietly, "Miller used to work for Jake Braun. Up until just a few years ago."

Billy nodded vigorously.

"Well then, Billy," Glynis went on, "did Mead go to see Jake Braun often?"

"I don't know. But I don't think so. He never told me if he did."

Glynis nodded, and turned to Cullen. "Is there anything else we should ask?" She turned back to Billy to say, "You know Constable Stuart, don't you?"

Billy looked uncertain.

Cullen smiled. "Yes, we've met, Billy and I, haven't we?"

Billy gave Cullen a tentative smile and stared pointedly at his badge. "Are you going to find out what happened to Mead?" he asked.

"I'm going to try," Cullen said. "Billy, if you remember anything else—anything you think could help me—will you get in touch with me? Or with Miss Tryon?"

"How can he, Cullen?" Glynis said. "He can't get into town."

"Yes, I can!" Billy suddenly exclaimed. "I got a horse now. Molly gave me one. And I can ride, too."

"Good," Cullen said to him. "Then you'll let me know if you think of something?"

Billy's forehead wrinkled, in either a frown or in concentration, before he nodded. "I guess so."

DO YOU THINK he understood?" Cullen asked as he turned the carriage horse around.

Glynis, who had been watching a curtain draw back from an upstairs window of the house, returned her attention to Cullen. "Yes, I think so. Billy's speech is unsophisticated and a little slow, but I think he can understand. And Neva seemed to agree—she thought he might have had a head injury, which could account for it. That and the problem with the left side of his body.''

She glanced back at the house as the curtain again moved across the window. ''Cullen, please—let's leave here!''

''Can't be too soon for me,'' Cullen agreed, climbing into the carriage and flicking the reins. ''Those are some mighty peculiar folks.''

To Glynis's surprise, Cullen steered the horse away from the drive. Instead they went some yards south and onto a narrow lane. The carriage bounced, the wheels finding old ruts overgrown with weeds.

''What's this?'' Glynis asked, gritting her teeth. ''I didn't realize there was another way out of the Grimms'. Where does this go?''

''It's an old farm lane. And it's the back way to Jake Braun's.''

ELEVEN

So from the world of spirits there descends
  A bridge of light, connecting it with this,
O'er whose unsteady floor, that sways and bends,
  Wander our thoughts above the dark abyss.
    —HENRY WADSWORTH LONGFELLOW,
      "HAUNTED HOUSES"

THE FARM LANE eventually leveled out enough for Glynis to speak without severing her tongue. "What did Lazarus tell you," she asked Cullen, "about what he and Pippa were doing?"

"Lazarus told me what you expected him to," he answered.

When she stared at him incredulously, Cullen grinned. "C'mon, Glynis! You'd never have left that shed before you found out what was going on—unless you were pretty sure you already knew."

Glynis gave him a pained look. "I think Lazarus is training Pippa to be a medium . . . a trance-speaking medium. It's said that the best way to establish contact with the spirit world is through young female clairvoyants."

"So Lazarus told me. Claims the girl's a natural medium; she has the gift, he says, whatever that means. How can anybody believe that nonsense?"

"But a lot of people do. Cullen, you can't have missed all the furor about this. It's been in the newspapers for years."

"You know the newspapers will print anything. That doesn't mean I have to read it. And apparently I haven't missed much."

If he had ignored it completely, Glynis thought, he'd missed quite a bit. It had been ten years since the young Fox sisters had sworn up and down that they'd communicated with some dead peddler's spirit in their house near Rochester. Although the notion had been around for some time, the Fox "visitation" was what had supposedly launched the spiritualist movement.

Glynis had thought at the time that it was something ready to happen anyway. There were too many people, and she admitted the majority of them were women, who felt the established churches had excluded them. The clergy of every major religious denomination had been, and still was, entirely male. And it was scarcely the first time in history that Americans had experienced what the preachers chose to call "a crisis of faith."

Cullen snorted in disgust. "This seance stuff . . ."

"Has mushroomed," Glynis interjected. "Yes, and now the Fox sisters are touring everywhere with lectures and demonstrations. Harriet saw them in Rochester. She said they were very impressive; they supposedly 'talk' with the dead by means of rapping sounds. They ask a question, and the answer comes by way of raps; so many raps for no, and for yes, and for an unknown . . . something like that. Although Harriet said they gave a spinetingling demonstration, she was skeptical. Thought it must be some sort of hoax."

"Good for Harriet!" Cullen retorted.

"But remember," Glynis said, "Harriet isn't very suggestible, and I doubt she wanted to hear from her dead husbands anyway."

Cullen laughed. "It's the most ridiculous thing I've ever heard of. Can you imagine anyone believing that?"

"It depends on how much someone wants to believe, I think. Horace Greeley does."

"I don't care if President Buchanan does."

"As a matter of fact, Cullen, I read somewhere that believers include some men in Congress."

"*That* doesn't surprise me!"

"Well, at this point," Glynis said, smiling, "there are not only thousands of mediums, but hundreds of spiritualist publications, including ten or twelve newspapers with large circulations."

In fact, the demand in town was so high, she had been forced to subscribe to several for the library. The most popular was *The Christian Spiritualist,* published by the Society for the Diffusion of Spiritual Knowledge. She hadn't trusted this name until she'd discovered it was one of the first such organizations; it had been formed about four years before in New York City, and that probably wouldn't surprise Cullen, either.

"Folks in Seneca Falls aren't reading this stuff, are they?" Cullen said skeptically.

"Absolutely, they are." Glynis gave him a sideways glance. "Don't you have even the slightest curiosity about it? Just a little? After all, there are well-known, supposedly reputable people who swear they've witnessed communication with the dead. Who is to say it isn't possible?"

"*I* am to say. It's crazy. And to think Lazarus Grimm is planning to use that sweet little girl—I'm amazed you aren't outraged about that, Glynis."

"Oh, I will be if he really does it. But you just saw Molly Grimm. You can't think she's going to allow her daughter to be involved in that—no matter how much Molly adores her brother—if for no other reason than that she's so possessive of Pippa."

"The woman does realize her brother Lazarus is one of the world's greatest confidence men, doesn't she?"

"I don't think that even matters to her, Cullen . . . *Cullen*!"

The rifle blast sounded so loud and so close she couldn't believe they'd either one survived it. But in seconds, Cullen had shoved her out of the carriage and landed beside her in the tall weeds.

"Stay down! Just stay down," he said, his voice tense in her ear. "Don't move."

Flat on her stomach, Glynis had no intention of moving. But who could have shot at them? And for heavens' sake, why?

Crouching beside her, Cullen drew his Colt from its holster. At the same moment, another blast sent a bullet winging over their heads.

"Damn it!" Cullen yelled, cautiously starting to rise. "Stop shooting. We're not game, for chrissake—" Another roar, another bullet, dropped him back into the weeds.

"Someone's really trying to kill us," Glynis whispered.

Her heart hammering, she tugged at Cullen's sleeve. "Please stay down!" she pleaded.

"And do what—just wait here until he runs out of ammunition? Or maybe gets lucky and hits us? Now listen, Glynis, you stay put. Right here! I'm going to try and get a look at him."

A whizzing sound this time, and a bullet thudded into the ground to their left. Then another, directly behind them. Cullen flung himself over Glynis, as moments later another flew over them.

Then there was silence. "You all right?" Cullen whispered, rolling off her.

Glynis tried to answer, but found her breath cut off by the goldenrod pollen she'd inhaled. She choked, gasped, fought for air as another bullet passed over their heads.

Glynis finally managed a deep breath, while Cullen whispered in concern, "Are you all right?" He reached out to touch her cheek.

She nodded. "Cullen, what are we—"

"We're going to crawl toward the brook on our bellies, very slowly. And carefully, so the weeds don't move. It sounds like he's using a revolver now—which means he can get off six shots without reloading. Damn Colts, everybody in the country's got one. Every lunatic—"

The firing began again, and Glynis felt Cullen nudge her ahead of him. She wriggled forward, trying not to agitate the weeds around her. After what seemed like a mile but in truth probably was only a few yards, her skirts snagged on the undergrowth and she had to stop to untangle herself. When she glanced over her shoulder—Cullen was gone! He couldn't be; if she had to die, she wanted him there with her. She brushed particles of dirt from her dry eyes. She must be too frightened for tears.

More bullets zinged over her head. She ducked and, counting to six, lay with her face on her hands, biting her knuckles to keep from screaming. The urge to stand up and let herself be shot, just to get it over with, all but overwhelmed her.

Suddenly, except for blood pounding in her ears, there was no sound other than the drone of bees in the goldenrod.

She had the terror-stricken thought that Cullen could have been hit. And if so, the killer might now be creeping up on her. If she raised her head, she would look directly into a barrel . . .

An angry shout. And another. She couldn't make out if it was Cullen's voice she heard.

A sudden rifle blast was followed immediately by another shout. It reached Glynis with breathtaking clarity. "Goddamn it, Jake—it's me! Cullen Stuart! Stop firing, you fool!"

Silence. Glynis pressed her face against her knuckles, hoping God could hear her. Then Cullen's voice again, "Glynis, c'mon! It's all right. C'mon out!"

She raised her head. What if it was a ploy? What if Cullen was being forced to call her?

"Glynis, it's O.K. But stay there if you want—I'll come get you."

He'd known what she feared. She rose slowly, pulling herself to a standing position only because Cullen kept talking to her, and because she could hear his voice getting closer. When he appeared through a cloud of pollen, apparently all in one piece, she stumbled forward to throw herself against him. He held her for much too short a time before he grasped her wrist and pulled her after him. When, moments later, they emerged from the weeds, a few yards away was a small, shingled farm house. And standing before it was Jake Braun. A Jennings rifle swung at his side.

She had seen the man a number of times. He'd always looked and sounded blustery, his stocky frame robust and his skin color that of a man who spent most of his time outdoors. But now Braun's face held a distinct pallor. His eyes looked bloodshot and red-rimmed, as if he'd not slept for days. Despite the man's evident loss of health, Glynis ardently wished she could swear as effectively as Cullen. That was the only appropriate response to Braun's sullen nod in her direction. But she was too frightened to say anything. So frightened she felt nauseated.

Cullen released her wrist and took several steps toward the man. "O.K., Braun, let's hear it again. You thought we were *who*?"

Braun's sullen expression didn't change. "Told you," he muttered.

"Tell me again!"

Braun's rheumy eyes shifted, then flew past Cullen's shoulder, and he jerked the rifle up into firing position. The gun wavered unnervingly. Braun's trembling had likely been the only thing, Glynis thought, that prevented him from killing both herself and Cullen.

"Put it down, Jake!" Cullen yelled. "There's nobody else here. Nobody!"

"Heard something," Braun said. He sounded genuinely terrified.

Cullen stepped forward and shoved the rifle barrel aside. Braun, caught off balance, staggered backward as Cullen wrestled the rifle away from him and thrust it at Glynis. She reached for it reluctantly as Jake Braun started toward her.

"Hold it," Cullen said, "right there!" He unfastened steel manacles from his belt. "C'mon, Jake, I'm taking you in."

"No!" Braun took several more steps toward Glynis before stopping. His face registered desperation as she, her own hands shaking, disarmed the rifle. Braun's revolver apparently had been confiscated earlier, as the handle now protruded from one of Cullen's back pockets.

"You can't leave me without no weapon!" Braun shouted.

"What makes you think I'm leaving you?" Cullen answered. "You're coming into town, to the lockup. In case you didn't know, it's against the law to try to kill a lawman. To say nothing of an unarmed woman."

"You was on my property. You sneaked in the back way."

"Makes no difference," Cullen stated flatly. "You can't just start firing at anybody who happens by, Braun. You must know that, man! So what the hell *were* you doing?"

"Protecting myself."

"Sure you were, Jake. Miss Tryon and I were coming by to ambush you, is what you thought, right?"

"Couldn't see you in the weeds. Thought you was somebody else," Braun countered.

"And just who, Jake, did you think we were?"

"Them that wants to kill me."

Cullen's face expressed distrust. "Oh? And just who might that be?"

"I dunno know who it is. Why don'tcha ask Turner? Ask Mead Miller! 'Cept you can't, cause they're dead!" Then Jake Braun's mouth clamped shut, as if he'd said more than he wanted.

Glynis suddenly felt as if she were going to be violently ill. She moved quickly to the cabin steps, where she sat and bent forward, her head toward the ground.

After Cullen had paused to watch her, he continued talking to Jake Braun, but Glynis heard his voice as if from far away. The nausea, however, began to subside.

"You telling me, Jake," asked Cullen, "that Turner's and Miller's deaths involved you?"

"I ain't saying no more."

"Well, then, I guess you can't give me one good reason why I shouldn't take you in, right?"

"You can't take me, Constable. Somebody's gonna kill me."

"Then it sounds as if I should take you in for your own protection."

Hearing the edge in Cullen's voice, Glynis glanced up; he might not think Jake Braun was terrified, but she had begun to believe it. And how could Cullen discount the fact that two men had been very recently murdered? She straightened up tentatively. The nausea seemed to have receded, but her head throbbed.

Jake Braun's mouth opened and closed several times. Finally he managed to spit out, "You take me into town, Stuart, I'm gonna git killed fer sure."

"I guess we'll just have to chance it, since you won't talk."

"Can't," Braun insisted.

"Why not?"

Braun shook his head stubbornly.

Cullen looked over at Glynis. "You O.K. now?"

She nodded and started to rise, but then sat back down

and said to Jake Braun, "How did you know about Mead Miller's death?"

Braun shook his head again.

"I can answer that," Cullen said to her. "Everybody in town knew by the time you and I left. And Lazarus Grimm told me Lily Braun was at the farm earlier this afternoon." He turned back to Jake Braun. "So I expect your niece Lily probably stopped by here and told you about Miller, didn't she?"

"No!" Braun yelled. "That filthy whore better not come here—"

"Watch it, Braun," Cullen growled. "Besides, I can remember a time when Lily was a nice girl. What was it that changed her? How'd it happen she didn't even turn up for her own father's funeral?"

Jake Braun looked away. He kneaded his reddened eyes with his fists, then muttered as if to himself, "My brother . . ." He stopped.

"What about your brother?" Cullen's eyes narrowed as he watched the man, while Glynis struggled to recall something about Otto Braun besides his name.

"Nothing," Jake Braun said. "Nothing about him." Glynis thought he still looked frightened. And a man that scared might do anything. She hoped Cullen would say they could leave.

"I'll tell you what, Jake," Cullen said. "You come on into town and tell me what the hell's going on around here—and I might be inclined to forget about charging you with attempted manslaughter."

"Can't do that. I'll git killed, I come into town."

Cullen looked exasperated. And angry. But Glynis decided he now at least half-believed Jake Braun's explanation. His problem remained, however, what to do with the man?

While her attention wandered, and with Cullen momentarily off guard, Jake Braun suddenly leaped to the steps. He grabbed Glynis, hauling her upright. Throwing a muscular arm around her neck, he spun her to stand in front of him. Cullen sprang forward, but not before Braun yanked a knife from his back pocket. He thrust the blade against her throat. She could feel the man's fear through his shaking hands even as her body went numb. Numb, and as cold as the steel blade poised at her jugular.

"Don't move, Stuart! You come one step closer, your woman's gonna git her throat slit. I mean it! Makes no never-mind to me if I kill 'er—'cause I'm a dead man anyway."

Glynis tried to hold her breath so she wouldn't move. As Braun's hands shook, the knife blade danced against her neck. She could feel small nicks being cut into the skin of her throat, but there was no pain. Her terror overrode everything.

She closed her eyes, knowing she had to regain her reason, telling herself that Jake Braun had nothing personal against her, that it was fear that drove him. So they had to lessen the fear!

Cullen stood absolutely still. Glynis could see the stark whiteness of his face, and prayed that he was thinking the same thing as she. *Lessen his fear!* Then the knife bit again.

"Mr. Braun," she gasped, "you're hurting me for no purpose. If you kill me, Cullen Stuart will shoot you in an instant."

Immediately, she knew she'd made a panicky error; Braun's grip tightened, and warm drops ran down her neck.

"Let her go," Cullen said, his voice cool and level. "You let her go, Jake," he said again, "and then we'll talk."

"No! No more talking. I got to git out of here—and she's gonna come with me. Go get me my horse, Stuart."

"Jake, you won't get far in your condition. Look at yourself, man! You need sleep."

Glynis gritted her teeth against the certainty that at any second the knife would bite deeper into her throat. The irony was that she still didn't believe Braun really meant to kill her. And if he did, it would be accidental, because he was out of control. Because of his overwhelming fear. *So lessen it!*

"Mr. Braun, I don't think you want to hurt me. And I do believe you. I believe that someone tried to kill you."

Ever so slightly, the pressure against her neck let up. That was the key! He needed to be believed. She gazed toward

Cullen, investing every ounce of energy she had left into making him hear her thoughts.

"Jake, listen to me," Cullen said. "Let's say I was wrong. Maybe somebody *is* trying to kill you. If you can't tell me the reason why, at least let me give you some protection. You have my word, Jake. My word that if you put down that knife, I'll give you the protection you need."

"How you gonna do that? You wanna put me in the lockup—somebody'll git me in there."

Glynis felt the knife blade move. It felt as if it had been turned, and now lay flat. She held her jaw rigid. *Please keep talking, Cullen.*

"No, nobody will get to you, Jake," Cullen answered. "I'll post my deputy on guard outside the lockup. I give you my word."

"Mr. Braun," Glynis said, trying not to move her chin against the blade, "if you let Cullen protect you, then you can at least get some sleep. How long is it since you've had any?"

"Dunno," Braun muttered. "Made two tries to git me already—I been watching for 'em ... three, maybe four days."

"When'd you last eat, Jake?" Cullen asked, and Glynis saw him take several almost imperceptible steps forward. She held her breath, feeling her heart slam painfully against her ribs.

"Dunno. A while, it's been."

"Jake, I give you my word." Cullen's voice sounded so patient, Glynis thought. But perspiration ran into her eyes, and she couldn't even see him clearly.

"I swear nobody will get at you," Cullen said again, "if you come in with me. Think about it, Jake—you can't go anywhere in the shape you're in now. How much longer can you last without sleep?" Cullen edged a little closer.

"Hold it there, Stuart!" Glynis felt Braun's arm tighten around her. She felt hope slipping away as despair raced to displace it. She was going to die. Any second now, Braun would rip the blade across her throat. She wouldn't be able to tell Cullen how much she cared for him. Even say goodbye.

But then Jake Braun's grip loosened somewhat. "You give me your word, Constable?" His voice had sounded increasingly groggy, and now his words slurred.

"My word! You've got it, Jake."

Glynis felt herself tipping backward, as if Braun was tottering. His hold on her slackened still more. She made herself concentrate only on what she should do, not on what could happen when she did. She had to do it fast.

Bringing her hands up to her chest, she slid them under his arm and flung it away from her, wrenching out of his grasp. Cullen leaped forward to grab her, and thrust her behind him.

Jake Braun took several slow steps backward. He swayed to and fro, as he might in a high wind. The knife dangled in his hand. Cullen reached out and snatched it, and tossed it into the weeds.

"You gave your word, Stuart," Braun said, now thoroughly glassy-eyed.

"Yes. Go get your horse, Jake, if you can manage it. We'll hitch it to the back of the carriage."

Braun looked at Cullen as if trying to focus, then shrugged and staggered toward the barn.

As Cullen now came toward her, Glynis had the sensation of black water rising swiftly around them both. It rose to her throat and she needed to warn Cullen, but she began to sink beneath the surface because she had no strength to swim . . . she should try to swim, she knew that . . . but she couldn't seem to move . . . it was so dark . . .

Suddenly she felt herself lifted into the air. And as Cullen carried her to the steps of the house, the water became the wetness of tears streaming down her face.

WHEN, SOME TIME later, their carriage bumped down a short grade, Glynis winced in pain as she turned to glance over her shoulder. His horse hitched to the rear of the carriage, Jake Braun slumped in the saddle, giving every appearance of a man asleep. She sincerely hoped this was the case.

Turning back, she flinched as fabric rubbed against her throat; Cullen had ripped her underskirt into strips with which he'd bandaged her neck. Glynis wasn't sure the amount of bleeding was worth the loss of a good petticoat, but she hadn't had the strength to argue.

Cullen now peered with concern at the bandage. His gaze moved to her eyes and he said gently, "Thank God you stayed calm back there, and didn't lose your head."

He was making some macabre joke, she thought for one shaky moment, but he apparently realized what he'd said, and grimaced convincingly. "Sorry! That's not what I meant."

"I hope not. I'm not ready to find anything about this humorous. I doubt if I will for quite a while."

Cullen reached to clasp her hand. And almost lost the reins as the lane dipped suddenly into a depression. Beyond was a small wooden bridge over Black Brook.

"What's this basin?" Glynis asked. "I've never noticed it before."

"You can't see it from the main road," Cullen answered. "It's the old dam site."

"Dam site? I didn't know Black Brook ever had a dam."

"It didn't. Almost did, though. Must have been before you came to Seneca Falls. A bunch of farmers got to-gether—Jake Braun was one of them, in fact," Cullen said, glancing over his shoulder, "with the bright idea that they'd dam the brook to give themselves more water for irrigation. You know how the brook gets wider north of here?"

Glynis nodded. "Just before the Grimm farm."

"Right. And since it flows north past Black Brook Reservation and on into the Montezuma Marsh, these farmers decided all that water was just going to waste. So they started building a dam."

"Could they do that? Legally?"

"They tried. Even made a stab at talking Obadiah Grimm into letting them build it at the north edge of his property, so he'd get more water, too. Obadiah said he wasn't interested. His refusal caused some real hard feelings."

"Is that when he became such a recluse?"

"Maybe." Cullen thought a minute. "I don't remember what he was like before that. But he did get called some interesting names. 'Indian lover' was about the only one I can repeat; some thought he refused because a dam would have cut off most all the water going into the reservation.''

"Cullen, that would have been a catastrophe for those people there. Good for Obadiah! I wouldn't have thought it of him.''

"I *didn't* think it of him. Because I don't believe that was the reason he refused to join the others. I think he was just too tight-fisted to spend money for the dam's construction. After all, he didn't really need it—it wouldn't have increased the brook's flow past his farm all that much.''

"Since the dam didn't get built," Glynis said, "what happened to prevent it?''

"One of the young Seneca men went to Jeremiah.''

"Mr. Merrycoyf got involved? That's a surprise. He doesn't like controversy, not at all.''

"Remember, he was a lot younger then. And don't believe everything Jeremiah says about that, Glynis. He's always liked a good fight. Bet he still does, if he thinks he can win.''

Glynis smiled, then winced and put a hand to her throat.

"It hurt?'' Cullen asked.

"A little.'' She looked over her shoulder at the sleeping Jake Braun. "It would feel worse if I thought he really meant to kill me. But I don't. You know yourself, Cullen, people do bizarre things when they're frightened. And you *do* believe his story, don't you?''

Cullen shrugged. "I intend to find out if it's true. Maybe after Jake's had some rest, he'll talk sense.''

The lane flattened out as it met Black Brook Road. Glynis turned to look north, then twisted on the seat. After some time, she turned back and asked, "So what did Jeremiah Merrycoyf do for the Indians?''

"Went to court. Stopped the dam's construction.''

"Stopped it how?''

"English common law—law that goes back centuries— that protects people who own along a waterway. Who own *land,* that is, because nobody owns the water itself. It's known as riparian rights. The law says one riparian owner can't do anything that would permanently interfere with the flow of water to another owner. That's oversimplified, of course, but it's the gist of it."

"And a dam to divert water for irrigating farms," Glynis said, "would certainly interfere with the flow of Black Brook."

"Right. That's what Merrycoyf argued, and the court agreed with him. Several courts, actually, because the farmers kept appealing the local judge's decision. They still lost in the end. Spent a lot of money doing it, too. But," Cullen added, "there was sure hell to pay for a while. Bad feelings against the Indians was the worst of it, even from folks who hadn't been involved in the dam project."

"Yes," Glynis sighed, "I can imagine. But who was the Seneca man with the good sense, to say nothing of the courage, to go to Merrycoyf in the first place?"

"It was so long ago I can't remember his name."

As they approached the village limits, Glynis put a hand to her throat. "Cullen, perhaps it would be better if . . ."

"Yes, I'll take you home first, then go the back way to the lockup with Jake. No sense letting the whole village know what went on."

"Harriet's going to have a fit when she sees me."

"She should. Better not tell her too much, though. Not while I've got Jake Braun in the lockup."

"No, of course not. He really might be in danger. But I hope you can get him to talk. The connection between . . ." Her voice trailed off.

"Glynis?"

"I just remembered something. Cullen, do you recall whether Cole Flannery was one of the men who tried to build that dam?"

"Well, yeah, come to think of it. He must have been— his farmland ran along Black Brook. Why?"

"I don't know precisely," she said. "But didn't Jack Turner say something to you about a brook—you know, the day before he died? We thought at the time it didn't make any sense. But maybe it did."

Cullen had shifted to stare at her. "Yes, I remember now—not Turner's exact words, though. What are you thinking?"

"I'm not sure," she told him. "Maybe nothing important."

Cullen had turned the carriage onto Cayuga Street, reminding her that she hadn't mentioned to him the black and white horse and its rider she'd seen earlier, just as they'd left Jake Braun's path for Black Brook Road.

Glynis tried to ignore the pang of guilt. And the uncomfortable question of why—why *again* she hadn't told Cullen.

She would tell him tomorrow.

TWELVE

❦

"MR. MERRYCOYF, SIR." Adam MacAlistair paused to clear his throat several times, and to rearrange his perfectly arranged neckcloth. "Ah, first of all, sir, please let me say how much I appreciate your referring Miss Hathaway to me. But I think I need to ask . . . that is, as you know, sir, I'm just starting out in the law." He cleared his throat again. "Well, is it possible that taking her case could . . . ah . . . hurt my reputation? Sir?"

From behind his desk, Jeremiah Merrycoyf studied the appealing young man standing before him. The lad's earnestness was no doubt sincere, and his concern under the circumstances quite appropriate. Still, he had to learn the practice of law somehow. And while encouraging Adam MacAlistair to represent Serenity Hathaway might resemble tossing a lamb into a lion's den, how the youngster acquitted himself—regardless of victory or defeat—could be significant. A rich experience for him, more important to his growth as a lawyer over the long haul than the flurry of public disapproval that would take place now.

Merrycoyf sighed and adjusted his spectacles. "My dear Mr. MacAlistair, I sympathize with your hesitancy. But— and it is a crucial *but*—the law must hold itself above and apart from mere personalities. Everyone is entitled to representation; surely they still teach that in law schools?"

"Oh, yes, sir, they do! And I quite agree with your premise, sir, Mr. Merrycoyf. It's just that this is . . ." The young man swallowed and ran a finger inside his starched white collar. "Sir, it's simply that this would be my first case, and Miss Hathaway my first client. I must question my worthiness to represent her with the competence she deserves."

Merrycoyf peered at Adam MacAlistair at length over his spectacles. After satisfying himself that no levity had been intended, he replied, "My dear fellow, while your humility is commendable, and your sentiment admirable . . ." Merrycoyf paused, recalling when he himself first began the practice of law. He'd all but forgotten how terrifying the responsibility appeared, how overwhelming his own inadequacy. And how failure loomed as fearsome as damnation.

While Adam MacAlistair stood fidgeting, Merrycoyf settled back in his chair and folded his hands over his stomach. "Let me put this bluntly, young man," Merrycoyf said. "You have to start somewhere! Now do sit down and stop squirming."

Adam MacAlistair sat.

"Now, then," Merrycoyf said, "I presume you have met Miss Hathaway, and that she has informed you of her difficulty?" The young man's sudden blush made answer to the first question unnecessary.

"Ah, yes, sir. Yes, I met with Miss Hathaway this very morning." His face reddened still more. "And she looks— that is, her case—very interesting."

"Indeed, yes," Merrycoyf agreed, concealing a smile. "And so, my young colleague, where do you intend to begin?"

"I believe I should make application for an injunction, sir. That the remedy for Miss Hathaway's distress is to stop those who wish to interrupt her business."

"Oh?" Merrycoyf steepled his fingers under his chin. "In other words, you wish to stop people from doing what they haven't yet done?"

"Well, yes," Adam MacAlistair frowned. "Because they are *going* to do it."

"And do you have sound reason for your application— that is, are those whom you wish to enjoin intending to do something illegal?"

Adam MacAlistair answered quickly, "I mean to find a

reason for arguing that they will be.''

Behind his spectacles, Merrycoyf's eyes twinkled. Yes, indeed, this bright young lawyer was on his way to a rich experience.

HEARING TEN CHIMES of the brass Seth Thomas clock in the downstairs hall, Glynis stretched and yawned, and pushed back the lightweight cotton coverlet. She had slept round the clock. Sunlight streamed through her open bedroom window. Any other year, by this time windows would be shut fast against bitter wind if not snow. Like nearly everyone else in Seneca Falls, she had begun to feel uneasy about the remarkable weather—and about what it might augur. For what should they prepare: the mildest winter in memory—or the harshest in history? Would each day of sunshine be followed by another, or would the sun tomorrow disappear in exhaustion for months? The paradox here, she thought to herself, smiling, was that while western New Yorkers complained religiously about their cursed winter weather, its absence provided grounds for anxiety, a sense of being lulled into complacency. The calm before THE STORM, it was feared. On the other hand, what could they do about it? They might as well enjoy it.

She stretched again, and winced in discomfort. Her neck hurt. So did her ribs. And memory of the day before brought her upright in the bed—although, truthfully, the whole thing now seemed more like a nightmare than reality. Her hand cautiously explored her neck. No—it had been real.

The previous night, after her landlady had examined her and hit the roof, Harriet had swabbed the cuts with witch hazel that stung and comfrey ointment that also stung, then wrapped Glynis in long strips of muslin from ear to collarbone. This had left her feeling partially mummified. She couldn't possibly appear in public this way.

When she reached the downstairs, the ruffles of her high-necked blouse fluttering against her bandages, Harriet was just waving good-bye to someone out the kitchen door.

''Who was that?'' Glynis asked, going quickly to the coffeepot on the stove.

Harriet shook her head and asked, "How are your wounds?"

"They're fine, Harriet."

"Good. Leave the bandages on until tonight, then I'll have a look." Harriet gestured to the table and the plate of graham muffins and glass jar of crabapple jelly.

After pouring her coffee, Glynis leaned over a pot of oatmeal porridge just to breathe in its familiar, comforting smell. "But who was just here?" she asked again on her way to the table.

"You sure you want to know?" Harriet's smile looked mischievous as she passed the jelly jar.

Glynis groaned. "That means it must have been Vanessa Usher. What was she doing here this early?"

"Early? It's near to noon."

"Then why was she here this late—except that Vanessa rarely gets up before noon."

"You'd better prepare yourself, Glynis. Because Vanessa came to invite us"—Harriet grinned—"to attend a seance! More than one, actually—she intends to hold them Saturday nights all winter."

"You're not serious." But on Harriet's face Glynis could clearly read that she was. "Well, I'm not attending, Harriet—don't even *try* to persuade me. I won't go."

"You know Vanessa will insist."

"Let her insist. I'm not the susceptible young thing she used to coerce so shamelessly. Not anymore. No."

"Aren't you even slightly curious about what Vanessa's up to?"

"No! Anyway, I can guess. In fact, I'll wager—whatever amount you'd like—that these seances involve Lazarus Grimm, don't they?" With some satisfaction, Glynis observed Harriet's surprise.

"How did you know?"

"I know Vanessa, that's how. Is she really in cahoots with him already? No, don't answer, I'm not interested. But tell me this—are they charging admission?"

"Well, as a matter of fact . . ."

"Aha!"

". . . there will be a donation requested."

"Aha, again! Where are they to be held—these spirited money-raisers?"

Harriet grinned and said, "I thought you weren't interested."

"I'm not. Are they going to use The Usher Playhouse?"

"For the first spiritualist meeting they will; the seances are to be at Vanessa's house. What do you suppose one wears to a seance?"

"A look of gullibility. How should I know, Harriet? In any event, I don't have to worry about what to wear because I'm—"

"Not attending. Yes, Glynis, I heard you the first time."

IT WAS MIDAFTERNOON before Glynis could leave the library and walk to the lockup. In the air hung the distinctive smell of burning leaves, and behind the church spires, huge white clouds billowed like sails before a shifting wind. Wind with a bite that announced the tardy autumn like a trumpet blast. The beautiful extended summer must be fleeing south.

When she rounded the firehouse and entered his office, Cullen was seated behind his desk. "Jake Braun hasn't said a word about this conspiracy to kill him," he grumbled. "In fact, sleep seems to have made him even more close-mouthed."

Glynis shook her head. "I don't understand his reluctance. Or does he feel that he's still in danger?"

"He hasn't mentioned it. But he's been as stubborn as ever. And he wants to leave."

"Do you think it's safe, Cullen, to let him go?"

"Hard to say. But I can't hold him here much longer without charging him. So . . . are you willing to swear out a complaint against Braun?"

"Me? For what?"

"For *what*! How about shooting at you, for starters? Attempting to kidnap you. Holding you against your will. Threatening to kill you?"

"Cullen, Jake Braun didn't intend—"

"How do you know what he intended?"

"Well, why don't *you* make the complaint?" Glynis asked. "And then—"

At that moment a florid man burst through the office door, shouting, "Constable, there's gonna be a riot! You'd better come quick."

Cullen got to his feet. "What're you talking about, Charlie?"

"My wife, she just went cross the bridge to meet up with those other crazy women. I'm telling you, Constable, there's gonna be trouble."

"You want to calm down and be a little more specific?"

"The tavern! They're gonna try and close down Serenity's Tavern."

Cullen groaned. "Oh, hell! This"—he frowned at Glynis—"is your friend Dr. Cardoza's doing."

"Please don't look at me like that, Cullen. I'm not even a participant. But I don't see how you can fault Neva for walking peaceably in front of a public building."

"It's not a public building."

"The public uses it."

"You've spent way too much time with Jeremiah Merrycoyf, you know that?" muttered Cullen as he buckled his holster. "Right, let's go, Charlie. And Glynis, would you tell Zeph to get somebody to stay with Jake Braun? Then have him meet me at the tavern."

"Cullen, you're not going to involve that boy in this?"

"He's not a boy—he's my deputy. And yes, he's going to be involved. Maybe your friend should think of the consequences before she does something so damnably stupid!"

Before Glynis could reply, Cullen strode out the door.

In the adjoining room, she found Zeph Waters, his boots up on a desk, reading. Glynis bent down to see the title and could make out only the name of Henry Wadsworth Longfellow on the book's spine.

"Poetry, Zeph?" she smiled. "I thought you said you'd never be caught dead reading that."

Startled, Zeph swung his boots to the floor and clapped the book shut. "Just looking at *Hiawatha*," he explained sheepishly.

"You needn't sound so embarrassed," Glynis said. "Longfellow's a master storyteller, and he's very popular."

Zeph shrugged, obviously still embarrassed, as he glanced

over his shoulder toward the holding cell.

"You're to find someone to stay here with Jake Braun," she told him, "so you can meet Constable Stuart down by the tavern on the canal."

"What's doing there?" Zeph asked, expectation bright in his eyes. He surely suspected what was doing, Glynis thought; there had been plenty of rumors about the temperance march.

"Zeph, why don't you just go and get someone as Cullen asked?"

He walked toward the door, then stopped and turned to look back at the cell and at Glynis. "How can I? Can't leave the prisoner."

"It shouldn't take you long. I'll stay here with Jake Braun," Glynis offered.

"Miss Tryon, I don't think that's such a good idea."

"It's a fine idea." Glynis looked pointedly at the wall-hung gun rack. "If anything happens . . . well, you're the one who taught me how to shoot, remember, Zeph? Now go ahead."

He looked hesitant, but she nodded at him, and he finally left, reluctantly. Once outside, though, Glynis knew he'd dash so as not to miss any of the goings-on down at the tavern. For that matter, she didn't want to miss them, either. But she had something to do before Zeph returned.

Quickly she went back to the holding cell, where its sole occupant, Jake Braun, sprawled on a cot, staring at the ceiling. Beside the cot, a tray holding several empty tin plates sat on the floor. A pack of playing cards lay on the gray wool blanket rumpled at the man's feet.

"Good afternoon, Mr. Braun," Glynis said as she went to stand before the bars of the cell.

Braun turned his head to give Glynis a nod. Otherwise, he didn't budge from his reclining position.

"Constable Stuart said you didn't care to talk about what happened yesterday," she began. "I don't understand how you expect him to help if you won't tell him anything."

"Don't expect him to help me none. It's not his business."

"Well, yes, it is. People getting killed violates the law."

Glynis kept her voice patient. "Two men have been murdered, and you said someone was trying to kill *you.* So it *is* the constable's business, Mr. Braun, whether you like it or not. But tell me, what is the connection between you and Jack Turner and Mead Miller? Because I'm certain there is one."

Braun turned his face to the wall.

Glynis searched for a way to jolt him out of his fatalism, if that's what was keeping him silent. "Mr. Braun, a few days ago, Sara Turner told me there would be more deaths." Braun rolled back to look at her. And Glynis now noticed beads of perspiration on his forehead. "How would Sara Turner know that?" she continued.

"She don't know nothin'," Braun mumbled.

"Oh, I think she does," Glynis disagreed.

Abruptly, Braun got to his feet. He looked at Glynis a moment, then walked to the cell window, where he stood staring out.

Why wouldn't he talk? She decided to try a stab in the dark. "How many of you farmers," she asked suddenly, "were involved some years ago in the attempt to dam up Black Brook?"

Braun whirled from the window. "Leave it alone—just leave it be!"

Although bewildered by the man's reaction, Glynis persisted, "Why should I leave it be? I think it may be a reason—"

"It ain't no reason, and you don't know what you're talkin' about! And you ain't never gonna know. Not from me, not from nobody, cause nobody else's left—"

He broke off at the sound of a door opening. Voices came down the short hall. As Zeph appeared with the young black man who worked at the livery, Glynis bit her lower lip in disappointment. Braun had been about to say something; she was sure of it.

Frustrated, she had no choice but to leave the lockup. When she headed down Fall Street for the bridge and Serenity's Tavern, Zeph caught up with her moments later. He sprinted past, anticipation spread thick as jam across his grinning face.

* * *

BY THE TIME Glynis crossed the bridge and started up Ovid Street, racing gray clouds had overtaken the white; a pale sun still managed to poke through now and then but a chill wind gusted from the northwest.

Glynis shivered and walked faster, pulling her shawl tightly around herself, while at the same time trying to keep her green merino wool skirt and her petticoats from blowing around too revealingly. After turning onto West Bayard Street she could see ahead to where a small crowd had formed. She walked on, then paused before turning down the short, well-worn dirt road that ran in front of the two-story clapboard tavern. The few oak trees on the shallow slope did not block her view of what was taking place below.

Wind ruffled the Seneca River beyond the tavern as it did the dark cloaks and shawls and the brightly colored bonnet ribbons of the gathered women. Blowing skirts exposed white flounced petticoats. From where Glynis stood, she could pick out Neva Cardoza and the strong, familiar profile of Susan Anthony. She looked for, but couldn't find, Elizabeth Cady Stanton; the only possible reason for Elizabeth's absence would be that she was trapped at home with her brood of six children. And in fact, although Glynis recognized a number of others—including Vanessa Usher's sister Aurora—many of the women seemed to be either beyond childbearing years or very young. There were, nonetheless, several children grasping their mothers' hands. Glynis counted roughly thirty-five women, but the voices carried upward by the wind sounded like a vastly larger number. And they sounded angry.

While Zeph stood at the far edge of the crowd, Cullen had stationed himself on the tavern steps; Glynis couldn't help smiling at his annoyed expression. The heavy oak door behind him remained closed. Over his head, the gilt scroll-work letters that spelled SERENITY'S TAVERN gleamed brilliantly in the darkening afternoon.

Glynis started down the road, but had gone only a few feet before she stopped again upon hearing Susan Anthony's clear, emphatic voice. The woman sounded exactly like the

schoolteacher she had been. "Ladies, please line up!" she
directed over the lively babble. A relative quiet descended
promptly. "Come now, let us move quickly! Please line up
behind Dr. Cardoza and me. Step smartly now—let us not
waste time."

Bustling like a mother hen among her chicks, Susan Anthony gestured and pointed until, after some minutes and a
great deal of confusion, the women seemed positioned to
her satisfaction. Glynis moved from the road, after catching
Cullen's eyes on her, to stand in the shadow of a still fully-
leafed oak. She didn't want to attract Susan and Neva's
attention for fear of being commandeered to join; Glynis
knew she wouldn't have the nerve to refuse, while at the
same time her age-old shyness cringed at this spectacle in
the making. Besides, she meant what she'd said to Neva;
though she agreed the tavern should be closed, she felt indebted to Serenity for help in the past. What she hadn't told
Neva or anyone else, and never would, was that, in spite of
herself, she rather liked Serenity.

Susan Anthony had placed herself beside Neva at the
head of two wavering columns of women, and now motioned for them to follow her. Stumbling forward—and jostling into and over each other—the women began a ragged
circular procession in front of the tavern.

Gradually the jostling eased as the participants found their
pace. The random chattering ended. In its place came a silence that Glynis found moving in its simple dignity; she
was also moved by the courage of the women below. Ordinary women, wives and mothers, risking their families'
severe disapproval and, in a few cases, their very well-being.
No, perhaps these women weren't so ordinary after all.
Some of them wouldn't feel they had even the right to defend themselves, or their children, against husbands who
came home, abusive and demanding, from the taverns. The
law certainly didn't give them that right. And yet here they
were.

The lines of women circled for some minutes without
incident. Cullen moved from the front steps to stand beside
Zeph at the far side of the building; this move quickly
proved fortuitous, as a stream of foul-smelling refuse sud-

denly poured from an upstairs tavern window. The mood of the march and its dignified silence was broken, pierced by shocked screams of those spattered when the offal hit the ground.

Susan Anthony whirled in her tracks, gesturing to the women to back away. Neva's small face, what Glynis could see of it, had reddened with fury; she whipped her skirts aside and stalked to where a large placard, attached to a pole, leaned against a tree. Snatching the pole, Neva hoisted the placard into the air, and quickly rejoined the women. The procession had regrouped under Susan Anthony's resolute guidance, and again began to circle, now well away from the tavern windows.

Glynis could now read Neva's sign: SPIRITS OF MISERY AND CRIME BOUGHT AND SOLD HERE! appeared on one side. The other side read, CLOSE DOWN THIS UNLAWFUL ESTABLISHMENT!

While Glynis didn't find these sentiments particularly inflammatory, the door of the tavern suddenly burst open. And through it, in all her henna-haired glory, stepped Serenity Hathaway. For women who before now had never seen the tavern's proprietor—which, Glynis assumed, would be most of them—Serenity's appearance must have come as something of a shock. For this was no debauched and dissipated hag, the wages of sin writ clear on her forehead. Standing before them was, without question, one of the most ravishing creatures ever to tread the soil of western New York. And the creature was plainly outraged.

With her hair tossing in the wind, Serenity swished the voluminous folds of her bustled taffeta gown around behind her. From where Glynis stood, the woman resembled nothing so much as the figurehead of a square-masted brigantine—chin high, breasts thrust forward, heading into a high gale—a pirate ship, primed for war.

For a long moment, a quiet held fast that only an act of God could have breached. Even the rouged and kohl-eyed women who now leaned out of every tavern window were apparently struck dumb. Serenity fixed her smoldering eyes on Neva Cardoza, who might very likely be, Glynis decided, the only female Serenity could recognize. Neva looked to be glaring just as fixedly back.

Glynis was reluctant to take her eyes from this standoff lest she miss something, but finally risked a quick glance at Cullen. He stood, feet apart, hands in his pockets, looking very much as though he were watching a performance at The Usher Playhouse.

Serenity's husky voice broke the silence. "Get off my property!" Turning to Cullen she ordered, "Constable Stuart, remove these persons!"

"Afraid I can't do that," Cullen said to her, not shifting his stance. Glynis observed that beside him, Zeph looked extremely uncomfortable. Well, it served him right, being so eager to get there!

"We have every intention of staying, *Madam* Hathaway," rang Neva's voice as clear as a ship's bell. "This is an illegal establishment, and we demand that it close. Furthermore, we intend to exercise our right to protest its illegality until it does close!"

Hoofbeats sounded on the road behind Glynis. She turned to see a chestnut mare with a good-looking young man astride, cantering briskly down the tavern road. Upon reaching the entrance, the young man dismounted, gave the assembled women an engaging and somewhat apologetic smile, and walked toward the steps. "Miss Hathaway, may we have a word?"

"About time you got here," Serenity said to him. "You going to get rid of these troublemakers?"

The young man, whose name, Glynis finally recalled, was Adam MacAlistair, shook his head briefly. He motioned to the near side of the tavern, and took Serenity's elbow to guide her there. They disappeared around the corner of the building.

Susan Anthony executed a sweeping motion with her arm. The women resumed their moving circle. But they did so now accompanied by catcalls from those hanging out the tavern windows.

Glynis stepped away from the oak, and crossed the road to make her way unobtrusively down the slope. She told herself this was none of her business, but curiosity managed to dislodge her sensibility. And no one would notice what she was doing, given the crowd and the noise.

When she reached the corner of the tavern, she heard voices and went forward along the building's side wall; the voices, she decided, must be coming from the towpath behind the tavern. Cautiously she peered around the corner. Nearby on the path stood Serenity and Adam MacAlistair.

Glynis had hoped this might be the case, as she didn't think Serenity would chance her customers or employees overhearing the battle plan. More to the point, Glynis felt certain that Adam MacAlistair—from what she remembered of him before he left for law school—would never set foot in a brothel. At least not when he might be seen.

Glynis had just started to go forward to show herself when Serenity suddenly said, "Now listen here, Mr. Smart Young Lawyer." She placed her hands firmly on the curve of her hips. "I expect you to do something *now*! Not tomorrow or next week, but now!"

"Miss Hathaway, I've tried to explain to you—"

"I'm not interested in explanations," Serenity interrupted. "I'm interested in results. I want those damn women gone. Can you think, for one minute, that we're going to get customers while those self-righteous shrews are parading back and forth? Not on your sweet ass, we're not!"

Glynis pulled back into the shadow of the tavern. Adam MacAlistair seemed to be doing an unusual amount of swallowing, and his face had taken on a pink hue. He ran a finger inside his white collar. "Ah, yes, Miss Hathaway—yes, you could be right."

"*Could* be? I *am* right! Half my customers are married men, and those could be their wives out there. You think those men are going to just waltz past them big as life? *Do you*?"

"Well, no . . . that is . . . no, probably not." Adam shook his head vigorously.

Glynis backed up against the tavern wall, pressing her hands over her mouth. It shouldn't have been funny, none of it, and she was ashamed of herself for laughing—but this poor young lawyer was really out of his depth. Why on earth had he agreed to represent Serenity in the first place?

"And I'm going to seek an injunction to stop them," he

was saying. "But I have to go to Waterloo, where the county court is, to request it."

"When?" Serenity snapped. "When is this going to happen?"

"Tomorrow, possibly. The very soonest I can get a hearing," he said earnestly. "But, Miss Hathaway, I must warn you, it won't be easy."

"That is *your* problem!" Serenity announced. "But I can tell you this much—you do whatever is necessary to get rid of those women. *Whatever!* Buy the judge, if you have to. I'll pay!"

Adam's face lost its pink color. All its color. "Oh, no! No, I don't think it would be wise to—"

"I'm not paying you to think! I'm paying you to look after my best interests," Serenity snapped again. "Now do it!"

She spun around and strode toward the tavern's rear entrance, her heels clicking angrily on the flagstones underfoot. Glynis waited while Adam MacAlistair followed her, wiping his pale forehead with a large handkerchief. He had one foot on the bottom step when he shook his head, stepped back down, and continued on around the far side of the building.

Glynis walked quickly back to the front entrance; she should be embarrassed, skulking like a common snoop.

She found the march coming to a straggling halt while the participants watched a small black buggy barrel down the dirt road. Surely not a customer! A second later she identified the driver of the buggy as Lazarus Grimm.

He reined in the horse close to the marchers, who stepped back hurriedly as he jumped from the carriage. "A doctor! I need a doctor!" Lazarus shouted. "Is Dr. Cardoza here?"

Glynis saw Neva start forward, then hesitate. Too late, as Lazarus had spotted her and rushed toward her. "Dr. Cardoza, please come with me. It's my father—I think he may be dying."

The assembled women let out a collective gasp, followed by murmurs of disbelief. Glynis, also disbelieving that something like death could befall Obadiah Grimm without his permission, moved closer to hear.

"Mr. Grimm," Neva asked, "when did your father become ill?"

"He's not ill! He . . . he seems to have taken a bad fall. Please, Dr. Cardoza, I truly think he may die." His face was ashen; he looked not only terribly upset, but as if he might himself keel over. "I tried to get Dr. Ives," he explained breathlessly, "but his wife said he'd gone to Tyre for a birth. Dr. Cardoza, I implore you to come!"

Neva turned and said something to Susan Anthony. She then turned to take Lazarus's arm, as if she thought he needed support. "Very well, Mr. Grimm. Of course I'll come with you." But her expression appeared distressed as she glanced around the crowd. Glynis hurried to join her.

"Oh, Glynis, I thought I saw you earlier. Is there any possibility that you could . . . ?"

"Dr. Cardoza," Lazarus broke in, his voice shaky. "We have to go right now!"

"Yes, Neva," Glynis said quickly, "you go ahead with Lazarus. I'll get a carriage and follow you out there."

Lazarus grabbed Neva's arm, and together they rushed to the buggy.

THIRTEEN

❧

To know the life of a wounded man, whether he shall live or die. Take the juice of lettuce, and give the sick to drink with water; and if he cast it up anon, he shall die; and if he do not, he shall live. And the juice of mouse-ear will [do] the same. Probatum est.

— A LEECHBOOK OR COLLECTION OF
    MEDICAL REMEDIES OF THE FIFTEENTH
    CENTURY

LAZARUS GRIMM GROUND his teeth and continued to urge the horse forward at breakneck speed, while Neva gripped the side panel of the wildly swaying buggy. She felt inescapably that she would be thrown out, her skull fractured, and left for dead. Grimm might not even note her absence. And just where, she'd like to know, was this quiet little town to which Constable Stuart had referred when she first arrived in Seneca Falls? The place was a hotbed of lunacy.

Of this, Lazarus Grimm was a prime example; he had said practically nothing since they'd careened on two wheels onto Black Brook Road, driving hellbent for leather. As the road evened out some, Neva let go of the buggy's side momentarily to hug around her shoulders the shawl Glynis Tryon had tossed to her just before Grimm goaded the horse up the tavern drive. Although the earlier wind had died, the twilight held a frosty chill. Neva again grabbed the buggy's side as it struck a bump in the road, launching them into the air to land with a bone-jarring jolt. She gave Lazarus Grimm a sideways glare; did he have to risk her life as well as his own?

She had tried without success to make him slow the reckless pace, so she decided to try once more for information. ''Mr. Grimm, what symptoms did your father exhibit after his fall? For example, did he appear to be unconscious?''

''No!'' Lazarus slapped the reins harder against the horse's flanks.

''So he was conscious?'' Bump. Jolt. ''You don't know? Well, did he speak to you?''

''No.''

''Did he move—for instance, try to sit up?''

''No.''

''Mr. Grimm, your monosyllabic grunts are not at all useful,'' Neva snapped. ''I'm simply trying to determine how serious your father's condition might be.''

Lazarus turned his gaunt face to her; he looked suitably contrite. ''I'm sorry,'' he said as the carriage took a great hop, then settled back on its undergear with a rattle like graveyard bones. Like *their* bones would sound if he didn't slow down.

''You do realize,'' Neva said to him, ''that I can't help your father if I'm lying dead in a ditch. Please exercise some prudence, Mr. Grimm.''

To her surprise, he flexed the reins and actually slowed the horse, again throwing her a contrite look. ''I apologize, Dr. Cardoza, if I've frightened you. The truth is, I'm not sure my father will even be alive when we get there. Molly insisted I go for a doctor, but if she hadn't . . .'' He shook his head at the futility of it.

''Mr. Grimm, I've met your father, and he struck me as an extremely hardy individual,'' Neva told him. ''He may just have sustained a slight concussion. That wouldn't be enough to—''

''No! He's hurt more seriously than that,'' Lazarus broke in. ''And I blame it all on that woman,'' he added tersely. ''Father was so disturbed after she left that . . . Who knows . . . ?''

''What woman?'' Neva asked, wondering who could have the wherewithal to disturb Obadiah Grimm.

''Lily Braun!'' Lazarus ground his teeth and, to Neva's distress, urged the horse to a faster pace.

Lily Braun had been at the Grimm place again? But why should Lazarus believe she had anything to do with his father's accident? Neva lost her next thought as the carriage took another mighty bounce. Her spine vibrated and her tailbone ached; her coccyx, she corrected herself. She'd obviously forgotten anatomical terms and likely everything else she'd learned in medical school. No surprise there. Since coming to Seneca Falls, she'd set exactly four fractures and assisted at six births—seven, including the Grimm's lambs. She had treated unsuccessfully a rash that had appeared mysteriously on the body of the mayor's wife and that, some days later, disappeared just as mysteriously. She had removed thorns from children's feet, a steel sliver from a man's earlobe, and several porcupine quills from the muzzle of a large, enraged dog. Also a shard of glass embedded in the snout of a six-hundred-pound sow who clearly hadn't wanted the glass removed.

On the other hand, in barely one month she'd assisted in two autopsies that had established death by means of poison. Some quiet little town!

But mostly her time had been occupied with the malnutrition of poverty, and bruises and swellings and cuts, nearly all attributable to intemperance. And for this Elizabeth Blackwell had exiled her from New York City? If it were the evils of drink Dr. Blackwell wanted her to experience, Neva thought she could have done this perfectly well in New York. And there, at least, she wouldn't have had her peace of mind disturbed by Abraham Levy. But this was no time to think of him!

As if pursued by demons, Lazarus now took the buggy into the Grimm drive. When he pulled to a stop in front of the barn, Neva felt so rattled that she was uncertain she could walk without assistance. She found this would not be necessary, however, as Lazarus seemed determined to drag her all the way to the barn. She eyed the sweating horse with resentment as they rushed past.

The twilight had shaded into dark blue, but when she stepped into the barn she still needed a minute for her eyes to adjust to the dimness. Gradually the shapes of farm tools, hung from hooks and leather loops, revealed themselves. It surprised Neva, even afforded her a perverse sort of pride, that as she walked past them, she could recognize objects she'd not known existed before she came to Seneca Falls: triangular spades, shovels and pitchfork, sheep shears, pruning chisels and saws, tree scrapers and long-handled, pronged gatherers for harvesting fruit without it bruising.

Stored on shelves next to the tools were powders, Epsom salts for purging, salt black, bottles of turpentine for de-lousing sheep, and several bags whose labels said they contained arsenic; Neva wondered if this was a safe place to keep it. But it was probably for barn rats, she decided, and thought fleetingly of Sara Turner.

Lazarus had sprinted on ahead. Neva looked to the far end of the barn, where lanterns illuminated a small group standing silently around a prostrate figure. Overhead was a hayloft. She hurried forward, clutching her black bag; it was fortunate she'd come to consider it as an appendage and had had the bag with her at the tavern, because Lazarus Grimm never would have consented to stop for it at Dr. Ives's.

Even before she reached Obadiah Grimm, Neva could hear his labored, raspy breathing. Those who were standing moved aside to let her through. No one spoke. She quickly knelt beside him on wisps of sweet-scented clover hay, opening her bag to extract her stethoscope.

Obadiah's skin held a waxy pallor the white of his hair and beard; however, beneath a glaze of sweat, his expression appeared markedly tranquil, as if he were experiencing no pain. It was shock, Neva decided, after drawing back his eyelids and noting that the pupils had so dilated that little of the irises showed, and blood suffused what white was visible. She carefully pulled away the blanket that had been placed over Obadiah's body. The shirt covering his torso was saturated with blood; when she'd unbuttoned it, she realized it would be impossible to remove entirely without incurring more blood flow.

After she positioned the stethoscope, the heartbeat she found was rapid and weak, and the pulse in his wrist thready. After listening for several minutes, Neva removed the stethoscope to sit back on her heels. She looked up at the silent assembly: Molly Grimm and her mother, Almira; Billy Wicken; and, of course, Lazarus. Two other women were also there, standing apart from the others, beyond the light cast by the lanterns.

"Was someone here when he fell?" Neva asked. "Did anyone see what happened?"

No one answered. They simply stared at her.

"Doesn't *anyone* know what happened?" Neva asked again, this time directing the question specifically to Molly. The woman's face was tear-streaked and, Neva noticed absently, slightly swollen on one side.

Molly seemed startled to be singled out, and she clenched spasmodically the torn lace trim that she'd been fingering on her collar. "We're not really sure . . ." she began, then paused to look with confusion at her brother.

"Can you just tell us how bad it is?" Lazarus asked.

"I'm afraid it's very bad," Neva answered quietly. She bent over Obadiah again and tried to locate the origin of the bleeding. When she probed the area directly over his heart the flow increased, and she found what felt like a small puncture wound.

She spoke to Lazarus. "I thought you said that he fell."

Lazarus nodded glumly. Neva looked over the heads of those standing around her. "Did he fall from up there—from that hayloft?" Not, she supposed, that it really mattered.

Gazing up at the loft, Lazarus again nodded. Neva scanned the others' faces. Billy Wicken's forehead wrinkled in apparent puzzlement; Almira, her face wooden, showed no response; and Molly indicated agreement with her brother.

Since she'd gotten there, Neva had run through her mind every medical procedure she could think of, but nothing would save this man now. Given his loss of blood, it almost defied belief that he had lasted this long. Frustrated by the sheer hopelessness of it, Neva bent forward to repeat her examination, and heard Obadiah's breathing stop. When it began again, it was faint and even more labored. And his heartbeat had slowed ominously.

"Could I have more light?" Neva asked.

Billy Wicken limped over to a lantern suspended from a beam. When he returned with it, Neva directed him to hold it above Obadiah's torso while she probed the wound and its surrounding area. She thought she'd found something, and had bent closer to see, when suddenly someone gave a harsh cough, and one of the two women Neva couldn't see stepped forward into the light. She now recognized her as the Seneca medicine woman, Bitter Root. Her companion was the sweet-voiced woman who had also been at Abraham's store.

Without even glancing down at the moribund figure, Bitter Root spoke directly to Neva. "Hole in his heart." The woman then pointed to Obadiah's chest.

"Yes," Neva agreed, somewhat surprised, "the heart's likely been punctured."

"Why don't you *do* something?" Lazarus's voice was frantic. "He's obviously dying. Do something!"

Before Neva could answer, Bitter Root replied, "Nothing to do. I told you before, he has heart hole. Nothing to do for that."

Molly moaned softly, "Oh, no—that can't be."

"I'm afraid it's true," Neva said as gently as she could. "We might try a pressure bandage, wrapping it around his chest, but I don't think he'll last long enough for us to do even that. I'm sorry." From the corner of her eye, she saw Bitter Root nod once in agreement. It occurred to Neva to wonder how the woman happened to be there.

"You have to try something!" Lazarus insisted.

Molly murmured a few words in a solicitous tone to Billy Wicken, who had been chewing on his lower lip and rubbing his withered hand against his side. He lowered the lantern he held, and gave Molly a searching look. While gazing up at Obadiah's family, Neva suddenly realized that his wife, the ordinarily voluble Almira, had remained completely mute. The woman's expression seemed almost dreamy; it was as if she were a thousand miles away. Neva chided herself for not recognizing sooner the possibility that Almira Grimm might be drugged. Opium addicted? Laudanum, most likely.

Suddenly, Obadiah gasped loudly. Those standing around him went rigid, then leaned forward, watching him warily as if they might miss his last moment. Neva was about to put her stethoscope to the man's chest when she realized his expression had altered. His face was contorting in a fierce grimace, his mouth opening and closing. His lips moved slightly as Neva bent over him.

The words came faintly, interrupted by the gasps and gurgling that indicated internal bleeding. Neva could barely hear him.

"Jere . . . Jeremiah . . ." the man sighed. His breathing abruptly stopped. It started again with a shallow wheezing like that of a perforated bellows.

"Mr. Grimm, can you say that again?" Neva asked.

Lazarus dropped to his knees and pushed Neva away with unnecessary force. He spoke agitatedly. "What is it, Father? What are you trying to say?"

The dying man's words were not quite loud enough for Neva to understand. She bent forward, despite a glare from Lazarus that made her wonder if there might be something he didn't want her to hear.

Obadiah sighed, "Jere . . . seven . . . tea he leaven . . ." This was followed by a rattle deep in his throat.

Lazarus frowned and shook his head. "What are you saying, Father—is it Jeremiah Merrycoyf you're asking for? Is there something you want us to tell him? Father?"

In reply, a small froth of blood bubbled from Obadiah's slack mouth, and his eyes stared unseeing at his son. Neva reached for the pulse in his neck. There was none.

As she got to her feet, Neva felt a sudden chill that had nothing to do with the dampness in the barn. Something seemed wrong with what she'd been told about Obadiah's fall; or rather, what she had not been told. She cast her eyes over the barn floor, at the same time nudging aside hay with the toe of her high-laced shoe.

Finally, though, the sense that she was intruding made her move away from the sounds of grief and from those who grieved. Glancing around, she saw with uneasiness that the Seneca medicine woman was staring at her intently. The sharp, dark eyes held Neva's own before they darted suddenly to the hayloft. Bitter Root gazed upward, then abruptly turned and went to stand beside her quiet companion.

Neva wondered if one of the family had summoned the women, or if, instead, they had been drawn there by some intuitive portent of death. Then, as if pulled by an invisible cord, she went to stand under the loft, and gazed upward.

CAN'T YOU MAKE that horse move any faster?'' Abraham Levy shouted to Cullen over the clatter of the carriage wheels.

Glynis, seated beside Cullen, thought the horse was moving quite fast enough. Obviously not, though, for Abraham, who, from the rear seat, had shouted the same thing several times since they'd left the Fall Street livery. He had arrived while she and Cullen waited for a horse to be harnessed; when he'd heard Neva was on her way to the Grimm farm, he'd insisted on going with them. Glynis wondered if he realized that his extra weight was what slowed their progress. If he did, he didn't seem to care.

Cullen didn't answer Abraham's question, but continued to peer intently ahead into the gathering darkness. The two small carriage lamps were not much help. Glynis herself had offered to take the reins; she told Cullen that during the past week she'd made this trip so many times she didn't require light. She needn't have bothered. No man was going to let a woman drive, not while he could still draw breath.

When they turned off Black Brook Road into the Grimms', the house ahead appeared dark. But from under the barn door shone a wedge of light. The three of them climbed from the carriage, the men walking directly to the barn, while Glynis paused to study a rectangular shape some yards away, under a clump of white birch. As her eyes adjusted to the darkness, she gradually confirmed it to be a wagon. Tied behind it, and what had first caught her eye, stood the distinctive black and white paint horse. She couldn't imagine what Jacques Sundown might be doing there.

As she began to walk toward the horse, Glynis heard voices coming from the barn. When she turned, the door had swung open, silhouetting the two men. A third figure was there also, dressed in a full skirt; it looked like Neva Cardoza. Glynis stood indecisively; if she went to join them, Jacques might leave before she found out why he was there.

As she watched, two of the backlit figures in the door

moved away from the barn. The other—from his height, Glynis determined it to be Cullen—went on inside. Glynis started toward the pair, but they hurried to stand under the low, spreading branches of an oak, remaining apart for only a moment before they merged into a single shape.

Although thoroughly astonished, Glynis smiled to herself and waited until the two separated before she went toward them. Neva, in a shaken voice, was saying, ". . . and I couldn't do anything for him . . . not anything!"

Abraham clearly intended to draw her close again; as she approached them, Glynis spoke loudly. "Neva, what's happened?"

The two jumped and hastily moved farther apart.

"Glynis, you frightened me," Neva said, her voice still unsteady. "Of course," she added belatedly, "I'm glad you're here."

Under the circumstances, Glynis did not find this convincing. "What's happened to Obadiah?" she asked again.

"He's dead," Abraham answered.

Glynis inhaled sharply at the abrupt announcement, and yet she wasn't totally surprised. Either Neva's words had prepared her, or she had begun to anticipate death at every turn. "But surely he didn't die from a fall?" she asked incredulously.

"He fell from the hayloft," Neva said. "That's what they all claim, the family, that is, and Billy Wicken. Although . . ." She hesitated, then went on, "although Lazarus and Molly were the only ones doing any talking."

"What about Pippa?" Glynis asked. "Was she there?"

"No. No, she wasn't, come to think of it. I don't know where she is."

"One of us should find her," Glynis said, glancing around at the horse and wagon. "But Neva, what did you mean, 'that's what they all claim'?"

"I'm not sure. But I won't sign a death certificate without an autopsy, even if they are opposed to it."

"Why do you think they'll oppose it?" Glynis asked with some surprise.

"Because they already have," Abraham answered her. He turned to Neva. "You told Cullen Stuart that as constable he could order an autopsy performed—you sure that's true?''

''Yes, I think so,'' Neva said. ''It was true in New York City, anyway, in the absence of a coroner.''

''What exactly did the family tell you,'' Glynis asked, ''about Obadiah's accident?''

''Not much. I never did find out if he was alone when he fell. And just before he died, he tried to say something—whether to me or to a family member, I don't know. It was very odd.'' Neva shrugged slightly, shaking her head.

''Did you hear him?'' Glynis pressed her.

''Some of it,'' Neva frowned. ''But nothing that made any sense. Something about Jeremiah Merrycoyf.''

A high-pitched alarmed voice came from the house as Molly Grimm, calling for Pippa, hurried down the porch steps. When she reached them, Neva asked, ''Isn't Pippa in the house?''

''I can't find her!'' Molly's hair tumbled over her shoulders, and her dirt-smudged skirt trailed bits of straw. ''I left her there inside, and now she's gone.''

Glynis was struck by the intensity of the woman's anxiety. Granted, Molly's father had just died; that certainly could account for it, except that the near-hysterical concern for Pippa had begun weeks ago.

''She's gone!'' Molly cried again. ''We have to find her!''

''The child certainly couldn't have gone very far,'' Abraham offered in an overly reasonable tone. ''After all, we've been standing right here. She couldn't have gone past without one of us seeing her, even if it is dark. And what would she be doing out here in the dark, anyway? She could get hurt.''

At this, Molly gasped, while Neva shot Abraham a black look. ''That wasn't the most helpful thing to say,'' she muttered to him.

Abraham appeared to be genuinely baffled by this reproof.

''Was Pippa in the barn, Molly,'' asked Glynis, suddenly anxious herself about the girl, ''when your father . . . when he fell? Could she have seen what happened?''

"No!" Molly's response was emphatic. "No, of course she wasn't there!" She turned toward the barn and said breathlessly, "But I'm afraid . . ." Her voice trailed off. She started back toward the house, followed by Neva and Abraham.

Glynis remained, determined to find out why Jacques Sundown was there, and why he didn't show himself.

A long, low whine made her whirl toward the paint horse and the wagon. Through the darkness gleamed two gold eyes, and the whine became short, imperative barks. A premonition of danger, not to herself but, unaccountably, to Pippa, made Glynis pick up her skirts and run toward the wolf.

But it had vanished when she reached the wagon. She stood in uncertainty and heard a faint noise some yards away. Even though her eyes had adjusted to the night, she narrowed them in nameless dread as she moved cautiously toward the sound. Then she sucked in her breath. Some distance ahead of her, a filmy white apparition appeared to hover just above the ground.

Glynis stood paralyzed while trying to reassure herself there were no such things as ghosts. Surely not.

Again a faint sound, now distinguishable as fabric rustling, made her take several cautious steps forward. The apparition took on corporeal identity, as Glynis could now see Pippa standing a few yards away, clad only in a white nightdress that fell to her calves. Below the nightdress, Pippa's legs and feet were bare, creating the illusion that she floated. But she must be half-frozen.

Her eyes were squeezed shut. Glynis wondered if the girl might be in some sort of trance again, and so said nothing, but moved quietly toward her. She stopped short after a few steps. Looking ahead, she saw where it was that Pippa stood—teetering on the edge of a ravine, at the bottom of which lay Black Brook. And there the brook flowed over an outcropping of rock and boulders. If Pippa took just one step backward . . .

Glynis stood stock-still, afraid of making a sound that might startle the girl. How could she reach Pippa without alarming her? As she debated, out of the darkness loped the gray wolf. It went straight for the girl. Glynis clutched her fists against her mouth, shutting off a scream, as the wolf clasped the hem of Pippa's nightdress in its jaws, braced its front legs, and tugged gently. Pippa was forced to take a few small steps forward. Glynis started toward her. But a rock in the girl's path made her trip, and for a moment she tottered unsteadily. Her eyes flew open, and when she flailed her arms, Glynis heard fabric tearing. The nightgown ripped apart, sending the girl stumbling backward. Glynis lunged for her. Too far away to catch her, she instead fell helplessly to her knees, watching in mute horror as Pippa, her arms raised as if in supplication, disappeared over the edge into the ravine.

Glynis heard a heartrending cry, and scrambled to her feet. Before she could get to the place where Pippa went over, Jacques Sundown appeared, climbing from the slope with the girl in his arms. Glynis rushed forward, but Jacques shook his head at her and walked toward the wagon. He gently deposited Pippa, her eyes closed again, on the wooden seat, while Glynis, right behind him, whispered, "Jacques, is she all right?"

"She's all right."

"How did you manage to catch her?"

"Circled around. Went partway down the slope. Thought the wolf could keep her from going over until I got behind her."

Glynis glanced around, but there was no sign of the gray wolf. She hadn't really believed there would be. "Jacques, what was Pippa doing out here, anyway?" Glynis wanted to ask what *he* was doing out there, but didn't think she'd get an answer.

Pippa made a soft sound, something between a sigh and a moan, and stirred a little on the seat. Her eyes opened sleepily, and she started to sit up, suddenly awake and seeming none the worse for her misadventure. But she began to tremble.

Her shaking increased, as if she were palsied. When Glynis hurried to her, the girl moaned and wrapped her arms around her knees, curling herself into a tight ball. She wrenched away from Glynis's hand on her shoulder, and cast her eyes about wildly.

Glynis climbed onto the seat and pulled Pippa to her, despite the girl's struggles to free herself. As Glynis spoke reassuringly to her, holding her close and stroking her hair, the struggles gradually ceased.

During this, Jacques had stood quietly by the wagon. Still holding Pippa, Glynis looked down at him to say, "Jacques, did you see how she got on the edge of the ravine? Was she sleepwalking?"

"Don't know what she was doing. Didn't see her until I heard the wolf."

"But how could she get from the house unseen by any of us?" Glynis asked him.

"Tunnel."

"Tunnel? What tunnel?" she said.

"Runs from the house to the barn. Grimm had it dug to use in winter when the snow got deep. Couple years back, he made it longer, so runaway slaves could get to the ravine and Black Brook. To head north without being seen."

"You mean this farm is a station on the Underground Railroad? I never knew that. So Pippa might have used the tunnel to . . ."

She stopped as Jacques's eyes suddenly shifted past her; a moment later, Cullen came striding out of the darkness. "Glynis, what're you doing out here? We've been looking all over the place for you. The girl's mother is beside herself, and Dr. Cardoza's trying to calm her . . . Sundown! I'll be damned. Where'd you come from?"

Given the fact that the two men hadn't seen each other in three years, Glynis thought Cullen's greeting a bit abrupt. He didn't smile, and she noticed that he made no move to shake his former deputy's hand. Probably he was still smarting from Jacques's indifference, but it wouldn't be like Cullen to hold a grudge.

"Jacques just kept Pippa from falling into the ravine, Cullen," she explained, and saw his expression change. She went on, "Somehow she'd gotten herself onto the edge there, and went over."

"How'd she get there?"

Glynis looked at Jacques, waiting for him to tell Cullen about the tunnel. Jacques said nothing.

But in the meantime, Cullen had stepped forward and extended his hand. "It's been a while, Jacques."

"Yeah." Jacques took Cullen's hand briefly. "A while."

Pippa squirmed against Glynis and gave a soft moan.

"We better tell her mother the girl's all right," Cullen said. "Wait around, will you, Jacques? Want to talk to you—I may need an extra deputy, the way things are going around here."

He lifted an oddly submissive Pippa from the wagon seat, and carried her off toward the house. Glynis wondered if he realized that Jacques hadn't answered him.

She waited until he was out of earshot to ask, "Do you think you'll accept Cullen's offer, Jacques?"

"No." Said without the least hesitation.

He went to the back of the wagon to untie his paint horse. Glynis climbed down and went toward him. He'd swung himself into the saddle and was looking down at her, about to say something, she was sure, when two women appeared, coming from the direction of the barn. Glynis recognized Small Brown Bird, then Bitter Root. She felt herself stiffen. What were they doing there?

Small Brown Bird stopped in front of Glynis, but Bitter Root brushed past her without a word. Before the woman climbed into the wagon, however, Glynis saw a veiled look pass between mother and son, a look that carried something disturbing; something Glynis interpreted as antagonism, at least on Bitter Root's part.

"Miss Tryon," Small Brown Bird said. "I didn't know you were here."

"I didn't know *you* were here, either," said Glynis, annoyed with herself for reacting so negatively to Bitter Root's presence. The older woman's obvious dislike of her didn't mean she'd done something to deserve it.

"We have been with the old Mr. Grimm," Small Brown Bird explained.

"How did you happen to be here tonight?" Glynis asked.

"The girl came for us after her grandfather was hurt."

"Pippa? Pippa went to the reservation—by herself?"

Glynis realized too late that her surprise might have sounded like mistrust.

Small Brown Bird seemed about to reply, but Bitter Root began to cough, and proceeded to choke out several unintelligible phrases. The younger woman quickly gave Glynis a shy smile before climbing into the wagon beside her sister. "Good night, Miss Tryon," was all Small Brown Bird said. She took the reins Bitter Root thrust at her, and flicked them over the horse's back.

Bitter Root looked over her shoulder at Jacques. She said a few short phrases to him, which were met with silence. With a jerk of her body, the woman turned from him to face front. And the wagon pulled away.

Jacques brought the paint to stand within a few feet of Glynis. Shivering now with cold she hadn't noticed before, she waited for him to say something. He gazed down at her; she raised her eyes to his and held them, until tension made her turn away. At last he said quietly, "You should stay away from here. Don't ask why."

Glynis swallowed her words; of course she'd been about to ask. Why *should* she stay away?

"At least tell me why you so flatly refuse Cullen's offer," she said.

"It's better you don't get mixed up in something you can't understand."

"That's not an answer, Jacques. Something strange—no, something diabolic—is happening in this town. I need to know if it in any way involves you; I feel that it does, even though I can't find a reason. But I never told Cullen how you appeared the night I found Mead Miller's body. Never told him I'd seen you at all. I—"

"Why?" he asked. "Why didn't you tell him?"

"I don't know. I don't even know why you *were* there. I don't know why you've come back to Seneca Falls, or why you won't take the deputy's job. Cullen needs you— there have been two murders, and maybe more." She could hear her voice rising, but couldn't stop herself. "I don't know why your mother's taken such a profound dislike to me—or why I even care about any of these things!"

But that wasn't true.

Jacques sat motionless, his eyes shadowed by darkness, and part of her urgently wanted to believe she could become indifferent to him if she chose. He suddenly leaned forward in the saddle. She saw his eyes harden into cold, glittering glass. Even his voice was hard when he said, "You should stay away from the reservation. Stay away from *me*. I don't want you hurt."

He turned the paint horse and rode off. He didn't look back.

A HALF MOON lit the road ahead of the carriage with pale light, and frost on tall dried thistles made them look to Glynis as if they'd been dusted with fine white flour.

Beside her Cullen flexed the reins and asked, "What d'you mean, Sundown said no to the job without any explanation?"

Teeth chattering, Glynis shook her head, then turned on the seat to look back at Abraham and Neva, following closely in a dray wagon that also carried Obadiah Grimm's body. Glynis pulled her share of the plaid carriage robe up to her chin, in a futile effort to keep from shaking with cold.

Cullen didn't press her further about Jacques, for which she was grateful. She couldn't talk about him. She didn't want to talk, period. It seemed like days since they'd driven out to the Grimms'. The final scene there, one that had ensued over the suggestion that a postmortem be performed on Obadiah, had left her, and, she assumed, everyone else drained.

She'd been surprised at Neva's dogged determination to take the body back to town that night. Molly and Lazarus had been equally opposed to it, he frowning and muttering about profanation and desecration and reincarnation. To Glynis's astonishment, Neva had replied, "If you had even the slightest knowledge of what you were talking about, you'd know that reincarnation means return of the soul in a *new* form. In which case, what happens to your father's present body is totally inconsequential."

In response to this, Molly had gasped, Cullen had scowled, Abraham sighed long and wearily, and Lazarus said simply, "Oh."

"In any event," Neva stated, "I'm not signing a death certificate until I satisfy myself as to what he died of."

Glynis, listening to Neva with mounting concern, had backed her without reservation. She felt she knew the young doctor well enough to be certain Neva's demand was not made capriciously. She must believe something was amiss. "And, Cullen," Glynis argued, "we've had more than our share of suspicious deaths lately."

The discussion continued at length, growing more and more acrimonious as Molly and Lazarus dug in their heels. They absolutely refused, they said, to allow their father's body to be moved anywhere but into consecrated ground.

"I'm not sure this is worth it," Cullen said in an aside to Glynis. "Give me one good reason why we can't wait until tomorrow, when I can get a court order for an autopsy."

"Because by tomorrow," Glynis responded, "they may already have buried him. Then you'll have to get an order to exhume him. And by that time . . . well, who knows?"

But Almira Grimm, who until then had looked totally disinterested, suddenly stunned them all. "Take him," she said to Neva. "Take him—it makes no difference."

"Exactly," Neva had said, whirling to face Cullen and Abraham, and motioning them toward Obadiah's body. "Strike while the iron's hot," she had whispered under her breath to Glynis. "No telling what that lady's going to do next."

And so, Glynis mused, here they were at close to midnight—a two-cart procession into Seneca Falls with the remains of a man who had avoided the town most of his life. She had no idea what Neva thought she'd find. But even Cullen had seemed impressed by her tenacity.

"She doesn't expect to do an autopsy tonight, does she?" he now asked.

"I expect so," Glynis said. "And if she wants to, do you think you can stop her?"

"No." Cullen shook his head. "Not for a minute!"

FOURTEEN

❦

*[Educated] girls come to marriage tired, and unequal to its
obligations . . . should pregnancy ensue, a big-headed child
and a narrow pelvis imperil her life and that of her offspring.*
—DR. WILLIAM GOODELL, C. 1850

RAIN MIXING WITH snow confronted Glynis the following
morning. She drew the hood of her black wool cape more
tightly around her face and, watching her feet, stepped cautiously to avoid thin patches of ice all but hidden in the ruts
of Fall Street. She'd nearly lost her footing several times,
though the ice came as no surprise; by the time the short
procession bearing Obadiah Grimm's body had arrived in
town the night before, the temperature had plummeted to
bone-chilling cold.

Receiving no response to her knocks on the Iveses' front
door, Glynis pushed it open, called out, then followed a flow
of warm air coming down the hall. Even before she reached
the back kitchen, she heard Cullen saying, ". . . and how
can you be sure?"

When Glynis approached the open doorway, she saw him
standing with arms crossed, leaning against the opposite
wall. He looked up and nodded to her distractedly. His gaze
then returned to Neva Cardoza, huddled in a chair directly
in front of the stove; black cast iron, the stove sat on four
curved feet near the central chimney of the house into which
it was vented.

Neva's hands were wrapped around a mug of steaming
coffee, coffee so strong that Glynis could smell it clear
across the room. She gave Glynis a brief half-smile before
she turned back to Cullen. "How can I be sure of *what*?"
Neva asked him. "If you mean how did I know someone
was lying, I suspected that even before I did the autopsy—
suspected it after I first examined Obadiah Grimm."

"So why didn't you say something when I got there?

Why wait until now?'' Cullen's question was put to her in a tight voice.

"Because I wasn't certain what I was looking for. I only knew there was a problem of logic with the family's story of Obadiah's fall, because they neglected to mention that he'd fallen *on* something. And I knew he must have—he sustained a punctured heart. And I found more than one wound.''

"Maybe they honestly didn't know,'' Glynis offered.

"That's what I first thought,'' Neva said. "But then I remembered that there was no sharp object near him when I got there. I checked the floor around him. Whatever he'd fallen on had been removed by the time I arrived—*if* he fell.''

"I still don't see why you suspected something was wrong right away,'' Cullen said, frowning.

"The wounds were in Obadiah's *chest*,'' Neva answered. "When I arrived, he was lying on his *back*. Now, when he fell, he either landed on his back—in which case, why the chest wounds?—or he landed facedown, somehow impaling himself on something. Something that should have been there, unless it had been removed. By someone.''

"How many chest wounds were there?'' Glynis asked.

"When Dr. Ives and I did the autopsy, we found three evenly spaced punctures, deep ones, including the one that pierced his heart.''

"Three . . . evenly spaced?'' Cullen repeated. "You mean''—he paused—"you mean caused by something like a pitchfork?''

"Something *exactly* like a pitchfork,'' Neva responded.

Glynis cringed at the image this aroused. "But that would seem to indicate,'' she said slowly, "that if Obadiah fell from the hayloft and landed facedown, impaling himself on the fork, then someone subsequently rolled him over and pulled it out . . .''

"And deliberately didn't tell me,'' Neva finished. "I say it was deliberate because I certainly asked, a number of times, if anyone knew what happened. The impression they all gave was that Grimm had been alone when he fell.''

"But obviously,'' Cullen said, "he couldn't have been,

at least not for long. Not unless he pulled out the fork himself and then . . .''

"Then wiped it clean and hung it back up with the other tools," Neva said with a sardonic smile. "And the pitchfork hanging in the barn had no blood on it. I checked."

"A farm that size surely would have more than one," Glynis said, frowning. "Why couldn't that particular pitchfork have been removed from the barn altogether? And who first discovered Obadiah, do we know that?"

"Billy Wicken told me he did," Cullen said.

"Was he alone?" Glynis asked. "Did Billy say he was alone when he found Obadiah?"

"That's what he said." Cullen's expression implied doubt. He turned to Neva. "Maybe he was afraid to tell you he'd removed the pitchfork. Could have thought that by doing it he'd made Obadiah's situation worse, and didn't want to own up to it."

"That's possible," Glynis agreed. "And he might have been reluctant to say anything about that in front of the family members. Did either of you ask him later, when he was by himself?"

Both Cullen and Neva shook their heads.

Glynis thought for a moment; it just didn't feel right. "No," she said, finally, "I don't believe that's what happened. Because if Billy had removed the pitchfork, why on earth would he wipe the tines clean and hang it back up? Unless . . . unless he thought he needed to protect someone."

"Or needed to protect himself?" Neva added.

Glynis and Cullen stared at her. Cullen spoke first. "You mean you think Billy speared Grimm with that fork on purpose? Meant to kill him?"

Neva lifted her shoulders in a small shrug. "Could be."

Glynis shook her head. "No, wait a minute. We're all three of us assuming the fork was removed by someone living there at the farm. What if it was someone else entirely? Someone who left immediately afterward and—"

She broke off abruptly. Jacques Sundown had been at the Grimms'—and she didn't know when he'd arrived. But he could have come with his mother and aunt when Pippa fetched them. Meaning *after* Billy had found Obadiah. That would make sense. With night coming, Jacques wouldn't have let the women go alone to the farm, so he'd ridden along with their wagon. Then something else struck her. Would Molly have let Pippa go for the medicine woman in the first place? Surely not. But if Pippa had used the underground tunnel to leave the house unseen, as she'd done later that night, Molly wouldn't have known.

"Glynis?" Cullen was frowning at her. "Glynis, I said, have you got any ideas about who might have had reason to kill Obadiah?"

Glynis said nothing, just shook her head. Something else was now bothering her, but she couldn't put her finger on it.

Cullen turned to Neva. "You?"

"No, I don't. But you do realize, Constable, that this is the third autopsy I've performed where the cause of death—"

"Yes!" Cullen's tone was harsh with annoyance. "Yes, of course I realize it. And, as the newspapers have trumpeted, I'm no closer to finding out who killed Jack Turner and Mead Miller than I was before this happened to Obadiah. Common sense tells me the first two deaths were connected in some way, but I'm damned if I can see how. If *you* can, I wish you'd say."

Apparently startled by Cullen's request, Neva's face lost its look of indignation. "Well, I can't, Constable. Arsenic in wine, snake venom delivered by dart, and pitchfork impalement—where could be the link?" she said, looking with question at Glynis. "Maybe there is no connection."

"I think there is," Glynis said. "Perhaps the very fact that the means of murder have been so dissimiliar, and also unusual, is a link in and of itself. Didn't you once tell me, Cullen, that in a series of murders committed by the same person, a pattern usually can be found?"

Cullen nodded. "Not that there's been all that many, at least not in this country."

"You mean that have been uncovered," Neva inserted. "After all, autopsies aren't performed that often, not without reasonable cause. And doctors haven't known how to identify most poisons, not absolutely, until this century—even this decade. So who knows how many there may have been?''

''Yes,'' Glynis agreed, ''and that's why these are so fiendishly clever. If Jack Turner hadn't alerted you, Cullen, you wouldn't have looked for anything suspicious when he died. The same was true of Mead Miller. Now there's Obadiah . . . and Jake Braun, who says *he's* going to be killed. But neither Jack Turner nor Jake would give you any explanation for their fear. Why? It seems fairly clear that if we could find the reason, we might find the murderer.''

''Well, it's not me,'' announced Abraham Levy as he entered the kitchen. ''I wouldn't know the first thing about poisoning someone.''

''You have a point,'' Glynis said to him.

Neva rose from the chair. ''I'll be ready to go in a minute,'' she told Abraham. She left the room, studiously ignoring Cullen's raised eyebrows.

''We'd best hurry. The train leaves in thirty minutes!'' Abraham called after her.

Cullen's eyebrows went higher. ''The train?'' he repeated.

Abraham obviously struggled not to smile. ''My monthly buying trip to Rochester,'' he said. ''The good doctor wanted to come along and see the new hospital that's just opened. A former medical professor of hers wrote to say a doctor's there that Neva might want to meet. He's supposed to be an expert on poison.''

''That's a piece of good luck,'' Glynis said, throwing Cullen a hopeful look. ''And there's a hospital?'' Her sister Gwen, in Rochester, had been complaining for years about the lack of such a facility. ''Who's opened it?'' she asked Abraham.

''Truthfully, I don't think it's much of a hospital,'' Abraham said. ''A woman named Hieronymo O'Brien—she's a nun with the Catholic Sisters of Charity—has opened it. And I hear it's just a couple of old, abandoned sheds.''

''I'm eager to meet this nun,'' Neva said, returning to the kitchen with a dark red wool cloak over her shoulders. ''Mr. Levy says she's caring for fifty or sixty people there.''

She and Abraham started for the door. But Neva looked back over her shoulder to say, "If you should need me, Constable Stuart, I'll be returning this evening. I just hope there's no occasion for another autopsy!"

She called good-bye to Glynis, who could then hear Neva's heels clicking lightly down the porch stairs, followed by the more substantial thump of Abraham's boots. Having detected in Neva's voice a certain unfamiliar lilt, Glynis glanced with a smile at Cullen, who stood staring after the departing pair with an expression of disbelief. He'd started to say something when the sound of boots running up the stairs stopped him. Someone banged on the door several times before it flew open, and Zeph Waters rushed inside.

The young deputy's face looked stricken. "Constable . . . Constable Stuart, I'm really sorry."

"You know, you're getting to be a regular standard-bearer of bad tidings, aren't you, Zeph? What's the matter now?" Cullen asked him.

Zeph stared at the floor, then took a deep breath and gazed at Cullen with an expression of abject misery. "It's Jake Braun, Constable Stuart. He's escaped." Following Cullen's explosive expletive, Zeph swallowed hard several times. "It's my fault, sir, and I still don't know exactly what happened, but . . . he's gone!"

"What d'you mean, you don't know what happened?" Cullen said with unconcealed exasperation.

Zeph shook his head. On the left side of his face, Glynis now saw a large angry-looking bruise. "What about your face, Zeph?" she asked. "Did Jake Braun do that to you?"

The boy looked so ashamed, Glynis was sorry she'd asked.

"C'mon, Zeph," ordered Cullen, "spit it out. How did Braun get away?"

"He . . . that is, I took him out to the privy like he asked. He'd just started to go inside, when the door flew open and caught me on the side of my head. Next thing I knew, I was lying on the ground and . . . and the prisoner was gone."

Cullen sighed deeply. "All right, Zeph. Can't be helped now. Braun was just waiting for the opportunity, and besides, I couldn't have held him much longer anyway without charging him. But, Deputy,'' he said sternly, ''I hope you learned something from this.''

Zeph, his expression now unmistakably one of relief, nodded vigorously. ''Yeah, let the prisoners shit in their trousers . . . Oh, I'm *sorry,* Miss Tryon!''

With difficulty, Glynis kept her face straight, while Cullen scowled darkly. ''No, that's not what I meant, Zeph! Keep a safe distance from the prisoners at all times, that's what you should have learned. And clean up your language!''

Clearly chastened, Zeph nodded again.

''Well,'' Cullen said to Glynis, ''I guess we'll just have to hope Jake Braun was wrong about somebody wanting to kill him.''

''You're not going after him?''

''Can't go chasing after a man without a reasonable charge—and I didn't hear you offering to place one against Braun. So to hell with him—he's on his own!''

IN THE WATERLOO courthouse, attorney Jeremiah Merrycoyf stood quietly before the bench of Seneca County judge Thaddeus Heath. While Judge Heath read over the legal papers Merrycoyf had presented him, the lawyer glanced at his client, who fidgeted beside him; Lazarus Grimm certainly hadn't wasted any time. His father had been dead a little less than twenty-four hours, and here he was, petitioning for appointment as administrator of Obadiah's estate.

''Mr. Merrycoyf,'' said Judge Heath, putting down the papers at last. ''It is stated here that Obadiah Grimm, the petitioner's father, died intestate. Without a will. Is that true to the best of your knowledge, sir?''

''Yes, Your Honor,'' Merrycoyf replied. ''The late Mr. Grimm had been my client, in matters involving real estate, for a number of years. Although I tried to persuade him otherwise, he repeatedly told me he saw no reason for a will.''

No reason to spend his money drawing one up, was what the tightfisted Obadiah really meant, Merrycoyf thought.

Judge Heath nodded. He picked up two sheets of paper and brandished them at Merrycoyf. ''These waivers from the next of kin—the wife, Almira, and the daughter,

Molly—were obtained without coercion on the part of the petitioner?''

"Oh, *no*, Your Honor!" Lazarus burst out. "I would never—''

"I'm not asking you, Mr. Grimm, I'm asking your lawyer," interrupted Judge Heath.

Ah, thought Merrycoyf, my client's reputation precedes him. But Molly Grimm and her mother had agreed to the waivers without a murmur. "No, Your Honor," Merrycoyf answered. "Both, to my knowledge, signed willingly."

"But why the rush here?" said the judge, scowling. "Obadiah Grimm hasn't even been buried yet, has he?"

"No, he hasn't. And this *is* an unusual circumstance," Merrycoyf agreed. "However, my understanding is that the Grimm family's crop of cabbage has been loaded onto a canal boat, and is now waiting to be transported to market in New York City. Before the load can leave, the boatman is demanding an authorized signature. And the canal is due to be drained any day now for the winter, Your Honor."

The judge nodded, apparently satisfied with Merrycoyf's explanation, and now addressed Lazarus Grimm. "I suppose," Judge Heath said, "that since under the law the estate of your father is to be divided among his surviving spouse—that is, your mother—Almira and his two children—yourself and your sister—which one of you is appointed doesn't matter that much."

"Yes, Your Honor," Lazarus replied. "But I consider myself well qualified to be the administrator."

At this, Judge Heath peered down at him with a skeptical expression, while Merrycoyf found himself wishing his client would keep his mouth shut. He then realized the judge had transferred his gaze from Lazarus to him.

"Mr. Merrycoyf," asked Judge Heath, "is there an issue of other surviving heirs?"

"As submitted in the petition, Your Honor," Merrycoyf answered.

"Very well. The request of the petitioner, Lazarus Grimm, is granted."

"Thank you, Your Honor," Merrycoyf said. Beside him, Lazarus smiled broadly at Judge Heath and seemed determined to comment further, but Merrycoyf took firm hold of the man's arm and turned him around. As he then nudged Lazarus somewhat ungently toward the center aisle, a clerk brushed by them on his way forward to the judge's bench.

"Judge Heath, sir," panted the clerk, "there is a request for a restraining order from the young gentleman attorney in the back of the room. He is quite insistent on being heard, Your Honor."

Merrycoyf looked toward the rear of the courtroom, where, to his surprise, he saw Adam MacAlistair dashing up the aisle with several rolls of paper under his arm.

As he went by, Adam shot Merrycoyf a cryptic look. But he kept on going, straight to the front of the room, saying to Judge Heath, "If the Court please, Your Honor, my name is Adam MacAlistair and . . . and with your permission, sir, may I approach the bench? Sir?"

"This is very irregular, young man," Judge Heath growled. "I don't believe you are listed on today's docket. In fact, I know you're not. Mr. Merrycoyf's was to be my last case."

"No, sir. That is, I mean, yes, sir—I'm not scheduled today. But if you will allow me to proceed, I think Your Honor will understand the reason for my . . . my irregular conduct, as it's a matter of some urgency. If you please, sir."

Merrycoyf had paused halfway down the aisle to observe Adam MacAlistair's less than refined approach. But his face carried such earnest appeal that Merrycoyf thought he himself would have found it difficult to deny the young lawyer a hearing. And Judge Heath, although ordinarily not noted for his charity, apparently was of like mind.

"Mr. MacAlistair, I trust this will not take long?"

"No, sir, not long at all."

"Very well. Proceed."

Merrycoyf suddenly remembered his client, and turned to find Lazarus Grimm standing directly behind him. "Mr. Grimm, I'd like to stay and listen to my young colleague present what will be his first case. If you don't mind." Merrycoyf avoided the possible objection from Lazarus by immediately seating himself.

He needn't have worried. He saw that Lazarus Grimm, too, had been watching the proceedings with curiosity and now slid into a chair readily enough beside Merrycoyf.

"... and proceed forthwith, Mr. MacAlistair," Judge Heath was saying.

"Yes, sir," Adam said as he finished unrolling on a table what appeared to Merrycoyf to be plat maps and deeds and titles that he'd carried forward with him. Adam straightened and said to the judge, "Your Honor, sir, I am applying for a restraining order on behalf of my client—my client who is a business owner in the village of Seneca Falls."

Merrycoyf nodded approvingly. Smart lad—don't reveal your client's name yet, not if the judge doesn't ask. Serenity Hathaway's lively establishment was surely known here in Waterloo if not through all of western New York.

"Yes, yes, Mr. MacAlistair," Judge Heath said. "Do get on with it."

"Yes, sir. My client, sir, is seeking an order that would prohibit certain people from exploiting the land on which the business is located."

"On what grounds is this order sought, Mr. MacAlistair?"

"Unlawful trespass, Your Honor," answered Adam. This said confidently, Merrycoyf noted, without a moment's hesitation. At least the young man had stopped stammering; in fact, MacAlistair seemed to be warming to his task. Unfortunately, it was difficult to see how he could possibly argue unlawful trespass. On a public road!

"Where is your client's business situated?" Judge Heath asked.

"Between the Seneca–Cayuga Canal and West Bayard Street, Your Honor."

The judge pulled himself upright in his chair. "Between Bayard Street and the canal?" Judge Heath leaned over the bench to peer down at the young attorney. "Perhaps you'd better tell me, young man—just what is your client's business?"

"A tavern, Your Honor. My client is a tavern owner."

Judge Heath nodded, his eyes narrowing. "And this tavern's name?"

"Serenity's, sir, and I should like the court to—"

"Just a minute! Am I correct in assuming that there is but one tavern in Seneca Falls called Serenity's?"

"Yes, sir, you are correct."

"Well, young man, I know the place in question, and—" Seeming to realize what he'd just inferred, Judge Heath quickly rephrased. "That is, I know the tavern and its owner by reputation. What reason could there be for asking relief against unlawful trespass? That tavern is notorious, Mr. MacAlistair, for its unrestricted access to those who wish to partake of gambling and alcoholic spirits and depraved behavior."

"But, Your Honor," Adam said firmly, "gambling and alcohol are not illegal. And yet there are those who wish to inhibit what you so rightly referred to as the tavern's previously unrestricted access."

Merrycoyf hid his grin behind a pudgy hand. And now what would Judge Heath do? Step into a quagmire by describing the activities *other* than gambling that took place at Serenity's? Just how would the good judge know about them? Young MacAlistair, despite his inexperience, had thus far played his hand shrewdly.

Judge Heath again peered down at the lawyer, and abandoned his previous line of questioning. "And what exactly does this trespass consist of, to which the owner of the tavern is objecting?"

"A hostile and disruptive mob of women who are parading in offensive fashion in front of my client's place of business, Your Honor. My client wants her property protected by an order prohibiting this activity."

"Be more specific," Judge Heath demanded.

"Miss Hathaway's business is such that potential customers are being discouraged—no, inhibited—from entering the premises."

"Indeed. Are you telling me, Mr. MacAlistair, that these little women are actually preventing grown men—"

"They are intimidating customers, yes, that's correct, Your Honor."

Judge Heath studied the earnest face before him as if seeking a wolf beneath the young man's impeccably tailored

wool suit. Apparently not succeeding, the judge said briskly,
"And just what is this female mob parading *on,* Mr.
MacAlistair—not thin air, surely, so it must be the street.
And Bayard Street is a *public thoroughfare,* young man."

Merrycoyf shifted in his chair and sighed regretfully.

"Yes, sir, Your Honor," Adam said. "Yes, Bayard Street
is a public thoroughfare. However, Bayard Street does not
run directly in front of the tavern. And the small dirt access
road that is off Bayard, and *does* front the tavern, is *not* a
public right-of-way."

"Can you demonstrate that?" said Judge Heath, his cold
blue eyes skeptical. But Merrycoyf straightened and leaned
forward.

Adam turned quickly, gathered the maps and deeds from
the table, and handed them up to the judge. "As you can
see from that deed, Your Honor, the dirt road in question
has been in use for only fifteen years—not for the twenty
years that legally is required to designate it a public thoroughfare."

Merrycoyf smiled as Judge Heath examined the plat
maps, and scrutinized what looked to be title to the land on
which the tavern sat. In the meantime, Adam stepped back
and sank into a chair in the front row. But not before he
sent Merrycoyf a long look across the room. Merrycoyf
could not precisely translate this look, but thought it might
ask: How am I doing? In reply, Merrycoyf simply nodded.
Anything more not only would have been unseemly, but
could encourage Mr. MacAlistair to let down his guard. And
this wasn't over yet.

Adam MacAlistair sprang to his feet as Judge Heath put
down the maps. "Young man," the judge said, "I must
admit your exhibits are fairly persuasive. Therefore, if you
want the public barred from using the tavern's dirt access
road, I can grant that."

Almost, Merrycoyf could hear what must be Adam's silent groan, and he wondered if Judge Heath might be testing
the young man's mettle. This judge was no recluse; he unquestionably knew of the recent law requiring taverns to be
licensed, and so could likely guess why the women were
demonstrating. And Heath also probably guessed that

Adam's tactics were delaying ones.

Lazarus Grimm, who, with eyes closed, had appeared to be snoozing, made a small motion with his hand. "What's going on?" he asked Merrycoyf softly. Merrycoyf whispered a brief explanation, while Adam MacAlistair recovered himself.

"Sir," Adam said, after a period of searching the ceiling, possibly for divine guidance. "Sir, Miss Hathaway does not want to bar *all* the public from using that road, certainly not her good cash-paying customers."

"I see. And just how," Judge Heath interposed, "am I to decide whom to restrict? Not being a total fool, Mr. MacAlistair, I am aware that Miss Hathaway does not wish males prohibited from accessing her establishment, however, does she expect all those of the opposite sex to be denied access?" He paused a moment to study Adam. "And," Heath then went on, "considering the nature of Miss Hathaway's business and particularly the gender of those whom she employs, does restricting females seem a plausible solution to you, Mr. MacAlistair?"

"No, sir, it does not," Adam responded quickly. "But my client, Your Honor, has a legal right that is being violated, and she asks for an injunction to prohibit specifically the aforementioned protesters from using *her* road for their dubious activity. Therefore," he said, whipping a folded document from his coat pocket, "I have taken the liberty of preparing such an order for your approval. If I may?"

Judge Heath quickly stifled a startled reaction, and said, "Yes, yes, hand it up here."

Scanning for some time the document Adam gave him, the judge said, "You propose, by way of a permanent injunction, to expressly prohibit Miss Susan Brownell Anthony, as well as members of the Women's State Temperance Society *and* their associates, from entering upon the lands owned by Miss Serenity Hathaway. Well, well."

Judge Heath looked down at the upright, clean-shaven, sober face of the young attorney. "Mr. MacAlistair, since this is your first appearance before me, I assume you are new to the practice of law. I warn you, sir, do not again strain the patience of this court by appearing unannounced.

"However, while I deplore your choice of client, young man, you *have* demonstrated sufficient cause for me to grant your restraining order. But only a temporary one, as the women have the right to respond and be heard, if they so wish. In the meantime, two exact duplicates of this order are to be prepared: one to be served on Miss Anthony, and one to be delivered to the constable of Seneca Falls, forthwith."

Judge Heath stood abruptly and immediately exited the courtroom. Adam MacAlistair stood quietly for a moment, staring after him, then whipped around to face Merrycoyf. He looked, the older lawyer thought, as the young Alexander might have, following his first military victory. The jubilant glow was near-blinding. Merrycoyf closed his eyes, remembering his own first courtroom triumph, and he suddenly felt very tired. Very tired and very old.

Perhaps it was time to step aside.

FIFTEEN

❦

Intreat me not to leave thee, or to return from following after thee: for whither thou goest I will go; and where thou lodgest I will lodge; thy people shall be my people, and thy God my God.

— *THE BOOK OF RUTH*, 1:16

ALTHOUGH MUCH OF the view from the train window had been obscured by thick, rainy mist, Neva found the trip from Seneca Falls to Rochester an enlightening one. Abraham Levy had given her an unrequested but nonetheless engaging history of the Jewish community in the city on the Genesee River.

Of German and English extraction, the first Jews in Rochester arrived during the 1840s wave of westward migration. Come as transient peddlers from New England and New York City, they found Rochester a receptive town, and settled in to become clerks and grocers and jewelers or, more often, clothing merchants. And by now, Abraham told her, the Jewish community consisted of some nine hundred persons. After years of holding their religious meetings in the third story of a rented hall, the Congregation Berith Kodesh had recently acquired its own synagogue.

Somewhere toward the end of Abraham's narrative, accompanied by the rocking motion of the train, Neva had dozed off. She jerked herself awake to discover him smiling down at her, apparently not in the least offended.

No, Abraham was not like her father. This man's warm, pleasant voice, his smell of wood shavings and pipe tobacco, his solid shoulder pressing against her own, made her feel what she could only describe as contented—inadequate as that description might be. But truly she was lost for words, as it was an entirely unfamiliar sensation. And this made her question just how long she had been angry. Perhaps anger was not something bred in the Cardoza bones, as she had believed. Perhaps it was more like a fracture that refused to knit—one that required continuous nursing by each member of the family. No wonder they were all miserable—they were all exhausted! Since she'd never considered this before, to do so now felt somehow disloyal, even a shade dangerous. Because her father had taught that if one became too contented, too happy, one also might become complacent. And thus ripe for catastrophe. A Jew, he had said, must be forever vigilant.

"Watch out!" Abraham shouted now, just as Neva stepped off a Rochester sidewalk into a gutter filled with rainwater. His arm curled around her waist, lifted her effortlessly, then set her down on higher ground. He grinned, and raised the black umbrella again over their heads although the rain had become only a light sprinkle. His arm remained around her waist.

"Wet feet, I imagine," he said, looking down at her lightweight boots. "Have to keep your eyes open."

"Yes, I know," Neva agreed. And was immediately surprised at herself for not snapping that she *had* been looking. "I guess I've gotten used to having no real sidewalks at home." At *home*? Why on earth would she describe Seneca Falls as "home"?

Abraham gave her a sideways glance. "I'd have thought you'd be used to cities."

"Oh, I am, and Rochester is . . . well, it's not as big as New York, of course, but it has much the same feel, the same dirt and disorder, everybody and everything moving constantly."

"Have you missed that?" Abraham released his grip on her waist to take her arm, as they moved onto the bridge crossing the Erie Canal.

Neva found she couldn't answer him. If he meant did she miss the fleas and cockroaches and rats that were one with life in every big city, like the squalor and the clamor that never ceased—well, no, she didn't. If it meant did she miss her father's and brothers' endless shouting at her to be something, anything, other than what she was—she didn't miss that, either. She *did* miss her mother. And her cousin Ernestine Rose.

She felt a gentle tug on her arm, and looked up into Abraham's face. "Did you hear what I said?" he asked, his steps slowing.

"Yes, I heard. I just don't know how to answer."

He looked strangely relieved. "I thought maybe you were homesick—all the time."

Voices broke through the gray mist, and they saw a number of people hurrying toward them; always rushing somewhere, strangers were another ubiquitous element of big cities. Neva and Abraham moved to the railing of the bridge to let the others pass. Neva watched them, the anonymous people, then gazed down at the partially drained canal.

"No," she said to him then, "actually I'm not homesick. I thought I would be. And I admit I expected to hate Seneca Falls. I believed that, isolated as I was out here in the hinterland, all of life that was worthwhile would pass me by. But now," she said carefully, "I'm not so certain."

Abraham made a small sound, and looked down at her with a sort of shine in his eyes that made her flush and turn away. "How much farther is this hospital?" she asked, mainly to divert his gaze.

"Not much farther," he said, letting out a long breath that smelled like the peppermints he liked so much. "But I hope you won't be too disappointed in the place."

Disappointed was not the word, Neva thought, when they reached the corner of Genesee and Brown Street, and what optimistically proclaimed itself on a small sign to be St. Mary's Hospital. A dilapidated woodshed, its roof sagging precariously, connected two small stables. Rags and straw had been stuffed into several broken windows, and mud oozed against the foundation stones. Planks lay over the mud as far as the shed door, but this improvised walk had sunk nearly out of sight. From the corner of her eye, Neva caught something grayish brown skittering under the straw, and she recoiled against Abraham's chest.

He pulled her back, saying, "It looks worse than I'd expected. Why don't we just leave?"

"No," Neva protested. "I want to see how they can call this wretched place a hospital."

"Sure'n it's not what it's called that counts," came a voice from the doorway. "And who might you be?"

Neva and Abraham exchanged an embarrassed glance, then went forward as a small woman in black nun's habit stepped to the plank walk. A white wimple covered her head to frame a round face and hide the ears that presumably supported the wires of her thick-lensed spectacles. Although the nun's face seemed pleasant enough, she appeared to be examining them rather closely.

Neva quickly introduced herself and Abraham. If the nun, who then identified herself as Sister Hieronymo O'Brien, was surprised to see two Jews at her establishment, she concealed it well.

"I'm a doctor," Neva explained, "from Seneca Falls." She started to correct herself and say New York City, but went on instead to explain further, "We don't have a hospital there, of course, and I'd like to look around. Would that be permissible?"

Sister Hieronymo, now smiling, said, "Oh, and I thank the good Lord it's not sick you are! We're full up. But sure'n you can look to your heart's content, my girl. And your gentleman friend, if he's of a mind, can wait in the kitchen."

The kitchen proved to be the ground floor of one of the stables, equipped with only one woodstove for both heat and cooking. Sister Hieronymo apparently saw Abraham studying with a puzzled expression the stove lids placed at intervals along the walls, because she sighed, "They're to keep out the rats, though the creatures come in just the same."

Neva and the nun left Abraham, and walked to the ground floor of the second stable, which housed the female patients; the loft over the kitchen of the other stable held the men, Sister Hieronymo explained. Neva counted perhaps twenty-five women on mattresses spread on the uneven wood floor. At the far end of the room, a man with stethoscope around his neck sat writing at a wobbly table. He eased his considerable bulk from a small wooden chair and stood, becoming perhaps the tallest man Neva had ever seen; he must be at least six and a half foot tall, she decided, and she put his weight at three hundred or more pounds. He didn't look obese, just big!

"Patrick Kelly at your service, Miss," he boomed, voice like a tympani. A few heads on the mattresses turned to look at Neva with dull-eyed apathy.

Sister Hieronymo laughed, a tinkle of sound that rang incongruously in the surroundings. "Not just 'Miss,' Patrick, but also 'doctor,' like yourself."

"Indeed. And where did you train, Miss Doctor?" He held out a huge paw of a hand.

Neva had to smile. That which might have sounded patronizing from another man had, from this one, a buoyant friendliness; he didn't intend to belittle her. And something suddenly shifted inside her, as if a long-carried burden had been eased. She gave Dr. Patrick Kelly her hand. When he gripped it, his hand completely enveloped hers.

"I trained in Philadelphia," she said, "at the—"

"Female Medical College, on Arch Street," Patrick Kelly said for her, smiling. "I know one of its founders, Joseph Longshore—he was a professor of mine."

"Yes, I know that," Neva responded. "And you also went to medical school there in Philadelphia. I've heard about you, you see."

A loud rap from directly below them sent Sister Hieronymo to the head of the rickety stairs. "I'll be leaving you, then," she called over her shoulder. "Young doctor wants to look 'round, Patrick—see to it, if you please."

At least an hour, maybe more, had passed, Neva realized, before she and Patrick Kelly descended to the kitchen. In front of the stove, feet up on a stool, Abraham sat reading Rochester's *Times-Union* newspaper. On the large table beside him lay a hammer and screwdriver and pliers, along with various items like a bucket handle that obviously had just been repaired. And Neva saw, too, that the room's broken windowpane had been replaced with new glass.

The outside door opened, and Sister Hieronymo bustled in, followed by a middle-aged nun, both of them with armloads of kindling.

"The kindness of people!" Sister Hieronymo remarked, putting down the wood. "Young carpenter left us this—and

him not a Catholic, either.'' She smiled at Abraham as he
got up to stack the kindling. The nun moved to the stove,
reaching for a long-handled spoon with which to stir the
soup simmering in a tin kettle. Whatever ingredients the
kettle held smelled delicious, Neva noted with relief; Patrick
Kelly had told her that when the hospital opened, several
weeks before, the main food supply had been water thick-
ened with flour.

"So what is it you think now, Dr. Cardoza?" asked Sister
Hieronymo, stirring her soup with relish. "We're not quite
so fancy as your New York hospital?"

Neva, helping the others stack the kindling beside the
stove, didn't know quite what to say. "I'm sure, Sister,"
she answered cautiously, "that when Rochester sees what
you're doing here, you'll soon have a splendid hospital."

Patrick Kelly smiled. "Good lass—just the right thing to
say. And it's true."

Abraham had returned to his chair at the table and, Neva
sensed uneasily, was studying her. Had he begun to understand that she couldn't be what she feared he wanted? He
had feelings for her, she knew that. But had those feelings
begun to wane, seeing her here with sick and diseased people, in surroundings that were not what he thought a woman's should be? And, as if to confirm this, he now rose
abruptly.

"We should be leaving," he said.

Sister Hieronymo turned from the stove, her eyes behind
the spectacles shrewdly measuring him, and Neva wondered
if the woman could be having the same thought she herself
had just had. But the nun said nothing to Abraham beyond
thanking him for the repairs. She then turned to ask Neva,
"Will you be having a proper clinic in Seneca Falls one of
these days?"

Neva lifted her shoulders in a shrug. "I'd be satisfied to
begin with just a simple shelter for mistreated or abandoned
women and their children."

"Ah, yes," Sister Hieronymo nodded. "Well, then, like
us all, you'll be needing the Lord's help for that. I'll ask
Him."

Neva smiled. "And it also takes money, but where to get it?"

"From those who most need to give it!" the nun said.

Neva had started to ask what she meant, when Abraham walked purposefully to the door. He had been more than patient, Neva recognized, and pulled her cloak around her. She said to Patrick Kelly, "When you write Dr. Thorndyke, you'll please ask him about what we talked of earlier—the snake venom?"

Abraham's eyes widened in question. "Snake venom?"

"Dr. Thorndyke studied under Robert Christison—the man I told you wrote that book on poisons," Neva said to him. "And Dr. Kelly here studied with Thorndyke."

Patrick Kelly nodded. "I'll ask him for certain. It sounds a bad lot you have there in Seneca Falls."

"You mean our quiet little town, where there's a murderer running loose?" Abraham said dryly. He opened the door.

NEVA HAD REFUSED to go to synagogue with Abraham. She had declined to meet Rochester's new rabbi, Isaac Mayer, or members of the Hebrew Benevolent Society to which Abraham belonged. Neither could she consider attending a dance and entertainment to be held later that evening, sponsored by the city's Jewish community. But he was most certainly free to go if he wished.

She now sat waiting for him at a table by the window of a small tearoom. It was several blocks from the former Tabernacle Baptist Church, where Congregation Berith Kodesh had newly located. The church had been purchased a year before, Abraham told her, despite Conservative opposition to the fact that there was no means in the former church for separation of the sexes. Women could not be properly segregated from men, it was argued, with simply an aisle between them.

"Oh, yes, that's right!" Neva said. "You men are so afraid you'll be contaminated by women."

"That's not the reason," Abraham replied. "Why are you so angry with your religion?"

"It's not *my* religion," Neva snapped. "I renounced it."

"You can't!" Abraham snapped back. "You were *born* a Jew. You can't just decide you're not Jewish."

"Can't I? Apparently you haven't been listening!"

They had argued all the way up Main Street. The earlier mood of closeness had been shattered by the time they climbed from the horse-drawn cab, and Abraham had stalked off to temple.

Neva fidgeted now in her chair and ordered another pot of tea. She would not recant her position. She had heard too often that her father, like other Jewish men, offered thanks every morning for having not been born a woman. She had listened to her cousin, Ernestine Rose, tick off on bejeweled fingers the inequities that existed, and would probably always exist, between Jewish men and their women. Neva wanted no part of it. Absolutely no part. No, not even a dance. It had been this last that sent Abraham steaming out of the tearoom into the rain. Well, let him steam!

She lifted something like her fifth cup of tea to her lips, determined to overcome the tears that threatened. If he didn't reappear soon, she would walk to the railroad station by herself. If something terrible happened to her—well, so be it. The high and mighty Mr. Abraham Levy could have that on his conscience!

But what if something had happened to him? She gripped the cup, then set it down, splashing tea into the saucer and onto the tablecloth. Hardly noticing it, she stared out at the wet street.

When, splashing through a downpour, he at last appeared outside the window, then came in the door, streaming water like a wet spaniel, she upset her cup of tea completely in her haste to get to him. Ignoring glances from the tearoom's other patrons, she drew him by the hand back to the table.

"Woman," he said wearily, just standing there, looking at her, "I don't know. I just don't know."

Neva pulled him down, still dripping, into the chair beside her. "I'm sorry," she said. "I'm truly sorry that I am such a trial to you, Abraham."

He brushed back curly wet hair from his eyes, gazing at her with such hope that her chest ached. "But," she said fiercely, ''I cannot be what I am not. I cannot say I believe what I do not.''

''You are a Jew,'' Abraham whispered, just as fiercely.

''All right! Have it your way. But I will never set foot again in a synagogue. I will never consider myself to be of a 'second sex,' inferior to men. Never, Abraham! Do you know how I had to fight to go to medical school? My brothers could go anywhere they liked, do what they liked. My father encouraged them, supported them, told them they were children he could be proud of. But me? No. Don't ask me to become a good Jewish girl, Abraham Levy—I can't!'' Hot tears streaked down her face.

Abraham reached across the table and grasped her hand. He held it tightly when she tried to pull away.

''We must try to understand each other,'' he said, the patience in his voice so profound that Neva wanted to throw something at him.

''Why must we?'' she choked. ''We *can't* understand each other, so what is the use of trying? Why?''

''Because,'' he said, ''I love you.''

Sixteen

❦

It is the custom of Indians when scouting, or on private expeditions, to step carefully and where no impression of their feet can be left—shunning wet or muddy ground.
—James Everett Seaver, *A Narrative
of the Life of Mary Jemison: The
White Woman of the Genesee*

JAKE BRAUN, SLOUCHED in the rocking chair, groaned fitfully. He twitched in nightmare, legs jerking in running motions, before he opened his eyes; with a start, he grabbed the Jennings rifle lying across his knees and leaped to the farmhouse window. An empty whiskey bottle rolled noisily across the floor and, as if he had left behind his ghost, the vacant chair continued to rock. At the window he peered out, then dropped to a crouch.

He positioned the rifle, his thumb ready on the hammer, and looked out into the gray dawn. Nothing stirred, not even the dry weeds. His glance went then to the door of the kitchen, latched and barricaded behind a chest of drawers. The door hadn't moved. He looked again through the window, then stood, and lowered the rifle slowly to his side.

"Damn it—damn it all to hell!" He rubbed his reddened eyes with a fist, then ran his fingers over the stubble on his chin.

"Gotta git outta here," he muttered to himself, and crossed to the opposite window, where a tin washbasin rested on the sill. He leaned over the basin to look out, then scowled when he saw that the narrow window was open several inches. Had he left it that way? He couldn't remember checking it the night before. "Can't think straight—gotta git outta here."

He squinted into the wavy glass hanging from a nail rusted into the window frame. "Gotta clean up, git out."

He hoisted a bucket of water from the floor, scooped out a few floating insects, and emptied it into the basin. Stripping off a grimy shirt, he grabbed the cake of soap on the sill.

After rinsing his arms and chest, only a milky film of soap on his face remained, and he reached for the straight razor. But his hand paused in midair—had that been a sound outside? He jerked forward to see out, then raced across the room to the other window.

Nothing. No telltale grass waving, no strange noises, nothing. He was spooked, was all. Hearing things. Hell, why wouldn't he be? He shoulda went when Turner got it. No—shoulda sold out and went when Dooley Keegan got it. But the rest of 'em, they called it a freak accident. Yeah! And for chrissake, it was so damn many years ago!

He went back across the room, and again reached for the razor. And found his hand was shaking so hard he could hardly hold the damn thing. Spooked.

After cutting himself a third time, he threw down the razor and fumbled for a rag to wipe his face. But he dropped the rag, suddenly clutching at his throat, trying to swallow. He tried again, and choked on his spit. What the hell? *He couldn't swallow!*

His breath now came in short gasps. He labored for air, fear turning to terror when his legs began to twitch uncontrollably, and the room suddenly went dark. Clawing at his eyes, he collapsed to his knees. His rifle—had to git his rifle. He crawled blindly, in quivering jerks, toward the rocking chair where he'd left it.

His ghost rose from the chair to meet him.

GLYNIS UNLOCKED THE door of the library and looked up again at the leaden cloud cover. Although she was fairly early—and had for once beaten even Jonathan Quant there—the morning had a darkened cast that made it seem like late afternoon. Though not particularly cold, the air held a strange stillness that raised the hair on the back of her neck. No doubt a storm brewing.

She'd just removed her cloak and hung it in her back office, when she heard the outer door open. Jonathan, probably. But then a familiar voice, which was not Jonathan's, called to her. She hurried out to the main room.

Elizabeth Cady Stanton, brown corkscrew curls clinging damply to her plump cheeks, stood by Glynis's desk. "Am I the first here?" she said breathlessly.

"Well, yes, you are. Why—who else is supposed to be here?"

"Susan is supposed to be. I got a note by messenger at the crack of dawn, saying to meet her here at eight-thirty." She glanced at the clock on Glynis's desk. "It's that now—and to think I practically undid myself getting here! I left Henry with the children, and he was not happy about it."

Henry Stanton was often unhappy about domestic matters, Glynis recalled. Curious that he didn't seem to understand why his wife complained of them.

The unmarried, childless Susan Anthony also complained. And her complaints stemmed from much the same source: too many babies! So many babies, in fact, that the National Woman's Rights Convention had not been held that year. There were too few available to organize it; women like Elizabeth Stanton, Lucretia Mott, Antoinette Brown Blackwell, and Lucy Stone, the pioneers of rights for women, had been either pregnant, or nursing mothers or, as Susan put it, were "awash in a rolling sea" of domestic obligations.

Just then the door flew open and Susan Anthony strode in, black wool scarf askew and cheeks flushed. She pulled off her gloves as she came toward them, saying, "Morning, Mrs. Stanton, Glynis. Is Neva Cardoza here yet?"

"Susan, what is going on?" Elizabeth said, a trifle testily. "Couldn't whatever it is have waited until a more civilized hour?"

"No! No, it could not. Because there is nothing the least bit civilized about what has happened."

Just then, Neva came through the door, looking, Glynis thought, remarkably cheerful for the hour. In fact, she very nearly glowed. Glynis observed her closely, and with some amusement, as Neva walked jauntily across the floor.

"Good morning, ladies. My, we are starting early—but such a lovely morning, isn't it?" Neva smiled expansively.

Glynis just stared at her, deciding that Neva was either on laudanum or in love.

Susan Anthony opened her purse and extracted from it a document that she handed to Elizabeth. "Read that," she said peremptorily.

"Susan, what—?"

"Just *read* it, Mrs. Stanton."

While Elizabeth scanned the document, Glynis pondered the oddity that though the women had known each other for years, Susan Anthony still called Elizabeth "Mrs. Stanton." At least in public, she did.

Now Elizabeth looked up at Susan with anger flashing back and forth across her face. "I can hardly believe this—it's an outrage!"

Glynis and Neva exchanged glances. "Do you suppose we might see that?" Glynis asked.

"Oh, yes, take it!" Elizabeth thrust the outrage at Glynis.

Neva moved to read it over her shoulder, and then exclaimed sharply, "But we have a right to freedom of speech! They can't do this. Can they?"

"They've done it!" Susan retorted. "They've actually given that *woman* a legal injunction that forbids us to set foot on a dirt road. And *she's* the one who's not complying with the law!"

"How can they do that?" Glynis asked. "None of you were in Waterloo at the hearing for this, I take it?"

"Certainly not!" Elizabeth snapped.

"Then how could the injunction be granted—if you weren't even there to plead your case?"

"How, indeed!" Susan said.

"And who is this Adam MacAlistair person who signed it?" Neva asked. "Is he the one who's representing that . . . that . . . that *woman*?"

Glynis noticed that the earlier glow in Neva's cheeks had begun to blaze. "He's a young lawyer from town here," she answered.

"A young whippersnapper is what he is!" Elizabeth said. "I know his family, and I just can't imagine what he is doing in league with Serenity Hathaway, of *all* people."

"What on earth do they teach these young men in law school?" Susan asked—rhetorically, Glynis decided as Susan answered it herself by saying, "And there, of course, is the obvious explanation—the only ones teaching and attending law schools *are* men!''

This sobering truth had the effect of silencing them all, until Susan said, ''Well, does anyone have a suggestion about what we might do?''

The pragmatic Miss Anthony returns, Glynis thought, wondering just how she herself had managed to get caught up in this. She hadn't even marched. Nor had Elizabeth, for that matter, although she would have, had her domestic duties not interfered. And Glynis could not imagine Henry Stanton saying something like, ''Oh, by all means, Elizabeth, go and close down a tavern or two. I'll be delighted to take care of things here at home until you return.''

''Glynis!''

She realized they had all been staring at her. ''Yes. Yes, I'm sorry, I didn't hear.''

''I said,'' sighed Elizabeth, ''could you talk to Jeremiah Merrycoyf about this? You know him better than we do.''

''You mean, would Mr. Merrycoyf represent you?'' Glynis asked.

Elizabeth nodded.

''Oh, I'm afraid not,'' Glynis said. ''At least I don't think so. Mr. Merrycoyf was the one, you see, who several years ago recommended Adam MacAlistair for a scholarship to law school. Even contributed to it himself. Although,'' she said quickly, ''I really shouldn't have mentioned that. No one was supposed to know. I don't think even Adam does.''

They stared at her again.

''But who, then,'' Elizabeth said, ''if not Jeremiah Merrycoyf?''

Glynis thought hard, discarding one alcohol-loving attorney after another. ''Well, there's always Orrin Makepeace Polk, in Waterloo,'' she finally offered. ''Mr. Merrycoyf doesn't like him personally, but says he's a fairly good lawyer. Mr. Polk might take your case because he's a Quaker.''

''Good!'' said Quaker Susan Anthony. ''I'll talk to him this very day. Neva, could you come with me? Neva?''

But Neva didn't immediately respond. She apparently had been wool-gathering, staring with fixed gaze at the gray sky beyond the tall library windows. And when she did answer

it was to announce, "Ladies, there might be another way."
She smiled broadly. "Didn't Constable Stuart tell you,
Glynis, that the Hathaway woman still needed one more
signature on her license petition?"

Glynis nodded. "Yes, but—"

"Yes!" Neva said, her earlier mood clearly restored.
"Then I may have an answer. Given me by a clever nun."

But before she could say any more, again the library door
swung open, this time to admit Jonathan Quant, who rushed
in, panting. "Sorry I'm late, Miss Tryon," he apologized,
"but Constable Stuart stopped me on the way here. He said
could you find Dr. Cardoza fast, and then meet him—"

Jonathan stopped and colored slightly. "Oh, Dr. Cardoza,
I didn't see you."

"Why does he want *me*?" Neva asked, suspicion shad-
owing her face.

"I don't know," Jonathan answered, unbuttoning his pea
jacket, "but whatever the reason, he'd like you to hurry. He
said he'll be at Dr. Ives's."

"IN THERE," CULLEN said, gesturing toward Quentin
Ives's examining room when Glynis and Neva arrived.
Glynis backed up against the wall for support. Though she
didn't want to believe it, she had guessed why they'd been
summoned. Her fear had been echoed by Neva, who
moaned, "Oh, no, not another!" as together they dashed
out of the library and hurried up Fall Street.

Neva shot Glynis a distressed look over her shoulder as
she went on into the room, then closed the door behind her.

Still leaning against the wall, Glynis said, "Cullen, it's
Jake Braun, isn't it?"

"Yes. Jake Braun."

"But how?"

"Don't know, not yet. He didn't have a mark on him,
though. I looked for punctures, stab wounds, bullet holes,
vomit from poison, you name it! Nothing. Nothing, that is,
but a couple of nicks on his face from shaving—his razor
was lying nearby."

"Who found him?"

"I did," Cullen said grimly. "Rode out to his place early

this morning to check on him.''

This didn't surprise her. When Cullen had said the day before that Jake Braun was on his own, she hadn't believed it. She knew he'd keep an eye on the man.

''Couldn't have been dead long when I got there—he was still warm. Dammit, I wish I'd gone last night.''

''Cullen, I doubt it would have made any difference. Whoever's killing these men is too clever by far to make an attempt when anyone's around. They've all died when they were alone.''

''No, not this time,'' Cullen said. ''This time's different—that's assuming Jake *was* murdered, and I expect Quentin Ives will tell me he was. No, this time somebody else was there.''

Cullen looked much more than upset, Glynis now realized; he looked almost as if he were in pain. And suddenly she was afraid. ''Cullen, who was there?''

''You want to tell me,'' he said hoarsely, as if his throat had tightened, ''why the hell my deputy would be skulking around Braun's place at the crack of dawn?''

''Your deputy! You mean—''

''My *former* deputy. Jacques Sundown.''

''He was there at Braun's?'' Glynis knew she was shaking her head, but couldn't seem to stop herself. Jacques couldn't have been there. Cullen must be mistaken.

''Yeah, he was there,'' Cullen said. ''Just after I found Braun—he was lying on the kitchen floor—I heard something outside. When I ran out, that black and white paint of Sundown's was galloping away in the direction of the reservation, hellbent for leather.''

Glynis bit down on her lip, plucking at her skirt and twisting the fabric between her fingers. Her previous deceit, in not mentioning Jacques's appearance after Mead Miller's death, now loomed so large she wondered how she ever could explain it to Cullen. ''Did you go after Jacques?'' she asked him, her stomach churning in apprehension.

''I yelled. Yelled my head off at him. Dammit, Glynis, I know he heard me! But I had to follow him on horseback half a mile before he stopped. Then he gives me some cock-and-bull story about how he was out exercising the horse.''

"And you don't believe him?"

"No, I don't believe him! Not after your friend Dr. Cardoza told us about Indians and snake venom, and the dart business."

"But, Cullen, that doesn't mean *Jacques* had anything to do with Mead Miller's death."

"But you were the one who said the deaths had to be linked, remember?"

Glynis cringed and bit down again on her lower lip. Her conscience jabbed her with painful urgency. She *had* to tell Cullen about Jacques, and tell him now. "Cullen, I—"

"And that's not all," he went on obliviously, but now scowling darkly. "I got to thinking about it, and you know the easiest way to deliver a dart?"

Glynis shook her head in mute fear.

"By air-gun," Cullen said. "A simple hollow tube. You stick an arrow, or a dart, inside the tube—the dart's got thistledown on it so it fits tight—and then you blow. In fact, we call them blow guns. And you know who invented this effective little weapon? Iroquois!"

"Cullen, aren't you jumping to a conclusion about this? About Jacques, I mean. There's no basis."

"No basis? Jacques and I used to hunt birds with air-guns. He's the one who taught me how to use the thing—and he was damn good at it. Don't know why I didn't remember it sooner. Maybe I didn't want to."

Cullen backed up to lean against the wall next to her. His face looked drawn and, completely uncharacteristic of him, his shoulders sagged. "Oh, hell, Glynis, you're probably right. I want to find the bastard who's killing all these people so bad, I'm grasping at straws in the wind."

Glynis started to agree, but Cullen went on as if he hadn't heard. "It's not that Sundown's incapable of killing—he's capable, all right. That night in the tavern, the night I first met him, backed up against the bar, I thought I was done for. Six drifters, mean-drunk, armed to the teeth—they were set to kill themselves a lawman that night. Didn't matter who—I just happened to be there. Sundown leaped over the bar from out of nowhere. I tell you, he appeared like one of Lazarus Grimm's spirits. He moved so *fast*. Before I knew what happened, he'd killed two of them in seconds with that knife of his. And as one of them went down, he grabbed the drifter's Colt and shot two more before they knew what hit them. The other two, well, they just threw up their hands."

Cullen stopped and bent over, his hands on his knees, staring at the floor. As if he were tired just thinking about it.

Although she'd heard some of this before, until now Glynis hadn't gotten the details. "What did Jacques do then, Cullen—when the two men gave up?"

Cullen straightened to look at her. "What did he do? Nothing. He just trained the Colt on them while I tied them up. Is that what you mean?"

"Yes. So he didn't keep firing, though he could have. He didn't kill them; he stopped shooting when the danger was over. Does that sound like a man who—"

"No," Cullen broke in, apparently seeing what she intended. "No, it doesn't sound like somebody who'd methodically kill off innocent men. But, Glynis, somebody's doing it!"

She moved away from the wall to face him. She had to do this, she *had* to. She and Cullen had never lied to each other. Never. What could she have been thinking that night?

"Cullen, I have to tell you something—no, please don't interrupt me. It's something about Jacques. And it's important!"

He'd started to speak, but he clamped his mouth shut and stared down at her. He must have believed it was serious, what she had to say, but she almost lost her nerve then. The way he just stared.

"When I found . . . right after I found Mead Miller's body," she began, with the knowledge that, in Cullen's eyes, she would be damning Jacques with every word, "well . . . Jacques appeared. He came riding up. No, not riding up, exactly, but he—that is, I don't know how long he'd been there, but it *couldn't* have been long."

"Glynis!" Cullen sounded astonished. He sounded astonished and he looked incredulous, and Glynis wanted desperately to take back the words. For Jacques's sake. For her own.

"Glynis, why didn't you tell me? *Why the hell didn't you tell me?*"

"I don't know. I really don't, Cullen, except that I was afraid you might think Jacques had—"

"You're right, I would have! I would have thought it was damn suspicious! I *do* think so." He looked down at her, shaking his head as if in confusion, then as if arguing with himself. Finally, "Glynis, what's going on with you and Sundown?"

"Going on? Nothing. Cullen, I don't know what—"

"Yes, you do know what I mean." The hurt in his voice was so acute, and was so painful to hear, that she took a step toward him, reaching out to touch his face. He brushed her hand away. The muscles in his jaw clenched, and there was a long pause until he said more. "I know you went out to the reservation a few days ago, Glynis—and now I bet it was to see him, wasn't it? *Wasn't it*?"

She heard the very instant Cullen's hurt became anger. His voice began to pound at her. "You know, Glynis, the last time Sundown hit town, a couple of years ago, I thought I saw something—something between the two of you. But I convinced myself it was only him. Only him pining after a woman he couldn't have. Fact is, I figured you were the reason he left again."

"Cullen," she broke in, "you're wrong about this. And please, please don't say something you'll be sorry for—that we'll both be sorry for. You're wrong."

"No, I don't think so." His voice was cold.

Amid her distress for him, for both of them, and the terrible guilt she felt, Glynis pictured everyone in the Ives house listening to this. "Cullen, could we step outside? Please?"

But then the door to the examining room opened, and Neva came out, followed by Quentin Ives. Her dark eyes, brimming with anxiety, flew to Glynis. Yes, she'd heard them.

"Cullen, I'm afraid we haven't got much," Quentin said. Apparently he was going to ignore whatever he'd overheard.

Cullen continued to stare at her as if she were someone he didn't know. Had never known. Then, without another word to her, he turned away. "Sorry, Quentin, I missed that."

Ives cleared his throat. "We haven't found the cause of Braun's death. Can't find it, other than some signs of convulsions and respiratory failure. But what caused those, we don't know. We can't do anything but guess," he said, now glancing at Neva.

Cullen's eyes followed the glance. "Dr. Cardoza? What about those cuts on his face?"

Neva shook her head. "Those seem to have been from the razor, as you thought, Constable. I don't really disagree with Dr. Ives, except that . . ." Her voice trailed off. She seemed extremely uncomfortable, and avoided looking at Glynis.

"Except what?" Cullen said, more harshly than normal, Glynis thought, although she wasn't sure she'd followed the conversation. She just wanted to leave. Leave and try to think of a way to right things with Cullen. He was upset— with good reason—but he couldn't really believe what he'd insinuated about Jacques and herself.

She suddenly realized no one was speaking. When she looked at the others' faces, she saw on Neva's something like agitation.

"Except *what*?" Cullen said to Neva again. "What don't you agree with?"

"Well," Neva said with uncertainty, "I'm not sure, of course, and I don't have anything firm to go on, but—it's his face. Braun's face. It's a strange color."

Quentin Ives added, "She thinks it could be the result of some kind of poison, Cullen. Something we can't identify."

Cullen turned and strode back into the examining room. Quentin Ives followed him.

"Glynis," Neva whispered, "are you all right? I heard."

"I'm sorry you did," Glynis said. "But there's nothing to do for it right now." She was determined to change the subject before she lost her fragile composure. "The color of Braun's face, you said. What color?"

Neva studied her a moment. Then she said, "Yellow. His

face, the lower part of it, is yellow. It almost looks stained. Quentin thinks it's jaundice, and he's probably right, but somewhere, in the back of my mind, there's something I should remember. And I can't. Something to do with a poisonous substance that causes a peculiar yellowing of the skin. What confuses things is that any poison might cause jaundice if enough red blood cells are destroyed. So you can see," she said, frowning, "that if I weren't so sure we were dealing with a murder here, I wouldn't have thought about it twice. The color, I mean."

"And we need to know definitely whether it *was* poison," Glynis said. "Is there something, some book perhaps, that would jog your memory?"

"Not that I can readily think of. And on top of everything else, Dr. Ives is leaving for Albany this afternoon. He'll be gone several days, so if I find something . . . well, I'm on my own." She looked at Glynis doubtfully. "You do think I'm right to pursue this?"

"Yes, Neva, absolutely you are. And Quentin Ives, fine doctor though he is, can't know everything. You said yourself that postmortem identification of poison has been fairly crude until—"

"Wait—of course!" Neva said suddenly. "I know where I can get information. Dr. Kelly—Patrick Kelly. I just met him in Rochester."

"But he can't examine Jake Braun's body," Glynis said.

"He doesn't have to! All he might need is a tissue sample." Neva whirled and rushed into the examining room, calling to Quentin Ives.

Glynis didn't know whether to leave or stay, whether to try to reason with Cullen now, or wait until he'd had time to think about it. But *why* had Jacques been at Braun's? There must be a logical explanation.

The door of the examining room swung open and Cullen came out into the hall, a slender oblong package in his hands. He looked at her only for a moment, his eyes shadowed, then started to walk past her.

"Cullen?"

"Let's just leave it, Glynis. For now. I've got a lot on my mind." He went down the hall, not even glancing at her, and on out the front door.

She went after him. ''Cullen, when can we talk about this?''

He took a few more steps, then stopped and turned. ''I don't know.'' But he must have reconsidered, because he said, ''I have to get this sample to Rochester. Then maybe . . . we'll see.''

She watched him stride toward Fall Street. Light snow had begun to fall, the flakes brushing his head and shoulders. Then he turned the corner and was gone.

For some time, Glynis stood there alone, until she was veiled in soft, lacy white.

SEVENTEEN

❦

The walls of the palace were snowdrifts, and in them sharp winds had carved windows and doors. There were a hundred halls, all illumined by flares of the northern lights; they were huge and barren and cold. Vast and empty and cold was the Snow Queen's palace.
> —HANS CHRISTIAN ANDERSEN, "THE SNOW QUEEN"

REIGN OF TERROR CONTINUES IN SENECA FALLS. So screamed the morning headline of the *Seneca County Courier.* Glynis winced at the newspaper's stark sensationalism, and glanced across the library at Jonathan Quant, who sat at his desk, hunched over the latest Mary Jane Holmes novel. Mrs. Holmes, Glynis thought, had nothing on the *Courier* in terms of lurid language. And it wasn't confined to the headline; the article under it began: "Seneca Falls remains gripped by the horror of two, and possibly three, unsolved murders. Citizens are said to be bolting their doors during daylight hours for the first time in village history."

Glynis tossed the paper onto her desk. The "possibly three" murders must mean those of Jack Turner, Mead Miller, and Obadiah Grimm. Since Jake Braun's body had been found by Cullen only that very morning, the newspaper's tally couldn't include him. Moreover, the newspapers had been told Obadiah's death might have been accidental; not that that would restrain the *Courier* beyond saying there had been *possibly* three murders.

She reached for the paper and continued to read.

> Seneca Falls Constable Cullen Stuart, in an interview conducted at his office in the No. 3 Firehouse, confirmed he has few if any suspects in the murder investigation, and no arrest is contemplated at this time. An unnamed source is reported

as saying that town councilmen are highly dis-
pleased by the lack of progress in solving the unprecedented wave of homicides. One council
member is said to have suggested that the investigation "may be beyond the resources of our
town constable."

Glynis put down the paper. She had picked it up only
because she couldn't concentrate on her work. But she had
to concede that, even without the *Courier* whipping up hys-
teria, people were frightened with good reason. And again
she felt the guilt, and the remorse, involving Cullen. He
didn't deserve any of this. Even Harriet Peartree, ordinarily
the most dauntless and understanding of women, had said
last night as she bolted the doors, "Glynis, this is terrible—
doesn't Cullen have *any* idea who's doing this? No? Well,
why not?"

But now he apparently thought he did. Glynis shook her
head and looked toward the windows, where clouds the sullen color of tarnished silver raced past. The flurry of snow
had stopped by the time she'd arrived at the library from
Ives', but a metallic smell in the air promised more. There
was talk of a storm coming in over Lake Ontario; as she'd
walked down Fall Street, shop owners had already begun
rolling up their awnings and taking in displays from the
plank sidewalks. November blizzards could be ferocious.

Storms from the Great Lakes didn't always track southeast and hit Seneca Falls head-on, but the New York Central
rail line in and out of town often closed. Cullen might get
caught in Rochester. Outside the library windows at that
moment, however, there was no snow.

Glynis propped her elbows on her desk and stared at the
beamed ceiling. The murders must somehow be connected.
They had to be. She refused to believe they had been random killings, and besides, as she'd said earlier, the bizarre
means of death linked them in one way.

She realized she had not even considered the possibility
that Jacques Sundown might be the killer. Because he
wasn't. There were some intuitive certainties that fell outside the tangible or the easily provable; Jacques's innocence

was one of those. And intuition had served her well in the past; she couldn't disregard it now.

She did know that intuition carried no weight in a court of law. But Cullen didn't have enough evidence to arrest Jacques. Being in proximity to a crime did not make one guilty. She smiled thinly, thinking of Cullen's comment that she'd spent too much time with Jeremiah Merrycoyf.

Too much time to ignore the compelling need to find some concrete answers.

Her chair scraped across the floor, as she pushed away from the desk and got to her feet. Jonathan started, and jerked his head toward her, sheepishly closing the novel.

"That's all right, Jonathan," Glynis said. "you might as well go ahead and read. With talk of a storm brewing, we won't get many more patrons in today. I'm leaving now to run an errand. If I'm not back by five, close up. But check the windows in case the storm comes tonight."

In her back office she retrieved her cloak and gloves. She had thought of something urgent, and it needed to be done before Cullen returned from Rochester.

AS SHE GUIDED the small gray mare onto Black Brook Road, the rear wheels of the carriage skidded on a patch of ice; the temperature had dropped several degrees since early morning. But still no sign of snow. Only the thick, fast-moving gray clouds that at this time of year habitually prowled the sky over western New York. Livery owner John Boone had repeated the rumors of bad weather to the north, but Glynis had told him not to fret, that she'd have his carriage back well ahead of any storm that might threaten.

But now, as she passed the Turner farm, she noticed uneasily that the metallic smell of the air had grown sharper. And the light wind, which had been blowing steadily from the northwest, suddenly gusted and shifted due north. Glynis drew on the reins, experiencing a moment of uncertainty; perhaps this was foolhardy, and she would do well to turn back. Still, she'd driven through snow before. She should have plenty of time to get to the reservation and back before it got too deep for carriage wheels.

Besides, if worse came to worst, she could always stop

at the Grimms'. And while this prospect did not enthuse her, she felt that what she needed to do would be worth the trouble. She shook the reins to urge the mare forward.

Just after she passed the abandoned Flannery farm, the wind abruptly picked up, its bite cold enough to pierce her sturdy hooded cloak; Glynis drew the hood around her face and now peered at the sky ahead with real misgiving. Layered like long rolls of fleece, dark clouds continued to scud swiftly southward. Then, as she watched with increasing alarm, the clouds began to tear apart, hurling themselves every which way like clumps of sodden wool. The entire sky suddenly appeared to be churning violently. When the wind began to rock the carriage, she knew she'd made a dangerous mistake. But now it was too late to turn back; she was far closer to the Grimms' than to town.

Overhead the clouds seethed like boiling stew. Turbulence created flashes of light as if a giant wick were being turned by a feverish hand. And the little mare had begun prancing skittishly and tossing her head, the wind blowing her mane parallel to the road.

The open carriage provided no protection. Glynis hunkered down to avoid being flattened against the seat, and the hair on her neck rose. The very air felt malevolent, and she cursed the stubbornness that had prevented her from turning back earlier. How much farther to the Grimms'? The mare kept slowing, shying from wind gusts and the dirt that whirled from the road, but Glynis urged her forward. Caught by the wind, a few flakes of snow spun haphazardly. Then, just ahead, stretched the long rise in Black Brook Road; the Grimm farm would be just a quarter-mile away. She might make it before the snow began in earnest.

The carriage started to climb the rise, and it was then, at the very moment her confidence returned, that Glynis heard the sound. A roar like a train, but louder. Her head came up into the wind, and her blood ran cold. Racing toward her was a wall of snow. It blotted out the sky and the road, the roar increasing until the ground trembled and the carriage shook. Even if she had known what to do, there was no time to act. She grabbed the side of the carriage as, with savage force, it struck. A great enraged beast howling out of its northern lair, it swept over the mare and the carriage as if they were trinkets. The carriage shuddered, and lifted off the road like a matchstick before it dropped with a sickening lurch. The snow came so thick, Glynis could barely see the mare, and within seconds she was shrouded in white. And blind.

Now she couldn't find the horse. Or the road. There was nothing but snow. The carriage shook, tilting one way, then another. She had to get out before it toppled. Closing her eyes against the driving pellets of snow, she held the reins tightly in one hand, in desperate fear of losing them, and groped for the carriage step. The wind fought her every move, buffeting her against the wooden frame until, just as she felt the carriage begin to lift again, she jumped. Landing in a heap of petticoats, the reins lost, she heard behind her a shattering crash. She got to her hands and knees and, facing away from the wind, crawled back toward the carriage. It lay smashed, upended, wheels still spinning. To her left, she heard a high whinny of terror. Dear Lord, the mare.

Avoiding the wheels, she inched forward in a crouch along the splintered shaft until the horse's tail lashed her face. The little mare was down, thrashing and entangling herself still more in the traces.

Glynis found she could stand nearly upright. The howling wind had slightly diminished, although it still blew hard enough to send the snow in horizontal sheets. She saw that the mare was on her side, her back to Glynis. To unbuckle the traces, she'd have to remove her gloves; she peeled them off and thrust them under one arm. Her fingers already ached with cold. Her hands were numb by the time she'd unfastened the shaft and the collar, and the freed mare scrambled up, mercifully not lamed. But the gloves had flown. And by this time both Glynis and mare were blanketed with a thick layer of white; even in one piece, the carriage would have been worthless.

The driving snow made it impossible to see any distance. Disoriented, Glynis grasped the retrieved reins, trying to determine if they were still on the road and from which way the swirling snow came. She dreaded the idea of walking into the wind, but it came from the north. And north lay the

Grimm farm. Now if she could only manage to stay on
Black Brook Road. She plunged forward with the mare beside her, praying they were headed in the right direction.

The farm was at least a hope, if they could remain on the
snow-covered road. If they wandered off . . . but she
wouldn't think about that. She wouldn't think about past
storms that had lasted for two or three days, or that she could
circle aimlessly until she dropped from exhaustion. It would
be better if she didn't think at all. Just kept plodding, she
and the mare. North.

Wind already had drifted the snow to above her ankles,
and her lightweight boots were soaked through; clad only
in cotton stockings, her feet throbbed painfully. Petticoats
and her long wool dress dragged her backward, making each
step forward exhausting. Her hair, loosed by the wind from
its knot, whipped across her face, while the hood of her
cloak billowed uselessly around her shoulders. The cold
made even her bones hurt. And she thought she had never
known such fear.

Isolated by the thick falling curtain of white, she prayed
it would part, if only for a moment, so she could find a
landmark—a fence, the brook, a bridge, *anything*. Several
times, to see if she and the mare were still on the road, she
went down on her knees to dig away the snow. But her
knuckles were scraped raw, her hands so stiff and painful
she had to give it up. She paused now and again to wipe
her face with her skirt. At these times, fatigue so overwhelmed her that she almost convinced herself she could
burrow down into the snow and rest. But that would be
suicidal. At last she turned to the mare.

Not since she was a child had she ridden bareback. But
surely it would be easier than walking. For several frustrat-
ing minutes she tried to pull herself up onto the mare's back.
She couldn't do it, not with the weight of wet petticoats.
She reached up under her skirt and yanked them off. Gripping one with her teeth, she tore it lengthwise into strips,
and wrapped the fabric around her hands like bandages. The
wind caught the remaining petticoats, tossing them away
like scraps of paper.

She was so cold. But if, in this nightmare, she could find

a single thing for which to be thankful, it was that this was November and not January, when the temperature might have been ten or twenty degrees below zero; that she couldn't have survived. But she wouldn't think about it.

Taking a deep breath, and with the muscles in her arms trembling, she managed to pull herself up onto the back of the mare. Flattening herself along its neck, she pressed her face against the coarse mane. The mare nickered softly. And they moved, very slowly, into the wind.

Glynis found she had no sense of time, no sense of how long they plodded forward. She wasn't even certain they still followed the road. They could have traveled a few yards or a few miles. The wind gradually lessened, but the snow continued to fall so heavily she couldn't see more than five or six feet ahead. It seemed as if they moved in place, not advancing or retreating, contained within a cocoon of white, spun by the fearsome Snow Queen.

The mare was tiring; Glynis felt it, and knew she should get off and let the animal rest. But while her thighs ached with the effort of gripping the horse, anything that meant relinquishing the warmth beneath her was unthinkable. Unwillingly, she gave the mare a poke with her heels. The horse took several quick steps forward—and balked. It happened so unexpectedly that Glynis had no time to ready herself. She pitched forward over the mare's head.

Landing hard, she heard a sharp crack, and felt herself breaking through a thin layer of ice. As she sank, water swirled up around her. Black Brook, she thought, frantically flailing her arms and trying to stand before the frigid water claimed her. Then her feet touched bottom. But the brook eddied around her, its current tugging at her with fiendish strength, determined to drag her under. She lunged forward, outstretched hands scrabbling for the bank. Her fingers found a tree root. Clutching it as best she could with numb hands, she used the root to heave herself out.

She crawled forward a few feet, then lay gasping in the snow. Her teeth chattered uncontrollably, and water streamed from her cloak and dress and hair, running down the bank to return to the brook. She had to get up. She *had* to. If she didn't, she would slide back into the water. It would not give her up again.

She managed to rise to her knees, calling to the horse for support. But the mare reared and shied away from her. Finally struggling to her feet, Glynis reached for the loose reins. She almost had them when the mare shied again, and the reins swung just beyond her fingers. She watched in frustration as the animal danced a few steps farther away. Whinnying once, a shrill, frightened cry, the mare took off in a whirl of white.

Glynis sank back into the snow. The horse couldn't leave her there alone. It couldn't. Again and again she called after the mare. But her only response was Black Brook; as if denied its rightful due, it slapped angrily against the bank. A terrible fear, like the wicked Snow Queen she had somehow held at bay, now loosed itself. And she thought then, for the first time, that she would die.

She had no strength left, not even to scream—and who would hear her? Soaked to the skin, her clothes growing stiff, without even the horse for warmth . . . She hauled herself upright and lurched forward, determined to move, if only away from the malignant sound of the water. It belonged to the Snow Queen, the brook; it had been watching for her, waiting to pull her under. It waited still.

Floundering through drifts, collapsing every few feet, she fought panic and fatigue more than cold. And she feared for her sanity when white apparitions began to twirl around her like whirligigs.

Suddenly, directly in front of her, a huge shape rose out of the dark. It towered over her, swaying with menace. She threw up her arms to ward it off, and plunged headlong against it. Crying out, her mouth filled with snow; gasping for breath, she clawed mindlessly at the thing until, in a moment of grace, she felt under her nails the jagged roughness of bark. Tree bark. She laid her cheek against the thick trunk, standing quietly to catch her breath before dropping to her knees. Under the tree, she might be sheltered from the full brunt of the wind. She sank into snow that had drifted against the trunk, and closed her eyes.

She remembered then that she had something to do . . .

something about Jacques Sundown. Perhaps she should call, and wait for him to come. It warmed her, the thought that he would find her. At least her body wouldn't be claimed by Black Brook. Not that it mattered very much . . .

A sudden gust of wind rocked her. She forced her eyes open. It didn't seem as cold. No, she told herself, that was death enticing her to sleep. She had to get up. Walk. Keep walking until Jacques came. She called to him, but the wind caught his name and threw it back to her.

Fatigue, like a massive weight, pressed her back into the snow. She would rest a little, then get up. She had to keep walking. Had to . . .

Something drifted into her consciousness. A faint, far-away sound—it might have been howling. Her eyelids strained to open, parted slightly, and fluttered closed again. It was only the wind, the wind howling through bare branches of the tree.

The sound grew louder, more insistent. Glynis struggled to swim through wet mist, and tried to lift her hands to rub her eyes. Her arms were too heavy. She must be sheathed with ice, imprisoned by the Snow Queen; but she was mortal and would die.

Now she heard from a distance a soft sound—the sound of snow being brushed? Warmth touched her cheek. Something crouched beside her, stroking her face. She found she could raise her lids. Two golden eyes looked into hers.

Now it would be all right. The wolf could break even the most evil spell. She stretched out her arms, suddenly weightless, and the wolf moved into them. Its breath felt warm, its lips moving over her cheeks and mouth, and when it held her tightly to its chest, she could feel the strong thud of its heartbeat.

It lifted and carried her into the eye of the storm.

SHE MOVED AGAINST the wolf's fur, and felt herself cradled, her head tilted back while heat poured down her throat. She slipped down between dark layers of fur and felt them close around her.

*   *   *

IT WAS A noise that woke her. A soft thump, then hissing. She smelled pine and dried corn and something sweet— maple sugar?—and when she opened her eyes, the shadow of flames danced beside her on a rough log wall. She thought she heard a door close.

When she tried to sit up, she slid back on silky fur. She was wrapped in some sort of pelt, and packed along either side of her were what felt like warm stones. Her hands slipped over the fur; when she breathed, it waved like short grass against her bare skin.

She struggled to sit up, lifting the fur to see what had become of her clothes. She still wore her cotton shift, although it felt unaccountably dry, but everything else was gone. Her eyes flew to a stone fireplace, beside which had been strung a line holding her bedraggled wool dress, long-sleeved muslin undergarment, and shredded cotton stockings.

Glynis felt her cheeks grow hot and thanked whatever good sense had made her wear the shift, however brief, instead of a boned corset. She let out a deep breath, and allowed herself to look around the one-room cabin.

A single chair, the cot she lay on, the stone fireplace with hooks holding cooking pots and a few utensils—and, surprisingly, next to it a bookcase of rough-hewn planks. The top shelf held a few earthen dishes, and wood carvings of what looked to be animals, an oddly curved pipe of black clay, and, positioned behind the rest, what must have been a javelin. Another shelf held a long, elaborately carved piece of wood ornamented with paint and feathers at one end, and what Glynis guessed was a piece of deer horn at the other; she shuddered involuntarily, as it was plainly an ancient war club and the horn would be honed razor sharp. The lower shelves held a goodly number of books. She squinted, but couldn't read the titles. Over the bookcase hung a rack holding a rifle and assorted knives. Ears of corn dangling from their braided husks were strung along another wall. Under these stood a pine chest, and hooks near the door held several deerskin garments, snowshoes, and what was her now tattered black cloak.

Beside her, a square pine table held a metal plate with

three corn cakes, and a small pottery jug from which came the smell of maple syrup.

As she reached for the plate, she found her hands were shaking, but managed to stuff the cakes into her mouth in a paroxysm of hunger. Then, seized by sudden need, she climbed from between the layers of fur robe. Shaking out the heated stones, she wrapped the robe around herself, and stood in indecision. Should she go outside? She glanced quickly around, but couldn't see her boots. Then, with relief, she spotted in one corner a covered chamber pot, and hurried to use it before Jacques came back. She had little doubt that it was his cabin.

Still alone a few minutes later, she went to the neat pile of wood beside the fireplace and placed another log on the fire. The corn cakes had made her feel stronger, and she was warm, warmer than she'd hoped ever to be again. Besides sorely scraped and reddened hands, and wind-burned cheeks, she could find no other signs of her ordeal. But there did remain a grinding fatigue. She thought she could sleep for days. Meanwhile, where was Jacques?

She drew up the chair in front of the fire, but couldn't sit down until she'd looked at what the bookcase contained. To her astonishment, two volumes proved to be Noah Webster's *American Dictionary of the English Language*. Furthermore, it was the 1841 revised edition, and had clearly been well thumbed. Jacques and a dictionary? It was as if she'd discovered Susan B. Anthony with a bottle of rum. Dickens, Hawthorne, Poe, and on across the shelves with authors Glynis herself would have recommended had he ever asked. The most startling, though, excepting the dictionary, were the Brontë sisters' *Jane Eyre* and *Wuthering Heights*. And all looked as if they'd been read, Glynis observed with a practiced eye, replacing the Brontës on the shelf.

She sank into the hard straight chair, her assessment of Jacques Sundown undergoing rapid revision. But where *was* he? The need to see him hadn't lessened, and in spite of the storm, she remembered what she'd originally intended. She glanced toward a cabin window, then got up, stiffly, to look out. The snow had stopped. And there was less of it than she would have imagined. Unless it had melted overnight. But then she realized she was seeing not the light of morning but the pale mauve dimness of a November afternoon. Late afternoon. But surely not—she had left Seneca Falls in early afternoon—it must be later than that. Or else . . . how long had she been here?

She had started back to the fire when a sound made her turn toward the door. Pushing loose hair from her face, she drew the fur robe more tightly around herself. The door opened and Jacques came in, brushing snow from his leggings and moccasins. He straightened, and Glynis saw him look toward the cot before he found her at the fireplace. His mouth curved slightly, and Glynis believed he might smile. Almost he did. "You all right—you look all right."

Not certain this was a question, Glynis nodded and asked, "How long have I been here?"

"A while." She must have looked confused, because he added, "Found you last night."

Last night?

Jacques came across the room, then stood looking down at her before he threw more logs on the fire. Glynis felt her face flush and, by way of pushing back her hair, pressed her hands against her cheeks. "I thought," she said with hesitancy, then with embarrassment as the memory gradually returned, "that the wolf found me."

Jacques seemed to be poking unnecessarily at the fire.

"Jacques, I said I thought," she repeated, "that the wolf—"

"Yeah."

"Yeah, *what*?"

"You thought the wolf found you." Jacques turned to stand with his back to the fire.

"Thank you," she said. "It's not adequate, of course, but thank you, Jacques. If you hadn't found—"

"What about the wolf?" And then, finally, he smiled.

"I don't know anymore," she said, smiling now herself, "whether the wolf is real or a figment of my imagination. Or is your spirit—your familiar, I think it's called. I don't know, and at the moment it's not as urgent to me as what we need to talk about." She added, "I was on my way here when the storm hit." But he probably knew that.

"O.K., what do you want to talk about?" he said, unexpectedly, as if he were initiating a normal conversation between them, which would be rare if not unprecedented.

"Why were you at Jake Braun's this—no, yesterday—morning? Cullen told me you were there when he found the body."

"Giving my horse a run."

"That's what you told Cullen. He didn't believe it. Neither do I, for that matter. Jacques, why were you there?"

"Stuart thinks I killed Braun, right?"

"That's not what I asked."

"O.K., you think I killed Braun."

"No! No, I don't. I know you didn't. But you're right, Cullen is suspicious. If you could just tell me what you—"

"No."

"Why not?" Glynis shrugged in irritation and felt the fur inch from her shoulders. She pulled it back up, and saw that Jacques watched her. She flushed again and looked away. They were alone here, isolated, and Glynis found to her distress that she was more flustered by her reaction to this truth than by Jacques himself. Which must mean it wasn't Jacques she worried about.

Going to the chair, she sat down firmly. She was determined to have this out, finish it, despite her inexplicable, unprincipled weakness for him. She supposed she should feel some relief at having finally confessed this—to herself, at least.

"Jacques," she said, thinking he must not realize how much danger he faced, "you surely know about the four deaths. And that Cullen has no real suspects."

"You said he suspected me," Jacques said, and she noticed his voice wasn't quite as flat as usual.

"You've shown up twice at a murder scene! Although Cullen didn't know you were there when I found Mead Miller—not until yesterday morning. I had to tell him, Jacques. I couldn't continue to deceive him."

"Why didn't you tell him before?"

"Because . . ." She stopped, then blurted, "Because I

was afraid for you, why else!''

Glynis saw the subtle shift in his eyes. But there was none of the confusion with which she'd responded to this in the past. Getting up from the chair, she went to stand beside him at the fireplace. They hadn't finished this yet, and she was determined to disregard the man himself and concentrate on his situation.

''Jacques, I am truly afraid. If Cullen focuses his attention on you, he won't be searching for the real killer. And it could go on—the killing could go on and on.''

''No,'' Jacques said. ''It's over.''

Stunned, Glynis suddenly recalled Jake Braun telling her in the lockup that ''nobody else was left.'' Nobody except him, he'd meant. But, she now realized, he'd told her that *before Obadiah Grimm had died*!

''How can you say it's over?'' she asked him. ''Jacques, what do you know about this?''

''That it's over. There won't be more killing.''

Glynis dashed at her eyes, at the tears that threatened. She wanted so much to believe him. ''How do you know that?'' she asked him again.

''You said you didn't think I did the killing. You mean that?''

''Yes! Yes, of course. But does it matter?'' Even as she asked, she doubted he would answer.

''Yeah. It matters. I don't care much about anybody else.''

She drew back slightly from the unfamiliar tension in his voice. But he reached for her and drew her closer, smoothing the fur at her shoulders, his fingers warm against her skin. Glynis tried to convince herself that no one would know what happened here. They were alone, she and Jacques. No one could possibly know. Not anyone . . . and most of all, not Cullen.

No, Cullen wouldn't know . . . but she would. And she couldn't do this. At least not now . . .

She reached up, reluctantly, to catch Jacques's hands, and a muffled noise outside made them both start. Jacques shoved her behind him with one hand, while with the other he pulled a knife from his belt.

The door burst open.

There, framed by the soft light, Colt revolver leveled in his hand, stood Cullen Stuart.

EIGHTEEN

❧❧

Her officials within her
are roaring lions;
her judges are evening wolves
that leave nothing till the morning.
  —ZEPHANIAH, 3:3

THERE FOLLOWED A silence so penetrating that Glynis barely registered the drip of snow melting from Cullen's boots. No matter how long she lived, she would not forget that silence, a charged, gravid stillness that stretched beyond her understanding of time itself, while Cullen stood there with his revolver aimed at Jacques Sundown.

At last, when it seemed they all three would turn to pillars of salt, Cullen said, "O.K. Sundown—lower the knife. Then don't move."

Jacques, the knife poised to throw, brought it down slowly. "Not going anywhere," he said evenly.

Glynis saw a muscle in Cullen's jaw move, then watched as his eyes raked the cabin. She didn't care to imagine what he must think—she and Jacques alone, his hand grasping her bare shoulder, her hair loose and tousled, her clothes hanging conspicuously on the line. And the rumpled cot.

In Cullen's single glance, Glynis felt years of her life, the years she had known him, plummet to where they could not be reached. And she could think of nothing to say or do that would bring them back. Or make it right.

"Drop the knife, Sundown. And let go of *her*."

Jacques released her shoulder in a slow, deliberate motion. The knife remained in his hand. Glynis began to tremble; she hadn't realized how cold it was in the cabin.

Except for an occasional tremor in his jaw, Cullen's face seemed cast in stone. He didn't look at her. In fact, he didn't appear to see her at all. She felt invisible, as though for him she'd never existed. And how could she blame him?

"C'mon, drop the knife!" Cullen repeated.

"If I was going to use it, I would've. You know that." Jacques's voice was flat; it held nothing menacing.

Glynis let out a breath she had not known she'd been holding, and moved from behind Jacques. "Cullen, I—"

"It's better you don't say anything," Jacques startled her by interrupting. "He won't believe you anyway. Not now, he won't."

Glynis looked at Cullen. His cold expression confirmed Jacques's judgment.

"You know, Sundown," said Cullen, "it's probably better if *you* don't say any more. You're under arrest."

"Cullen, you can't believe Jacques killed those men," Glynis protested. "There's absolutely no evidence."

Cullen ignored her. He stepped forward, the hand without the gun pulling manacles from his jacket pocket. And Jacques raised the knife, not fast, but with calculation. Cullen stopped, and Glynis heard the revolver in his hand click as he drew back the hammer.

"Cullen, stop it," she cried. "You *can't* shoot him."

"Oh, I sure as hell can," Cullen said softly, not taking his eyes off Jacques.

Glynis stepped to Jacques's side. "Give me the knife, Jacques, please. Please. Cullen can't hold you with no evidence. You must know that anything he has is circumstantial."

Cullen's jaw tightened. This made her even more frightened for Jacques, but she repeated to him, "Please, just give me the knife. If Cullen is determined to take you in, let him. I'll go to Jeremiah Merrycoyf. He'll have you free in no time—and you know that, Cullen," she said, turning to him. "So why are you doing this?"

"Give her the knife, Sundown."

There was, again, a long silence. Glynis, in desperation spurred by guilt, stepped forward to reach for the weapon. "Stay away from him!" Cullen ordered.

"Are you considering shooting me, Cullen?" Glynis heard herself say with an eerie composure; she was terrified one of them would be killed, if this absurd standoff didn't end. It would be unintentional if it happened, but someone would still be dead.

And Cullen—this just wasn't like him. With a resurgence of guilt, she surmised his vindictive attitude involved her. But it still wouldn't be like him. Cullen had never before let anger get in the way of his job. And Jacques had been his deputy—had saved his life, in fact. How could he believe Jacques had murdered all those men? And, dear Lord, for what reason?

Jacques, his eyes still on Cullen, said to her now, "This is dangerous. I don't want you hurt. Him either." He handed Glynis the knife.

Cullen moved fast, pushing Glynis out of his way to clamp the manacles on an unresisting Jacques. Glynis thought she had control of herself, so the fierceness in her voice surprised her when she said, "Why are you doing this, Cullen?"

"Because," he said harshly, not to her but to Jacques, "you're under arrest, Sundown, for the murder of that poor pathetic woman."

Glynis gaped at him, then whirled to Jacques. His head had snapped toward Cullen, while across his impassive features raced a fleeting expression. Glynis felt certain what she saw was surprise. But in the flick of an eye it was gone.

"Woman?" she asked in bewilderment. "Cullen, what on earth are you—"

"C'mon, Sundown," Cullen said, "let's go." He gave Jacques a shove toward the door, and said over his shoulder to Glynis, "I'd like to think you didn't know about this. So maybe you should take a look out back. By the woodpile. Take a good look. What you'll see is a dead woman—with Sundown's knife in her chest."

"No." Dazed, Glynis shook her head. "No, Cullen, you must be mistaken." Which sounded preposterous; he couldn't be mistaken about something like that. But he must be. "Who?" she whispered, still shaking her head, as if that might make it untrue. "Cullen, who is it?"

"Lily Braun."

Glynis swayed in disbelief, and to brace herself, she reached for him. But Cullen shook off her hand. When he pushed Jacques ahead of him out the door, Glynis heard, from the woods behind the cabin, a chilling sound. Unearthly in its tone and intensity, the howl rose on the air, climbing higher and higher in pitch until it became a prolonged cry of mourning. As if the wolf foretold its own death.

"AND SO AS you can see, Jeremiah, Jacques Sundown's situation is very serious." Glynis moved to the edge of the chair and folded her hands on the lawyer's desk to study his reaction.

Seated behind the desk, Jeremiah Merrycoyf laced pudgy fingers over the rounded bulge of his waistcoat. His eyes glinted thoughtfully at her from behind the wire spectacles. "I daresay it sounds serious, Miss Tryon."

All these years, Glynis thought distractedly, and he still insisted, most of the time, on calling her "Miss Tryon." But until now he'd not said a word. Not once during her recital had he interrupted with so much as one question.

"Then I assume," she said to him, "you know why I'm here. I want you to represent Jacques. And I realize the bald facts look incriminating."

"Yes, they certainly do," Merrycoyf agreed. A little too readily, Glynis thought.

"There's a reasonable explanation, Jeremiah, I'm sure of it. Jacques Sundown did not kill that woman. Or anyone else. But why," she asked with some misgiving, "haven't you questioned me about what I've told you?"

"It's been my experience, Miss Tryon," Merrycoyf said, unlacing his fingers and sitting forward, "that you are a very reliable witness—so no, I don't question your account. Not of those things which you yourself have seen. But *someone* killed the woman Lily Braun. And someone has also been quite actively dispatching other citizens of our fair village. We won't speculate right now on whether this might be the *same* someone. But—"

"Remember, though," she interrupted, "that Jacques wasn't charged with the deaths of those men. Only with Lily Braun's."

"But," Merrycoyf continued, as if she hadn't spoken,

"one can understand the inclination of Constable Stuart to arrest Mr. Sundown. That inclination does not seem to me to be an unreasonable one. The body of Lily Braun was discovered, if I understand you correctly, behind Mr. Sundown's cabin. Beside Mr. Sundown's woodpile. In the victim's body was what the constable believed to be Mr. Sundown's knife. I will venture to say Constable Stuart had the right, indeed the obligation, to suspect that Mr. Sundown had dispatched the victim."

"I told you, Jeremiah, that Jacques Sundown is not a stupid man. Far from it. So why would he murder Lily Braun and then leave her body behind his own cabin?"

"Because he hadn't had time to remove it to less incriminating surroundings."

"But *I* was there—I could have stumbled onto it inadvertently."

Merrycoyf's eyes glinted. "Indeed. Perhaps Mr. Sundown had reason to believe you wouldn't be interested in stumbling around outside his cabin."

Glynis flushed furiously. "I told you very clearly *why* I was in Jacques's cabin."

Merrycoyf sighed. "Yes. Although I don't suppose you told me all of it. However," he went on as she tried to interrupt, "I can't take Mr. Sundown's case in any event."

"Why? Why not?"

"Because, my dear Miss Tryon, I am tired. I am an old man, ready to retreat to a quieter life. For the rest of my days, however short they may be."

"That's rubbish, Jeremiah! You're not one bit older than Harriet Peartree."

"Ah, the delightful Mrs. Peartree, yes. She, if I recall rightly, has buried three husbands. That alone might make one forget one's own years."

Despite her anxiety, Glynis had to smile. "What's happened to make you feel this way?"

"I've been observing the vigor of the young, the sharp wits of those newly launched in this profession—a profession that requires every ounce of vitality one can muster. But I, alas, no longer have that with which to muster."

Glynis sat back to think. What really had brought this on?

Merrycoyf was normally the most equanimous of men. She wondered if . . . "Was it you, by any chance, who inflicted Serenity Hathaway on poor Adam MacAlistair?"

Merrycoyf straightened with alacrity. "Mr. MacAlistair did a commendable job in a most unusual circumstance."

"Oh, he certainly did. And he now has a significant portion of the women in town outraged at him."

Merrycoyf smiled benignly.

Ordinarily she might find this as comical as Merrycoyf did, but not with Jacques's welfare at stake. He had been denied bail and now sat in the lockup, vulnerable to the town's mounting anger. She must somehow persuade Merrycoyf to defend him.

"Jeremiah, perhaps I have the answer to your despondency."

"I am not despondent, Miss Tryon, merely realistic."

"Very well. But I believe you owe young Mr. MacAlistair a debt of gratitude. He has undoubtedly, because of his association with Serenity Hathaway, lost a number of potential clients. Clients who will most certainly now turn to you. So you owe it to Adam to let him redeem himself in those clients' eyes by assisting you in an important trial. You were the one who encouraged him to go into law, and even contributed to his—"

"Miss Tryon! That is not public knowledge. You acquired that information in confidence."

"Yes, so I did. But consider this: I also have several debts owed me by you. You might say, in fact, that I am calling in my markers." She gave him a wintry smile. "Do I need remind you of the time, for instance, that I traipsed all over Henrico County, Virginia, for you? Or the time that I rescued your client, Mr.—"

"I think I have underestimated you," Merrycoyf broke in. "I had no idea you were educated in the parlance of gamblers, Miss Tryon. Calling in your markers, indeed."

He sounded very stern, and Glynis remembered a time when it would have intimidated her. Now she looked for, and found, the twinkle behind the glasses.

"Then you'll take Jacques's case?"

Merrycoyf's sigh was profound. "My dary, calling in

your markers—as you so colorfully put it—will not produce a spirited or vigorous defense for your friend Mr. Sundown. Which, from what you've told me, he requires in large measure. No, although I apologize most sincerely, I cannot do it.''

Glynis bit her lower lip in distress. What more could she say? Oh . . . perhaps . . . yes, it was worth a try.

She rose from the chair and pulled on her gloves. "Very well, Jeremiah, if that is your last word. Needless to say, I am disappointed."

She started toward the door; then, as if it were an afterthought, she turned to say, "But I would imagine that the prosecutor assigned to Jacques's trial will be most gratified. He will, in a sense, finally have beaten you."

Merrycoyf's head came up sharply. "Who *is* the prosecutor?" he asked with more than casual interest.

Glynis waited for his interest to build.

"Miss Tryon, *who*?"

"Who else, for what promises to be a much publicized trial, than your old adversary, Orrin Makepeace Polk."

"Polk!" Merrycoyf half rose from his chair. "Why, he's older than I am! By several years, at least."

"At least," Glynis replied, and waited.

Merrycoyf sighed deeply. "For shame, Glynis." He stared at the ceiling, sighed again, then rose quickly from his chair; he'd managed to muster his frail resources remarkably well, she thought. "It appears that the first thing to do," he said, "is to remove my client from the charged atmosphere of the Seneca Falls lockup."

Glynis nodded, too troubled to savor her victory. "Yes, I agree," she said. "But would you tell me, Jeremiah, if you recently performed some service for Obadiah Grimm? Something for which he might have owed you money?"

Merrycoyf seemed taken aback by her question; behind his spectacles, his eyes blinked slowly. "No," he said, shaking his head. "No, I'd done nothing for Grimm in the past several years."

Something nudged at Glynis, but it remained just beyond her grasp. "Well, then," she asked, "can you tell me who was involved, some years ago, in an action brought by you for a Seneca man? It was to stop the building of a dam on Black Brook. The landowners, I believe, lived either on or near the brook. And Mr. Polk represented them.''

Merrycoyf looked distinctly non-plussed. Then he sat back down to stare at her, comprehension gathering in his eyes. ''There were eight men, eight *white* men, who were opposing my client,'' he said at last. ''Yes, they all lived along Black Brook. And one of them was Otto Braun, Lily Braun's father.''

''Jeremiah! Do you think—''

''What I think, Miss Tryon,'' he interrupted, ''is if we travel down that particular path, we might well trip over Pandora's Box. Which, if opened, could prove quite dangerous.''

Dangerous for whom, she wondered uneasily, Merrycoyf didn't say.

AS GLYNIS WALKED up Fall Street between the two lawyers, it became obvious to her that, if need be, Adam MacAlistair possessed vigor enough for both men. He seemed exuberant over the summons from Merrycoyf, and Glynis was beginning to resent the excessive eagerness with which Adam anticipated Jacques's trial.

Merrycoyf was more taciturn. ''We are not going to a church picnic, young man,'' he growled, ''and I suggest you temper your enthusiasm until we know more. As of now, Miss Tryon may be the sole resident of Seneca Falls who believes our client innocent. And you can thank her for recommending your assistance.''

Adam MacAlistair smiled at her warmly. She was certain he had not missed Merrycoyf's reference to ''*our* client.''

As they neared the turn to the firehouse, loud, aggressive voices reached them. Glynis walked more rapidly over the thawing road, sweeping her petticoats out of the mud's way. When she turned the corner, she stopped short. As did Adam and Merrycoyf behind her.

Cullen had positioned himself on one of the firehouse steps with a rifle in the crook of his arm. In the road just below him stood a group of men whose postures were clearly belligerent.

"What're you protecting him for, Stuart? He's killed off four good men—he don't deserve no protection."

Glynis strained to see the man who had asked the question. It was bootmaker Sam Carson, one of those who'd been in the agitated crowd at Levy's hardware.

"No-account red Indian!" shouted Lemuel Tyler, much more mouthy, Glynis noticed, in the absence of his wife, Tillie. "He's fixin' to kill all us white folk—I say hang 'im now."

Beside her, Adam had gone very quiet, but Glynis heard Merrycoyf's tongue cluck in disapproval. This seemed to her an inadequate response. "Jeremiah, don't you think this is a precarious situation?"

"No question about it, Miss Tryon. Precisely what we needed, in fact." Merrycoyf ambled forward, nodding pleasantly to the assembled men. He stopped and said something to Sam Carson, whose head then bobbed with apparent agreement.

"What's Merrycoyf doing?" Glynis whispered to Adam.

"I think he might be verifying a hostile atmosphere," Adam suggested.

"A hostile atmosphere appears unquestionable," Glynis retorted. She glanced around. More men were moving toward the firehouse; they appeared to be younger than those already there, and these new arrivals acted more truculent. It couldn't be a worse time of year, she thought anxiously; the hard work of the harvest was done, and these men not only had a craving to let loose, but the spare time for deviltry.

Cullen had now come down a step, and stood listening to Merrycoyf. When the lawyer turned to motion Glynis and Adam forward, the young man grasped her elbow to steer her through the men; although she heard some muttering, no one said anything directly to her or to Adam. As they went around the corner of the firehouse, she glanced back at Cullen, still on the step; when she'd passed him, she thought he'd looked in her direction, but if so, he had swung back to face the crowd again.

As she and Adam followed Merrycoyf into the lockup, Zeph Waters jumped to his feet. He nodded to her, then looked at the floor, scuffing his boots in obvious embarrassment. He *should* be embarrassed, Glynis thought. Jacques Sundown had once befriended Zeph when the boy sorely needed it. And now here he was, guarding the man in a cell. But in the next instant she forgave him and nodded in turn, sighing softly to herself; Zeph was only doing his job as Cullen directed. None of this had been his fault.

Jacques was in the back cell, seated on a cot—the same one Jake Braun had occupied before his fatal escape. Zeph unlocked the cell door, then stood rocking from one foot to another.

"You may leave us now, young man," Merrycoyf said to him.

"Ah, sir, I don't know if I should."

"I can assure you that you should," Merrycoyf said, but not unkindly.

Zeph, looking miserable, shot Glynis a distraught glance.

"I think it's all right for you to leave us, Zeph," she told him. "But go and ask Cullen about it, if you'd rather. In the meantime, if it would make you feel better, you can lock the cell door."

He sent her a look of gratitude. Before he relocked the cell, Merrycoyf and Adam slipped in with Jacques, while Glynis remained outside the bars.

As Zeph hastened off in search of Cullen, Adam folded his arms across his chest and leaned back against the bars, while Merrycoyf walked to the cell window and stood peering out. Glynis took the opportunity to study Jacques. After two days in a cell, he looked the same. No better, no worse. He turned on the cot slightly and saw Glynis, apparently for the first time. His eyes flickered over her face, creating in her the now familiar tension, but his expression remained impassive. And he said nothing.

An hour later, he still had said nothing. Merrycoyf and Adam had certainly tried, Glynis thought with increasing despair. Both in turn had been persuasive, firm, sympathetic, annoyed, and, finally, had all but pleaded with Jacques to say *something*.

"Look here, man," Adam said, his tone exasperated, "how do you expect us to defend you if you won't defend yourself? If you won't answer a single question we put to you? We're not wizards."

Merrycoyf had turned back to the window, and was silent.

"Jacques," Glynis said, "Mr. MacAlistair is right. They can't help you without some cooperation."

Jacques turned to look at her. For a split second she saw a suggestion of something new in his eyes, a shadow of emotion, not fear certainly, not even discomfort; it seemed more like resignation.

And then, "I don't want help," he said flatly.

They were the first words he had uttered, and Merrycoyf spun away from the window to stand in front of his client.

"Mr. Sundown, because—and *only* because—Miss Tryon has interceded persuasively in your behalf, we are committed to defending you. Whether you want our help or not. Now, if you wish us to spend the next weeks of trial preparation simply wandering around in the dark, so be it."

Jacques didn't look away from Merrycoyf, but his eyes betrayed nothing. And he remained silent.

"Jacques, please," Glynis urged him, "give these lawyers something to work with. You must see how dangerous your situation is—Lily Braun stabbed with *your* knife, in back of *your* cabin. Just tell us, at the very least, who could be trying to make it look as if you killed her."

For a bewildering moment, Glynis thought that Jacques might actually smile!

"Jacques," she said, despair raising her voice to a cry, "if you don't cooperate, you'll hang!"

He gave her a long, steady look, then got up from the cot and went to the window. She saw a barely discernible tautness in his shoulders, nothing more.

"Very well, Mr. Sundown," Merrycoyf sighed. "Constable Stuart has conceded that you need more protection than he can provide. You will be moved immediately, therefore, to the prison facility in Waterloo to await trial. I beg you to reconsider your position, and furnish us with that which we need for your defense. Otherwise, we will see you in court."

NINETEEN

*The wampum codes of De-ka-na-wi-da [founder of the
League of the Haudenosaunee] and his helper, Hiawatha,
furnished an almost ideal code for the ethnic culture with
which it was designed to cope. By holding to their old laws
the Iroquois became the dominant power east of the Missis-
sippi. . . .*

— ARTHUR C. PARKER, *THE LIFE OF
GENERAL ELY S. PARKER*

GLYNIS STOOD AT the top of the steps that led into the
Seneca County Courthouse. She blew on fingers that were
turning purple, and stiff with cold. Clenching her teeth to
stop their chattering, she raised the ruffled hood of her dark
green wool mantle, then drew up her hands inside its wide
sleeves. She should go inside now. And she would, if she
was able to ignore the conflict below on the Waterloo village
square. Although apprehensive, she still believed a violent
confrontation might be averted.

Snow mostly concealed the dry brown grass on the square
in front of the courthouse; the ground underneath had frozen
so hard it seemed inconceivable that, just weeks before,
clumps of chrysanthemums and asters had bloomed there.
Or that a few months from now, patches of snowdrops and
fragrant violets would nestle against stone foundations of
the two white-steepled Protestant churches facing the
square. That they were dormant this day proved fortunate;
flowers would not have fared well against the townsfolks'
buttoned gaiters and boots, and the buckskin moccasins of
the Iroquois.

The white men from Waterloo and surrounding towns
looked to be some thirty or forty in number. And it first
appeared to Glynis as if every male Seneca and Cayuga
Iroquois from Black Brook Reservation also had gathered
below on the green. But as she again scanned the crowd,

she saw that probably no more than twenty copper-skinned men stood silently before the taunts and threatening gestures of four or five Seneca County residents. Just how long their Iroquois stoicism could last was the question.

Glynis could hear snatches of the derision being leveled at the Iroquois. "Heathens! Murderers!" jeered one burly white man with his raised fist but a few feet from the flat stares of the silent men. Another sullen-faced white yelled something mercifully indistinct, then whooped in mockery while hopping from one foot to the other. Directly behind these, Glynis could see other white men, clustered in small groups, who seemed to be simply watching. Some were grinning.

Cullen Stuart and Zeph Waters had positioned themselves between the Iroquois and the troublemakers. From where she stood, Glynis could make out Zeph's young black face tightened in resolve. And she knew he would remain at Cullen's side, no matter what happened. Or however frightened Zeph might be.

Somewhat the same spectacle had taken place the day before, while inside the courthouse the jury was being selected. Cullen had managed to defuse that first confrontation. But overnight the mood had grown uglier, and Glynis saw Cullen's hand resting on his hip, next to the butt of the Colt revolver in its holster. She assumed everyone else could see this. If trouble erupted, nonetheless, how long could Cullen and Zeph maintain control? The afternoon before, Cullen had wired the U.S. marshal's office in Auburn for assistance; the return wire had indicated it could be some time until reinforcements could be spared.

Suddenly, on a narrow drive to the far side of the square, a horse and a small carriage appeared, clattered over the cobblestones, and drew up in front of the courthouse. Judge Thaddeus Heath stepped down. He walked a few feet, then stood scowling at the groups of men, while Glynis cautiously descended several steps to bring herself closer.

"What is going on here, Constable?" demanded Judge Heath brusquely of Cullen. His voice came as a surprise to Glynis; it was much larger than his slight stature would indicate.

"Nothing much, Your Honor," Cullen answered evenly. "Just a bunch of folks waiting on you. And now you're here, I'd guess they can get on their way. Right?" Cullen spoke this last to the crowd, but stared directly at the handful of troublemakers.

"Constable, I want these men dispersed!" Judge Heath ordered. "This crowd could intimidate the jury. I want the area cleared now!"

Glynis clutched the hood of her mantle around her face as a sharp gust of wind carried away the responding mutters of the crowd. Not a one of them moved. Cullen's greatest concerns, he'd told Merrycoyf the day before, were that Senecas and Cayugas would begin pouring into Waterloo from the other Iroquois reservations in western New York, and that the town's troublemakers would grow even bolder. That this hadn't happened yet was encouraging, but then it might be a lengthy trial. And either verdict, innocent or guilty, would likely inflame one of the factions.

Judge Heath continued to scowl as Cullen gestured to the men. "All right, fellas, let's move," he said affably. "C'mon, my friends—move along!"

Zeph Waters stood rocking back and forth on his heels. Glynis saw the fingers of his right hand twitching above his holster, but they didn't touch the revolver. The youngster must be terrified. And for a long moment it looked as if none of the men were prepared to go anywhere. Glynis knew Cullen would not summarily order them to move unless Judge Heath forced his hand; without other lawmen to back him up, Cullen wouldn't risk a possible showdown. Moreover, he always preferred persuasion.

Glynis held her breath.

But then—whether it was simply Cullen's calmness, the diversion of the judge's arrival, or the severe figure of Judge Heath himself that broke the crowd's mood—with some grumbling the men began to disperse. Most of the whites ambled in the direction of Waterloo's main street; the Iroquois moved purposefully toward the courthouse.

Judge Heath himself came briskly up the steps toward Glynis. He started to go past her, then paused, his cold blue eyes giving her such brief but thorough scrutiny that she wondered what he knew about her—and possibly about her connection to Jacques. She stood there, flushed and uneasy, until Judge Heath, with a cursory nod, went on inside. His black morning coat swung from side to side with each assertive step.

After glancing down once more at the emptying square, Glynis turned to follow the judge into the courthouse. She certainly could not blame the Iroquois for this volatile situation. And other than individual troublemakers, she could not really blame the townsfolk or even Cullen, who, she'd eventually been forced to concede, had only done his job. As he saw it, at least. No, the one to blame was the killer.

GAZING OUT THROUGH the courthouse windows an hour later, Glynis watched a red-tailed hawk circle. Some small unfortunate creature was about to die. Finding herself twirling a strand of hair around her fingers, Glynis tucked the strand back inside her topknot—but not before she had plucked from it one long gray hair. After jabbing a hairpin into place, she laced her fingers firmly in her lap.

She glanced up again at Judge Heath's bench, and the door behind it that led to his chambers. What could be taking so long? Glynis sighed heavily and watched snowflakes strike the windowpanes; windowpanes that only hours before had seen watery sunlight and blue sky. But, three days from the winter solstice, a cloak of white now swirled seasonably over a gray landscape. And brown bears finally had been observed shuffling irritably into their winter quarters.

The coal stove at the front of the courtroom now emitted a series of snaps and hisses, and Glynis became aware of the smell of damp wool and the heat of bodies tightly packed. But she remained chilled from the near hour-long sleigh ride from Seneca Falls; despite the carriage robes and oven-warmed bricks at her feet, only her hands tucked inside a beaver muff had been tolerably warm, and now she continued to clutch her mantle around herself. She let out her breath slowly. Then, after smoothing the green skirt of her winter walking dress, she tried to find comfort on the hard wooden chair. Failing this, she sighed again.

Across the center aisle, Cullen turned to give her a searching frown. Lines drawn by weather creased around his eyes and mouth; the lines seemed deeper than she remembered.

"Why do you suppose," she asked, addressing the aisle space between them, "this is taking so long?" Her voice sounded more curt than she had intended.

Under his frock coat, Cullen's shoulders lifted in a shrug, but he said nothing. Stretching his long legs into the aisle, he gave an impression of nonchalance. Glynis knew better. She glanced up at the grandfather clock standing against the far wall. They had been in conference, the judge and two lawyers, for over half an hour. Meanwhile, the jury had been removed to one back room, the defendant to another. Almost as if Judge Heath had expected the prisoner would try to escape.

As if Jacques Sundown were the dangerous and brutal killer he was accused of being.

Glynis gradually became conscious of the low hum of restrained conversation. She didn't need to turn and look to know they were all there: those who had been subpoenaed; those who had reason to fear the trial's outcome, whatever it might be; those who hated Indians on general principles; and those Waterloo and Seneca Falls people who were merely observers, mixed among the others like seasonings in a stew. Therefore the courtroom was filled. Had been filled on the day previous, when jury selection took place—before and during which Jeremiah Merrycoyf argued that a panel composed entirely of white men could hardly be construed as the defendant's peers, and therefore did not qualify to sit in judgment.

Merrycoyf's arguments had been denied. Judge Heath had ruled, late the previous afternoon, that the trial would proceed with the jurors who had been impaneled.

Glynis now looked up as the door to his chambers opened and Judge Heath reappeared.

"Oyez! Oyez!" called the bailiff. "Let all who have business before the court come forward and you shall be heard. The trial of the People of the State of New York versus Jacques Sundown, also known as Walks At Sundown, is now in session. All rise!"

Chairs scraped against the floor as people scrambled to

their feet. Judge Heath stepped to the bench and waited for the courtroom to reseat itself before saying, "This lengthy delay was necessary. There were several questions to be resolved, pertaining to expert witnesses whom the People and the defendant expect to call. We can now proceed, but I will repeat what I said yesterday. There will be no more outbursts of any kind in my courtroom. Those who do not abide by this admonition will be removed by the bailiff forthwith."

The judge straightened his black robe while directing a baleful eye over those seated below him. Because he had, the day before, ordered several agitators removed, Glynis had small doubt that Judge Heath meant what he said. But his statement did nothing to lessen the silent hostility vibrating throughout the courtroom. The presence of threat remained barely suppressed.

"Bailiff," Judge Heath ordered, "bring in the jury."

Twelve men filed into the jury box. They were sober-faced, ordinary-looking citizens of Seneca County; Glynis hadn't yet observed one of them who could not be described as such. Whether this meant Jacques Sundown would receive justice at their hands remained to be seen. As they were seating themselves, Glynis turned to glance back at Neva Cardoza, who had chosen to sit next to the aisle in the last row.

Neva shot Glynis an angry look. Unquestionably, Neva believed that the witness whose expert qualifications the prosecutor had challenged was she. And that because she was female, she would be found wanting, no matter what her professional background. She might not be allowed to testify at all. Glynis bit down on her lower lip, and turned back to watch the two lawyers enter.

Orrin Makepeace Polk, prosecutor for the People of New York, stepped briskly to his table. But *stepped*, Glynis decided, would not be the most accurate word—*darted* better characterized Polk's entrance. His sharp features, like those of a ferret, and whip-thin body were fairly quivering with anticipation. And Glynis now fretted that Polk's personal antagonism toward Jeremiah Merrycoyf would heighten his usual combativeness.

Behind Orrin Polk, Merrycoyf entered and lumbered to his table. In contrast to the ferretlike prosecutor, Merrycoyf resembled one of the bears whose winter sleep was commencing. A pipestem protruded from the pocket of his black morning coat. He settled into his chair with a sharply expelled breath, then sat forward and straightened his wire-rimmed spectacles as Jacques Sundown was brought to the defense table by the bailiff.

Jacques's wrists were manacled. But he looked no more concerned than ever, and moved, even in these circumstances, with lithe, easy grace. His impassive eyes focused straight ahead. Glynis heard behind her soft exclamations of surprise from Waterloo's female spectators, those who had never before seen Jacques Sundown and were probably expecting, given the charges against him, someone more in common with the creature in Mary Shelley's *Frankenstein*. But it didn't matter; Jacques's striking looks could not save him. In fact, Glynis worried, his appearance might serve to convict him more readily with the all-male jury.

Judge Heath leaned over his bench to address Orrin Polk. "Mr. Prosecutor, we are ready for your opening statement."

As Polk gathered together his notes and rose to speak, Glynis glanced sideways at Cullen. His face, as he watched Polk go forward, bore a grim stillness that distressed her more than if he had scowled. He studiously avoided looking at her—did he still believe Jacques guilty as charged?

As Orrin Polk began what undoubtedly would be a lengthy oration, Glynis gazed again toward the snow-spattered windows.

AND SO, GENTLEMEN of the jury," Polk said dramatically, coming at last to what sounded like his conclusion, "we will establish, without so much as a scintilla of doubt, that the defendant, Jacques Sundown, had the motive, the opportunity, and the means to commit the heinous crime of which he stands accused."

Glynis twisted with discomfort on the stiff wooden chair, and glanced to the rear of the courtroom. The Iroquois men stood ranged against the wall, shoulder to shoulder, arms crossed over their chests. Their dusky faces mirrored the

impassive, stonelike stillness of Jacques, exhibiting no external reaction to Polk's words. Nonetheless, the tension created by their silent presence alone could be felt as a palpable
force.

Before the prosecutor started back to his table, he nodded
to the jury and Judge Heath, then bestowed on Merrycoyf
a brief and self-satisfied smile.

The door of the heating stove clanked on its hinges when
the bailiff pulled it open, and the fire inside hissed noisily
as he shoveled in more coal. Glynis realized she suddenly
felt hot. With a sigh, she untied the grosgrain ribbon of her
mantle, and let the garment drop over the back of the chair;
her wool dress was now more than warm enough.

Conventional wisdom said the stove must remain ablaze
when it was too cold to open the windows, and yet everyone
around her looked uncomfortably overheated. Glynis sighed
again, inhaling the smell of moist woolens, scent bags
packed with dried lavender, pouches of pungent tobacco,
and assorted other odors, not necessarily as agreeable, riding
the close air.

From her seat on the aisle, two rows behind the defense
table, she watched Merrycoyf get to his feet and nod when
Judge Heath asked, "Does the defense wish to make an
opening statement?"

Before he addressed the jury, Merrycoyf glanced toward
the rear of the courtroom. Adam MacAlistair still hadn't
returned. The young lawyer had shot out of the judge's
chamber after the earlier conference; dashing by Glynis, and
in answer to her raised eyebrows, he'd murmured, "Telegraph office." Glynis wondered, with a new surge of un-
ease, what had prompted the sudden need to send a
telegram.

"We surely do wish to make a statement, Your Honor,"
Merrycoyf now said as he shifted to face the jury. "Gentlemen, you have just heard the prosecutor describe the death
of the woman Lily Braun as a heinous crime. While that is
undoubtedly true, the crime was not committed by the defendant. Scientific evidence will clearly demonstrate that my
client, Mr. Sundown, is innocent. And furthermore . . ."

Glynis guessed Merrycoyf's statement would, of necessity, be short. There wasn't much to say. In the past weeks, she and the two lawyers had learned nothing from Jacques Sundown that would shed light on the death of Lily Braun. They had learned some things from other sources, although by no means enough to ensure Jacques's acquittal. But they did know that the day on which Dr. Neva Cardoza first arrived in Seneca Falls, the same one on which Jack Turner voiced his premonition of death, had not been the beginning of this tragedy; that day, in retrospect, had marked only the beginning of the end. The true genesis of what they now confronted had been many years before.

Glynis glanced across the aisle at Cullen. She didn't know if he still believed what he thought he'd seen that day in Jacques's cabin. They had exchanged few words in the past weeks, and their encounters had been brief—as brief as a curt nod on Fall Street—as if the two of them were of remote acquaintance; as if they had experienced over the years simply a single, but unpleasant, encounter. Although one bitterly cold day she had tried to explain.

"Cullen, I'd like for us to talk."

"I'm working right now." This said with frosted breath as he watched skaters on the shallow frozen canal, plainly not wanting to look at her, and plainly not working at anything other than his own anger.

"But you need to hear what really happened that day," she'd persisted.

"Not now."

"When?"

"I don't know, Glynis."

But she had heard something catch in his voice, when he said her name, that made her grasp at hope. So she'd stood there shivering, rubbing her frigid hands together, waiting. He did condescend, finally, to look at her. But his face held such anger, and pain, that she flinched, hurrying away before tears could reveal her own unhappiness. She remained well aware that, while she hadn't done what Cullen tacitly accused her of doing, she'd been more than a little tempted. And this guilty knowledge kept her from yielding to anger of her own.

She'd been staring at her hands clenched in her lap, and

now looked up to see Merrycoyf trudging back to the defense table, where Jacques sat silently, facing the judge's bench. The lawyer's opening had been short indeed.

Yet Merrycoyf had done all within his power to stall the opening week of the trial. In this he had succeeded, as it was now Friday. They would need the weekend recess, he'd said, to weigh the testimony of the prosecutor's opening witnesses; when Polk submitted the names of those he intended to call, Merrycoyf had expressed concern. Most jarring had been the prosecution's subpoena received by Dr. Quentin Ives. And now they must simply wait and see.

Because Jacques would not help them.

Glynis just had turned to rearrange her mantle when Adam MacAlistair came up the aisle. He went to the defense table and said something behind his hand to Merrycoyf before he seated himself to the other side of Jacques; Merrycoyf looked disturbed.

Judge Heath cleared his throat, poured from a carafe into a cup what looked to be tea, and said, "The prosecution may call its first witness."

Mr. Polk rose from his chair. "Yes, Your Honor. The prosecution calls Cullen Stuart."

Cullen moved into and up the center aisle without a glance at Glynis. The women in the courtroom sat a little straighter and watched from the corners of their eyes as he strode past them; several even gave their hair a quick pat. Cullen, however, looked neither right nor left. Nor did he look at Jacques after he'd reached the witness chair.

While he was being sworn, Glynis noticed dark smudges under his eyes, and again marked the deepening lines around his mouth. He also seemed pale. Since most of the time Cullen looked uncommonly healthy, the paleness worried her. But she knew she looked a little peaked herself, and a small spark of anger flared when she wondered if he, like her, had had trouble sleeping. She rather hoped so. And instantly felt ashamed.

Judge Heath leaned forward over the bench, his wintry eyes watching Cullen with interest. Glynis supposed the judge must know that Jacques had once been Cullen's deputy.

"State your name and your place of residence for the record, please," said the court clerk.

"Cullen Stuart, constable of the village of Seneca Falls, Seneca County, New York." He appeared at ease in the witness chair, and if he was at all troubled, he didn't display it. Orrin Polk stepped forward, not missing the opportunity for an ingratiating smile at the jury. "Constable Stuart, would you tell the court how long you have been a law-enforcement officer?"

"Sixteen years, more or less."

"Continuously?"

"Yes, except for several months in '54."

"And what did you do during those months, Constable?"

"I was employed by Pinkerton's Detective Agency."

"Ah, yes, Pinkerton's. In that case, I think we can safely assume that you are experienced in law enforcement. And what was your education?"

"Four years of college, and one year of law school."

Glynis caught Adam MacAlistair's surprised look. He wouldn't know that Cullen had hated law school, and had left mostly because he'd discovered he might be compelled to represent the guilty as well as the innocent. He'd concluded that he preferred putting them in jail to getting them out.

Glynis stole a glance back at Neva Cardoza; Abraham Levy had arrived and now sat beside her, and Neva no longer looked quite as angry. Although that was probably subject to change, depending on what the judge had decided about her future testimony.

Polk restated at length Cullen's expertise in law enforcement—as if there were some question, Glynis thought in irritation.

"Constable Stuart," Polk at last began, "how long have you known the defendant, Jacques Sundown?" He pronounced it "Jacks Sundown," hissing the *s*'s like an irritated snake.

"Around ten years, on and off."

"On and off?"

"Jacques would leave town every so often—for extended periods."

"I see—yes, I see," Polk said as if giving this statement weighty consideration. "And what was your association with the defendant?"

"He was my deputy for some of that time."

"Your deputy. So he worked for you?"

"Yes."

"Constable Stuart, did you have any contact with the defendant other than your work affiliation? Did you, for instance, spend time together when you were both off duty?"

"In a small town, Mr. Polk, a constable is never off duty."

Glynis heard a few chuckles, and saw several members of the jury smile. But why was Polk going on about this at such length?

"So you had close contact with the defendant?"

Cullen seemed to be considering his answer overly long, before he said, "I don't know if I'd call it close. Jacques Sundown's not an easy man to know. He tends to avoid contact."

Glynis saw Adam glance at Merrycoyf, who shook his head slightly. She thought the young lawyer probably wanted to object to Polk's leading questions, but she didn't think Merrycoyf would, not without serious cause. A lot of niggling objections could provoke the jury, and Merrycoyf could safely assume, because he'd dealt with Polk before, that breaches of conduct would get even worse later on. She almost could see him sending Adam the message: Save the objections until they count.

"Tends to avoid contact," Polk echoed loudly. "I see. Would you, then, characterize the defendant as a taciturn man, Constable?"

"Yes."

"A solitary individual—a lone wolf, so to speak?"

"Yes."

"Please, Your Honor," Merrycoyf now said, "while I have great respect for Constable Stuart's judgment, he has already stated that he didn't socialize with Mr. Sundown. So why is he being asked to describe anything about my client other than his deputy's professional conduct?"

Judge Heath gave a brief nod. "Yes, Mr. Polk, I fail to

see where your questions are leading. Please move along.''

Polk snapped out his next question. "Constable Stuart, would you describe *your deputy* as an aggressive man?"

Adam MacAlistair twitched in his chair, staring pointedly at Merrycoyf. Again the older attorney shook his head.

"Aggressive? Yes, I'd say Sundown could be aggressive," Cullen agreed.

"Would you give us an example of this character trait?" Polk asked.

"Well," Cullen answered, "I've seen him attack in situations where most men would back off. Given the opportunity, Sundown would always put himself in an offensive position rather than a defensive one. But maybe," Cullen added unexpectedly, "that just means he has more courage than most men."

Jacques's shoulders stiffened imperceptibly; if Glynis hadn't been watching for his reaction, she never would have seen it. And Adam received a smile from Merrycoyf. Glynis imagined what he was thinking: You see, young man—give Mr. Prosecutor Polk enough rope and he'll hang himself.

As if to keep Cullen from further gratuitous speculation, Polk hurried on. "Do you recall, Constable, the defendant being present at the scene of several recent murders?"

"Objection!" Merrycoyf was on his feet. Adam MacAlistair wore a stunned expression, and was staring at Polk in disbelief.

"Your Honor," Merrycoyf said, "Your Honor, I object to the prosecutor's tactic most strenuously. He is attempting to inflame the jury. My client is not on trial for *several* murders!"

"Your Honor," Polk jumped in, before Judge Heath could speak, "I am simply laying the groundwork here. I intend to connect these murders by means of motive."

"I object!" Merrycoyf stood, bending forward, the fingers of his hands pressing the table. "Your Honor, there is no foundation for the prosecutor to use the word *murder*. Cause of death has not been established, and my learned colleague knows it!"

"Yes, Mr. Polk," Judge Heath said, frowning. "Mr. Merrycoyf's objection to the word *murder* is well taken. I sustain his objection. But I will allow the prosecution some latitude if you intend to establish motive here.''

''Your Honor—'' Merrycoyf began, but the judge cut him off with, ''Proceed, Mr. Polk.''

Polk nodded and smiled appreciatively. ''Constable Stuart, did you arrive at the scene of the . . . the untimely death of the man Jake Braun?''

''Yes, his body was still warm when I found him.''

''Describe the scene, please.''

''I got to Braun's house in the early morning. Inside, the victim was lying on the kitchen floor, not breathing. I found no heartbeat. I heard a horse out back, and when I went to the door, I saw Sundown riding off. Fast. I went after him on my own horse. Had to chase him—''

''Objection,'' Merrycoyf said. ''The word *chase* is subjective and prejudicial. How does the witness know that my client was fleeing? He doesn't.''

''Would you rephrase that, Constable Stuart?'' the judge said.

Cullen looked vaguely annoyed, Glynis thought, before he said, ''I *followed* Jacques Sundown to the edge of Black Brook Reservation before he pulled up.''

''And did you ask him how he happened to be at the scene of a mur—of an untimely death?'' Polk said.

Merrycoyf glared at him.

Cullen said, ''I asked him. He said he was exercising his horse.''

''And did you believe him?''

''No,'' Cullen said. ''No, I didn't.''

''Why is that?''

''Jake Braun's place is pretty remote. You have to know where it is to find it. And since it's not on the main road, or on the way to anywhere else, it's not easy to just stumble on it—exercising your horse, for instance. Then there was Braun's attitude. He'd been sure he was being hunted. Insisted he was.''

''Being hunted,'' Polk repeated unnecessarily. ''You mean, Constable, that Mr. Braun knew he would be murdered—''

''Objection.'' Merrycoyf interrupted, adopting a we've-been-through-this-before expression.

"Mr. Polk," said Judge Heath, "I've admonished you about that once. Objection sustained."

"Yes, Your Honor," said Polk, not at all bothered, Glynis observed, since the damage, as far as the jury was concerned, had already been done.

"Constable Stuart," Polk went on, "did Jake Braun tell you *why* he felt endangered?"

"No. Wouldn't talk at all about why. He did make some comments to the effect that others had recently died. And he was genuinely terrified of something, I'll swear to that."

"Very good, Constable. I'm certain the court is quite willing to take your word for it. Now then, I'd like to ask you about another untimely death—that of one Mead Miller. Did you have the opportunity to locate Mr. Miller's body?"

"Yes. It was along Black Brook, about a mile out of town."

"Would you tell the court what you observed about Mead Miller prior to his demise?"

"On what turned out to be the night of his death, I saw Miller at a tavern, drunk and disorderly. He was obviously agitated, and he was thrown out of the tavern for fighting."

"Did you see him after that?"

"The next time I saw him, he was dead."

"And, Constable, did you become aware sometime later that the defendant had been at or near the vicinity of Miller's death?"

"Objection," Merrycoyf said. "Hearsay."

"Overruled," Judge Heath snapped. "The witness can certainly testify as to what he became aware of."

"Do you recall the question, Constable Stuart?"

"Yes. Jacques Sundown appeared at the time Miller's body was first discovered. Miss Glynis Tryon, who found the body, told me—"

"Objection!" Merrycoyf growled. "That is hearsay, Your Honor."

"Sustained." Judge Heath leaned over his bench. "Mr. Polk, that is rank hearsay."

"Yes, Your Honor," Polk said, sounding not in the least chastened, Glynis observed. She herself wanted to crawl under the chair. Both Polk and Cullen knew very well that Cullen couldn't testify to what someone had told him. To what were they leading?

"Constable, some days before the untimely death of Mead Miller, was there yet another untimely death in your village?"

"Objection!" Merrycoyf said firmly. "Immaterial and irrelevant."

"I will establish this as part of the pattern providing motive, Your Honor," said Polk.

"Objection overruled," said Judge Heath.

As the judge spoke, Glynis could see both Adam and Merrycoyf furiously making notes on their pads. Merrycoyf had said that the judicial rulings regarding testimony on previous deaths would be crucial. He had hoped against hope that the judge wouldn't allow them. An unavailing hope, it now seemed.

Polk cleared his throat dramatically. "Do you recall the question, Constable Stuart, regarding another death—*untimely,* of course?"

"Yes. Man's name was Jack Turner. His body was brought into town by his wife and some neighbors."

"And did you have some pertinent contact with the victim, Mr. Turner, before his death?"

Merrycoyf scowled but didn't object.

"The day before Jack Turner's death, he stopped me on Fall Street, insisting he was going to be killed."

"Did he say by whom?"

"No, he refused to say."

"I see. Now, then, would you please tell the court, Constable Stuart, if, some years ago, you were at the scene of a fatal fire at what was known as the Flannery farm?"

Glynis bit her lower lip. They were going to tie that fire in, she knew it. And she was the one who'd suggested to Cullen that there *was* a connection.

"Yes. I was there. Two men were killed in the fire—Cole Flannery and Dick Davis, a hired hand."

"When was the fire?"

"In '52."

"Did you observe anything at the scene that looked out

of the ordinary, Constable Stuart?''

For a moment it appeared to Glynis that Merrycoyf would object. But he held his peace, although he seemed disturbed.

''The two men's bodies were found next to the barn door, as if they'd been trying to get out. But the door had been bolted from the outside.''

''Did you inquire as to how this might have occurred?''

''Yes, but no one there, fighting the fire, came forward to say anything. I decided at the time that someone had done it by mistake during the initial confusion.''

''And do you still think that was the case, Constable?''

''I don't know. I think it's possible that the fire was set, and the two men deliberately locked inside.''

''Objection,'' Merrycoyf called. ''That's pure conjecture on the witness's part.''

''Yes, I'll sustain that objection,'' the judge said. ''The jury is ordered to disregard the last statement.''

''Tell me, Constable Stuart,'' Polk asked, ''was there anyone else in the Flannery family at the farm that night?''

''No. Cole's wife had taken their children to visit relatives in Syracuse. Seems it was only the second time she'd ever been off the farm overnight without her husband.''

''Your Honor,'' Merrycoyf complained, ''I must object again to this immaterial and irrelevant line of questioning. We have gotten very far afield, here. Does the prosecutor really intend to question the constable about every death that's ever taken place in Seneca Falls?''

''If I have to—'' Polk began. But he was interrupted by Judge Heath.

''Mr. Polk, I said I would allow you some latitude. But do you intend to connect this testimony to the matter at hand before this court?''

''Yes, Your Honor. As stated earlier, I intend to establish a pattern that will clearly demonstrate the motive for the crime of murder!''

Polk fairly shouted the word *murder*.

Adam sprang to his feet; he looked over Jacques's head at Merrycoyf and received a curt shake of the older lawyer's head.

Adam sat back down as Merrycoyf said sharply, ''Your

Honor, the prosecutor is clearly attempting to prejudice the jury with inflammatory assertions that have nothing to do with the case at hand. I cannot object strongly enough to this tactic. And I am shocked that the learned prosecutor would stoop to this chicanery.''

"Your Honor," Polk protested, "I am merely establishing a foundation for the crime we are now prosecuting."

"Then I suggest you get on with it, Mr. Polk," Judge Heath said. He took a swallow from his teacup, and set it down with an emphatic *clunk*.

Polk walked to the witness chair to stand beside Cullen. "Constable Stuart, have you had occasion to go to the defendant's residence?"

"Yes."

"Describe where it is located, if you please."

"It's an isolated cabin on the southeastern edge of Black Brook Reservation. Backs up to the woods."

"Isolated, you say?"

"Yes."

"And is there a woodpile near the cabin?"

"Yes, a short distance behind it."

"Now, Constable, please tell the court for what purpose you went to the defendant's isolated cabin."

Cullen's jaw tightened, which Glynis recognized in him as proof positive of strain. Not that he looked as strained as she undoubtedly did. "The day after last month's severe storm," he began, "when I returned from a trip to Rochester, I was told by . . ."

Cullen paused, obviously anticipating Merrycoyf's objection, and quickly corrected himself by saying, "That is, I *became aware* that a horse, rented by Miss Glynis Tryon a few hours before the storm hit, had returned alone, and without a carriage, to the livery. Since no one, including her landlady, had seen Miss Tryon after that time, I assumed she'd been caught in the storm. I went in search of her."

Glynis had the distressing sense that every head in the courtroom was swiveling toward her, and again wished she could crawl under her chair. But she gripped her hands anxiously in her lap and stared straight ahead, praying for some semblance of dignity, and hoping she didn't look as flushed as she felt. Moreover, she had still worse to fear from Cullen's testimony.

She wondered, though, why in his search he would have headed north. Then she realized that the livery owner, John Boone, probably had seen her turn onto Black Brook Road. Going toward the reservation!

". . . and alongside the road," Cullen now was saying, "I found the carriage badly smashed. And some yards away I found a glove that I knew belonged to Miss Tryon."

Yes, he certainly would know it was hers; Cullen had given her those fur-lined gloves the previous Christmas.

"The carriage and glove," Cullen went on, "were about a quarter-mile from the Grimm farm. But when I stopped at the Grimms', no one there had seen her, so I went on north. I thought, if Miss Tryon was on foot, she might . . . she might have become disoriented in the storm. And ended up at the reservation."

Had Cullen *really* believed that? Or had he, right from the start, guessed she had gone to see Jacques? Glynis swallowed with difficulty; this was the part of his testimony she had been dreading the most. She had no way of knowing if Cullen, angry as he was with her, would try to protect her reputation. Whether he would actually testify that she'd been with Jacques. Unless Cullen had told Orrin Polk, no one else knew—no one but Merrycoyf. And she'd been told by Jeremiah that if he had to—to provide Jacques with an alibi—he'd compromise her in a second. But he'd vowed to avoid it if he could.

And so she just had to suffer the waiting.

But not for long, as Orrin Polk now asked, "To relieve our concern, Constable Stuart, did you locate the missing lady?"

Glynis wanted to duck her head, but before she could, Cullen's eyes found her. She forced herself to lift her chin and meet his gaze, and even hold it for an interminable moment.

Cullen's eyes swung back to Polk. "Yes," he said. "She'd found shelter, and she was . . . she was all right."

Glynis slowly let out her breath, and looked at Cullen

with what she hoped conveyed gratitude. But his face had turned toward the jury.

"Well, splendid," Polk said, smiling. But then, in a flash, his expression transformed to something less pleasant. "Did you also then find the defendant's cabin?"

"Yes," Cullen said, now turning to look for the first time at Jacques.

"Tell the court what you found there."

Cullen's eyes narrowed, and he continued to stare at Jacques, while he said, "I saw some tracks—they looked as if they'd come out of the trees and led to the woodpile. When I went to check, back of the woodpile, I found the body of Lily Braun. It was partially covered with snow. There was a knife in her chest."

The courtroom had become very still. Though all must have been aware of what was to come, they waited with breathless attention.

"Constable Stuart, did you recognize the knife?"

"Yes. The blade was buried in the victim's chest, but the handle was visible. It was of bone, and distinctively carved."

"How?"

"With the head of a wolf."

"And had you seen this carved handle before?"

"Many times."

"And to whom did this vicious weapon belong, Constable?"

"To Jacques Sundown."

Polk waited until, after a collective intake of breath, the spectators had quieted before he said briskly, "Thank you, Constable Stuart. I have no further questions of this witness, Your Honor."

"Mr. Merrycoyf," Judge Heath said, "do you wish to cross-examine the witness?"

Glynis knew Merrycoyf would be assessing the damage. And would only question Cullen if he could be certain to blunt the previous testimony. Otherwise he would pass, not wanting to emphasize the harm already done.

"Yes, Your Honor," Merrycoyf said amiably, "I have just a few questions." Judge Heath motioned him to proceed. Merrycoyf remained seated while he said, "Constable Stuart, you mentioned some tracks behind Mr. Sundown's cabin. Did you follow those tracks to ascertain from where they came?"

"Couldn't follow them," Cullen said. "The snow had drifted over them by that time, and they were covered except for the few that went, as I said, to the woodpile."

"So those tracks might have originated anywhere, correct?"

Cullen shrugged. "I don't know where they came from, if that's what you mean, Jeremi—Mr. Merrycoyf."

"No, you couldn't know, my friend. Just one more question. My learned colleague, Mr. Polk, has led you to describe Mr. Sundown's character as—"

"Your Honor," Polk interrupted, "if counsel for the defense had a complaint, he should have voiced his objection earlier."

Judge Heath peered down at Polk and said, "I don't hear counsel complaining now, Mr. Prosecutor. And let us please keep this sniping to a minimum, gentlemen. Proceed, Mr. Merrycoyf."

"Thank you, Your Honor. Constable Stuart, you described your deputy, the defendant, as aggressive. Had you ever seen Mr. Sundown behave aggressively toward a non-aggressive person? Someone not able to defend himself?"

Glynis recalled what Cullen had told her about the night he first met Jacques; she hoped Cullen remembered it. If he did, she knew he wouldn't lie about it. He didn't lie.

"No," Cullen said. "No, I never saw Sundown do that."

"Ever see him attack a woman?"

"Never."

"Thank you, Constable. No further questions."

"Your Honor," Orrin Polk said suddenly, "May I have leave to ask one last question on redirect?"

Judge Heath scowled, but said "Yes."

"Constable Stuart," Polk asked, "would you tell the court whether there have been any more untimely deaths, any at all, *since* the defendant has been incarcerated?"

"No."

"Thank you very much, Constable Stuart."

As Cullen left the witness chair, Judge Heath said, "Mr. Prosecutor, do you anticipate a lengthy examination of your next witness?"

"Oh, yes, sir, I do," Polk replied; the enthusiasm with which he said this, Glynis found alarming.

"In that case, we will recess one hour for mealtime. Court adjourned."

TWENTY

❦

For ache of womb [stomach] of man or woman that hath
eaten venom. Take green rue and wash it, and temper it with
wine, and give to drink.
    —*A Leechbook or Collection of*
      Medical Recipes of the Fifteenth
      Century

GLYNIS WENT DOWN the courthouse stairs and into a small
room off the entrance lobby. Merrycoyf and Adam Mac-
Alistair had located chairs and seated themselves around a
small table, as had Neva and Abraham Levy, and they'd
begun eating whatever cold lunch they had brought from
home. They did not present a cheerful picture.

The smell of coffee wafted in from somewhere. "I'll go
find it," offered Adam, with what Glynis had begun to believe was inexhaustible vitality. Merrycoyf watched his
young colleague bound out the door, and expelled a heavy
sigh. He chewed slowly, not seeming to pay much attention
to his food, which Glynis knew to be a very bad omen.
Finally he turned to Neva, who'd been looking pointedly at
him since Glynis arrived. And Merrycoyf sighed again.

"Does that sigh mean what I think it means?" Neva questioned him, anger poised in her tone.

"Yes, Dr. Cardoza, I'm afraid so. Judge Heath ruled that
you cannot testify in the capacity of an expert witness."

"The wretched bastard!" Neva erupted, bringing a stran-
gled sound from Abraham, and a long look over his spectacles from Merrycoyf. Adam had just come back through
the door with several mugs of coffee, which, following Neva's outburst, sloshed alarmingly.

"I suppose I shouldn't bother to ask why," Neva added
sharply, ignoring Adam's rueful inspection of a stained shirt
cuff.

"No, probably not," Merrycoyf agreed.

"Well, *I* will," Glynis said, blotting the coffee on Adam's cuff with his handkerchief. "I take it Judge Heath has denied that Neva is a qualified doctor—because she's a woman?"

"Why else?" Neva snapped.

Merrycoyf sighed again. "We really don't have time to address the issue now," he said. "I intend to ponder it later, as this ruling could be to our advantage." Neva's head came up at this, as did Glynis's. "But frankly, young woman"— he peered at Neva—"it is not the most serious of our immediate troubles."

Neva's lips pressed tightly together, and Glynis expected to see steam pour from her ears. And she didn't blame Neva. But Jeremiah was right; there was no time now for this. She turned to Adam and asked, "Why did you go to the telegraph office earlier this morning—to send a wire to whom?"

Adam answered, "To Dr. Patrick Kelly in Rochester. Let's hope he can get here by Monday." He said to Merrycoyf, "Do you think he'll complete his case today? The ferret-face, I mean?"

Merrycoyf jerked erect in his chair. "Mr. MacAlistair!" he said sternly. "Please never let me hear you speak of a colleague in such a disparaging manner. Mr. Polk has had a notable career"—noted for what, Glynis observed, Jeremiah didn't say—"and he deserves respect whether you agree with his approach or not. Do I make myself clear?"

Adam nodded readily enough, but Glynis saw his mouth twitching, as was her own and Abraham's. Neva, however, still looked irate.

"Insofar as your question, young man," Merrycoyf went on, if somewhat less sternly, "it all depends. If things proceed as depressingly apace as they did this morning, I'd imagine Mr. Polk will rest his case today."

All of them were silent. There would be so little time to act.

"MR. POLK," JUDGE Heath directed, "call your next witness."

"The prosecution calls Dr. Quentin Ives."

As Ives came forward to be sworn, carrying a number of file folders, Glynis glanced back at Neva, who shook her head and mouthed, "No."

Glynis nodded with relief and turned to face the bench. Either Quentin Ives hadn't said anything to Neva, or hadn't yet discovered that his files had been rifled. Two nights before, after the subpoena had arrived, and while the Ives family had slept upstairs, she and Neva had crept with lighted candles into Quentin's small downstairs office. They worked as fast as they could by candlelight, not wanting to risk the brighter glow of lanterns. It took half the night to find the files for which they searched. They had had to go through patient records that went back ten years.

Not that their findings would do Jacques much good, but at least the defense would be spared the shock that this afternoon's testimony would undoubtedly bring. She and Neva hadn't told Merrycoyf how they had come by their ill-gotten information. And Merrycoyf, pragmatic soul that he was, hadn't asked. But Glynis suspected that he guessed and probably Adam did, too.

Quentin Ives was just now finishing his qualifications, and Merrycoyf had slumped in his chair as if asleep. Glynis knew better, but Adam, glancing over at him repeatedly, looked concerned.

"Dr. Ives," Polk began, "did you conduct an autopsy on the deceased Jack Turner?"

"Yes."

"Objection, Your Honor," Merrycoyf rumbled. Adam looked relieved. "Same objection of irrelevance and immateriality as previously made."

"Overruled, Mr. Merrycoyf," said Judge Heath. "Same ruling as previously made, subject to prosecutor's establishing motive. Continue, Mr. Polk."

"Dr. Ives, would you tell the court what you found?"

"We found Jack Turner's death to be a result of arsenic poisoning. By 'we,' " Quentin Ives turned to the jury, "I mean Dr. Neva Cardoza and myself."

Bless Quentin for that. Glynis imagined Neva was grateful, even though Judge Heath and Polk would ignore her participation. The physician now recited the medical findings on which they had based their conclusions about Turner's death.

"Did you also, Dr. Ives, conduct an autopsy on the deceased Mead Miller?" Polk asked.

"Yes, again with Dr. Cardoza. Our findings indicated that he had died as a result of poisoning." Ives again described their process of discovery, giving Neva credit for suggesting rattlesnake venom.

"Did you make any conclusion about how this poison was delivered to the victim?" Polk said.

"Not conclusively."

"Given your professional experience, have you an opinion, Dr. Ives?"

"Objection!" Merrycoyf said perfunctorily, as if expecting it to be overruled. It was.

"A hole in the victim's neck indicated that it had been pierced with a pointed object."

"Such as an arrow, Dr. Ives?" Polk asked loudly.

"Probably something smaller."

"For instance?" Polk prodded.

"Your Honor, I object," Merrycoyf said. "The good doctor has just testified that he found inconclusive evidence—"

"I'll restate the question," Ives jumped in. "Dr. Ives, could the poison have been delivered by means of a dart?"

Quentin Ives hesitated. Then, reluctantly, he said, "It could have."

"Are you familiar, doctor, with the Iroquois weapons known as air-guns, sometimes called blowguns, that use—"

"Objection!" This time, Merrycoyf sounded angry. "The witness has not been established as an expert in weaponry. And let the record show that I restate my previous and continuing objection—a strenuous objection—to the prosecutor's repeated inclusion in this proceeding of immaterial and irrelevant deaths. My client is not being tried for those deaths, Your Honor."

"Mr. Polk," Judge Heath said irritably, "I expect you to show a connection shortly with that of the victim Lily Braun, sir. And I will sustain the defense's objection to your last question of this witness.''

But again, Glynis thought, the damage had been done. The jury might be ordered to disregard the prosecutor's question, but how could they? Their eyes had all swept to Jacques when Orrin Polk mentioned Iroquois air-guns. It would surely stick in their minds.

"Moving on, Dr. Ives," said Polk. "Did you conduct an autopsy on the body of Jake Braun?"

"Yes, again with Dr. Cardoza."

"Yes, yes, doctor. And what did you discover to be the cause of death?"

"Actually, I didn't discover the cause of death," Ives answered quickly.

Polk hesitated, then wheeled around and went to his notes on the table. The spectators in the courtroom stirred restlessly, as if waking from a monotonous dream, Glynis thought, wondering how Polk would handle this. She looked back at Neva, who sent her a smug smile.

"Ah, yes, Dr. Ives," Polk said, returning to stand by the witness chair. "I see now that a tissue sample of Braun's was sent to Rochester—to a Dr. Patrick Kelly. Why was that?"

"It was Dr. Cardoza's idea. She felt that Braun's death might be the result of nicotine poisoning, owing to the odd yellow tinge of his facial skin. It was somewhat different from the jaundiced color associated with liver failure, but we didn't have the expertise or equipment to determine that. Dr. Cardoza knew that Dr. Kelly was considered an expert in that area."

Polk stroked his clean-shaven chin momentarily, then seemed to make some kind of decision, as he said, "Dr. Ives, this Miss Cardoza—"

"*Dr.* Cardoza," Quentin Ives corrected him.

"Yes, well, she's just some sort of trainee under your supervision, isn't she?"

"No, Dr. Cardoza already has a medical degree, Mr. Polk. She's now simply fulfilling a residency requirement before being admitted to the staff of a New York City hospital."

Glynis didn't dare look around at Neva, who must be

rubbing her hands with glee over the pompous Polk's blunder.

But Judge Heath suddenly said, "Mr. Prosecutor, shall we move along? This discussion hardly seems relevant to the case at hand."

"Yes, Your Honor," said Polk, in the relieved voice of one who had been tossed a rope as he sank in quicksand. "Yes, certainly. Tell us, Dr. Ives, did this Dr. Kelly in Rochester send you a report on his findings?"

"Yes. He verified that the postmortem tissue sent by Dr. Cardoza indicated that Braun's corpse did indeed exhibit signs of nicotine poisoning. And this would be consistent with Dr. Cardoza's observation of the discoloration of the victim's face."

"Meaning what?" Polk said, looking dubious.

"Meaning that the poison was applied to Braun's face. Very likely it was put in something as innocent-looking as shaving lather or soap."

"And that could have caused his death?"

"Absolutely."

Polk seemed to have regained his bearings, as he now asked, "How soon would death have occurred after the application of the nicotine?"

"It could have been quickly."

"*How* quickly? Dr. Ives. Give us your best estimate."

Quentin Ives clearly recognized what Polk was driving at, because he sounded reluctant when he answered, "Death could have occurred anywhere from five minutes to four hours afterward."

"Five minutes? You did say *five minutes,* Doctor?"

"Well, that's the lowest estimate that—"

"Yes, of course," Polk cut him off. "Thank you very much," he said with obvious satisfaction. "Now, Dr. Ives, can you tell us the findings of your autopsy on the poor woman, Lily Braun?"

"No, I can't."

"I beg your pardon, Doctor?"

"I can't tell you what I found, because I didn't conduct the autopsy. I had been called out of town. So Dr. Cardoza did—"

"Thank you, Doctor. I have a few last questions." Polk went to his table and picked up a sheet of paper, then returned to stand by the witness chair. "Dr. Ives, have you brought those files requested by me and pursuant to this court's subpoena?"

"Yes." Ives indicated the files on his lap.

"Fine." Polk glanced at the paper in his hands. "Now, Dr. Ives, did you sign a death certificate for one Otto Braun on the sixteenth of April, 1848?"

Ives opened a folder and shuffled through several papers.

Glynis glanced back at Neva, who shrugged and shook her head slightly. In their nocturnal search, they'd left the physician's own duplicate death certificate on top of the other papers in the folder labeled BRAUN, OTTO, Glynis was sure of it. Still, she exhaled with relief when Ives stopped shuffling the papers, and nodded at Polk.

"Yes," he said, staring at what Glynis knew to be his duplicate of Otto Braun's death certificate. "Yes, here it is, and the date is as you stated—April '48," he told Polk.

"How old was Otto Braun at his death?"

"It says here that he was forty-two."

"And what did you list as the cause of death, Doctor?"

"Cardiac failure."

"At the time, did you have any reservations about your conclusion, Dr. Ives? I ask this because the victim was brought to you after having just been in a terrible wagon accident—or I should say *perhaps* it was an accident."

"I really don't remember, it was so long ago," Ives said.

"Were you aware at the time, Doctor, that wheels of Braun's wagon had unaccountably fallen off, going down a steep grade? Or that this wagon's hand brake was later found to be broken? Do you remember?"

"Objection!" Merrycoyf said angrily. "Not only is this testimony irrelevant and totally immaterial, but the event in question took place almost ten years ago. Does the prosecutor really expect the good doctor to remember every death he attends?"

"Overruled," said Judge Heath. "The witness is capable of stating whether or not he remembers."

"I don't remember," Ives now said.

"From your records, was there any indication before his deadly *accident* that the victim's heart was weak?"

"Objection!" Merrycoyf had lunged to his feet. "Your Honor—"

"Sustained," said the judge.

"I'll rephrase that for you, Dr. Ives. Did Otto Braun have any history of heart trouble?"

"No, but that doesn't mean that—"

"Thank you," Polk cut him off. "Dr. Ives, were you aware that the Otto Braun in question was the father of Lily Braun?"

Merrycoyf looked about to object, but instead sank back silently in his chair.

"Yes," Ives answered, "I seem to remember that."

"And that the Jake Braun mentioned earlier in your testimony was the brother of Otto Braun and the uncle of Lily Braun?"

"Perhaps I knew that. I'm not sure I made the connection," Quentin Ives said, looking puzzled.

Glynis felt so warm, she was experiencing lightheadedness. Or it could be from the intensity of the prosecutor's attack, she thought miserably. She watched Polk go to his table and retrieve more papers. This was proving worse than they had feared. But it was not, thanks to the midnight foray, completely unexpected.

"To continue," said Polk, "do your records, Dr. Ives, indicate that you signed a death certificate for one George Jackson in June of 1854?"

Again Ives shuffled. "Yes, apparently I did," he responded, grasping a document. "But I don't recall this at all."

"How old was George Jackson when he died?"

Ives scanned the duplicate certificate. "Thirty-four."

"The cause of George Jackson's death?"

"I have here that it was due to liver failure," answered Ives. He glanced through the file.

"Did Jackson have a history of liver problems?"

"Apparently not. I really don't recall this."

"Did you perform an autopsy, Dr. Ives?"

"No. An autopsy isn't usually done—"

"But why did you conclude that the cause of death was liver failure?"

"Probably because he was jaundiced."

"Jaundiced. You mean yellowish? Yellowish like Jake Braun?"

"Objection, Your Honor," Merrycoyf said, exasperation in his voice.

"Sustained," Judge Heath ruled. "Mr. Polk, would you please conclude whatever it is you are leading to? And I assume you *are* leading to something?"

"Yes, Your Honor. One last death certificate, Dr. Ives— that of a Dooley Keegan, signed by you in October of 1855. Do you recall Mr. Keegan's death?"

"Yes, I do."

"The cause of death was cardiac failure?"

"That's what I wrote here," said Ives, looking unhappily at the document in his hand.

"And Keegan's age?"

"He was thirty-one."

"Only *thirty-one*? And did he have a history of heart—"

"No," Ives broke in.

"You seem quite definite about that, Doctor. Did you have some question about your diagnosis at the time?"

Ives hesitated and stared down at the open folder he held. "Well, yes," he said finally. "Thirty-one is a young age for death from heart problems. But it's not unheard of, certainly."

"But you felt it was, perhaps, suspicious?"

"Objection!" said Merrycoyf. "Leading the witness."

"Overruled," said Judge Heath. "Answer the question, Dr. Ives."

"I thought it was unusual, yes. Especially since Dooley Keegan had no history of any illness at all that I was aware of."

"Dr. Ives, in retrospect, do you find the deaths of the three relatively young and healthy men just discussed to be, shall we say, questionable?"

"Objection! Irrelevant and immaterial!" Merrycoyf protested.

"Overruled. The witness is directed to answer."

"Well," Ives said slowly, "I suppose that in retrospect it might seem that way. But the deaths were separated by years. And young men occasionally do die suddenly. At the time, I had no reason to believe that the deaths involved anything other than natural causes."

"But now, Dr. Ives?"

"Your Honor," Merrycoyf said firmly, "Dr. Ives has already answered the prosecutor's question, several times. I object strongly to this harassment of a witness."

"He's not even your witness!" Polk snarled.

"Gentlemen!" Judge Heath admonished. "I believe, Mr. Polk, that the doctor has answered to the best of his ability. Objection sustained."

"Thank you, Dr. Ives," Polk said. "I have no further questions of this witness, Your Honor."

Glynis saw Adam lean behind Jacques to confer momentarily with Merrycoyf. Merrycoyf nodded and then stood.

Judge Heath said, "Do you wish to cross-examine Dr. Ives?"

"Yes, just briefly," Merrycoyf said, going toward the witness chair. "Please tell us, Dr. Ives," he directed, "if you recently signed a death certificate for one Obadiah Grimm?"

"Yes, I did."

"What did you list as the cause of death?"

"Death was due to a punctured heart," Ives stated emphatically.

"No question about it?"

"No question."

"Did his death look suspicious, Dr. Ives?" Merrycoyf turned to glower at Polk as if daring him to object.

Polk seemed to be considering it, but said nothing.

"Yes, it looked odd," Ives said. "Dr. Cardoza seemed to think—"

"Objection! Hearsay and conjecture," Polk said.

"Sustained."

"What did *you* think, Doctor?"

"I thought Mr. Grimm impaled himself on a sharp object that punctured his heart."

"An accident?"

Ives hesitated. "I don't know," he said finally.

Polk was on his feet, probably ready to call this irrelevant, Glynis guessed, because Obadiah Grimm didn't fit into the pattern he was trying to establish.

In any event, Merrycoyf quickly said, "No more questions, Dr. Ives. Thank you."

As Quentin Ives went back to his seat, Glynis turned to look at Neva, who gave a sideways bob of her head. Glynis followed her gaze and was startled to see the sweet-voiced Seneca woman, Small Brown Bird, seated in the last row by the door. The woman's head was down, staring at her hands folded in her lap. Glynis supposed she shouldn't be surprised; after all, she remembered, Small Brown Bird was Jacques Sundown's aunt.

She turned back as Judge Heath said, "Mr. Polk, call your next witness."

"The prosecution calls Mr. Theobald Fedmore."

A tall, lanky man with thinning hair made his way up the aisle; under his arm he carried a bulging file folder. Glynis thought she recalled seeing him in court earlier, but couldn't identify him. She was afraid, though, that she knew what he did and why he was there.

"Your name and your residence?" the court clerk asked after the witness had been sworn.

"Theobald Fedmore, and I live in Waterloo."

"Mr. Fedmore," Polk began, "what is your occupation, sir?"

"I'm the Seneca County clerk."

"And as such, Mr. Fedmore, do your duties include maintenance of the civil litigation records for the Supreme Court of Seneca County?"

"Yes."

"Very good. Mr. Fedmore, at my request, and pursuant to a subpoena issued by this court, have you brought with you documents concerning the case of Many Horned Stag versus the following: Jake Braun, Otto Braun, Dick Davis, Cole Flannery, George Jackson, Dooley Keegan, Mead Miller, and Jack Turner?"

"Yes, I have them here." Theobald Fedmore indicated the file folder on his lap.

Polk asked now, "And who was counsel of record for the parties named?"

Mr. Fedmore must have just reviewed the case, Glynis decided, as he didn't even open the folder before he answered, "Jeremiah Merrycoyf for the plaintiff, Many Horned Stag, and Orrin Makepeace Polk for all the defendants named."

Glynis looked at Merrycoyf, who again appeared to be drowsing, but now had a small smile on his lips.

"Mr. Fedmore," continued Polk, "are you acquainted with the pleadings?"

"Yes, I have reviewed them."

"Fine. And what was the nature of the claims?"

"Plaintiff Many Horned Stag, for the benefit and in the right of the Seneca Indian Nation, sought an injunction to prohibit the defendants from constructing a dam on Black Brook. This dam, the plaintiff claimed, would reduce the flow of water to the Black Brook Reservation, which is situated on the brook itself."

"And what," Polk asked, "was the position of the defendants regarding this worthwhile project?"

Glynis frowned at Polk's puffery, but saw that Merrycoyf's smile had broadened.

"The position of the defendants was that they all had farms situated on or near Black Brook," Fedmore answered, himself beginning to smile ever so slightly.

Mr. Polk now turned toward the window to ask in an uncharacteristically quiet voice, "What was the disposition of the case?"

Fedmore answered, "Plaintiff Many Horned Stag for the Seneca Nation was granted injunctive relief prohibiting the damming of water under the protection of riparian rights."

Adam MacAlistair's face bloomed into a wide grin, while Merrycoyf just continued to smile and doze.

"Mr. Fedmore, was a judgment of injunction issued and served upon each of the eight defendants?" Polk asked, rather peevishly.

"Yes."

"As of what date was this done?"

"The nineteenth of September, 1847."

"Thank you, Mr. Fedmore. No further questions."

"Cross-examine, Mr. Merrycoyf?" asked the judge.

Merrycoyf opened his eyes and sat forward. "How long have you been a clerk in Seneca County, Mr. Fedmore?"

"Fifteen years."

"And during that time, sir, were other injunctions rendered on any of those eight defendants in Seneca County Supreme Court cases?"

"Objection," Polk said, frowning. "That's totally irrelevant."

"It's not in the least irrelevant, my dear Mr. Polk," snapped Merrycoyf unexpectedly. "Not if you intend to try to somehow prove my client guilty by connection with this dam project you've burdened us with today."

The prosecutor howled "Objection!" again and again over the noise of laughter. Judge Heath was compelled to bring his gavel down a number of times before quiet finally was restored. Even Mr. Fedmore, Glynis noticed, had allowed himself a chuckle.

"Mr. Merrycoyf," said Judge Heath harshly, "I warn you against making any further such prejudicial statements during this trial. Do I make myself clear?"

"Yes, Your Honor," said Merrycoyf cheerfully. "But will the court direct the witness to answer?"

"I have objected," Polk said irritably.

"Mr. Polk, you brought up this issue in direct examination," Judge Heath said. "Objection overruled."

"I don't suppose you remember the question at this point, Mr. Fedmore?" said Merrycoyf.

"Actually I do, Mr. Merrycoyf. And yes, there were some other issues that involved a few of the defendants previously named—issues concerning fences and property lines and the like."

"I see," Merrycoyf said. "And can you tell me, Mr. Fedmore, to the best of your knowledge, did any of those injunctions result in someone's death?"

Polk's face was mottled red, and Glynis could see he longed to object if he could but find grounds. Before he did,

Mr. Fedmore answered, "No. Not to my knowledge."

"Thank you," said Merrycoyf. "I have one last question. Did landowner Obadiah Grimm, whose farm also bordered Black Brook, take any part in the dam injunction case discussed here?"

"Obadiah Grimm?" Mr. Fedmore repeated. "No. No, sir, his name does not appear anywhere in that record."

"Thank you again, Mr. Fedmore. No further questions."

Merrycoyf returned to his seat beside Jacques at the table, while Judge Heath bent forward over the bench to ask Orrin Polk, "Mr. Prosecutor, do you intend a lengthy examination of your next witness?"

"I can't say, Your Honor. Perhaps."

"In that case," said the judge bringing down his gavel, "we will take a short recess. Court will reconvene in fifteen minutes."

"All rise," the bailiff called as the judge left for his chambers.

TWENTY ONE

⤞⤝

*The present Iroquois, the descendants of that gifted race which
formerly held under their jurisdiction the fairest portions of
our Republic, now dwell within our limits as dependent
nations, subject to the tutelage and supervision of the people
who displaced their fathers.*
> —LEWIS HENRY MORGAN, *LEAGUE OF THE
> HO-DE-NO-SAU-NEE, OR IROQUOIS*

GLYNIS SLIPPED INTO her mantle and made for the rear
door. The courtroom had become oppressively hot, and even
now the bailiff shoveled more coal into the stove. She
inched past a clutch of people and headed for the stairs.
When she reached the first-floor entrance, she saw a hand
stretch over her shoulder to push open the door, and Adam
MacAlistair's engaging grin followed her outside.

"Hot in there," Adam offered, his own overcoat unbuttoned.

"Like an oven," Glynis agreed. "This fresh air feels
good—even if it's cold."

The snow-sprinkled square beyond the courthouse lay
empty. Across it swept the long purple shadows of church
spires as December's watery sun hung low in the south-
western sky. The darkest, dreariest month of the twelve,
Glynis reflected, and she and everyone else should be at
home, reading Dickens and preparing for Christmas.

"Do you think the jury sees yet what Polk is setting up?"
Adam asked quietly.

"I don't know," Glynis answered. "It's hard to tell with
juries—this one especially, because the men are all so un-
responsive, or they seem to be. I'll admit I'm worried,
though."

Adam nodded. "It doesn't look good." He had plainly
lost his earlier exuberance.

"No, it doesn't," she conceded. "The worst thing is just

sitting there, not able to do anything.''

"Well, our client certainly hasn't helped. It's as if Sundown's been struck deaf, dumb, and blind. During the most damaging testimony, he didn't even blink.''

"Just as he's been for the past weeks. And you know, Adam, we haven't any of us figured out why.''

Adam frowned. "What is there to figure out? He won't talk.''

"But *why* won't he?''

"I assume it's some Iroquois ritual of silence. After all, this whole week you've heard those Indians insisting Sundown shouldn't be in a white man's court to begin with. Lord help us if he's found guilty—''

"*If,* Adam!'' Glynis broke in. "You haven't given up?''

He looked off at the gathering twilight. "I don't want to. But despite the fact that I dislike the prosecutor, he's doing a decent job, old ferret-face is.''

He grinned, and Glynis forced a halfhearted smile. "But we still don't know the most crucial thing,'' she said. "If Jacques didn't kill Lily Braun, then who did?''

"Any ideas?''

Glynis sighed. "A few. And I keep thinking there's something obvious that we've missed, something right in front of us. Every so often, I feel a tug at my memory confirming it. Have you ever had that happen?''

"Yes, all the time during law school exams.''

Glynis laughed. How young he was. And he did lift her spirits. *Spirits!* "You know, Adam, what we need is a seance.''

Adam wrinkled his nose as if he'd smelled something unpleasant. "A seance?''

"Yes, we could raise Lily Braun's spirit and ask who killed her . . .'' Glynis stopped. Her memory had again thrust something almost to the surface. But it slipped away. She shook her head in frustration.

Adam pulled a watch from his waistcoat. "Time to go in, I'd think.'' As they went through the door to the lobby, he asked her, "Have you ever been to a seance?''

"No. But my neighbor, Vanessa Usher, has become deeply involved with the spirit world. There's a seance held at her house every week, I'm told, and these sessions include, unfortunately, Lazarus Grimm and young Pippa."

"I've met Lazarus Grimm," Adam said, "but who's Pippa?"

They began climbing the stairs with others heading toward the courtroom, and Glynis answered him over her shoulder. "Pippa is Molly Grimm's daughter."

"Molly Grimm?" Adam said, sounding puzzled.

"Yes, she's Lazarus's sister."

Adam paused on the top step. "But that's not possible," he said.

BY THE TIME Glynis and Adam hurried to their seats, Judge Heath was already seated on the bench, and Merrycoyf's annoyed gaze swept the room. He gave Adam MacAlistair a fierce scowl as the young man hurled himself into his chair.

Judge Heath glowered down at the defense table before he said, "Mr. Polk, call your next witness."

"The prosecution calls Sara Turner."

Glynis felt great sympathy for Sara Turner as she came slowly up the aisle, the poor woman—hadn't she had enough hardship without this? But Sara didn't look quite as frail as she had previously. She seemed to have gained some weight, and her face no longer looked cadaverous, nor did it have bruises. But she still held one wrist at an awkward angle. Her other arm cradled an old, dog-eared Bible.

As she sat down in the witness chair, Sara plucked at the seams of her flowered cotton dress; it was not what most women would have worn on a cold winter day. Not if they had the choice. Perhaps Jack Turner hadn't left much money after all.

This made her think of Cullen, and while Sara gave her name and address, Glynis took a quick look across the aisle to the row where he'd been seated. He wasn't there. Glynis found him standing under the windows, watching the Seneca and Cayuga men, although they didn't seem to have shifted since the trial began.

Her gaze returned to Sara Turner as Polk walked up to the woman and asked his first question. "Mrs. Turner, did you hear the testimony of Dr. Quentin Ives concerning your husband's unfortunate and untimely death?''

''Yes.''

''And did you hear Mr. Fedmore, the Seneca County clerk, testify?''

''Yes.''

''Now, I must ask you some questions, Mrs. Turner, but before I do so, I want to extend my sympathy to you for your untimely loss.''

''Then why'd you make me come here?'' Sara said softly.

''Because we must find the truth,'' Polk explained condescendingly, as if Sara were a child. ''But I apologize for intruding on your grief.''

''Weren't no grief,'' Sara Turner replied harshly.

Polk looked startled. ''I beg your pardon, Mrs. Turner?''

A pin could have been heard to drop in the courtroom as Sara Turner repeated, ''It weren't no grief.''

''Ah, well . . . I see . . . I see,'' Polk stammered, looking very much as if he didn't. But he recovered admirably fast. ''Well, in that case, Mrs. Turner, we'll just proceed forthwith. Yes. Now then, did you hear the names Mr. Fedmore gave during his testimony—the names of the defendants in the action involving the Black Brook dam?''

''I heard.''

''Were the names familiar to you?''

''I knew 'em.''

''You knew these men—they were your neighbors and friends, were they not?''

''Not mine, they wasn't. They was *his* friends.''

''Your late husband's?''

''Yes.''

''Now, Mrs. Turner, please think carefully. Do you know of any subsequent events—that is, any other things—that involved those eight men and the Indian man called Many Horned Stag.''

Sara Turner appeared to shrink in the witness chair. It reminded Glynis of when she herself had questioned Sara in the Iveses' kitchen, and the woman had all but disappeared, as if she were but someone else's shadow.

''Yes. I know,'' she said in a whispered voice.

"Could the witness speak louder?" requested the court clerk.

"*I know!*" repeated Sara, without more prompting.

Polk took several steps backward. "Ah, yes. Mrs. Turner, would you tell the jury how you know of this subsequent event? For instance, did your husband tell you?"

"He told me nothin'. I followed them's how I know."

Glynis felt a chill shoot down her spine. She looked at Merrycoyf. He, and Adam too, sat perfectly still, attention riveted on Sara Turner. The jury, who couldn't know what was coming, looked mildly interested. And Jacques Sundown stared straight ahead.

"You say you followed them, Mrs. Turner. Can you tell us what happened to make you follow these men?"

Sara looked at Polk, then shook her head.

"Mrs. Turner," Judge Heath said in a surprisingly benevolent tone, "you must answer the prosecutor's question."

Sara's eyes darted around the courtroom. She was truly frightened, Glynis believed; no doubt she had lived with this fear for ten years.

"Mrs. Turner," Polk said, "do you remember telling Constable Stuart about this several weeks ago?"

Sara nodded slowly.

"Please tell the court what you told Constable Stuart."

Glynis looked back at Cullen. He was watching Sara Turner, and his face expressed real concern. He moved up the aisle toward the front of the room, nodding at the small woman in the witness chair.

Sara had obviously seen Cullen, because she nodded back at him and took a deep breath, then said, "I couldn't never talk about this before. Not while's he was alive, I couldn't."

"Your husband, Mrs. Turner?" said Polk.

"Yes."

"What made you follow the men?" Polk repeated.

"He comes to the door, that Otto Braun does, and tells him—"

"Tells your husband?"

"Yes, him—Otto Braun tells him to get his horse and come with them all. He says they're gonna get them that

Indian. Because he raped his daughter . . . Braun's daughter.''

"Who was 'them,' Mrs. Turner?" asked Polk.

"*Them!* The ones you named.''

"All the men I named earlier, were they *all* there?''

Sara nodded.

"Let the record show," Polk said, "that the witness has identified the eight defendants in the Black Brook injunction proceeding, including her husband, Jack Turner.''

Polk and Judge Heath both looked at Merrycoyf.

Not taking his eyes from Sara Turner, Merrycoyf said, "No objection.''

"Where did the men go, Mrs. Turner?''

"They went to the reservation—must have done, 'cause I got a horse and rode up Black Brook Road after 'em, and then I seen 'em come across the brook with the Indian. I knowed somethin' bad was gonna happen. Just couldn't do nothin' to stop it.''

Sara's hands had begun to shake; squirming on the chair, she tried to twist a handkerchief out of her dress pocket. Mr. Polk stepped forward and handed her a large white square from his own pocket. Sara took it and rubbed it across her eyes.

The courtroom was silent, motionless, as if all were framed in a daguerreotype. Glynis, too, couldn't take her eyes from Sara; she couldn't even begin to imagine what Jacques must be going through. And Small Brown Bird, she suddenly remembered. But she couldn't bring herself to look around.

Sara drew another deep breath. "Anyhows, they took that Indian into them woods . . . and they . . . and they strung him up.''

It seemed to Glynis as if an eternity passed before Judge Heath brought down his gavel. It wasn't so much the noise—which was strangely muted—that needed attention, as the commotion of people moving in and out of the rear doors. When the rustling of skirts and clumping of boots ceased, Glynis turned around. The Iroquois hadn't moved. Neither had Small Brown Bird, who was still staring at her hands. Neva and Abraham, who, like Glynis, had known beforehand, hadn't left their seats. Otherwise, half the room had rearranged itself. A number of empty chairs had appeared. And there was a great deal of noise coming from outside the open door.

"Bailiff, make those people quiet down," Judge Heath ordered, "and close the door."

Glynis turned back to Sara Turner, aware of more rustling behind her as people apparently hurried back to their seats, while in the meantime, Sara hunched in the chair, clutching Polk's handkerchief over her face.

Glynis desperately wanted to go to Jacques, to say something to him—at the very least, to tell him how sorry she was. But of course she couldn't. How many in the courtroom, she wondered, knew that Many Horned Stag was Jacques's brother? Merrycoyf knew, but hadn't until several days ago. It was Cullen who had told him—Cullen, who Merrycoyf said was more disturbed than he'd ever seen him before, and who related that for years there'd been rumors of a lynching near the reservation. But no body had been found, no proof offered, and no one had come forward with information.

Judge Heath now said shortly, "Continue, Mr. Polk."

"Mrs. Turner," said Polk, waiting until the handkerchief was lowered, "again I am sorry to have to ask you these questions. But there are just a few more. Did you actually see these men hang the Indian man?"

"No, not do it." Sara seemed to have composed herself; perhaps it was a relief to have it out after all these years.

Sara went on, "Man was already hangin' from a rope, time I got there. 'Cause I left the horse and went afoot till I found 'em. But I couldn't do nothin'. Nothin'."

"Then what did they do—the men, I mean?" Polk asked.

"They just goes ridin' off."

"Mrs. Turner, why haven't you come forward with this before?"

Sara Turner stared at Polk as if he were the stupidest man she'd ever laid eyes on. "You makin' a joke?" she asked.

"No, no, of course not," Polk assured her. "Were you afraid—afraid of your husband, for instance?"

"No 'for instance' about it! He said he'd kill me, I ever

talked about what I seen. He'd a' done it, too. Sent my kids off, said they'd never come back if I talked about it. He sent 'em away!''

Sara, her hands trembling again, brought the handkerchief up to her face, her thin frame racked with silent anguish. How had Sara survived, married to a man like Jack Turner?

Glynis looked at Sara Turner, and thought of Jacques's mother, Bitter Root; it seemed as if women had forever grieved for their children. The Bible still tucked under Sara's arm made Glynis think again of the passage "Rachel weeping for her children." What Old Testament book was that from? A librarian should know; Obadiah Grimm would have known in an instant. Glynis drew in her breath and stared up at Sara Turner's Bible, and suddenly it came: Jeremiah. It was from the Book of Jeremiah.

Polk had cleared his throat, and now said, "Who else was at the scene of this . . . this hanging, Mrs. Turner?"

"There was a couple Indian squaws, and a boy." She jerked her head toward Jacques.

"Let the record show that the witness has identified—"

"Objection," Merrycoyf retorted. "The witness said 'a boy.' This dreadful event happened years ago—how could the witness know what that boy looks like now?"

"Sustained," Judge Heath said.

"Very well," said Polk with disturbing confidence. "Mrs. Turner, did your husband ever indicate that he feared for his life?"

"Yes. 'Specially after some of the others died."

"Ah, yes—after the others died. And did he say whom he was afraid of?"

"Well, he says more'n once, it must be that Sundown."

Glynis clenched her hands in her lap, thinking she might feel better if she could hate Sara Turner. But Sara was almost as much a victim in this as was Jacques.

"Just one more question, Mrs. Turner. Was there anyone else present at the scene of this tragedy? Other than those you've already mentioned?"

"Yes, there was. I seen her in the woods, watchin'."

"And who was that watching?"

"It was a girl. It was Lily Braun."

Glynis gasped in astonishment with the rest of the court-room. Lily Braun? Why on earth had *she* been there? But then, abruptly, the memories that for days had eluded her rose to the surface of her mind. Glynis held them tightly. They might be the last hope for Jacques.

"Do you wish to cross-examine the witness?" Judge Heath asked Merrycoyf.

"No, Your Honor, no cross-examination."

Mr. Polk now approached the bench. "Your Honor, to save the inconvenience of subpoenaing the defendant's mother, who I understand is ill, I request the following: that I, as counsel for the People, and Mr. Merrycoyf, as counsel for the defense, do stipulate for the record that the Seneca man, Many Horned Stag, was the half brother of the defendant Jacques Sundown."

The courtroom reaction to this was as expected, and Glynis cringed as Judge Heath's gavel banged. But most of the jury members just leaned forward to look at Jacques: their expressions ranged from surprised to indifferent to antagonistic, with one or two sympathetic glances. Glynis noted these last carefully.

Merrycoyf now answered Polk, "I so stipulate."

Judge Heath said to the clerk, "The stipulation is received and made part of the record. And now, Mr. Polk, do you have any idea how much more time you need to finish? It's late, and I would like to adjourn until Monday morning."

"Please, Your Honor. I have but one more witness, and the gentleman has traveled here under subpoena from Rochester. May we extend this session slightly so he won't need to return here?"

"Do you anticipate that your examination of this witness will be lengthy, Mr. Polk?"

"No sir, I do not."

"Very well, call your witness," directed Judge Heath, a trifle wearily, Glynis observed.

"The prosecution calls Mr. Lewis Henry Morgan."

Glynis twisted in her chair to watch Morgan stride briskly forward. She had met him several times in Rochester, and when he had traveled through Seneca Falls. As he passed her aisle chair, he nodded to her briefly before proceeding to the witness chair to be sworn.

Morgan did not appear to age; he must be close to forty, but an engaging boyish face, and a ready smile, made him look more like fourteen. Trained in corporate law, he'd made a fortune early in life by speculating in railroads and mining. Glynis knew enough about him to assume he did not want to be here. Not under these circumstances.

"Mr. Morgan, sir, we appreciate your taking time from your busy schedule to testify here," Polk said unctuously.

Morgan said nothing. Just sat there with his hands folded, studying Polk. Glynis noticed that Morgan already had taken a long look at Jacques.

"Mr. Morgan," Polk began, "you are the author, sir, of a work entitled *League of the Iroquois,* are you not?"

"Yes, but it's *League of the Ho-de-no-sau-nee, or Iroquois,*" Morgan gently corrected him. "The name Iroquois is a French invention, more or less."

"Yes, I see. Well, how long ago did you write this, Mr. Morgan?"

"Actually, I didn't write it alone. I collaborated with a Seneca man, Ely S. Parker, to whom the book is dedicated. And it was published six years ago, in '51."

"The book has been received with very great enthusiasm," Polk said, while Glynis watched Merrycoyf slouch in his chair and close his eyes, as if to disassociate himself from the prosecutor's obsequious behavior.

Polk spent no small amount of time extolling Morgan's professional and scholarly background, until at last even Judge Heath apparently had heard enough. He leaned over his bench to say, "Mr. Merrycoyf, would you be willing to stipulate that you accept Mr. Morgan's qualifications as an expert?"

"Oh, *yes,* Your Honor! Yes, indeed. Immediately."

A ripple went through the room, and Morgan himself grinned at Merrycoyf.

Polk shot Merrycoyf an annoyed look, then walked to his table, picked up Morgan's book, and opened it with a flourish to a bookmarked page. "Mr. Morgan, will you please identify the following passage for the court: 'To He'-no, he'—that is, the Great Spirit," Polk inserted, " '—committed the thunderbolt; at once the voice of admonition, and the instrument of vengeance.' '' Polk stopped reading and waited for Morgan to answer.

"You want me to identify that, Mr. Polk?" Morgan smiled. "Well, I wrote it, if that's what you mean."

"That's what I mean," said Polk, looking unaccountably pleased with himself. "Now, sir, to what were you referring?"

Morgan stared at Polk for a moment. "That requires a fairly involved answer. How long do we have today?" He smiled again.

"Your Honor," said Merrycoyf, "while it is pleasant to hear the prosecutor's mellifluous voice, I am still waiting, as I'm sure everyone else is, to discover *why* the prosecution has called Mr. Morgan here."

"Are you placing an objection, Mr. Merrycoyf?" Judge Heath asked.

"Yes, I am. With no insult meant to Mr. Morgan, whose work I admire, this examination is irrelevant and immaterial."

Polk's response was passionate. "I intend to show motive for the defendant's murder of Lily Braun, Your Honor."

"Objection!" Merrycoyf spat.

"Yes, sustained," Judge Heath agreed. "Mr. Polk, it is late. Please come to the point."

Polk flipped rapidly to what Glynis could see was another bookmarked page. "And did you also write this, Mr. Morgan?" Polk paused dramatically before he read, " 'The greatest of all human crimes, murder, was punished with death. . . . Unless the family were appeased, the murderer, as with the ancient Greeks, was given up to their private vengeance. They could take his life whenever they found him, even after a lapse of years, without being held accountable.' ''

The courtroom had become very quiet, and when Polk slapped the book shut, it sounded like a thunderclap. And so perhaps it was, Glynis thought with despair.

"Did you write that, Mr. Morgan?" Polk asked.

"Yes. But what must be understood is that—"

"Mr. Morgan," Polk cut him off, "did you write that this

Iroquois code of vengeance is an obligation—not a choice, but an *obligation*—that a victim's kin must fulfill?''

"That's not the precise language, but . . . it's approximate. However—''

"Thank you, Mr. Morgan. No further questions.''

Glynis realized full well what a blow had been struck. What could Merrycoyf do to soften it?

"Cross-examine, Mr. Merrycoyf?''

"Yes.'' Merrycoyf remained seated, saying to Morgan, "Is this vengeance obligation an absolute?''

"No, by no means,'' Morgan answered quickly. "For instance, if certain symbolic acts of contrition were performed, the victim's family could accept them as appeasement. The debt of revenge could be wiped out, so to speak.''

"So the obligation is not unequivocal under every circumstance?''

"No. And, as you might suspect, the older Iroquois are much closer to the tribal ways than are the young,'' Morgan said, looking first at Jacques Sundown, and then turning to the jury.

"Thank you very much, Mr. Morgan,'' Merrycoyf said. "No further questions.''

Polk grabbed Morgan's book and jumped to his feet. "I have one question on redirect, Your Honor.''

"Just one question, Mr. Polk,'' responded Judge Heath.

"Mr. Morgan,'' Polk said, "in the Iroquois code of vengeance, if attempts at conciliation with the victim's family were not successful, then what happened?'' But before Morgan could answer, Polk opened the book and read: " 'If the family, however, continued implacable . . . the question was left to be settled between the murderer and the kindred of his victim, according to the ancient usage.' Tell us, Mr. Morgan, did you write that passage, sir?''

Lewis Henry Morgan again looked at Polk for a long moment before he answered, "Yes.''

Polk said, "No further questions, Your Honor. The prosecution rests.''

"Then this court is adjourned,'' Judge Heath said, "until Monday.''

"All rise,'' called the bailiff.

TWENTY TWO

∞

The Shapes we buried, dwell about,
Familiar in the Rooms—
Untarnished by the Sepulchre,
The Mouldering Playmate comes. . . .
　　　　　　—EMILY DICKINSON

THE FOLLOWING EVENING, when Glynis walked into Vanessa Usher's parlor, her impression was that the familiar room had been redecorated by Edgar Allan Poe. Black velvet draperies had been hung from ceiling to floor, covering the four walls and the windows; the carpet beneath the heavy folds of fabric was a somber gray. All furniture had been removed, save a round table and eight chairs in the center of the room, and a black-lacquered, hinged screen positioned across one shadowed corner. Another deft touch of the bizarre was a pot of white lilies from the Ushers' conservatory, from which drifted a sickly sweet funereal odor.

Near the table a floor-standing, wrought-iron candelabra held two candles; this provided the sole illumination, barely enabling Glynis to see a handful of people standing about in the gloom. She took a wary step forward, concluding that this was very much like entering a sepulchre—unquestionably Vanessa Usher's desired effect.

The one vibrant note in the gloom was the carved rosewood frame of Vanessa's dulcimer. The lovely Vanessa herself, garbed in floor-length dove-gray velvet, sat as if suspended in thin air; closer inspection revealed a three-legged stool beneath her. She lightly struck the strings with the dulcimer hammers, producing a delicate resonance all but absorbed by the drapery. After listening a minute or two, however, Glynis recognized the melancholy refrain of an old Irish ballad.

She trusted that Neva had arrived earlier than the others,

according to plan, and had concealed herself behind the screen. Vanessa had opposed their intrigue vehemently until they'd bribed her with a subscription to the new spiritualist newspaper *Banner of Light*. And told her that without their intervention, Pippa might be in danger. Still, Vanessa had consented only with extreme reluctance.

Those present included two women and a man unfamiliar to Glynis, in addition to Lazarus Grimm and Molly, and of course Pippa. The girl looked distressingly unwell.

"Miss Tryon, hello," Pippa said listlessly as Glynis went across the room to greet her, noting the girl's dull, red-rimmed eyes and slouched bearing, and she asked Pippa if she'd again been ill.

"Oh, she's just a little tired is all," answered Molly quickly, standing behind her daughter with her hands resting lightly on the girl's shoulders. "Isn't that so, Pippa?" she said softly, pressing her cheek against the girl's buttery-yellow hair.

"Yes, Mama."

Before Glynis had the opportunity to ask more, Vanessa set down her dulcimer and hammers, and rose to say, "Now that everyone's here, we should begin." She motioned them to the table, obviously an unnecessary gesture for all but Glynis, as the others already had begun seating themselves. Lazarus led Pippa quickly to a chair, then seated himself directly beside her.

"This is Miss Glynis Tryon, for those of you who don't know her," Vanessa announced. "Miss Tryon is a skeptic, but we can fervently hope for her enlightenment, and ask the spirits' indulgence. Do sit right here, Glynis, between Lazarus and me. No, no, Molly, let Sylvia sit next to Pippa—she never has before."

Molly looked concerned, and glanced protectively at Pippa before she went with obvious unwillingness to the only remaining chair. Glynis sat as directed, thankful that at least Vanessa had cooperated in the seating arrangement. On the other side of Vanessa sat one of the unfamiliar women, then the man, then Molly, the woman called Sylvia, and finally Pippa, beside Lazarus. Immediately upon settling themselves, the participants grasped the nearest hand of the person beside them. Before doing this herself, Vanessa reached out to snuff a candle; the one remaining gave the room only the dimmest of light, like a match struck in a dark cave, Glynis thought with increased misgiving.

Seated beside Lazarus, she watched him closely from the corner of her eye. After the day she'd seen him in the shed with Pippa at the Grimm farm, she had gone to Neva, who'd guessed Pippa might have been in a deep trance, or mesmerized. Glynis then had collected for the two of them what little information she could find on the eighteenth-century physician Franz Mesmer. They found the answer, they thought, in the material on Mesmer's philosophical successor, Dr. James Braid; only a decade before, in the 1840s, Braid had coined the term *hypnotism*.

"I'll wager," Neva had declared, "that it's what these crazy spiritualists are doing—some kind of hypnotism."

"Which would mean that they aren't all charlatans," Glynis said. "At least some of them must truly believe they're in touch with the hereafter."

"They're deluding themselves," Neva retorted.

"Maybe so, but not intentionally."

"But Pippa is simply being used by Lazarus," Neva protested. "I'm told that the 'contributions' he requests at the spiritualist meetings are substantial."

Glynis frowned, then offered, "It's certainly true that Lazarus Grimm has a dubious reputation, but what if he really believes this otherworldly plane exists? If that's true, he could be unaware or ignorant of what he's doing when he hypnotizes Pippa. And it could be dangerous for her."

"Yes, in terms of what we've read about Mesmer," Neva readily agreed, "if Pippa is concealing from herself the memory of an event too overwhelming to recall."

The night before on the ride home from Waterloo, Glynis had insisted that she and Neva attend Vanessa Usher's weekly seance. That this might help Jacques as well as Pippa, she didn't mention at the time.

Vanessa now grasped Glynis's hand and that of the woman to her right, intoning dramatically, "Our spirit circle is closed." She looked expectantly at Lazarus.

Lazarus's tone contained a not-so-subtle reproach. "You

all should realize," he said pointedly, "that because we have a disbeliever present, the spirits may choose not to communicate."

Glynis was aware that all eyes swung her way. She was also aware that this was a common excuse of mediums: an unsympathetic presence would keep the spirits from revealing themselves. So far, researchers of psychic phenomena had found this circular argument to be invincible.

Lazarus continued, his voice growing ever more intense, "I must emphasize to you that if you have questions, they *must come through me* to the medium. This is imperative, otherwise she could become perilously confused. Do you all understand this?"

What Glynis understood was that Lazarus demanded to remain in control. And although she found his transformation from aesthete to commanding general nothing less than extraordinary, she nodded earnestly with the others.

He turned to Pippa. "Close your eyes. Go to sleep, Pippa. Sleep. Sleep . . . sleep . . . sleep . . ."

Pippa's eyes closed, and instantly she seemed to sink lower in her chair. Lazarus repeated the command until Glynis began to feel her own lids droop. She quietly took a deep breath, concentrating on the need to shut out Lazarus's voice and watch the others. Their eyes had closed. All but those of Lazarus. He didn't seem to notice Glynis's scrutiny as his attention focused steadily on the girl beside him.

He stopped talking. The room was still. Only the sound of soft breathing intruded.

"Sylvia," said Lazarus quietly, "you wish to talk to your daughter?"

"Yes. Oh, yes. Please ask Pippa to bring her here."

In response to this plea, Glynis felt a strong distaste. There was something of the indecent, even the obscene, in this summons to the dead. She tried to distract herself by wondering what Neva was thinking. But she probably didn't need to wonder. She half expected Neva at any minute to come flying out from behind the screen and denounce the entire business.

Gradually, though, Glynis became aware of an odd, repetitive sound, almost as if someone were humming.

Someone *was* humming, though who it was among them she couldn't tell. Except that it sounded like a female voice.

"Oh, dear Lord," Sylvia cried out suddenly, "it's my baby. It's my little girl."

Everyone's eyes shot open; they closed again quickly. Glynis was relieved that she saw no acknowledgment of the muffled snort that had just come from behind the screen.

Sylvia's face, though tear-streaked, had become radiant. In embarrassment, Glynis looked away; she felt unclean at being a party to this. Naturally Sylvia wanted to believe that what she heard was her beloved dead daughter; was there a grief more devastating than losing one's child? Undoubtedly this was the root of the spiritualist movement's appeal: people believed what they needed to believe. And while the spiritualists weren't the first to recognize the importance of promised immortality in easing death's anguish for survivors, they surely did offer better theater than had most of their predecessors.

Glynis shifted slightly in her chair so she could watch Pippa. The girl's eyes remained closed. But suddenly, in the midst of Sylvia's ecstatic sobs, a high-pitched voice said, "Grandfather, are you there? Is that you?"

With their eyes closed, the others wouldn't see that Pippa's lips hadn't moved. Glynis felt Vanessa's grip on her hand tighten, while Lazarus's hold on her other hand went oddly limp. As if he'd forgotten he was grasping it. But she couldn't concern herself with Lazarus just then. She kept her eyes fixed on Pippa, who as yet exhibited no reaction.

"Grandfather," came the voice again. "Grandfather, be careful. No! No, don't do that to my—"

Pippa's eyes flew open, just as Lazarus leapt to his feet. "Who's doing that?" he demanded. "Who said that?"

Pippa had begun to whimper. The whimpers rose to a keening wail. Glynis and Molly both sprang forward, but Lazarus prevented them from reaching the girl by wrapping his arms around her like a shield. "Keep away from her!" he ordered.

"Lazarus," pleaded Molly, "please let me—"

"No, keep away," Lazarus repeated. "Everyone must leave now. It's over. It's over for tonight."

With looks of confusion, and one of despair from Sylvia, the two women and the man moved toward the door, casting frightened backward glances at Pippa. The weeping girl had begun to writhe in Lazarus's grasp, striking at him in a frenzy while she battered her head against his chest.

Molly stood frozen with fists pressed against her mouth, and Vanessa glared at Glynis, snarling, "I knew I shouldn't have let you come. You ruined it!"

Lazarus, his back to the screen, didn't see Neva when she emerged from behind it. "Pippa," she said, "listen to me—"

"Stay away from her!" Lazarus ordered Neva, his expression as forbidding as his voice. But he didn't register any surprise at finding her there, Glynis observed, so complete was his preoccupation with Pippa.

"No, I won't stay away from her. The girl needs help," Neva stated firmly. "Pippa, listen to me. There's no reason for you to be frightened. Nothing is going to happen to you! I promise."

Pippa's sobs, though they persisted, seemed to lessen in severity. Neva reached forward to grasp the girl's shoulder, and for a moment Glynis thought Lazarus would shove her aside. But Pippa managed to squirm from his grasp to hurl herself against the young doctor. Glynis glanced at Molly, who stood several feet away. The woman's face expressed such stark agony that Glynis wondered if Molly would ever forgive any of them for this, including her brother.

"Perhaps Pippa should stay at the Iveses' tonight," Neva suggested, speaking over the girl's head.

"No! Absolutely not," Lazarus objected. "She needs to be at home. With her mother, with her family."

"Her *family*," Neva retorted, "haven't done much to protect her, have they? I think—"

"Please," Molly broke in, her voice pleading, "please let us take her home."

"You don't need to beg," Lazarus said to his sister with a sudden gentleness, "she has no right to keep the girl here."

"No, but I strongly advise it," said Neva, still holding Pippa close.

"Pippa," Lazarus said, his eyes fastened on the girl, and his tone now one of concern, "don't you want to come home? You don't want to stay here, do you?"

Pippa's sobs had slowly diminished; she looked up at Lazarus as if seeking forgiveness. When Neva tried, unsuccessfully, to insert herself between the girl and her uncle, Glynis saw how far Lazarus's influence over his niece extended. Pippa pulled away from Neva and, wiping her eyes, said, "Yes, I want to go home. I'm sorry for what I did, Uncle Lazarus, but I'm all right now."

Lazarus smiled, and stroked the girl's wet cheeks. After a nod from him, Molly rushed with a faint cry to her daughter. Vanessa, who had been unexpectedly quiet all this time, now said cheerily, "Well, I suppose these things do happen—but we certainly can't let a little unpleasantness dissuade us from communicating with our loved ones on the other side."

While Glynis stood gaping at her, Vanessa escorted the Grimms to her door, chirping banalities at every step.

"Neva, do you think she'll be all right?" Glynis asked. "Pippa, I mean."

"I didn't think you meant the Witch of Endor, there," Neva said, watching Vanessa with a look of disgust. "And I don't know how the girl will be. When she gets back to the farm," she added, somewhat anxiously, "there'll be Almira. And Billy Wicken."

"Yes. I know that." It was all Glynis could bring herself to say.

"I suppose," Neva went on as if she hadn't heard, "there's nothing we can do about it. Lazarus was right. We can't keep Pippa here against his and her mother's will."

"But I think we *can* do something," Glynis said. "Not tonight, certainly, but I think you and I need to go out to the Grimm farm tomorrow."

Neva scowled. "They won't exactly welcome us, you know, none of them. I doubt we'll get anywhere near Pippa."

"I don't think that's necessarily true," Glynis protested. "Not if we can persuade the constable's deputy to come with us."

"How can we do that? And why do we want to?"

"We'll have to ask for Zeph, that's how. I think Cullen will listen to me about this, especially if it involves Pippa's welfare. But if he won't, we'll get Jeremiah Merrycoyf involved."

"Do we have to rely on one of those men? You and Cullen Stuart are barely speaking!"

"Yes, and I'd rather not involve him. But, Neva, we're *women,* and whether we like it or not, we don't have one jot of authority. Besides, at this point, I'll rely on whomever I have to."

"But why do we need to go to the Grimms'?" Neva insisted. "We already know that Pippa saw—"

Shaking her head, Glynis interrupted, "To prove Jacques Sundown didn't kill Lily Braun."

Neva caught her breath. "Do you know who did?"

"Yes, I think so," Glynis said slowly, "but I haven't put it all together yet. And we'll need more than my suppositions to keep Jacques from hanging."

TWENTY THREE

❦

[Dr. Elizabeth Blackwell] *has quite bewildered the learned faculty by her diploma, all in due form, authorizing her to dose and bleed and amputate with the best of them. Some of them think Miss Blackwell must be a socialist of the most rabid class, and that her undertaking is the entering wedge to a systematic attack on society by the whole sex.*
—*NEW YORK JOURNAL OF COMMERCE,* 1849

GLYNIS PAUSED TO look over her shoulder before she entered the Waterloo courthouse. The Monday morning sunlight came pale and hazy above the southeast horizon on this day of the winter solstice, and the weather had taken an erratic swing; the air felt as warm as April. Melting snow ran in rivulets and turned the roads into bogs, but the only ones truly grumbling about it were the liverymen. They'd had to put aside their cutters and retrieve the recently stored carriages.

On the square below Glynis, where scenes of the previous trial days had been played out, the mood had changed significantly. The townsmen were still there, but the rabble-rousers were fewer and were mostly, if not completely, ignored. The Iroquois stood just as silent, just as remote, and their bearing revealed little of the underlying tension as they waited to see what this white man's judge and jury would do to Jacques Sundown. History surely had given them grounds for distrust.

Word of Sara Turner's testimony the previous Friday had swept through Seneca County, and it was that, Glynis knew, which explained the subdued atmosphere below. Sara's account of the lynching had produced a firestorm of revulsion from Quakers and abolitionists, most Christian pulpits, and, to their credit, the newspapers—although Neva insisted this was simply because it made good copy. Nonetheless, the confrontations had been minimal this Monday in Waterloo.

Cullen came briskly up the steps. "Quiet, down there," he said to Glynis, "and I hope it lasts. Until this is over at least. Then I expect we'll go back to the normal mutual dislike. But if Jacques is convicted . . ." He shrugged.

Glynis turned toward the door. She didn't want to think about it—about any of it. The more she learned concerning the events of ten years before, the more wretched she felt.

Behind her, Cullen said, "Glynis?" and reached for her shoulder. She stood in place, not walking away, not turning to face him. He released her shoulder and came around to stand in front of her. "Glynis, you want to tell me what happened that day? Day of the blizzard?"

Startled, all she could think to say was, "Why? Why now, Cullen?"

"I think maybe we should get this sorted out before . . ." He broke off as she frowned. And the silence wavered there between them until she said, "Before Jacques is convicted? Before he's hanged, you mean?"

"No, that's not what I mean."

"Cullen, you wouldn't talk to me about it before. Wouldn't talk to me at all, for weeks. And now . . . well, I don't want to talk."

"You think you have a right to be angry about this?"

"Oh, you're absolutely correct, Cullen! At this point I think I have every right to be angry. You haven't allowed me to explain, haven't allowed me a word in my own behalf for all these weeks. Even accused criminals are supposed to be assumed innocent until proven otherwise! But you've apparently had no doubt about what you *think* you saw that day. Well, go ahead and continue to think it—think whatever you like. I'm not going to explain myself at this late date regarding something I didn't do!"

She walked away, into the lobby and up the stairs, without looking back. And if she hadn't been angry before, she told herself, she was angry now.

Entering the courtroom with her heart beating rapidly, Glynis paused to calm herself. She then went directly to the defense table and stood waiting until Jacques was escorted in from the jail. Because of the weekend's events, Merrycoyf had gone to the judge's chambers to revise his list of witnesses, and she realized she might not have another opportunity to speak with Jacques alone. Every time she'd visited him at the jail, there had been a guard present. Even now, after seating his prisoner, the bailiff stood just a few feet away. She moved in close to the table.

"It would have been so much easier, Jacques," she said softly, "if only you had told me."

Jacques looked at her with what might have been amusement. "You think you're a good spirit, a Ho-no-che-no'-keh? Think you can bargain with He'-no for my life?"

Glynis felt her face flush. "No, of course not. But if you had just explained it to me."

"No."

"You don't think I would have understood?" she asked him.

"You cannot understand."

"Yes, I think I can. What took place ten years ago created an afterlife of its own. As a result, and in addition to what is happening to you, three women's lives have been destroyed—one way or another. Perhaps a child's life as well."

"You know, then." And suddenly his eyes, no longer flat, held pain so graphic that Glynis had to look away.

When she turned back to him, she said only, "Yes, Jacques, I know. And while I've been torn in two directions about it, I told Jeremiah what I know; it's his decision now."

The door opened, and Merrycoyf emerged from the judge's chambers. He gave her a brief nod, then looked anxiously toward the rear door.

"Have you seen Mr. MacAlistair?" he asked Glynis.

"No, I haven't. Jeremiah. What if he doesn't get here with Dr. Kelly?"

"I do not care to consider that," Merrycoyf said.

While they'd been talking, Jacques's hands, lying together on the table, had clenched reflexively, and Glynis now pressed them quickly with her own. Hearing the bailiff behind her, she held Jacques's eyes momentarily, before she went back to the seat she'd had the previous week.

*   *   *

"THE DEFENSE MAY now present its case," said Judge
Heath after completing the preliminaries. "Mr. Merrycoyf,
call your first witness."

The men of the jury, Glynis noted, had been tight-lipped
since they'd entered the courtroom; most tellingly, they did
not look at Jacques. They undoubtedly felt that the defense
presentation would be a waste of time, no more than a for-
mal requirement of the legal system. Their faces indicated
the trial had been all but over the previous Friday. Several
of them even looked disgusted as Merrycoyf got to his feet.

"The defense calls Dr. Neva Cardoza."

Orrin Polk also rose. "Your Honor," he said querulously,
"we discussed this witness in your chambers before the trial
began. You made a ruling at that time; consequently there
is no reason for defense counsel to try to present this woman
as a doctor."

"Yes, Mr. Merrycoyf," Judge Heath said, scowling, "I
have denied this woman the status of medical expert on the
grounds that she lacks the proper qualifications."

Unlike everyone else in the courtroom, Glynis didn't turn
to look at Neva. Both of them knew that the "proper qualifications" involved gender. But even Merrycoyf, although
he was no staunch feminist, had been somewhat surprised
when Judge Heath denied expert status to Neva solely because she was a woman. Glynis had not been surprised. Not
with medical schools across the country rewriting their ad-
missions policies to specifically prohibit women.

"Your Honor, with all due respect," Merrycoyf now said,
"although this witness is denied the status of expert, she
may surely testify. It is a basic tenet of law that any witness
called is qualified to say what *she saw* and what *she did*, if
relevant to the issues."

Judge Heath's scowl remained; he nodded, however, saying with a touch of testiness, "Very well, counsel. But Miss
Cardoza may not give expert opinion as to the findings."

"Of course, Your Honor," said Merrycoyf as he turned
and gestured to Neva.

Glynis was relieved to see, as Neva came forward, that
her face did not reflect outrage; the young doctor walked up

the aisle quickly, looking straight ahead with no expression whatsoever. In fact, Glynis marveled, Neva did not appear in the least nervous.

Merrycoyf's first question, after Neva was sworn, concerned her educational background. Even this innocuous inquiry made Orrin Polk bristle. He half rose from his seat and, with his neck extended like a weasel about to strike, seemed prepared to remain in that position indefinitely.

"I attended the Female Medical College of Pennsylvania," Neva answered in a clear voice.

"And did you receive a medical degree, Dr. Cardoza?" Merrycoyf asked.

"Yes, last spring."

"And why did you come to Seneca Falls, Dr. Cardoza?"

"To train with and assist Dr. Quentin Ives, in preparation for a staff position in a New York City hospital."

"And have you, since coming here, been offered that position in New York?"

"Yes, one week ago. But I declined the offer, choosing instead to remain in Seneca Falls."

Although Glynis already knew this, she couldn't help turning around for a look at Abraham Levy. His smile warmed the entire courtroom. Possibly the entire county.

Judge Heath leaned forward to say, "Mr. Merrycoyf, please move along with the witness."

"Yes, Your Honor. Dr. Cardoza, shortly before his death occurred, were you called to the farm of Obadiah Grimm?"

"Yes."

"And were you present at the moment of Mr. Grimm's death?"

"Yes."

"Did Mr. Grimm say anything to you in the moments prior to his death?"

Before Neva could answer, Polk said, "Objection! That would be hearsay."

"No, Your Honor," Merrycoyf argued, "a dying declaration is an exception to the hearsay rule."

"That is correct, Mr. Merrycoyf," said the judge. "However"—he turned to Neva—"young woman, did Obadiah Grimm expire immediately following his words to you?"

"Yes, he did."

"Then the objection is overruled," Judge Heath said. "The witness may answer."

Polk sat down; he looked disconcerted, Glynis thought, but apparently not enough so to debate the judge about whether Neva, if she wasn't an expert, could recognize death when she saw it.

"What did Obadiah Grimm say, Dr. Cardoza?"

"He said, 'Jeremiah,' several times. That much was clear. He also said something that sounded, to me at least, like 'seven tea he leaven.' "

"Did that mean anything to you, Dr. Cardoza?"

"Not at the time, no. I thought perhaps it had to do with you, Mr. Merrycoyf."

"I will state for the record," Merrycoyf said, "that I had not seen or heard from Obadiah Grimm for several years."

"Do you object, Mr. Polk?" Judge Heath asked.

"No objection," said Polk, looking puzzled.

"Did you have occasion later to discuss these words with anyone other than the Grimm family, Dr. Cardoza?"

"Yes, I discussed them with Miss Glynis Tryon, who had known the family longer than I."

"Objection!" Polk yelped. "Hearsay."

"Mr. Polk," said Judge Heath, "we will never finish here unless some leeway is allowed. Now I can plainly see that Miss Tryon is here in court, and so defense counsel could call her for corroboration of this testimony should it be necessary. But if we can save time, let us by all means do it. Proceed, Miss Cardoza."

Neva answered, "I related to Miss Tryon what Mr. Grimm had said. We discussed this a number of times, but came to no conclusion about what he meant. Then, last Friday evening, she asked me to again repeat his words. She said she thought that Obadiah Grimm, given as he was to biblical quotations, might have been referring to a passage from the Old Testament Book of Jeremiah.

"Miss Tryon thought that 'seven tea' might be chapter seventeen—not seventy, because there is no seventieth chapter in Jeremiah—and that what I heard as 'leaven' could be verse eleven."

Neva stopped there, and looked at Merrycoyf.

"And subsequently," Merrycoyf said, "did you and Miss Tryon locate the passage in Jeremiah, chapter seventeen, verse eleven?"

"Yes, we did."

Merrycoyf walked back to the table, where he picked up a Bible. Opening it to a marked page, he now said to Neva, "Will you identify this as the passage to which you believe Obadiah Grimm referred?" Merrycoyf read: " 'As the partridge sitteth on eggs, but hatcheth them not; so is he that getteth riches but not by right . . . ' Is that the one, Dr. Cardoza?"

"Yes," Neva said.

Merrycoyf closed the Bible and returned it to the table, before he said, "Thank you, Doctor. Now I would like to question you in regard to another death. Did you, Dr. Cardoza, perform an autopsy on the deceased Lily Braun?"

"Yes."

"Had you ever performed such an autopsy before?"

"Since I've been in Seneca Falls, I've assisted Dr. Ives in four of them."

Polk sprang to his feet, apparently to object, but when Judge Heath frowned forbiddingly at him, he clamped his mouth shut and sank back into his chair.

"And why did you not assist Dr. Ives on this occasion, Dr. Cardoza?"

"He had been called out of town. Constable Stuart brought the Braun woman's body to the Iveses' house and asked me to do the autopsy."

"Constable Stuart asked you to do it?"

"Yes."

"And as a result of your autopsy, Dr. Cardoza, what did you see—"

"Objection!" Polk protested. "The witness is not an expert. She cannot testify to anything medical in nature."

"Your Honor," Merrycoyf responded, "the witness can testify as to what she saw."

"Yes, yes, counsel," Judge Heath said. "Objection overruled. Please, Mr. Polk, exercise some discretion in your objections. Unless counsel asks this witness for a cause of death, I will allow her to answer his questions."

"Again, Dr. Cardoza," said Merrycoyf, "what did you *see*?"

Neva hesitated, presumably to choose her words with care. "What I *saw*," she said, "was a knife in the deceased's chest. I saw no air in the surrounding tissue or chest wall or under the skin. Also, I saw no evidence whatever of external bleeding and also none of an internal nature, not even in the pleural cavity."

Judge Heath leaned over the bench. "Dr. Cardoza, was that unusual?" he frowned.

Clearly astonished to be addressed at all by this judge, not to mention his use of *Dr.* Cardoza, Neva blurted, "Unusual? It defied the laws of nature!"

Merrycoyf, observed Glynis, was having some difficulty restraining a smile. Orrin Polk, on the other hand, looked incendiary. Neither said a word, however. And Judge Heath continued frowning as he nodded at Merrycoyf to continue.

"What else did you see, or not see, Dr. Cardoza?" Merrycoyf asked.

Neva looked beyond him at Glynis, who nodded encouragement, and then went on with regained composure as she said, "Most important was the evidence that the deceased had eaten shortly before she died. The stomach contents contained a quantity of tea and biscuits. And there was acute inflammation of the stomach, as well as patches of bright scarlet on the mucous membrane."

"Was that, or anything else, *unusual,* Dr. Cardoza?" Merrycoyf asked, careful to emphasize Judge Heath's own word.

"Yes. And there was something else. Adhering to the stomach lining were small particles."

"Could you see what those particles consisted of?"

"Yes. They consisted of approximately three and a half grains of arsenic."

As the courtroom erupted in a bedlam of noise, Judge Heath, scowling furiously, pounded his gavel. The jury had long since stopped looking bored, and now for the most part wore expressions of total confusion. Orrin Polk was objecting, although he could barely be heard over the commotion.

Glynis threw a quick glance to the rear of the courtroom; no one was leaving this time. And against the back wall, the Iroquois stood as still as death.

The gavel brought results only after Judge Heath further ordered the bailiff to remove those who would not comply with his order for silence. Gradually the noise abated.

"There will be no more such outbursts in my courtroom!" Judge Heath ordered. "In the event another occurs, the bailiff is instructed to immediately empty the room of spectators. I hope I have made myself clear."

With one more stroke of the gavel, he said, "Mr. Merrycoyf, do you have further questions of this witness?"

"No, Your Honor."

"Cross-examine, Mr. Polk?"

"Yes, indeed, Your Honor." Polk already was on his feet. "Would you tell the court, Miss Cardoza, whether, since coming to western New York, you have worked with anyone other than Dr. Quentin Ives?"

"Do you mean another doctor?"

"Yes, my dear, that's what I mean."

"Well, I worked several days with Dr. Witherspoon."

"Dr. Witherspoon the *dentist*?"

"Yes."

"And just how often does a dentist perform autopsies?"

"Objection!" Merrycoyf said.

"I withdraw the question." Polk smiled graciously. "Now tell us, did you usually discuss the autopsy findings with Dr. Ives, my dear?"

"I am not your 'dear,' Mr. Polk, and you will kindly refrain from addressing me as such. And yes, of course Dr. Ives and I discussed our findings."

"And did you discuss with Dr. Ives the findings to which you have testified today?"

"Yes."

"And did he correct any of your observations?"

"No, he did not."

"He didn't tell you what to say here?"

"No, he most certainly did not."

"Just answer the questions yes or no, Miss Cardoza.

Didn't Dr. Ives suggest what you might say about the deceased's—''

"No, he did not!" Neva interrupted. "And for you to infer—''

"I have no further questions of the witness Cardoza," Polk said.

"In that case," said Judge Heath, "the defense will call its next witness. Thank you, Dr. Cardoza, and you may step down."

Before she left the witness chair, Neva favored Judge Heath with a very small smile.

At the rear of the courtroom, two men—one of them extremely tall—started up the aisle, inducing a prolonged sigh from Merrycoyf. He stood quickly to say, "The defense calls Dr. Patrick Kelly."

Glynis, too, sighed with relief. Adam MacAlistair's telegram had reached Kelly's housekeeper in Rochester, who had wired back that the doctor was spending his weekend at the fashionable Inn at Hemlock Falls. It was now obvious that Adam, having raced to Hemlock Falls by carriage, had succeeded in locating Kelly. Glynis imagined the young lawyer had probably enjoyed the escapade immensely, and Merrycoyf looked not only relieved, but distinctly impressed.

"Dr. Kelly, would you state your educational background for the court?" Merrycoyf now asked.

"I received my degree from Harvard Medical School. Before setting up practice in Rochester, New York, I studied in Philadelphia under Dr. Paul Mercutio, a specialist in toxicology, who himself studied under Dr. Robert Christison."

"Dr. Christison is the author of *Treatise on Poisons*, is he not?"

"Yes."

"Dr. Kelly, were you in the courtroom to hear Dr. Cardoza's testimony?"

"Yes, I was standing in the back."

"Based on her testimony, Dr. Kelly, can you formulate an opinion as to the cause of death of the woman Lily Braun?"

"Yes."

"What is your opinion?"

"As described by Dr. Cardoza, the appearance of the deceased's internal organs, specifically the stomach, indicates acute poisoning. It seems clear that prior to her death, the victim ingested arsenic, probably introduced in tea. And three and a half grains of it would be more than enough to kill an adult woman."

"Can you attribute the victim's death, then, to the arsenic?"

Kelly didn't hesitate. "I'll put it this way, Mr. Merrycoyf; her death was probably caused by arsenic poisoning, because it most certainly did not result from a knife wound."

"Can you explain that?"

"Yes, but Dr. Cardoza already has done so. She testified that she saw no blood."

"What would that mean?"

"It means that the woman was dead, again almost certainly of arsenic poisoning, *before* the knife ever entered her body."

"Objection!" snapped Polk.

"On what grounds are you objecting?" said Judge Heath.

"That it is conjecture on the part of the witness."

"The witness is a physician and an expert in toxicology," Merrycoyf retorted.

"Objection overruled. Continue, Mr. Merrycoyf."

"Thank you, Your Honor. Now, Dr. Kelly, can you draw a conclusion about the presence of a knife in the victim's body? Could that have been planted evidence to obscure the real cause of death?"

"Yes—"

"Objection!" Polk broke in shrilly. The man looked beside himself, and continued in a piercing tone, "That is an outrageously leading question on defense's part."

"Sustained," said Judge Heath. "The jury should ignore this conjecture of counsel for the defense."

Ah, yes, Glynis reflected, watching the jury hang on every word. Tit for tat, Mr. Polk.

"Thank you, Dr. Kelly." Merrycoyf smiled fulsomely. "No further questions."

"Do you wish to cross-examine, Mr. Polk?"

"I certainly do, Your Honor!" Polk jumped from his chair. "Isn't it true, Dr. Kelly, that you never met the woman Lily Braun—alive *or* dead?"

"Yes, that's true."

"And so you formulated your opinion about the cause of her death based solely on the testimony given by the witness Cardoza in response to questions by counsel for the defense?"

"There is little doubt that—"

"Please answer yes or no, Dr. Kelly?"

"Yes."

"And, Dr. Kelly, is that ordinarily the way you prepare to testify in court?"

"Now, just a minute—"

"No further questions of this witness, Your Honor."

"The witness may step down," Judge Heath said.

Patrick Kelly appeared very much, Glynis observed, as if he'd like to punch Orrin Polk in his sharp little nose. But Kelly settled for a withering look as he stepped from the witness chair.

Judge Heath stood up, saying, "At this time we will take a fifteen-minute recess."

"All rise!"

TWENTY FOUR

❦

You will wait for me, my Gray Wolf,
For I soon shall come to join you.
O, my Gray Wolf, my Tah-yoh-ne,
Hear the voice of your Ah-weh-hah,
Only wait a few days longer
And I then will walk beside you.
    —MOURNING SONG OF SENECA
    WOMAN AH-WEH-HAH, FROM
    ARTHUR PARKER, *THE LIFE OF*
    GENERAL ELY S. PARKER

"WILL YOU CALL your next witness, Mr. Merrycoyf?"

"Yes, Your Honor," Merrycoyf said. "The defense calls Small Brown Bird, member of the Seneca Nation."

Necks craning, the courtroom spectators turned to watch the woman come up the aisle. When she went past, Glynis gave her what she hoped would be interpreted as a sympathetic look; anything more than that, a smile for instance, would have been ludicrous given the ordeal Small Brown Bird now faced.

Immediately there followed a flurry of discussion, instigated by Polk, which involved himself, the judge, and the court clerk, concerning the prospective witness's mandatory oath before a Judeo-Christian God. Glynis scarcely could believe her ears—not when considering some of the thoroughly ungodly people in the past who, with nary a challenge put to them, had sworn and given testimony in this very courtroom.

Small Brown Bird stood quietly, exhibiting little emotion and a great deal of dignity. This day her pantalettes were not of bright calico but of deerskin, their elaborate border above her moccasins embroidered with shell beads and porcupine quills, as was the hem of her deerskin overdress, which was buttoned with silver brooches. She fingered a

chain of silver beads that disappeared under the neckline of
the dress. During a momentary pause in the deliberation
swirling around her, she tilted her head slightly toward the
men arguing, then pulled out the chain to reveal a large
silver cross, saying in her musical voice, "I am a Christian."

Glynis swallowed a smile at the faces of the startled men,
who stared dumbly at the Seneca woman, until the clerk
scurried forward with the Bible. When presumably sworn to
everyone's satisfaction, Small Brown Bird was permitted to
sit in the witness chair.

"Will you give your name and place of residence to the
court clerk," said Judge Heath, in an unusually subdued
tone of voice.

"I am called Small Brown Bird. I live at the Black Brook
Reservation."

Merrycoyf rose and went to stand next to the jury box—
probably, Glynis determined, to verify that the jury could
hear the delicate voice.

"How long have you lived there at the reservation?"
Merrycoyf began.

"Many . . . fourteen years."

"And where did you live before that?"

"The Cattaraugus Reservation, near Buffalo."

"Are you related to the defendant?"

"I am sister to Walks At Sundown's mother."

"So you are his aunt?"

"As you say."

Merrycoyf shook his head at her slightly, and Small
Brown Bird then said, "Yes."

"And so you were also aunt to the defendant's half
brother, Many Horned Stag?"

"As you say. Yes."

"Miss—excuse me, Small Brown Bird—were you at the
reservation on the day ten years ago that eight men came
and took Many Horned Stag from his home?"

"Yes."

"Did you yourself witness this act?"

"I saw it. Yes."

Merrycoyf, apparently satisfied the jury could hear, and

indeed the woman's voice carried well despite its lightness of tone, now moved back to the defense table and picked up a pad of paper. While he leafed through it, Glynis glanced at Orrin Polk. The prosecutor had perched at the edge of his chair and continually lifted from it, up and down, as if he sat on a hot griddle. He had risen several times, ostensibly to object, but lowered himself back down without speaking. He was uneasy about this witness for good reason: Polk didn't know, Glynis was fairly certain, why the Seneca woman had been called.

Merrycoyf now went to stand beside the witness box. "Were you in the courtroom last Friday?" he asked Small Brown Bird.

"Yes."

"Did you hear the testimony of the prosecution witness Sara Turner?"

"Yes."

"And did you hear Mrs. Turner connect the lynch-killing of your nephew, Many Horned Stag, with the Black Brook dam litigation—that is, the legal battle? And with the alleged rape of Otto Braun's daughter, Lily?"

"Yes, I heard."

"Do you share her view? Do you think that the Black Brook dam, and the fact that your nephew won the case, was the reason he was killed?"

"Revenge was not all of the reason."

"Or that he was said to have raped Lily Braun?"

"No. Many Horned Stag would not do that."

"Would you now describe the reason as you know it to be?"

Small Brown Bird sat quietly with her hands folded in her lap. Before she spoke, she looked down at her nephew. Jacques sat equally still; his face, from where Glynis sat, seemed without expression, but she couldn't see his eyes. Orrin Polk fidgeted in his chair, and looked ready to pounce for any reason he could find.

Small Brown Bird drew in her breath, and began, "Ten summers ago—when the dam trouble was happening— Many Horned Stag and the girl Lily, they knew each other—"

"Pardon me," Merrycoyf broke in, "but do you mean Lily Braun and Many Horned Stag met during the dam dispute? The dispute that her father and uncle were involved in?"

"Yes. That."

"Thank you. Please go on," Merrycoyf said.

"Many Horned Stag and the girl, they"—Small Brown Bird hesitated as if searching for the words—"they were in love. They wanted to marry, but her father, the girl's, would not allow it. All that autumn the girl asked her father to let them marry, but it was of no use. Then the girl told Many Horned Stag and me and his mother that—"

"Objection," Polk argued. "This is a recollection that is ten years old, and—"

"No, Mr. Polk," interrupted Judge Heath. "Your objection is overruled. We will hear the woman out. The fact that it *was* ten years ago that this lynching occurred, and that this is the first any of us have heard of it, means it is high time the truth was uncovered. I want to know what happened. Please continue . . . ah . . . Miss Brown Bird."

They had been so afraid; but Judge Heath *would* listen, Glynis thought with relief that nearly brought tears.

"What was it that the girl Lily Braun told Many Horned Stag?" Merrycoyf asked.

"She said that she was with child."

"His child—Many Horned Stag's?"

"Yes."

After a few outraged whispers, the courtroom again quieted. Remarkably quiet also was Orrin Polk, who had sat back in his chair after the judge's last ruling with an angry expression, but now looked almost as inquisitive as everyone else.

"Small Brown Bird, do you recall whether the defendant also knew of his brother's coming child?" Merrycoyf asked.

"He knew. He is the one who said they had better run away."

"Jacques Sundown—your nephew Walks At Sundown— told his brother and Lily Braun that they should leave?"

"He said it was dangerous for them to stay."

Merrycoyf nodded. "Yes. What happened next?"

"They planned to go the next day. The girl went to her parents' house to get things to take with them. She was coming back to the reservation the next morning."

"So she and Many Horned Stag could leave together?"

"Yes."

"What time of year was that?"

"The same time as now. Early in winter."

"Were the other men who lived on the reservation—other than Many Horned Stag and his brother Walks At Sundown—were they there at that time of early winter?"

"No. They were gone hunting, three or four days gone, all but the very old men."

"So the only able-bodied men on the reservation at that time were the defendant and his brother."

Small Brown Bird frowned in apparent confusion, before her forehead smoothed and she answered, "No. No, Walks At Sundown, he left in early morning of that day to go and get the other men hunting."

"Why did he do that?"

"He thought there would be trouble. But not so soon."

"You mean he thought that trouble would come sometime after the two lovers had gone?"

"Yes."

"After Walks At Sundown left that morning, what next occurred?"

"The girl did not come back. Many Horned Stag waited and waited until it was afternoon. Then he said that her father must have found out and stopped her. Many Horned Stag said he would go to her father's house and get the girl."

"And did he do that?"

"He was getting his horse ready. Then they came."

"They? You mean the men—the eight white men?"

"Yes."

Small Brown Bird's fingers knotted in her lap. Glynis could see her knuckles draw taut, and could see the glitter of tears that did not fall. She herself knew what was coming and wished she could leave the courtroom, but to do so would be to abandon Jacques. And Small Brown Bird.

Merrycoyf, his voice kind, now said to Small Brown Bird,

"So eight men came into the reservation. I know this is difficult for you, but please tell us what happened then. Take as much time as you need."

The woman first gave Jacques a poignant look, then she turned and said to Merrycoyf, "The men took Many Horned Stag. They pulled him off his horse and tied a rope around his neck, and they dragged him into the woods. We tried to stop them, but they were too many. We followed them. They dragged him to a clearing in the trees, and they . . ."

Small Brown Bird's voice broke, but she shook her head and went on, "The men, they looped the rope around Many Horned Stag's neck over a tree limb. Before they pulled the rope, they . . . they took his manhood."

Glynis was vaguely aware of rustling skirts and the rear door opening; she didn't have to turn to know people were leaving. Otherwise the room was quiet, until Merrycoyf said, "They took his manhood. I'm sorry to have to clarify this, but do you mean they castrated him?"

Small Brown Bird, now choking back tears, nodded and said, "Yes." It was all but lost in the scuffle that broke out in the back of the room.

Glynis turned to see Seneca and Cayuga men standing in front of the rear door, preventing those attempting to leave from doing so. Cullen stood talking quietly and obviously trying to reason with them. When women's cries of protestation reached Glynis, distracting her from her anxiety for Cullen, she turned to look at Judge Heath. Merrycoyf was also watching the judge, while members of the jury were, for the most part, staring either toward the back, or at Small Brown Bird.

Judge Heath's gavel struck loudly. "I want this courtroom quiet," he said. "It is understandable that some are upset by the testimony and wish to leave. But we need order here immediately."

Suddenly a Seneca man called out, "Everyone should sit down. There is a need for all to hear this." His voice sounded determined but controlled, not as reckless with fury as it might have been, Glynis recognized with relief.

In response, Judge Heath stood up and moved away from the bench. His black robes made him look like a monk—or an executioner. Glynis waited with anxiety like the rest of the courtroom, but her glance shifted back and forth between Cullen and Jacques, who had turned around for a quick glance, but now looked straight ahead at Small Brown Bird.

"Your Honor," Cullen said from the back of the room, "Your Honor, these men," he gestured to the Iroquois, "do have a point. They say that whatever happens here today will go beyond this courtroom in its consequences. And for that reason we should all listen. They have agreed, though, that the women wanting to leave can go. But everyone else, having been here for the prosecution's case, should stay to hear the defense. While it's an unusual approach, I don't think that under the circumstances it's entirely without merit, Your Honor."

"Constable Stuart, I don't like being dictated to in my own courtroom," Judge Heath said. "However, if these men will allow the ladies to leave, and if they themselves give you their solemn word that they will go peaceably back to the reservation at the conclusion of this trial—*no matter what the jury's verdict*—then we can proceed."

Glynis thought this posture of Judge Heath's to be either naive or sublimely arrogant. Didn't he understand that the Iroquois, and not he, were in control? That their goodwill would decide the outcome of this standoff? Cullen's approach had been far more conciliatory.

But when a male voice just behind Glynis said, "Well done, Judge Heath," he received for his effort a glare from the judge. Who perhaps did understand after all.

"Your Honor," Merrycoyf said loudly, "would you instruct the constable that no one who has been subpoenaed to testify should be allowed to leave?"

Glynis breathed more easily after she saw Cullen nod his agreement to Merrycoyf; she had worried about that. But perhaps the crucial person did not yet realize the implications of Small Brown Bird's testimony.

The rear door was then opened and many of the women, but not all, hurried out. Some men did also, as the Iroquois at this juncture didn't stop anyone. They had made their point, as Cullen had put it.

It was a few more minutes before order was entirely restored. While her sympathy centered on Jacques, Glynis felt most sorry just then for Small Brown Bird. The woman had composed herself admirably during the uproar, but her hands still lay knotted in her lap. She looked over at Glynis once, her expression one of sorrow. And Glynis herself felt again the smart of tears.

"May we proceed?" Merrycoyf asked Judge Heath. Glynis had earlier noticed Orrin Polk leaving quietly by way of the judge's door, but, after peering out to see that order had been accomplished, he now returned to the prosecution's table.

"Yes, Mr. Merrycoyf, proceed, if you please!" Judge Heath directed.

"I hope to finish soon," Merrycoyf said to Small Brown Bird. "After the eight men had hanged your nephew, what happened?"

"They left. They rode away. And then Walks At Sundown came. The wolf had found him . . ." She broke off at a gesture from Merrycoyf.

"Yes, please go on," he said to her quickly, obviously trying to avoid an explanation of his client's familiarity with wolves.

"Walks At Sundown first cut his brother loose, and we, after a little while, carried his body back to the reservation."

"When you say 'we,' " Merrycoyf asked, "do you mean you yourself, the young men's mother—Bitter Root—and Walks At Sundown?"

"Yes."

"But had there been anyone else in the woods while this despicable deed was taking place?"

"Yes, there was the girl Lily. She was hiding behind some trees, but we knew she was there."

"Did she go with you when you took Many Horned Stag back to the reservation?"

"No. We didn't see her again that day—Bitter Root and I didn't."

"Did you see Lily Braun sometime after that?"

"Yes. Walks At Sundown later found her lying in the woods. She had near frozen to death. He was afraid for her and for the child, so he took her on his horse to the nearest white people's house.''

"Are you saying," Merrycoyf asked her, "that the defendant saved the life of the very woman whom he is now accused of killing? The woman who was the mother of his brother's child?"

"Walks At Sundown would not kill a woman," Small Brown Bird answered.

"No," Merrycoyf said. "No, I don't think so either. But to whose house did he take Lily Braun?"

"To Obadiah Grimm's house."

"And did Lily Braun stay at the Grimms'?"

"She stayed until the child was born, in the spring."

"Were you present at the birth of this child?"

"Yes, and my sister too. The Grimm family asked us to come to the farm to help because my sister, Bitter Root, she is a medicine woman."

"And was the child healthy at birth?"

"Yes, healthy." For the first time that day, Glynis saw Small Brown Bird's face relax slightly.

"What happened after the child was born?"

"Lily left the Grimms'."

"Had the Grimm family asked her to leave?"

"Yes, that is what she told us."

"And the baby?"

"Lily left the baby with the Grimms. Because she had no money, she said."

"Do you know," Merrycoyf asked, "if Lily Braun planned to leave the child there at Grimm's for long?"

"She said she would not come back—is that what you mean?"

"That's what I mean," agreed Merrycoyf. "Small Brown Bird, I know this has been very difficult for you. But your testimony has been important, and I thank you for coming. I have no more questions."

Judge Heath looked at Orrin Polk. "Do you plan to cross-examine this woman, Mr. Polk?"

Given the way the judge scowled when he said this, Glynis thought that even if Polk had planned to cross-examine, he might not now. And when he said, "No, Your

Honor, no questions,'' the jury looked distinctly relieved.

As Small Brown Bird left the witness chair, she gave Jacques a forlorn, almost apologetic look before she started down the aisle.

"You have another witness, Mr. Merrycoyf?" Judge Heath asked.

"Yes, Your Honor. The defense calls Billy Wicken."

Toward the back of the room, a small commotion broke out and several people got to their feet. Glynis couldn't see exactly what was happening, but Cullen, in the meantime, had moved toward the source of the noise. He stood beside the last row of chairs, motioning with his hand. Glynis heard "No," several times, then a distinct "I don't want to!" But Cullen kept gesturing, and at last Billy Wicken moved with reluctance toward the center aisle. When he reached it, Cullen put his hand on Billy's shoulder, said something to him, then gave him a small push forward.

Despite herself, Glynis felt a rush of pity as Billy limped up the aisle. He looked so miserable, his expression so confused. Someone had made an effort to smooth his unruly hair; the result was an unfortunate cowlick that stood up like a rooster's comb, while his large, pointed ears still protruded through the mop of straw hair. Billy's chameleon eyes, now an indeterminate gray, darted from side to side as if looking for a means of escape.

There was some difficulty with his swearing in, and when he finally ended up in the witness chair, his voice sounded tremulous as he gave the clerk his name. Merrycoyf spoke briefly to Adam before he went forward; he seemed to take rather a long time before he asked his first question, but Glynis was aware that Merrycoyf needed to proceed with caution.

"Mr. Wicken, how long have you lived at the Grimm farm?"

"I . . . I don't know. A long time, maybe . . ." Billy shrugged.

"Would you think twelve years was about right?"

"Yeah, about right."

"Mr. Wicken—but would you mind if I call you Billy?"

"It's O.K., I don't mind."

"Good. Billy, where did you live before you went to work at the Grimms'?"

"Around. I lived around. No place, really."

"Were you hired as a handyman at the Grimms'?"

"Yeah. I did lots of things."

"What do you do now?"

"Not so much now. I take care of the sheep. I used to do it with Mead Miller until he . . . you know."

"Until Mead Miller was killed?"

"Yeah."

"Why don't you do as much now as you used to, Billy?"

Billy gave Merrycoyf a shaky grin, and held up his withered hand. "Why do you think?"

"Isn't your leg injured as well? How did that happen?"

Billy's eyes darted to the sides of the room.

"How did your injuries happen, Billy?" Merrycoyf repeated.

"Accident. I had a accident."

"What kind of accident?"

"Went down the stairs."

"You fell down some stairs?"

"Well—that's not right. I kind of was pushed."

"I see. Who pushed you?"

"It was a accident. He didn't mean to do it. He was just mad, is all."

"Who was just mad, Billy?"

Orrin Polk cleared his throat loudly before he said, "Objection, Your Honor. This line of questioning is totally irrelevant."

"I agree, Mr. Merrycoyf," Judge Heath responded.

"Your Honor," Merrycoyf said shortly, obviously annoyed at being interrupted just as he was gaining Billy's trust, "I need to establish a pattern here. Or, as my esteemed colleague would say, a motive for behavior."

"And I will allow you the same leeway, but only for a short time," Judge Heath growled. "Objection overruled."

"Billy," Merrycoyf immediately asked again, "who pushed you down the stairs?"

Billy shook his head. When Judge Heath leaned forward and ordered him to answer, he looked about to cry. But finally he said, ''Mr. Grimm did—but he didn't mean to. He said so.''

''Which Mr. Grimm was that, Billy?''

Billy looked surprised at the question. As if there couldn't be more than one, Glynis thought. ''You know,'' he said to Merrycoyf, ''*Mr.* Grimm.''

''Do you mean Mr. Obadiah Grimm?''

Billy nodded. ''Yeah.''

''So as a result of being pushed down the stairs by Mr. Obadiah Grimm, you suffered paralysis in your hand and your leg—and a severe head injury, too, didn't you?''

''Your Honor!'' Polk whined. ''What in the name of heaven does defense think he is establishing?''

''Your Honor, I can recall Quentin Ives if necessary,'' said Merrycoyf, ''to establish the extensive nature of Billy Wickens's injuries.''

''The injuries appear to be self-evident,'' Judge Heath said. ''If the prosecutor has an objection, it is overruled. Now get on with it, Mr. Merrycoyf!''

''Do you remember when the girl Pippa was born, Billy?''

''Yeah, I do.''

''Did your accident happen before or after that?''

''After. It was after Pippa came.''

''So, because of your injuries, did you spend a great deal of time with Pippa when she was small?''

''Yeah, I did. And Molly too, because they liked me.''

''And Molly Grimm too. Very good. Would you say you took care of Pippa and Molly?''

Billy smiled broadly. ''Yeah, I took care of them.''

''Would you agree with me if I said that you wouldn't allow any harm to come to them—not if you could help it?''

''I wouldn't let anybody hurt them, you mean?''

''Yes, Billy, that's what I mean.''

''You're right!''

''Good. Now tell me this, Billy—did there come a time, some months ago, when a woman named Lily Braun came to visit Pippa?''

Billy scowled, and nodded. "Yeah, she came. It wasn't good."

"Why wasn't it good?"

At that moment a sound from the back of the room made Glynis and everyone else turn to look. Lazarus Grimm was making for the door, gesturing to his sister behind him. Molly, however, sat with her eyes glued on Billy Wicken. Cullen stepped in front of the door, barring Lazarus's way, saying, "Back to your chair, Grimm. Nobody's leaving just now."

"Yes, take your seat back there!" Judge Heath ordered.

Lazarus shot the judge a frown, but Cullen took his shoulder and pushed him into a recently vacated chair on the aisle. Then he himself took a seat opposite, and nodded to Judge Heath.

During this, Billy had been moving his head and shoulders from side to side, and Glynis now saw why Merrycoyf appeared to pace in front of his witness. In fact, Merrycoyf had done this from the beginning of Billy's testimony, deliberately blocking his view to the rear of the courtroom.

Merrycoyf resumed his pacing now, and repeated, "Why wasn't it good when Lily Braun would visit the Grimms, Billy?"

"Molly got upset. Everybody got upset."

"Do you know why Lily Braun kept going to the Grimm farm?"

"No. Just that she wanted something."

"She wanted something. All right, Billy, now were you at the farm the day that Obadiah Grimm died?"

Billy frowned. " 'Course I was there."

"Did Lily Braun visit that day too?"

"Yeah, she did."

"And did people get upset again?"

Billy's head bobbed, trying to see past Merrycoyf's broad frame. Finally he said, "Yeah, real upset."

"And did you see what happened to Obadiah Grimm in the barn? Did you see him before he fell?"

Billy's face took on a stricken cast, and he weaved back and forth. Glynis assumed Judge Heath could observe from the bench what was going on. And Orrin Polk had begun to look worried.

"Billy, you have sworn on the Bible to tell the truth," Merrycoyf said, but very gently. "Now, what did you see in the barn that day?"

"A accident. It was a accident."

"Another accident, Billy? Like the one that happened between you and Obadiah Grimm?"

"Yeah, like that," Billy said readily.

"Tell us," Merrycoyf said in a sympathetic voice, while taking a few steps closer to Billy. "Tell us what happened to Obadiah Grimm."

"He was mad at Molly after she climbed up in the hayloft with him—to talk to him, I think."

"What was Obadiah Grimm doing in the hayloft?"

"Forking hay."

"Do you know why he was mad at Molly?"

Billy seemed to consider this, then said, "I think it was about Pippa. They were talking real loud, that's how I know."

"What happened while they were talking loudly?"

"He . . . he hit Molly!" Billy said excitedly. "He hit her hard in the face. She almost fell off the hayloft—just like I fell down the stairs."

"After Obadiah Grimm hit you?"

"Yeah. But Molly, she didn't fall. So he grabs her dress and he starts to shake her and she's crying . . ." Billy lifted from his seat now in a desperate effort to see the Grimms in the back of the room. But Merrycoyf again blocked his view.

"Did Molly grab his pitchfork to protect herself?" Merrycoyf asked kindly, reassuring Billy by saying, "It would be a natural thing to do."

Billy frowned and said, "Yeah, she got the pitchfork and old Obadiah he was so mad, he . . . he looked like he mighta run right into it."

"Yes. And then he fell backward off the hayloft."

"Yeah, he did."

"Billy, was Pippa there in the barn when this happened?"

"She *was* there, but then she was gone when me and

Lazarus looked for her. I think she went in the secret passage.''

"The passage from the house and barn, you mean?'' Merrycoyf asked. "The one that takes you out to Black Brook?''

"That one.''

"Why didn't you tell anyone what you saw, Billy? For instance, when Dr. Cardoza came and asked what happened?''

"I wouldn't tell. It was a secret, she said.''

"She? Do you mean Molly Grimm?''

Billy's head bobbed. "And I wasn't sorry he got killed!''

"That's understandable, Billy. Now I want to ask you a few questions about the day of the blizzard. Do you remember the storm last month?''

Billy looked troubled, and didn't answer. He fidgeted in his chair, until Judge Heath bent toward him, saying, "Billy, you need to answer Mr. Merrycoyf's question.'' Like Merrycoyf, the judge spoke kindly.

Billy sighed loudly. "I remember the storm.''

"Do you remember that Lily Braun came to the farm that day?''

Orrin Polk rose, beginning to object, although it seemed to Glynis that the prosecutor's heart wasn't in it.

Judge Heath interrupted him. "Let Mr. Merrycoyf finish this, Mr. Polk. I'm going to allow wide latitude with this witness.'' He said this quietly, as if not wanting to interfere with Billy's tenuous trust of Merrycoyf.

"Did Lily Braun come that day before the storm started?'' Merrycoyf prodded gently.

Billy frowned and slowly nodded.

"What happened after she came?''

"She got mad.''

"Lily Braun was mad at whom—at Molly?''

"No, Molly was being nice, real nice, to her. She got mad at Lazarus. So Molly told him to leave.''

"Leave where?''

"The house.'' Billy looked as if he thought this should be obvious. Glynis wanted to turn and look behind her, but was afraid to do anything that might upset the delicate balancing act Merrycoyf was attempting. And the rest of the spectators, those that were left, seemed equally fixed in place.

"What did Lily Braun do then, Billy? After Lazarus left the house?"

"She got sick."

"Sick? How did she look?"

"She looked real sick. She was holding her stomach and making noises and then she fell off her chair onto the floor. I thought she was going to die. Then she did."

"She died? Lily Braun *died,* there in the Grimm house?"

"Yeah, she did."

While sounds of astonishment rippled softly through the room, Glynis had her eyes on Jacques. All she saw in the way of reaction was a shake of his shoulders, before he leaned back against his chair. And Orrin Polk just stared at Merrycoyf. But he said nothing.

Merrycoyf looked up at Judge Heath, who was glaring at the spectators, and received a nod. "Continue with your witness, Mr. Merrycoyf."

"Billy, after you saw that Lily Braun had died, what did you think?"

"I thought I should do something."

"Why?"

" 'Cause it was bad for her to be dead in the house. I knew that because Molly was crying. So I took the dead lady to the barn."

"Took Lily Braun's body—did you carry it?"

"Yeah, she wasn't very big. Not even as big as a sheep. I took her and put her on my horse. Molly gave me the horse, you know that?"

Merrycoyf nodded. "Go on."

"So I put the lady on the horse and I took her into the woods. It was snowing real hard."

Glynis started, and half-turned as a hoarse sound came from the back of the room. She didn't turn around; she didn't need to.

"Where in the woods did you take the lady's body?"

"To the end, by the reservation. There's a cabin right there. So I left her and the horse by the woodpile, and I looked in the cabin's window 'cause I thought I could find a shovel and bury her. And nobody would know. But when I looked in the window, I saw some knives on a rack. Nobody was around, so I went in and got one. A big one, with a wolf. I thought it would be better than a shovel."

"And you put the knife in the lady's chest?" Merrycoyf asked.

"Yeah."

"Why did you do that?"

"So people would think she got killed by Indians."

"As indeed they did," Merrycoyf said. "What happened next? Did you leave then?"

"No, I was going to put the lady inside the cabin. But I heard something. Somebody was coming."

"Who was it, did you see?"

"Yeah, I hid behind the woodpile and I saw him." Billy pointed his finger at Jacques. "He was carrying Miss Tryon to the cabin, and she was covered with snow and looked like she was dead, too. And I got scared, 'cause I thought maybe he really had killed her—Miss Tryon. And I pulled my horse into the woods and then I went back to the farm."

"Thank you, Billy," Merrycoyf said. "You've done a fine job. And I have just one or two more questions. Tell me, when Lily Braun was in the Grimm house, was she drinking something just before she died? Something like tea, perhaps?"

Billy nodded. "Yeah, she was drinking tea."

"Who had made the tea for her?"

Billy smiled broadly. "Molly. She made it."

Glynis turned then, to look at Molly Grimm. The woman sat with her arms wrapped around herself, rocking back and forth, her sobs quiet but nonetheless heartrending. Cullen stood directly behind her. He responded to Molly's anguish by very gently placing his hands on her shoulders. And Glynis wondered how she ever could have felt anger toward this man.

Zeph was stationed by the door with Lazarus Grimm, who stared at his sister as if dumbfounded. Glynis questioned how much of this was an act. Was it possible he hadn't known? But if she had managed to figure it out, surely Lazarus could have. Granted that her initial guess was driven

by the need to free Jacques; Lazarus might well have been
blinded by affection. Because he almost certainly knew that
Molly had killed their father, if only accidentally. He had
lied to Neva that night to protect his sister. And perhaps to
protect his access to Pippa.

When Glynis first began to speculate about the Grimm
siblings, she had suspected Lazarus, as the proximity of the
farm to Jacques's cabin seemed all-important. And when
she'd figured out Obadiah's dying quotation, it certainly
seemed to implicate Lazarus: "... he that getteth riches but
not by right ..."

But last Friday, Adam MacAlistair had said it was impossible for Pippa to be Molly's daughter. He told her that
he'd reviewed the material submitted by Merrycoyf on Lazarus's petition for administration of his father's estate: Lazarus had sworn that Obadiah Grimm had no grandchildren.
Then she recalled Almira Grimm saying, after a visit from
Lily Braun, "that girl of mine got trouble—big trouble."
When asked if she meant Pippa, Almira had laughed and
said, "No, she never told nobody *she* had a husband." So
Molly might not have been married—no one had ever actually seen a husband, just heard about one. Had Pippa been
conceived out of wedlock? In that case, why did Lazarus
swear there were no grandchildren? When Glynis asked
Merrycoyf about this, he said he'd been told that Pippa was
a foundling.

Obadiah's quotation from Jeremiah then took on an entirely different cast: "As the partridge sitteth on eggs, but
hatcheth them not ..." It pointed a cruel finger at Molly.

Just as important was the indisputable fact that Molly became distraught whenever Lily Braun appeared—and why
had Lily kept returning to the Grimms'? In retrospect it was
clear: to get her daughter back. Had Obadiah threatened to
give Pippa to her natural mother? That he was capable of it
was borne out by his brutal dying words. They would probably never know if Molly used the pitchfork in self-defense
or to deliberately kill him—Glynis believed the former—
but they did know she had done it.

Given Pippa's behavior that night, Glynis had suspected
that the girl might have witnessed something terrible; thus

the reason she and Neva had contrived to have Neva interrupt the seance with "Pippa's" voice. Then, armed with the certainty, when she and Neva had gone to the Grimm farm with Zeph, they'd found a scrap of Molly's lace collar caught in the flooring of the hayloft—the torn collar they all had seen the night Obadiah died. Almira had told them, among other things, exactly where to look.

Glynis now glanced again at Molly Grimm, who was being taken from the courtroom by Cullen; the eight men who murdered Jacques's brother had made this woman their victim as well. Molly had raised the child of Lily Braun and Many Horned Stag as her own; only to be threatened with having her beloved Pippa torn from her by a woman she viewed as abandoning her baby—and as a prostitute unfit to raise a child.

And yet it could be argued, Glynis now believed, that other than Many Horned Stag himself, Lily was the most tragic victim of that lynch mob.

Cullen had just returned to the courtroom as Merrycoyf, who had been talking to Judge Heath, stood back from the bench to say, "Your Honor, I move that the indictment charging the man Jacques Sundown with the murder of Lily Braun be dismissed."

Orrin Polk, staring toward the windows, merely said, "No objection." His shoulders drooped, and Glynis wished she could spare some sympathy for him. But Mr. Polk had taken a little too much relish in his job.

"Case dismissed," Judge Heath said. "The prisoner is free to go. But, Constable Stuart, I believe your investigation is not over yet—do you agree?"

"I agree, Your Honor," Cullen responded.

No, Glynis thought, with a bone-deep sadness; this was not yet over.

Epilogue

ॐ

I will live in the Past, Present, and the Future. The Spirits of all Three shall strive within me.
—CHARLES DICKENS, *A CHRISTMAS CAROL*

WHEN CULLEN ARRIVED unexpectedly the following morning, Glynis already had been up since dawn, dressed and brooding over coffee in the Peartree kitchen. She had not slept well.

"I figured you'd want to go out to the reservation today," he had said when she opened the door to him.

"I'd planned to, yes."

"I have a carriage out front."

"You want us to go out there . . . together?" Glynis asked, surprised and unable to disguise it.

"Yes, I believe we should," was all he said.

She could find no reason to refuse, and wrapped herself in her new, wine-colored merino wool cloak, no longer regretting the loss of the somber black one destroyed by the blizzard. They said little, but the silence between them did not feel as uncomfortable as Glynis had feared.

And, she now thought, this must be done today. The weather was changing again, and behaved more like the three days before Christmas that it was; a few snowflakes spun around them, and a watery sun appeared every so often. But once the winter snows began in earnest, everything north of town would be isolated for weeks at a time.

Passing the Grimm farm, Cullen broke the silence: "You probably haven't heard about Serenity's tavern license?"

Glynis, thinking of the ravaged Grimm family, was startled by this non sequitur, and murmured, "No, I haven't."

"You did know we're apparently going to have a Jewish wedding in Seneca Falls next spring?"

At that, she had to smile. "Yes, at least Abraham thinks so. But what does that have to do with Serenity Hathaway?"

"When I got back from Waterloo yesterday, Serenity and her sidekick, Brendan O'Reilly, came by to announce they'd finally gotten the last signature they needed on her petition."

"Oh?" Glynis said, simply to be polite, but not particularly interested one way or the other.

"The last petition signer was Lazarus Grimm."

"*Who?*"

"That's exactly what *I* said. But it seems that crafty little Neva Cardoza came up with a scheme some weeks ago. She went to Serenity—"

"Neva did?"

Cullen nodded. "She talked Serenity into making a generous contribution to Lazarus's spiritualist group, in return for Lazarus's signature on the petition, which he could give now that he's a landowner."

"I can't believe it. Neva didn't tell me. And besides, she wanted the tavern closed!"

"She didn't tell you," Cullen said, "because she knew you wouldn't approve."

"I don't."

"Well, there you are." Cullen nodded again.

"But *why?*"

Cullen's smile, the first she'd seen of it in some time, swept across his face. "Seems Neva then finagled Lazarus into giving *her* the money Serenity gave him."

"What . . . whatever for?"

"For a shelter. For abandoned wives and children of drunks. Neva suggested to Lazarus that it would be better for him to give the money to charity than to keep something, as she put it, 'so obviously tainted'!"

"No!"

"And, as you might guess, our Dr. Cardoza plans to run this shelter herself, now she's staying. But she told Lazarus he could hold his spiritualist meetings there once a week, if he'd split the donations with her charity."

"Oh, Cullen!" Glynis felt laughter catch in her throat. She couldn't release it, not with what lay ahead, but it was good to know she was still able to feel it. And then she thought of Molly Grimm.

No one, including Cullen, had known what to do with the

woman. Molly did not seem to comprehend, or even remember, what had happened. She could not grasp anything
other than the certainty that she would lose Pippa. Jailing
her, then putting her on trial for Lily's murder, struck everyone, even Judge Heath, as inhuman if she couldn't understand what it was she had done. Neva Cardoza had come
up with an answer that, while unsatisfactory in some regards, seemed to most the reasonable course. Thus Neva and
Abraham and Zeph were now on the train with Molly, taking her to the Rochester Asylum for the Insane. A terrible
penalty, Glynis thought with sorrow, for a woman driven
mad by desperation at the prospect of losing her child.

A few minutes later, as they started down the grade into
Black Brook Reservation, Cullen said, "Glynis, I expect
you know what I have to do?"

Apparently he'd come to the same conclusion she had
some days before, and he didn't sound any more comfortable with it than she had been.

"I'd like to talk with her before you do anything, Cullen."

"I thought you would. All right, go ahead—there's certainly no hurry at this point."

But, ironically, the "hurry" was exactly what had trig-
gered the answer. Why, she'd asked herself over and over,
had the three remaining members of the eight-man lynching
party been killed in a period of several weeks, when the first
five had been spread over almost ten years? Because, for
some reason, time was running out. Then, of course, there
had been Jacques's uncompromising refusal to defend himself; at last she had come to realize that his was the silence
of a protector. And finally, as she'd guessed early on, the
methods of murder provided the key. Not one had been
committed with a standard male weapon: a rifle or pistol or
knife. None had involved physical proximity, as would have
strangulation or suffocation. And none had required
strength. Tenacity, daring, patience, and knowledge of poisons, yes. Not strength. Even loosening wagon wheels could
be done by a woman. And if Jacques had taught Cullen to
use the Iroquois air-gun, then who might have likely taught
Jacques?

Cullen now brought the carriage up next to the bridge, and tethered the horse to the same willow that Glynis had used weeks before. When he swung her down from the carriage, as he had so many times in the past, Glynis felt a sudden longing for what once had been between them—for what seemed unlikely to be again.

"I'll wait here, outside," he said to her. "You go ahead."

As she went toward the house, she saw Small Brown Bird standing in the open doorway. "How is she?" Glynis asked from the foot of the shallow steps.

"She is not good. It will be soon now."

Glynis nodded. "Yes, I thought as much. It's consumption, isn't it?"

Small Brown Bird tilted her head in acquiescence.

"I'd like to talk to her. Constable Stuart said he would wait."

"I was expecting him to come. You also, I hoped, would come. You helped Walks At Sundown. She knows that," Small Brown Bird said, inclining her head toward the house interior.

"But why didn't she help?" Glynis asked. "Her own son?"

"Ask her," Small Brown Bird said. "Only she can tell you."

As Glynis went up the steps, she saw Jacques come across the bridge. She didn't wait for him, but went on into the house.

Hovering inside was a faint turpentinelike odor, which suggested poultices of beth root and willow bark. Bitter Root lay on a narrow cot, covered with a thick woven shawl. She was coughing weakly when Glynis entered the room; the paroxysm lasted several minutes, during which Pippa, kneeling on the floor beside the cot, lifted the woman's head to wipe blood from her lips. Glynis was at first confused when she saw the girl there, before she recalled what the trial had revealed: that Bitter Root was, in fact, Pippa's grandmother.

And Bitter Root was dying; even Glynis could see that.

She went to stand by the cot, waiting for the coughing to subside. When it did, Bitter Root fell back against a blanket roll, plainly exhausted. She stared up at Glynis with eyes that, while dulled with pain, still held a flicker of hard light. She motioned with a feeble gesture for Pippa to go outside.

"I don't understand," Glynis said, after checking that Pippa was safely beyond earshot. "Oh, not about those eight men—*that* I understand. It's not uniquely Iroquois, your code of vengeance. 'An eye for an eye' is probably as old as the human race. What I don't understand is how you could let your son stand trial without coming forward."

"I didn't kill the woman," Bitter Root said hoarsely. "You know that."

"But your son didn't either, and you knew *that*. You also must have known that the eight men you did kill would rise like ghosts to condemn him during the trial. They very nearly got him convicted of Lily Braun's murder, because he couldn't say a word in his own defense. Not without betraying you and your acts of retribution."

Bitter Root motioned to Small Brown Bird, who moved the blanket roll so the woman's head was slightly elevated. Bitter Root wheezed as she choked out, "Walks At Sundown was to perform the obligation to his brother. He would not. He tried to keep me from this duty."

"How?"

Bitter Root began to cough again. When Small Brown Bird tried to assist her, the woman waved her away.

"Miss Tryon," Small Brown Bird said, "my sister is weak. She is dying. This is very hard for her."

"Yes, it's been hard for everyone," Glynis said to her. "But then you tell me, if you know, how Walks At Sundown could keep this woman from doing whatever she wanted."

"He took her away, many times."

"Away?"

"After the first man, Lily Braun's father, had been . . . I think you would say *executed,* then Walks At Sundown took his mother to the Cattaraugus Reservation."

"So she wouldn't be suspected?"

"So she couldn't kill again. But as soon as he would leave, she always came back here."

"How many times did he do this?"

"Every time. Every time but this. He knew she was dying. He could not interfere."

"You mean that whenever she executed another man, Jacques would take her away? No wonder he kept leaving Seneca Falls with no explanation," Glynis said with astonishment. And no wonder he had turned up at the murder scenes, checking on the men that were left—Mead Miller and Jake Braun. He had suspected that, even sick as she was, she would find them.

Small Brown Bird said, "It was difficult for her."

"For *her*! What about him—what about her son?"

Bitter Root raised her head slightly. "He was never whole Seneca—his father was a good man, but white. Walks At Sundown, he thinks like Seneca sometimes, thinks like the white man too many times. He believes in the white man's law. I say he should have his trial, he thinks the white man's law is so good!"

A shadow fell across the room as someone came through the doorway. Glynis turned to see Jacques. He walked to within several feet of her, then stood looking down at his mother. Glynis wondered how long he had been standing outside, and how much he had heard.

"There's no question," she said to Bitter Root, "that you succeeded—brilliantly, I would add—in avenging your son. Your other son. But keep in mind that the white man's law you despise so much did function. Walks At Sundown is free. From hanging. I suppose the question now is, will *you* free him?"

"He is free," Bitter Root said. "He has no more duty to his brother. I did this for him." She looked at her son then. There remained none of the antagonism that Glynis had witnessed before. In fact, a faint smile appeared on the woman's face.

She took several steps away from the cot to stand beside Small Brown Bird, who said softly, "She is content. She has finished the duty to her son, and she has her granddaughter here. It is enough."

Glynis nodded, and before leaving she gave Bitter Root a long last look. She received no concession from the woman. She hadn't thought that she would. When she turned to go, she saw Cullen standing in the doorway. He stepped aside to let her pass, and followed her out.

"Did you hear?" she said to him.

"Yes, I heard."

"What are you going to do . . . about her?"

Cullen sighed. "Glynis, what do you expect I'll do—haul a dying old woman into jail? Or have we gotten so far apart that you really don't know the answer?"

She did know. But he might not believe her if she told him that. Not anymore. No more than Bitter Root would have believed that, had Glynis herself been a mother, and forced to watch done to her son what had been done to Many Horned Stag, her need for revenge undoubtedly would have been just as great. And she knew, as surely as did Bitter Root, that even if those eight men had been brought to trial, they almost certainly would never have been convicted.

Glynis turned to walk toward Black Brook and the carriage. But she stopped by the bridge, listening, with the sudden awareness that for some time she had not heard the wolf. Nor had she seen it. Not since the day, she now realized, when Cullen had arrested Jacques. Or in all the time he'd been in jail and on trial.

In Jacques's absence, had the wolf been killed by white men for a few dollars in bounty? Or pushed farther and farther north to die out like the rest of its kind? Glynis wiped at her eyes as a tide of tears threatened, more so than at any other moment in all the moments of recent time.

She became conscious of footsteps behind her, and heard Jacques say, "I need to talk to you."

She turned to face him, and to see Cullen standing at the foot of the house steps with Small Brown Bird. He kept glancing toward her and Jacques.

Jacques stood just looking at her. She felt again the involuntary attraction, and her cheeks began to burn.

"Thanks." His flat voice did not correspond to the expression in his eyes.

"It's not needed," Glynis said quickly. "I'm just so very sorry you had to go through so much. But, Jacques, you've saved me more than once. I'm not sure we're even yet."

"You sound like a white man. Or, maybe, He'-no."

"I certainly don't mean to!"

"Then don't talk about us being 'even'." His eyes warmed her despite the snow that now fell around them in cold, wet flakes, and Glynis remembered the moment in his cabin. The moment before Cullen arrived. But what would Jacques do now—go or stay? She was too afraid to ask.

Cullen had started walking, quickly, toward them. When he got to within a few yards, he said to Jacques, "Sundown, your mother is dying. Obviously there's no point in . . ." He broke off, just shaking his head. "Look," he went on, "I can't apologize for arresting you. I'm sorry it all happened, sure sorry for you, but I was doing my job."

"Yeah, doing your job. I know."

A long look passed between them. Neither man held out a hand to the other. "Well," Cullen said, "probably after your mother goes, you'll be moving on, right?"

"Moving on."

"Yes, I'd guess you might not want to stay after—well, you know."

"No. I don't know."

Glynis stood watching them, holding her breath as she waited for Jacques to say he was leaving.

Then, "No, I don't think I'll leave," Jacques said. "Think I'll stay around for a while." He came very close to smiling.

Glynis let out her breath, giving in to her own smile.

Cullen looked narrowly at her, then back to Jacques. "So that's the way it's going to be?" Then he shook his head, and Glynis saw his jaw harden. "No, I don't give up that easily," he said to Jacques; he didn't sound particularly angry, simply determined. "So I guess we'll all three of us just wait. And we'll see."

Flushing, Glynis turned and hurried to the carriage.

It was as Cullen steered the horse out of the reservation that she heard it. The first notes. The howl soared up and over her as if riding currents of cold air. And then Glynis saw it. A flash of gray in the corner of her eye, it streaked past the carriage, heading up the long rise of Black Brook Road to disappear into the silvery winter sky.

HISTORICAL NOTES

❧

AIR-GUNS, IROQUOIS

Present-day usage of the term *air-gun* usually implies an actual gun that fires pellets propelled by compressed air or gas. And the term *blowgun* tends to be associated with Amazonian Indians. However, Lewis Henry Morgan, in his *League of the Ho-de-no-sau-nee, or Iroquois,* says the following: "The air-gun is claimed as an Indian invention. It is a simple tube or barrel, about six feet in length. It is made of alder, and also of other wood, which is bored by some artificial contrivance . . . a very slender arrow, about two feet in length, with a sharp point, is the missile. The arrow is discharged by blowing."

BANNER OF LIGHT

The spiritualist publication *Banner of Light* was but one of many such nineteenth-century newspapers. The *Banner* began publishing in Boston in 1857, and professed to have subscribers in every state. The newspaper also held a free public "spirit circle" at its offices, and published the results each week. In addition, the *Banner* served as a conduit of communication between the various groups from which the Spiritualist movement drew its members. As Glynis Tryon pointed out, the majority of followers were women: those dissatisfied with the principal religious denominations; those already involved in social issues such as women's rights, abolition and temperance reform; and those who wanted radical changes in existing marriage laws.

BERITH KODESH

The first Jewish congregation in Rochester, Berith Kodesh was founded in October of 1848; its earliest history has been recounted in the body of the novel. It is thought that the congregation was originally Orthodox, but became

Reform around 1871. The spelling of Berith Kodesh was changed at the beginning of the twentieth century, and today the synagogue of B'rith Kodesh is situated in a beautiful parklike setting in the Rochester suburb of Brighton.

BLACK BROOK

Until some seventy-five years ago, Black Brook was a flowing body of water of substantial size. Although parts of it today still can be traveled by canoe, it has been ninety percent channelized for irrigation, so its flow is greatly diminished except in spring. The brook flows north from Seneca Falls into the Montezuma National Wildlife Refuge. Prior to the turn of this century, the Montezuma Marsh extended twelve miles north from Cayuga Lake and was, in some places, eight miles wide. The earliest human inhabitants of this area were Algonquins, followed by the Cayugas of the Iroquois nation; much of the Iroquois livelihood was supported by the marsh's plants and fish and birds. During construction of the New York State Barge Canal, which included a dam at the outlet of Cayuga Lake and subsequent alteration of nearby existing rivers, most of the marsh was drained. In 1937 the U.S. Fish and Wildlife Service purchased 6,432 acres of the former marsh. Since Montezuma lies in the middle of one of the most active flight lanes in the Atlantic Flyway, it is today an important refuge and feeding ground for migratory birds.

BLACKWELL, EMILY (1826–1910)

The older sister of Dr. Elizabeth Blackwell, America's first licensed female physician, Emily had been rejected by eleven medical schools before being accepted at Rush Medical School in Chicago in 1852. However, one year later the college yielded to pressure from the state medical society and revoked her admission. Not without a significant struggle did she manage, several years later, to complete her course work, with honors, at Western Reserve Medical College in Cleveland. In 1857 she was joined by her sister Elizabeth and the German-born Dr. Marie Zakrzewska (1829–

1902) in founding the New York Infirmary for Women and Children (see below).

DULCIMER

The hammered dulcimer dates from the tenth century, but the modern dulcimer, with its standard trapezoidal design, was developed during the sixteenth century. In the early to middle nineteenth century the dulcimer was a familiar instrument to American musicians. Easier to transport than its bulky cousin the piano, the dulcimer traveled west with the pioneers, and accompanied both folk dancers and singers, as well as religious services. Dulcimers were played at picnics, parties, contests, and clubs, or at any event at which rural and small-town peoples were gathered. Most pertinent to *Blackwater Spirits,* however, is the fact that, during the decade of the 1850s, the center of American dulcimer production was Chautauqua County, in western New York.

FEMALE MEDICAL COLLEGE OF PENNSYLVANIA

A group of Philadelphia doctors, thwarted in their attempts to place their private female students in regular medical schools, established the Female Medical College of Pennsylvania in 1850. (Its name was changed in 1867 to Woman's Medical College of Pennsylvania, and in 1970 to Medical College of Pennsylvania.) The first regular medical college for women anywhere in the world, it began with a student body of forty, and a faculty of six. At its first commencement exercises, it has been recorded that fifty policemen stood guard against a threatened disruption by male medical students. On this occasion, one of the college's founders, Dr. Joseph Longstreet, said: "[The community] will expect as *much,* nay, *more,* than of your professional brethren. . . . Do not, because you are *women* regard yourselves as inferior."

FOX, MARGARET (1833?–1893) AND CATHERINE (1839?–1892)

The nineteenth-century Spiritualist movement had its beginnings in 1848, with these two young girls, and what came to be known as the "Rochester rappings." The noises were attributed to spirits by the girls, and they began to attract sizable audiences for their demonstrations. Their older, married sister Ann Leah Fish began organizing regular public presentations of the girls' mediumistic abilities. Spiritualism took on a life of its own when Horace Greeley became convinced of the Fox sisters' authenticity, and endorsed them in his *New York Tribune*. Both girls' lives subsequently became tragic examples of unmitigated exploitation. Both underwent a severe slide into acute alcoholism from which they did not recover. Margaret eventually conceded that the whole thing had been a hoax, that her sister and she had produced the rappings by cracking their toe joints. But confirmed spiritualists at that point (1888) denounced this confession as a result of drunkenness. And Margaret soon retracted her confession and returned to spiritualism. Both sisters' later years were spent in poverty.

HOLMES, MARY JANE (1825–1907)

Although born in Massachusetts, Mary Jane Holmes resided for most of her life in Brockport, New York. In close to fifty years, she wrote thirty-eight full-length novels and hundreds of magazine stories; these sentimental romances, uncompromisingly moralistic in tone, were immensely popular with women and girls, selling upwards of two million copies per book, many of them in paperbound editions. During her literary career, Holmes gave a substantial portion of her earnings to religious and charitable causes. A significant portion of her work may be found in the local history division of the Rochester Public Library's Rundel Memorial Building.

JEMISON, MARY (1742?–1833)

Familiarly referred to by western New Yorkers as "The White Woman of the Genesee," Mary Jemison is best known through her own account, given at age eighty to James Seaver, M.D., and first published in narrative form in 1824. But most people initially meet Mary Jemison at her monument in Letchworth Park, New York. It was in this area that Jemison lived for a good portion of her life, after she was taken prisoner at age twelve in Ohio by Shawnees. She was adopted as a sister by two Seneca women, later married and outlived two Seneca husbands, owned a substantial plot of land—now part of Letchworth Park—and refused to leave her adoptive people when given the opportunity to return to the white world. Her monument's bronze statue depicts Mary Jemison as a young mother who, in the season of early winter, walked hundreds of miles from Ohio to her future Seneca home in New York with her nine-month-old baby strapped to her back. In her own words, "Those only who have travelled on foot the distance of five or six hundred miles, through an almost pathless wilderness, can form an idea of the fatigue and suffering that I endured on that journey."

One of Jemison's descendants, the Seneca artist Peter Jemison, is today the historic site manager of the Ganondagan State Historic Site in Ontario County, New York, just outside of Rochester. Ganondagan was a seventeenth-century Seneca village; it is the only historic site in New York State dedicated to Native Americans that is operated by the New York State Office of Parks, Recreation and Historic Preservation.

A LEECHBOOK OR COLLECTION OF MEDICAL RECIPES OF THE FIFTEENTH CENTURY

Warren R. Dawson transcribed this manuscript, and he states in his introduction to the book that nothing is known of its history: "It has been in the library of the Medical Society [of London], founded in 1773, since its earliest days." Dawson made a complete transcript of the document in March 1932. The manuscript is a small quarto volume of ninety-eight folios of vellum; the leechbook occupies folios 1–95; the remainder of the manuscript is filled with the beginning of a botanical glossary in Latin. It contains therapeutic recipes including preparations of drinks, confections, salves, and other medicants. There are surgical directions, such as the use of an anaesthetic drink to render the patient unconscious before operating. An example of the original

manuscript is: "ffor kestynge that comyth of cole. Ete myn-
tis that be soden with flesshe." Translation by Dawson: For
casting (vomiting) that cometh of cold. Eat mint that is sodden (boiled) with flesh."

MORGAN, LEWIS HENRY (1818–1881)

The pioneering ethnologist Lewis Henry Morgan has
been called "the father of American Anthropology." His
League of the Ho-de-no-sau-nee, or Iroquois, published in
1851, is considered the first scientific account of an Indian
tribe; Morgan wanted to describe the Iroquois in their own
terms, and while the work is flawed in this respect, as it
contains many examples of white ethnocentrism, it remains
a classic of research for its time. Morgan also must be cred-
ited with being the first to propose the admission of women
to the all-male student body of the University of Rochester.
His will contained the following clause: "I desire to use my
estate for the purpose of female education of high grade in
the city of Rochester."

NEW YORK INFIRMARY FOR WOMEN AND CHILDREN

Opening its doors at 64 Bleecker Street in New York
City on May 1, 1857, the infirmary was begun by Drs. Elizabeth Blackwell, Emily Blackwell, and Marie Zakrzewska.
It was the first hospital to be run entirely by women, its
practice consisting of both medical and surgical services.
Despite criticism from the male medical establishment,
threatening mobs armed with pickaxes and shovels, and fi-
nancial uncertainty, the infirmary quickly outgrew its original facilities and, by August 1859, moved to a new location
on Second Avenue, with a dispensary as well as space for
several female medical students. The infirmary received the
sanction of a number of prominent male physicians who
served as consultants.

O'BRIEN, SISTER HIERONYMO (1819–1898)

A native of Washington, D.C., Sister Hieronymo came
to Rochester, where she opened the city's first hospital, St.

Mary's, in 1857. She presided over its growth from a stable to a building that, during the Civil War, housed as many as seven hundred soldiers. She later went on to establish a Home of Industry for young needy girls. The above is only a cursory sketch of this remarkable woman, who was the center of much controversy in Rochester, during and after the Civil War.

O.K.

Readers of previous novels in the series have questioned the appearance of *"O.K.,"* frequently used by Cullen Stuart and Jacques Sundown, as perhaps anachronistic. But it is one of the oldest and most durable of Americanisms. A number of explanations surround its origin; the most favored, however, is that it began as an abbreviation of *oll korrect*—"all correct." In any event, *O.K.* originated early in the nineteenth century.

PARKER, ELY S. (1828–1895)

Ely Parker, a Seneca Indian, was born on the Tonowanda Reservation in western New York, and he collaborated on Lewis Henry Morgan's study of the Iroquois. Well-educated, Parker was trained in the law and also became an accomplished civil engineer. He served as a military staff officer to General Ulysses S. Grant and, acting as Grant's secretary, copied the terms of surrender which ended the Civil War. In 1869, Parker was appointed Commissioner of Indian Affairs by President Grant, becoming the first Native American to hold that position.

ROSE, ERNESTINE (1810–1892)

The *Boston Examiner* said of Mrs. Ernestine L. Rose that she was "an excellent lecturer, liberal, eloquent, witty, and we must add, decidedly handsome." Rose had left Poland and her Jewish family soon after her mother died and her rabbi father remarried. Several accounts exist as to why she emigrated. Some contend that her father insisted she marry someone whom she despised—and that her refusal to do so came after a substantial dowry had been committed. Others insist that she was forced to leave following a dispute with her father over her rejection of Jewish teaching concerning the inferiority of women, and after her subsequent renunciation of the Jewish faith. (Readers can see in the above the inspiration for the character of Rose's fictional cousin, Neva Cardoza.) Before Rose left Poland, and as a gesture of her independence, she turned over a sizable inheritance to her father. She then moved to Berlin, where she supported herself by inventing and selling a household deodorant. After marriage, she and her husband lived in New York City, where she spent most of the remainder of her life working for abolition, temperance, and women's rights.

WATERLOO COURT HOUSE

Also known as the Seneca County Court House at Waterloo, it was built in 1804 at a cost of fifteen hundred dollars. It stands today with the square in front, but the elms of yesterday are gone.

WATERS, SUSAN CATHERINE MOORE (1823–1900)

Born in Binghamton, New York, Susan Catherine Moore began earning her tuition at a female seminary by still-life and animal drawings. After marrying William Moore, a Quaker, she became an itinerant portrait painter while traveling with her husband in southern New York State. Her greatest artistic interest was the depiction of sheep, and she kept her own models in a pen in her backyard. Indeed, possibly her best-known work is the oil painting *Sheep in a Landscape,* in the collection of the Newark Museum.

Items that appeared in the Historical Notes sections of *Seneca Falls Inheritance* and *North Star Conspiracy* have not, for the most part, been included in the above, although some notes in those volumes may also be pertinent to *Blackwater Spirits*. Since there is frequent historical overlap, this choice was made to avoid repetition and to prevent these sections from eventually becoming longer than the novels themselves.